CITY OF SAINTS AND MADMEN

E.S.

JEFF VANDERMEER

men. If you cannot buy *City of Saints and Madmen*, chain yourself to the library steps until they bring in a copy for you, then steal it from the library. Loan it only to those over whom you have a sure hold. It is your guide to Ambergris, and you may just find that you live there."
—*SF Site*

"VanderMeer may well be the best fantasist working today. He slips past your defenses and seeds the hidden recesses of your imagination with spores that fruit in unexpected ways. You owe it to yourself to give him a try."
—*Revolution SF*

"This isn't a book, it's an experience. It's not for everyone, but if you delight in running weird rabbit trails of thought, being dazzled by description, or simply picking out the strange flecks floating in the interstices of the mundane world, then this book is definitely for you."
—*Tangent Online*

"Examining VanderMeer one is reminded of the glories of Angkor and Anudhapura combined with the bustle and swagger of Captain Conrad's Indonesia, the adventurous intrigues of Byzantium and Venice, the brutal Spice Wars of the Dutch. But sometimes it is as if Proust intrudes, incensed and reminiscent. VanderMeer describes a world so rich and exaggerated and full of mysterious life that it draws you away from any intended moral or pasquinade deep into the wealth of the world's womb . . . we should admire the rare texture of the writing, the engaging vividness of his description and the quirks of his idiosyncratic mind which conducts its network of realities with celebratory panache. Make the most of the tapestry of tales and visions before you. It is a rare treasure, to be tasted with both relish and respect. It is the work of an original. It's what you've been looking for." —Michael Moorcock

OTHER BOOKS BY THE AUTHOR

The Book of Frog
Lyric of the Highway Mariner
Dradin, In Love
The Book of Lost Places
Dradin, In Love & Other Stories (Greece)
The Hoegbotton Guide to the Early History of Ambergris
The Exchange (with Eric Schaller)
Veniss Underground
Shriek: An Afterword
Now Entering Ambergris
The Refraction of Light in a Prison
The Zamilon File
Fragments from a Drowned City
The Importance of Bibliographies to Squidfiction (nonfiction)
The Drunk but Repentant Life of Cadimon Signal (nonfiction)
The Further Adventures of the Torture Squid
A Sudden Dislocation of the Spirit
In a Strange and Distant Land
The Fear of Unfamiliar Streets
Red Flags at Dusk
Do You Know Where You Are Now? (self-help/travel guide)

CITY OF SAINTS AND MADMEN

JEFF VANDERMEER

Introduction by
Michael Moorcock

BANTAM BOOKS

CITY OF SAINTS AND MADMEN
A Bantam Spectra Book

PUBLISHING HISTORY
Prime Books hardcover edition published 2002
First Tor (UK) edition published 2004
Tor (UK) mass market edition published 2005
Bantam trade paperback edition / March 2006

Published by
Bantam Dell
A Division of Random House, Inc.
New York, New York

Book design by Garry Nurrish, except for "King Squid" and title pages, designed
by John Coulthart

Library of Congress Cataloging-in-Publication Data
VanderMeer, Jeff.
City of saints and madmen/Jeff VanderMeer
p. cm.
ISBN-10: 0-553-38357-4
ISBN-13: 978-0-553-38357-7
I. Title.

PS3572.A4284 C58 2006   2005048289
813/.54 22

Printed in the United States of America
Published simultaneously in Canada

www.bantamdell.com

BVG 10 9 8 7 6 5 4 3 2 1

꧁꧂

"What can be said about Ambergris that has not already been said? Every minute section of the city, no matter how seemingly superfluous, has a complex, even devious, part to play in the communal life. And no matter how often I stroll down Albumuth Boulevard, I never lose my sense of the city's incomparable splendor— its love of ritual, its passion for music, its infinite capacity for the beautiful cruelty."
—Voss Bender, *Memoirs of a Composer*, Vol. No. 1, page 558, Ministry of Whimsy Press

꧁꧂

For Ann, who means more to me than words

Contents

THE BOOK OF AMBERGRIS

APPENDIX

A Letter from Dr. V to Dr. Simpkin
X's Notes
The Release of Belacqua
King Squid
The Hoegbotton Family History
The Cage
In the Hours After Death
A Note from Dr. V to Dr. Simpkin
The Man Who Had No Eyes
The Exchange
Learning to Leave the Flesh
The Ambergris Glossary

The Book of Ambergris

JEFF VANDERMEER

THE REAL VANDERMEER
AN INTRODUCTION

"You'll be familiar, of course, with VanderMeer." Schomberg's fat red fingers fondled the notes he had counted. He placed them in his box and took a sideways look at me before pretending to hide it under the table. "Captain VanderMeer? First mate of *The Shriek* until she hit that reef. Master of *The Frog* when he next came back to the Islands."

"There was a woman involved, I take it?" I sipped my vortex water. It was locally made and suspiciously piquant.

"He knew Shriek himself and did his dirty work." Schomberg grimaced with his habitual distaste for every villainy and moral weakness not his own. The big fans overhead fluttered and rattled and stirred the thick, damp air. "Dradin did it to him. That's the view round here. You can tell what happened. It's all in the final story, if you're not afraid to give it your full attention."

"So X was, after all, his muse, his love?"

Schomberg shrugged. It was clear he wanted me to leave. As I removed myself from his story, I heard him breathe heavily in relief. I would miss his earthy explanations, but my presence made him uneasy. I strolled back to my place and was again absorbed in VanderMeer . . .

—Josef Conrad, *The Rescued*, 1900

In those earlier years, to which we all look back with long-ing, there was no captain more respected than Vander-Meer. He sailed the Mirage Islands and the Ambergris Peninsula. His memoirs had been eagerly awaited by the cognoscenti of the ports from Jannquork to San Francisco; but when they were published not everyone was satisfied the account was genuine. The methods he chose were often grotesque, baroque and fantastical, as if he strove to mirror in his writing style the visions he had witnessed. To be sure, this density of narrative was a little demanding to the reader used to the single sentimental plot which passes for story in most modern tales, as if there were only one truth, and only one way of uttering it, one character of central interest, one view to which you should be sympathetic.

If our author's response to his own experience was instinctively post-modern, this should be no reason for anyone's surprise. As one of a remarkable group of con-temporary captains who follow their own psychic maps, Captain VanderMeer is a master of keel and sail and at the wheel can take his vessel anywhere he chooses, whether skimming over rocky shallows or plunging her prow ag-gressively into the crowded waters of the Further Depths. For curiophilia, a wild curiosity and a love of exotic trea-sure, a fascination with complex architecture, a taste for the strangeness in the apparently ordinary, is what drives him on, carrying a peculiar miscellany of equipment into cor-ners of the universe no intelligence has explored before and returning with remarkable rarities, so valuable they have yet to find their true price or, indeed, connoisseurs.

While we are inevitably reminded of Captain Smith's *Mercury* or Ashton Smith's *Zothique*, Jack Vance's *Dying*

Earth, 'Crastinator Harrison's *Viriconium* or Lady Brackett's *Old Mars* or of the borderlands explored by the famous Hope Hodgson expedition, while Dunsany and even Lovecraft can be used in respectful comparison, we perhaps find more useful similarities in those recent reporters from the imagination's margins.

We recall Captain Aylett's *Beerlight* and Pilot Etchells' *Endland*, whose mores and customs are at once so familiar and so strange to us. Since the great expansion, Captains DiFilippo, Constantine, Miéville, Gentle and Newman all return with alien currency from new worlds. Others with a taste for exotic geographies continue to seek the Unending Parallel. All have left accounts.

Yet of course few of these have the weighty grandeur of *Ambergris*, which is reminiscent more of Peake's fine, almost-finished *Titus Alone*. Here is the complex surreality of fresh-discovered history, only a shade or two inland from our most familiar harbors. It shares resonances with Sir David Britton's monumental wasteland offered to us in the dark memories of *Lord Horror* and *The Auschwitz of Oz*. We are also reminded of labyrinthine Whittemore of the *Sinai Tapestry* and lands explored by the Welsh captains from Cowper Powys to Rhys Hughes and the strangely named Captain Taffy Sinclair. Robert Irwin, the *Arabiste*, has been another to draw his own maps and follow them. With VanderMeer, all are commanders of their chosen literary destinies, as courageous a company of psychic navigators as any you could hope to find.

Examining VanderMeer one is reminded of the glories of Angkor and Anudhapura combined with the bustle and swagger of Captain Conrad's Indonesia, the adventurous intrigues of Byzantium and Venice, the brutal Spice Wars of the Dutch. But sometimes it is as if Proust intrudes, insensed and reminiscent. VanderMeer describes a world so rich and exaggerated and full of mysterious life that it draws you away from any intended moral or pasquinade deep into the wealth of the world's womb. There is, I know, some suspicion he made over-free, even fictional, use of his material, perhaps to point an irony or two, even to present some kind of personal vision? Has this created a material change in his world? Would the Ambergris we next visit be anything like VanderMeer's romantic version? And what of the rumor that there is a delicious tinge of an obscure heresy in these pages?

I believe I am not the only one to have calibrated the references to Giant Squid and detected emotional involvements more appropriate in a child to a mother than in man to cephalopod. But it isn't our place or intention to analyze Captain VanderMeer's character or predilections, such as he offers us in these pages. Rather we should admire the rare texture of the writing, the engaging vividness of his description and the quirks of his idiosyncratic mind which conducts its network of realities with celebratory panache.

Make the most of the tapestry of tales and visions before you. It is a rare treasure, to be tasted with both relish and respect. It is the work of an original. It's what you've been looking for.

Michael Moorcock
Circle Squared Ranch
Lost Pines, Texas

Dradin,
In Love

I

RADIN, IN LOVE, BENEATH THE WINDOW of his love, staring up at her while crowds surge and seethe around him, bumping and bruising him all unawares in their rough-clothed, bright-rouged thousands. For Dradin watches *her,* she taking dictation from a *machine,* an inscrutable block of gray from which sprout the earphones she wears over her delicate egg-shaped head. Dradin is struck dumb and dumber still by the seraphim blue of her eyes and the cascade of long and lustrous black hair over her shoulders, her pale face gloomy against the glass and masked by the reflection of the graying sky above. She is three stories up, ensconced in brick and mortar, almost a monument, her seat near the window just above the sign that reads "Hoegbotton & Sons, Distributors." Hoegbotton & Sons: the largest importer and exporter in all of lawless Ambergris, that oldest of cities named for the most valuable and secret part of the whale. Hoegbotton & Sons: boxes and boxes of depravities shipped for the amusement of the decadent from far, far Surphasia and the nether regions of the Occident, those places that moisten, ripen, and decay in a blink. And yet, Dradin surmises, she looks as if she comes from more contented stock, not a stay-at-home, but uncomfortable abroad, unless traveling on the arm of her lover. Does she have a lover? A husband?

Are her parents yet living? Does she like the opera or the bawdy theatre shows put on down by the docks, where the creaking limbs of laborers load the crates of Hoegbotton & Sons onto barges that take the measure of the mighty River Moth as it flows, sludge-filled and torpid, down into the rapid swell of the sea? If she likes the theatre, I can at least afford her, Dradin thinks, gawping up at her. His long hair slides down into his face, but so struck is he that he does not care. The heat withers him this far from the river, but he ignores the noose of sweat round his neck.

Dradin, dressed in black with dusty white collar, dusty black shoes, and the demeanor of an out-of-work missionary (which indeed he is), had not meant to see the woman. Dradin had not meant to look up at all. He had been looking *down* to pick up the coins he had lost through a hole in his threadbare trousers, their seat torn by the lurching carriage ride from the docks into Ambergris, the carriage drawn by a horse bound for the glue factory, perhaps taken to the slaughter yards that very day—the day before the Festival of the Freshwater Squid as the carriage driver took pains to inform him, perhaps hoping Dradin would require his further services. But it was all Dradin could do to stay seated as they made their way to a hostel, deposited his baggage in a room, and returned once more to the merchant districts—to catch a bit of local color, a bite to eat—where he and the carriage driver parted company. The driver's mangy beast had left its stale smell on Dradin, but it was a necessary beast nonetheless, for he could never have afforded a mechanized horse, a vehicle of smoke and oil. Not when he would soon be down to his last coins and in desperate need of a job, the job he had come to Ambergris to find, for his former teacher at the Morrow Religious Academy—a certain Cadimon Signal—preached from Ambergris' religious quarter, and surely, what with the festivities, there would be work?

But when Dradin picked up his coins, he regained his feet rather too jauntily, spun and rattled by a ragtag gang of jackanapes who ran past him, and his gaze had come up on the gray, rain-threatening sky, and swung through to the window he now watched with such intensity.

The woman had long, delicate fingers that typed to their own peculiar rhythms, so that she might as well have been playing Voss Bender's Fifth, diving to the desperate lows and soaring to the magnificent highs that Voss Bender claimed as his territory. When her face became, for the moment, revealed to Dradin through the glare of glass—a slight forward motion to advance the tape, perhaps—he could see that her features, a match for her hands, were reserved, streamlined, artful. Nothing in her spoke of the rough rude world surrounding Dradin, nor of the great, un-mapped southern jungles from which he had just returned; where the black panther and the blacker mamba waited with such malign intent; where he had been so consumed by fever and by doubt and by lack of converts to his religion that he had come back into the charted territory of laws and governments, where, sweet joy, there existed women like the creature in the window above him. Watching her, his blood simmering within him, Dradin wondered if he was dreaming her, she a haloed, burning vision of salva-tion, soon to disappear mirage-like, so that he might once more be cocooned within his fever, in the jungle, in the darkness.

But it was not a dream and, of a sudden, Dradin broke from his reverie, knowing she might see him, so vulnerable, or that passersby might guess at his intent and reveal it to her before he was ready. For the real world surrounded him, from the stink of vegetables in the drains to the *sweet* of half-gnawed ham hocks in the trash; the clip-clop-stomp of horse and the rattled honk of motored vehicles; the rustle-whisper of mushroom dwellers disturbed from daily slumber and, from somewhere hidden, the sound of a baroque and lilting music, crackly as if played on a phonograph. People knocked into him, allowed him no space to move: merchants and jugglers and knife salesmen and sidewalk barbers and tourists and prostitutes and sailors on leave from their ships, even the odd pale-faced young tough, smiling a gangrenous smile.

Dradin realized he must act and yet he was too shy to approach her, to fling open the door to Hoegbotton & Sons, dash up the three flights of stairs and, unannounced (and perhaps unwanted) and unwashed, come before her dusty and smitten, a twelve o'clock shadow upon his chin. Obvious that he had come from the Great Beyond, for he still stank of the jungle rot and jungle excess. No, no. He must not thrust himself upon her.

But what, then, to do? Dradin's thoughts tumbled one over the other like distraught clowns and he was close to panic, close to wringing his hands in the way his mother had disapproved of but that indicated nothing unusual in a missionary, when a thought came to him and left him speechless at his own ingenuity.

A bauble, of course. A present. A trifle, at his expense, to show his love for her. Dradin looked up and down the street, behind and below him for a shop that might hold a treasure to touch, intrigue, and, ultimately, keep her. Madame Lowery's Crochets? The Lady's Emporium? Jessible's Jewelry Store? No, no, no. For what if she were a Modern, a woman who would not be kept or kept pregnant, but moved in the same circles as the artisans and writers, the actors and singers? What an insult such a gift would be to her then. What an insensitive man she would think him to be—and what an insensitive man he *would* be. Had all his months in the jungle peeled away his common sense, layer by layer, until he was as naked as an orangutan? No, it would not do. He could not buy clothing, chocolates, or even flowers, for these gifts were too forward, unsubtle, uncouth, and lacking in imagination. Besides, they—

—and his roving gaze, touching on the ruined aqueduct that divided the two sides of the street like the giant fossilized spine of a long, lean shark, locked in on the distant opposite shore and the modern sign with the double curlicues and the bold lines of type that proclaimed *Borges Bookstore,* and right there, on Albumuth Boulevard, the filthiest, most sublime, and richest thoroughfare in all of Ambergris, Dradin realized he had found the perfect gift. Nothing could be better than a book, or more mysterious, and nothing could draw her more perfectly to him.

Still dusty and alone in the swirl of the city—a voyeur amongst her skirts—Dradin set out toward the opposite side, threading himself between street players and pimps, card sharks and candy sellers, through the aqueduct, and, braving the snarl of twin stone lions atop a final archway, came at last to the *Borges Bookstore.* It had splendid antique windows, gilt embroidered, with letters that read:

JEFF VANDERMEER

> ## GIFTS FOR ANY OCCASION:
>
> * THE HISTORY OF THE RIVER MOTH *
> * GAMBLING PRACTICES OF THE OUTLANDS *
> * THE RELIGIOUS QUARTER ON 15 s. A DAY *
> * SQUID POACHING *
> * CORRUPTION IN THE MERCHANT DISTRICT *
> * ARCHITECTURE OF ALBUMUTH BOULEVARD *
>
> ALSO, *The Hoegbotton Series of Guidebooks & Maps to the Festival, Safe Places, Hazards, and Blindfolds.*

Book upon piled book mentioned in the silvery scrawl and beyond the glass the quiet, slow movements of bibliophiles, feasting upon the genuine articles. It made Dradin forget to breathe, and not simply because this place would have a gift for his dearest, his most beloved, the woman in the window, but because he had been away from the world for a year and, now back, he found the accoutrements of civilization comforted him. His father, that tortured soul, was still a great reader, between the bouts of drinking, despite the erosion of encroaching years, and Dradin could remember many a time that the man had, honking his red, red nose— a monstrosity of a nose, out of proportion to anything in the family line—read and wept at the sangfroid exploits of two poor debutantes named Juliette and Justine as they progressed from poverty to prostitution, to the jungles and back again, weepy with joy as they rediscovered wealth and went on to have wonderful adventures up and down the length and breadth of the River Moth, until finally pristine Justine expired from the pressure of tragic pleasures wreaked upon her.

It made Dradin swell with pride to think that the woman at the window was more beautiful than either Juliette or Justine, far more beautiful, and likely more stalwart besides. (And yet, Dradin admitted, in the delicacy of her features, the pale gloss of her lips, he espied an innately breakable quality as well.)

Thus thinking, Dradin pushed open the glass door, the lacquered oak frame a-creak, and a bell chimed once, twice, thrice. On the thrice chime, a clerk dressed all in dark greens, sleeves spiked with gold cufflinks, came forward, shoes soundless on the thick carpet, bowed, and asked, "How may I help you?"

To which Dradin explained that he sought a gift for a woman. "Not a woman I know," he said, "but a woman I should like to know."

The clerk, a rake of a lad with dirty brown hair and a face as subtle as mutton pie, winked wryly, smiled, and said, "I understand, sir, and I have *precisely* the book for you. It arrived a fortnight ago from the Ministry of Whimsy imprint—an Occidental publisher, sir. Please follow me."

The clerk led Dradin past mountainous shelves of history texts perused by shriveled prunes of men dressed in orange pantaloons—buffoons from university, no doubt, practicing for some baroque Voss Bender revival—and voluminous mantels of fictions and pastorals, neglected except by a widow in black and a child of twelve with thick glasses, then exhaustive columns of philosophy on which the dust had settled thicker still, until finally they reached a corner hidden by "Funerals" entitled "Objects of Desire."

The clerk pulled out an elegant eight-by-eleven book lined with soft velvet and gold leaf. "It is called *The Refraction of Light in a Prison* and in it can be found the collected wisdom of the last of the Truffidian monks imprisoned in the Kalif's dark towers. It was snuck out of those dark towers by an intrepid adventurer who—"

"Who was not a son of Hoegbotton, I hope," Dradin said, because it was well known that Hoegbotton & Sons dealt in all sorts of gimmickry and mimicry, and he did not like to think that he was giving his love an item she might have unpacked and catalogued herself.

"Hoegbotton & Sons? No, sir. Not a son of Hoegbotton. We do not deal with Hoegbotton & Sons (except inasmuch as we are contracted to carry their guidebooks), as their practices are . . . how shall I put it? . . . *questionable*. With neither Hoegbotton nor his sons do we deal. But where was I? The Truffidians.

"They are experts at the art of cataloguing passion, with this grave distinction: that when I say to you, sir, 'passion,' I mean the word in its most general sense, a sense that does not allow for intimacies of the kind that might strike the lady you *wish to know better* as too vulgar. It merely speaks to the general—the *incorporeal,* as one more highly witted than I might say. It shall not offend; rather, it shall lend to the gift-giver an aura of mystery that may prove permanently alluring."

The clerk proffered the book for inspection, but Dradin merely touched the svelte cover with his hand and said no, for he had had the most delightful thought: that he could explore those pages at the same time as his love. The thought made his hands tremble as they had not trembled since the fever ruled his body and he feared he might die. He imagined his hand atop hers as they turned the pages, her eyes caressing the same chapter and paragraph, the same line and word; thus could they learn of passion together but separate.

"Excellent, excellent," Dradin said, and, after a tic of hesitation—for he was much closer to penniless than penniful—he added, "but I shall need two," and as the clerk's eyebrows rose like the startled silhouettes of twin sea gulls upon finding that a fish within their grasp is actually a snark, he stuttered, "A-a-and a map. A map of the city. For the festival."

"Of course," said the clerk, as if to say, *Converts all around, eh?*

Dradin, dour-faced, said only, "Wrap this one and I will take the other unwrapped, along with the map," and stood stiff, brimming over with urgency, as the clerk dawdled and digressed. He knew well the clerk's thoughts: *a rogue priest, ungodly and unbound by any covenant made with God.* And perhaps the clerk was right, but did not canonical law provide for the unforeseen and the estranged, for the combination of beauty and the bizarre of which the jungle was itself composed? How else could one encompass and explain the terrible grace of the Hull Peoples, who lived within the caves hewn by a waterfall, and who, when dispossessed by Dradin and sent to the missionary fort, complained of the silence, the silence of God, how God would not talk to them, for what else was the play of water upon the rocks but the voice of God? He had had to send them back to their waterfall, for he could not bear the haunted looks upon their faces, the disorientation blossoming in their eyes like a deadly and deadening flower.

Dradin had first taken a lover in the jungles: a sweaty woman priest whose kisses smothered and suffocated him even as they brought him back to the world of flesh. Had she infected his mission? No, for he had tried so very hard for conversions, despite their scarcity. Even confronted by savage beast, savage plant, and just plain savage he had persevered. Perhaps persevered for too long, in the face of too many obstacles, his hair proof of his tenacity—the stark black streaked with white or, in certain light, stark white shot through with black, each strand of white attributable to the jungle fever (so cold it burned, his skin glacial), each strand of black a testament to being alive afterwards.

Finally, the clerk tied a lime green bow around a bright red package: gaudy but serviceable. Dradin dropped the necessary coin on the marble counter, stuck the map in the unwrapped copy and, with a frown to the clerk, walked to the door.

Out in the gray glare of the street, the heat and the bustling confusion struck Dradin and he thought he was lost, lost in the jungles that he had only just fled, lost so he would never again find his lady. His breaths came ragged and he put a hand to his temple, for he felt faint yet giddy.

Gathering his strength, he plunged into the muddle of sweating flesh, sweating clothes, sweating cobblestones. He rushed past the twin lions, their asses waggling at him as if they knew very well what he was up to, the arches, and then a vanguard of mango sellers, followed by an army of elderly dowager women with brimming stomachs and deep-pouched aprons, determined to buy up every last fruit or legume; young pups in play nipped at his heels, and, lord help him, he was delivered pell-mell in a pile, delivered with a stumble and a bruise to the opposite sidewalk, there to stare up once again at his lady love. Could any passage be more perilous than that daylight passage across Albumuth Boulevard, unless it was to cross the Moth at flood time?

Undaunted, Dradin sprang to his feet, his two books secure, one under each arm, and smiled to himself.

The woman had not moved from her station on the third floor; Dradin could tell, for he stood exactly as he had previous, upon the same crack in the pavement, and she was exactly as before, down to the pattern of shadows across the glass. Her rigid bearing brought questions half-stumbling to his lips. Did they not give her time for lunch? Did they make a virtue out of vice and virtually imprison her, enslave her to a cruel schedule? What had the clerk said? That Hoegbotton practices were *questionable*? He wanted to march into the building and talk to her superior, be her hero, but his dilemma was of a more practical kind: he did not wish to reveal himself as yet and thus needed a messenger for his gift.

Dradin searched the babble of people and his vision blurred, the world simplified to a sea of walking clothes: cufflinks and ragged trousers, blouses dancing with skirts, tall cotton hats and shoes with loose laces. How to distinguish? How to know whom to approach?

Fingers tugged at his shoulder and someone said, "Do you want to buy her?"

Buy her? Glancing down, Dradin found himself confronted by a singular man. This singular soul looked to be, it must be said, almost one muscle, a squat man with a low center of gravity, and yet a source of levity despite this: in short, a dwarf. How could one miss him? He wore a jacket and vest red as a freshly slaughtered carcass and claribel pleated trousers dark as crusted blood and shoes tipped with steel. A permanent grin molded the sides of his mouth so rigidly that, on second glance, Dradin wondered if it might not be a grimace. Melon bald, the dwarf was tattooed from head to foot.

The tattoo—which first appeared to be a birthmark or fungal growth—rendered Dradin speechless so that the dwarf said to him not once, but twice, "Are you all right, sir?"

While Dradin just stared, gap-jawed like a young jackdaw with naive fluff for wing feathers. For the dwarf had, tattooed from a point on the top of his head, and extending downward, a precise and detailed map of the River Moth, complete with the names of cities etched in black against the red dots that represented them. The river flowed a dark blue-green, thickening and thinning in places, dribbling up over the dwarf's left eyelid, skirting the midnight black of the eye itself, and down past taut lines of nose and mouth, curving over the generous chin and, like an exotic snake act, disappearing into the dwarf's vest and chest hair. A map of the lands beyond spread out from the River Moth. The northern cities of Dradin's youth—Belezar, Stockton, and Morrow (the last where his father still lived)—were clustered upon the dwarf's brow and there, upon the lower neck, almost the back, if one were to niggle, lay the jungles of Dradin's last year: a solid wall of green drawn with a jeweler's precision, the only hint of civilization a few smudges of red that denoted church enclaves. Dradin could have traced the line that marked his own dismal travels. He grinned, and he had to stop himself from putting out a hand to touch the dwarf's head for it had occurred to him that the dwarf's body served as a time line. Did it not show Dradin's birthplace and early years in the north as well as his slow descent into the south, the jungles, and now, more southern still, Ambergris? Could he not, if he were to see the entire tattoo, trace his descent further south, to the seas into which flowed the River Moth? Could he not chart his future, as it were? He would have laughed if not aware of the impropriety of doing so.

"Incredible," Dradin said.

"Incredible," echoed the dwarf, and smiled, revealing large yellowed teeth scattered between the gaping black of absent incisors and molars. "My father Alberich did it for me when I stopped growing. I was to be part of his show—he was a riverboat pilot for tourists—and thus he traced upon my skin the course he plotted for them. It hurt like a thousand devils curling hooks into my flesh, but now I am, indeed, incredible. Do you wish to buy her? My name is Dvorak Nibelung." From within this storm of information, the dwarf extended a blunt, whorled hand that, when Dradin took it, was cool to the touch, and very rough.

"My name is Dradin."

"Dradin," Dvorak said. "Dradin. I say again, do you wish to buy her?"

"Buy who?"

"The woman in the window."

Dradin frowned. "No, of course I don't wish to buy her."

Dvorak looked up at him with black, watery eyes. Dradin could smell the strong musk of river water and silt on the dwarf, mixed with the sharp tang of an addictive, *ghittlnut*.

Dvorak said, "Must I tell you that she is only an image in a window? She is no more real to you. Seeing her, you fall in love. But, if you desire, I can find you a woman who looks like her. She will do anything for money. Would you like such a woman?"

"No," Dradin said, and would have turned away if there had been room in the swirl of people to do so without appearing rude. Dvorak's hand found his arm again.

"If you do not wish to buy her, what do you wish to do with her?" Dvorak's voice was flat with miscomprehension.

"I wish to . . . I wish to woo her. I need to give her this book." And, then, if only to be rid of him, Dradin said, "Would you take this book to her and say that it comes from an admirer who wishes her to read it?"

To Dradin's surprise, Dvorak began to make huffing sounds, soft but then louder, until the River Moth changed course across the whorls of his face and something fastened to the inside of his jacket clicked together with a hundred deadly shivers.

Dradin's face turned scarlet.

"I suppose I will have to find someone else."

He took from his pocket two burnished gold coins engraved with the face of Trillian, the Great Banker, and prepared to turn sharply on his heel.

Dvorak sobered and tugged yet a third time on his arm. "No, no, sir. Forgive me. Forgive me if I've offended, if I've made you angry," and the hand pulled at the gift-wrapped book in the crook of Dradin's shoulder. "I will take the book to the woman in the window. It is no great chore, for I already trade with Hoegbotton & Sons, see," and he pulled open the left side of his jacket to reveal five rows of cutlery: serrated and double-edged, made of whale bone and of steel, hilted in engraved wood and thick leather. "See," he said again. "I peddle knives for them outside their offices. I know this building," and he pointed at the solid brick. "Please?"

Dradin, painfully aware of the dwarf's claustrophobic closeness, the reek of him, would have said no, would have turned and said not only no, but *How dare you touch a man of God?*, but then what? He must make acquaintance with one or another of these people, pull some ruffian off the dusty sidewalk, for he could not do the deed himself. He knew this in the way his knees shook the closer he came to Hoegbotton & Sons, the way his words rattled around his mouth, came out mumbled and masticated into disconnected syllables.

Dradin shook Dvorak's hand off the book. "Yes, yes, you may give her the book." He placed the book in Dvorak's arms. "But hurry about it." A sense of relief lifted the weight of heat from his shoulders. He dropped the coins into a pocket of Dvorak's jacket. "Go on," and he waved a hand.

"Thank you, sir," Dvorak said. "But, should you not meet with me again, tomorrow, at the same hour, so you may know her thoughts? So you may gift her a second time, should you desire?"

"Shouldn't I wait to see her now?"

Dvorak shook his head. "No. Where is the mystery, the romance? Trust me: better that you disappear into the crowds. Better indeed. Then she will wonder at your appearance, your bearing, and have only the riddle of the gift to guide her. You see?"

"No, I don't. I don't see at all. I must be confident. I must allow her to—"

"You are right—you do not see at all. Sir, are you or are you not a priest?"

"Yes, but—"

"You do not think it best to delay her knowing of this until the right moment? You do not think she will find it odd a priest should woo her? Sir, you wear the clothes of a missionary, but she is no ordinary convert."

And now Dradin did see. And wondered why he had not seen before. He must lead her gently into the particulars of his occupation. He must not boldly announce it for fear of scaring her off.

"You are right," Dradin said. "You are right, of course."

Dvorak patted his arm. "Trust me, sir."

"Tomorrow then."

"Tomorrow, and bring more coin, for I cannot live on good will alone."

"Of course," Dradin said.

Dvorak bowed, turned, walked up to the door of Hoegbotton & Sons, and—quick and smooth and graceful—disappeared inside.

Dradin looked up at his love, wondering if he had made a mistake. Her lips still called to him and the entire sky seemed concentrated in her eyes, but he followed the dwarf's advice and, lighthearted, disappeared into the crowds.

II

Dradin, happier than he had been since dropping the fever at the Sisters of Mercy Hospital, some five hundred miles away and three months in the past, sauntered down Albumuth, breathing in the smell of catfish simmering on open skillets, the tangy broth of codger soup, the sweet regret of overripe melons, pomegranates, and leechee fruit offered for sale. Stomach grumbling, he stopped long enough to buy a skewer of beef and onions and eat it noisily, afterwards wiping his hands on the back of his pants. He leaned against a lamppost next to a sidewalk barber and—aware of the sour effluvium from the shampoos, standing clear of the trickle of water that crept into the gutter—pulled out the map he had bought at Borges Bookstore. It was cheaply printed on butcher paper, many of the street names drawn by hand. Colorless, it compared unfavorably with Dvorak's tattoo, but it was accurate and he easily found the intersection of streets that marked his hostel. Beyond the hostel lay the valley of the city proper; north of it stood the religious district and his old teacher, Cadimon Signal. He could make his way to the hostel via one of two routes. The first would take him through an old factory district, no doubt littered with the corpses of rusted out motored vehicles and railroad cars, railroad tracks cut up and curving into the air with a profound sense of futility. In his childhood in the city of Morrow, Dradin, along with his long-lost friend Anthony Toliver (Tolive the Olive, he had been called, because of his fondness for the olive fruit or its oil), had played in just such a district, and it did not fit his temperament. He remembered how their play had been made somber by the sight of the trains, their great, dull heads upended, some staring glassily skyward while others drank in the cool, dark earth beneath. He was in no mood for such a death of metal, not with his heartbeat slowing and rushing, his manner at once calm and hyperactive.

No, he would take the second route—through the oldest part of the city, over one thousand years old, so old as to have lost any recollection of itself, its stones worn smooth and memory-less by the years. Perhaps such a route would settle him, allow him this bursting joy in his heart and yet not make his head spin quite so much.

Dradin moved on—ignoring an old man defecating on the sidewalk (trousers down around his ankles) and neatly sidestepping an Occidental woman around whom flopped live carp as she, armed with a club, methodically beat at their heads until a spackle of yellow brains glistened on the cobblestones.

After a few minutes of walking, the wall-to-wall buildings fell away, taking the smoke and dust and babble of voices with them. The world became a silent place except for the scuff of Dradin's shoes on the cobblestones and the occasional muttering chug-chuff of a motored vehicle, patched up and trundling along, like as not burning more oil than fuel. Dradin ignored the smell of fumes, the angry retort of tailpipes. He saw only the face of the woman from the window—in the pattern of lichen on a gray-stained wall, in the swirl of leaves gathered in a gutter.

The oldest avenues, thoroughfares grandfatherly when the Court of the Mourning Dog had been young and the

Days of the Burning Sun had yet to scorch the land, lay a-drowning in a thick soup of honeysuckle, passion fruit, and bougainvillea, scorned by bee and hornet. Such streets had the lightest of traffic: old men on an after-lunch constitutional; a private tutor leading two children dressed in Sunday clothes, all polished shoes and handkerchief-and-spit cleaned faces.

The buildings Dradin passed were made of a stern, impervious gray stone and separated by fountains and courtyards. Weeds and ivy smothered the sides of these stodgy, baroque halls, their windows broken as if the press of vines inward had smashed the glass. Morning glories, four o'clocks, and yet more ivy choked moldering stone street markers, trailed from rusted balconies, sprouted from pavement cracks, and stitched themselves into fences or gates scoured with old fire burns. Whom such buildings had housed, or what business had been conducted within, Dradin could only guess. They had, in their height and solidity, an atmosphere of states-craft about them, bureaucratic in their flourishes and busts, gargoyles and stout columns. But a bureaucracy lost to time: sword-wielding statues on horseback overgrown with lichen, the features of faces eaten away by rot deep in the stone; a fountain split down the center by the muscular roots of an oak. There was such a staggering sense of lawlessness in the silence amid the creepers.

Certainly the jungle had never concealed such a cornucopia of assorted fungi, for between patches of stone burned black Dradin now espied rich clusters of mushrooms in as many colors as there were beggars on Albumuth Boulevard: emerald, magenta, ruby, sapphire, plain brown, royal purple, corpse white. They ranged in size from a thimble to an obese eunuch's belly.

Such a playful and random dotting delighted Dradin so much that he began to follow the spray of mushrooms.

Their trail led him to a narrow avenue blocked in by ten-foot high gray stone walls, and he was soon struck by the notion that he traveled down the throat of a serpent. The mushrooms proliferated, until they not only grew in the cobblestone cracks, but also from the walls, speckling the gray with their bright hoods and stems.

The sun dimmed between clouds. A wind came up, brisk on Dradin's face. Trees loured ever closer, darkening the sky. The street continued to narrow until it was wide enough for two men, then one man, and finally so narrow—narrow as any narthex Dradin had ever encountered—that he moved sideways crablike, and still tore a button.

Eventually, the street widened again. He stumbled out into the open space—only to be met by a *crack!* loud as the severing of a spine, a sound that shot up, over, and past him. He cried out and flinched, one arm held up to ward off a blow, as a sea of wings thrashed toward the sky.

He slowly brought his arm down. Pigeons. A flock of pigeons. Only pigeons.

Ahead, when the flock had cleared the trees, Dradin saw, along the street's right-hand side, the rotting columbary from which the birds had flown. Its many covey holes had the bottomless gaze of the blind. The stink of pigeon droppings made his stomach queasy. Beside the columbary, separated by an alleyway, stood a columbarium, also rotting and deserted, so that urns of ashes teetered on the edge of a windowsill, while below the smashed window two urns lay cracked on the cobblestones, their black ash spilling out.

A columbary and a columbarium! Side by side, no less, like old and familiar friends, joined in decay.

Much as the sight intrigued him, the alley between the columbary and columbarium fascinated Dradin more, for the mushrooms that had crowded the crevices of the street and dotted the walls like the pox now proliferated beyond all imagining, the cobblestones thick with them in a hundred shades and hues. Down the right-hand side of the alley, ten alcoves had been carved, complete with iron gates, a hundred hardened cherubim and devils alike caught in the metalwork. The gate of the nearest alcove stood open and from within spilled lichen, creepers, and mushroom dwellers, their red flags droopy. Surrounded by the vines, the mushroom dwellers resembled human head-stones or dreamy, drowning swimmers in a green sea.

Beside Dradin—and he jumped back as he realized his mistake—lay a mushroom dweller that he had thought was a mushroom the size of a small child. It mewled and writhed in half-awakened slumber as Dradin looked at it with a mixture of fascination and distaste. Stranger to Ambergris that he was, still Dradin knew of the mushroom dwellers, for, as Cadimon Signal had taught him in Morrow, "they form the most outlandish of all known cults," although lit-tle else had been forthcoming from Cadimon's dried and withered lips.

Mushroom dwellers smelled of old, rotted barns and spoiled milk and vegetables mixed with the moistness of dark crevices and the dryness of day-dead dung beetles.

Some folk said they whispered and plotted among themselves in a secret language so old that no one else, even in the far, far Occident, spoke it. Others said they came from the subterranean caves and tunnels below Ambergris, that they were escaped convicts who had gathered in the darkness and made their own singular religion and purpose, that they shunned the light because they were blind from their many years underground. And yet others, the poor and the under-educated, said that newts, golliwogs, slugs, and salamanders followed in their wake by land, while above bats, nighthawks, and whippoorwills flew, feasting on the insects that crawled around mushroom and mushroom dweller alike.

Mushroom dwellers slept on the streets by day, but came out at night to harvest the fungus that had grown in the cracks and shadows of graveyards during sunlit hours. Wherever they slept, they planted the red flags of warning, and woe to the man who, as Dradin had, disturbed their wet and lugubrious slumber. Sailors on the docks had told Dradin that the mushroom dwellers were known to rob graves for compost, or even murder tourists and use the flesh for their midnight crop. If no one questioned or policed them, it was because during the night they tended to the garbage and carcasses that littered Ambergris. By dawn the streets had been picked clean and lay shining and innocent under the sun.

Fifty mushroom dwellers now spilled out from the alcove gateway, macabre in their very peacefulness and the even hum-thrum of their breath: stunted in growth, wrapped in robes the pale gray-green of a frog's underbelly, their heads hidden by wide-brimmed gray felt hats that, like the hooded tops of their namesakes, covered them to the neck. Their necks were the only exposed part of them—incredibly long, pale necks; at rest, they did indeed resemble mushrooms.

And yet, to Dradin's eye, they were disturbingly human rather than inhuman—a separate race, developing side by side, silent, invisible, chained to ritual—and the sight of them, on the same day that he had fallen so irrevocably in love, unnerved Dradin. He had already felt death upon him in the jungles and had known no fear, only pain, but here fear burrowed deep into his bones. Fear of death. Fear of the unknown. Fear of knowing death before he drank deeply of love. Morbidity and sullen curiosity mixed with dreams of isolation and desolation. All those obsessions of which the religious institute had supposedly cured him.

Positioned as he was, at the mouth of the alley, Dradin felt as though he were spying on a secret, forbidden world. Did they dream of giant mushrooms, gray caps agleam with the dark light of a midnight sun? Did they dream of a world lit only by the phosphorescent splendor of their charges?

Dradin watched them for a moment longer and then, his pace considerably faster, made his way past the alley mouth.

Eventually, under the cloud-darkened eye of the sun, the maze of alleys gave way to wide, open-ended streets traversed by carpenters, clerks, blacksmiths, and broadsheet vendors, and he soon came upon the depressing but cheap Holander-Barth Hostel. (In another, richer, time he never would have considered staying there.) He had seen all too many such establishments in the jungles: great mansions rotted down to their foundations, occupied by the last inbred descendants of men and women who had thought the jungle could be conquered with machete and fire, only to find that the jungle had conquered them; where yesterday they had hacked down a hundred vines a thousand now writhed and interlocked in a fecundity of life. Dradin could not even be sure that the Sisters of Mercy Hospital still stood, untouched by such natural forces.

The Holander-Barth Hostel, once white, now dull gray, was a salute to pretentiousness, the dolorous inlaid marble columns crumbling from the inside out and laundry spread across ornately filigreed balconies black with decay. Perhaps once, jaded aristocrats had owned it, but now tubercular men walked its halls, hacking their lungs out while fishing in torn pockets for cigars or cigarettes. The majority were soldiers from long-forgotten campaigns who had used their pensions to secure lodging, blissfully ignorant (or ignoring) the cracked fixtures, curled wallpaper, communal showers and toilets. But, as the hansom driver had remarked on the way in, "It is the cheapest" and had added, "It is also far away from the festival." Luckily, the proprietors respected a man of the cloth, no matter how weathered, and Dradin had managed to rent one of two second-story rooms with a private bath.

Heart pounding now not from fear, but rather from desire, Dradin dashed up the warped veranda—past the elderly pensioners, who bowed their heads or made confused signs of Truffidian ritual—up the spiral staircase, came to his door, fumbled with the key, and once inside, fell on the bed with a thump that made the springs groan, the book thrown down beside him. The cover felt velvety and smooth to his touch. It felt like her skin must feel, he thought, and promptly fell asleep, a smile on his lips, for it was still near midday and the heat had drained his strength.

III

MOUTH DRY, HAIR TOUSLED, AND CHIN SCRATCHY WITH stubble, Dradin woke to a pinched nerve in his back that made him moan and turn over and over on the bed, his perspective notably skewed, though not this time by the woman. Still, he could tell that the sun had plummeted beneath the horizon and where the sky had been gray with clouds, it now ranged from black to a bruised purple, the moon mottled, the light measured out in rough dollops. Dradin yawned and scrunched his shoulders together to cure the pinchedness, then rose and walked to the tall but slender windows. He unhooked the latch and pulled the twin panes open to let in the smell of approaching rain, mixed with the sweet stink of garbage and honeysuckle.

The window looked down on the city proper, which lay inside the cupped hands of a valley veined with tributaries of the Moth. It was there that ordinary people slept and dreamt not of jungles and humidity and the lust that fed and starved men's hearts, but of quiet walks under the stars and milk-fat kittens and the gentle hum of wind on wooden porches. They raised families and doubtless missionaries never moved amongst their ranks, but only full-fledged priests, for they were already converted to a faith. Indeed, they—and people like them in other cities—paid their tithes and, in return, had emissaries sent out into the wilderness to spread the word, such emissaries nothing more than the physical form of their own hopes, wishes, fears; their desires made flesh. Dradin found the idea a sad one, sadder still, in a way he hesitated to define, that were it not for his chosen vocation, he could have had such a life: settling down into a daily rhythm that did not include the throbbing of the jungles, twinned to the beating of his heart. Anthony Toliver had chosen such a life, abandoning the clergy soon after graduation from the religious institute.

Around the valley lay the fringe, like a roughly circular smudge of wine and vulgar lipstick. The Holander-Barth Hostel marked the dividing line between the valley and fringe, just as the beginning of Albumuth Boulevard marked the end of the docks and the beginning of the fringe. It was here, not truly at a city's core, that Dradin had always been most comfortable, even back in his religious institute days, when he had been more severe on himself than the most pious monks who taught him.

On the fringe, jesters pricked and pranced, jugglers plied their trade with babies and knives (mixing the two as casually as one might mix apples and oranges). The life's blood swelled at a more exhilarating pace, a pace that quickened beyond the fringe, where the doughty sailors of the River Moth sailed on barges, dhows, frigates, and the rare steamer: anything that could float and hold a man without sinking into the silt.

Beyond the river lay the jungles, where the pace quickened into madness. The jungles hid creatures that died after a single day, their lives condensed beyond comprehension, so that Dradin, in observation of their own swift mortality, had sensed his body dying, hour by hour, minute by minute, a feeling that had not left him even when he lay down with the sweaty woman priest.

Dradin let the breeze from the window brush against him, cooling him, then returned to the bed, circling around it to the bed lamp, turned the switch, and lo!, a brassy light to read by. He plopped down on the bed, legs akimbo, and opened the book to the first page. Thus began the fantasy: that in some other room, some other house—perhaps even in the valley below—the woman from the window lay in her own bed by some dim light and turned these same pages, read these same words. The touch of the pages to his fingers was erotic; they felt damp and charged his limbs with the short, sharp shock of a ceremonial cup of liqueur. He became hard, but resisted the urge to touch himself. Ah, sweet agony! Nothing in his life had ever felt half so good, half so tortuous. Nothing in the bravely savage world beyond the Moth could compare: not the entwining snake dances of the Magpie Women of the Frangipani Veldt, nor the single, aching cry of a Zinfendel maid as she jumped headfirst into the roar of a waterfall. Not even the sweaty woman priest before the fever struck, her panting moans during their awkward love play more a testimonial to the humidity and ever-present mosquitoes than any skill on his part.

Dradin looked around his room. How bare it was for all that he had lived some thirty years. There was his red-handled machete, balanced against the edge of the dresser drawers, and his knapsack, which contained powders and liquids to cure a hundred jungle diseases, and his orange-scuffed boots beside that, and his coins on the table, the gold almost crimson in the light, but what else? Just his suitcase with two changes of clothes, his yellowing, torn diploma from the Morrow Institute of Religiosity, and daguerreotypes of his mother and father, them in their short-lived youth, Dad not yet a red-faced, broken-veined lout of an academic, Mom's eyes not yet squinty with surrounding wrinkles and sharp as bloodied shards of glass.

What did the woman's room look like? No doubt it too was briskly clean, but not bare, oh no. It would have a bed with white mosquito netting and a place for a glass of water, and her favorite books in a row beside the bed, and beyond that a white and silver mantel and mirror, and below that, her dresser drawers, filled to bursting with frilly night things and frilly day things, and filthily frilly twilight things as well. Powders and lotions for her skin, to keep it beyond the pale. Knitting needles and wool, or other less feminine tools for hobbies. Perhaps she kept a vanilla kitten close by, to play with the balls of wool. If she lived at home, this might be the extent of her world, but if she lived alone, then Dradin had three, four, other rooms to fill with her loves and hates. Did she enjoy small talk and other chatter? Did she dance? Did she go to social events? What might she be thinking as she read the book, on the first page of which was written:

THE REFRACTION OF LIGHT IN A PRISON
(Being an Account of the Truffidian Monks Held in the
Dungeons of the Kalif, For They Have Not Given Up
Sanity, or Hope)

BY:
Brother Peek
Brother Prowcosh
Brother Witamoor
Brother Sirin
Brother Grae
(and, held unfortunately in separate quarters,
communicating to us purely by the force of her
will, Sister Stalker)

And, on the next page:

BEING CHAPTER ONE:
THE MYSTICAL PASSIONS

The most mystical of all passions are those practiced
by the water people of the Lower Moth, for though
they remain celibate and spend most of their lives
in the water, they attain a oneness with their mates
that bedevils those lesser of us who equate love
with intercourse. Surely, their women would never
become the objects of their desire, for then these
women would lose an intrinsic eroticism.

Dradin read on impatiently, his hands sweaty, his
throat dry, but, no, no, he would not rise to drink water
from the sink, nor release his tension, but must burn, as his
love must burn, reading the self-same words. For now he

was in truth a missionary, converting himself to the cause of love, and he could not stop.

Outside, along the lip of the valley, lights began to blink and waver in phosphorescent reds, greens, blues, and yellows, and Dradin realized that preparations for the Festival of the Freshwater Squid must be underway. On the morrow night, Albumuth Boulevard would be cleared for a parade that would overflow onto the adjacent streets and then the entire city. Along the avenues, candles wrapped in boxes of crepe paper would appear, so that the light would be like the dancing of the squid, great and small, upon the midnight salt water where it met the mouth of the Moth. A celebration of the spawning season, when males battled mightily for females of the species and the fisher folk of the docks would set out for a month's trawling of the lusting grounds, hoping to bring back enough meat to last until winter.

If only he could be with her on the morrow night. Among the sights the hansom driver had pointed out on the way into Ambergris was a tavern, *The Drunken Boat*, decked out with the finest in cutlery and clientele, and featuring, for the festival only, the caterwauling of a band called The Ravens. To dance with her, her hands interwoven with his, the scent of her body on his, would make up for all that had happened in the jungle and the humiliations since: the hunt for ever more miserable jobs, accompanied by a general lightening of coin in his pockets.

The clocks struck the insomniac hours after midnight and, below the window, Dradin heard the moist scuttle of mushroom dwellers as they gathered offal and refuse. Rain followed the striking of the clocks, falling softly, as light in touch as Dradin's hand upon *The Refraction of Light in a Prison*. The smell of rain, fresh and sharp, came from the window.

Drawn by that smell, Dradin put the book aside and rose to the window, watched the rain as it caught the faint light, the drops like a school of tiny silver-scaled fish, here and gone, back a moment later. A vein of lightning, a boom of thunder, and the rain came faster and harder.

Many times Dradin had stared through the rain-splashed windows of the old gray house on the hill from his childhood in Morrow (the house with the closed shutters like eyes stitched shut) while relatives came up the gray, coiled road: the headlights of expensive motored vehicles bright in the sheen of rain. They resembled a small army of hunched black, white, and red beetles, like the ones in his father's insect books, creeping up the hill. Below them, where it was not fogged over, the rest of Morrow: industrious, built of stone and wood, feeding off of the River Moth.

From one particular window in the study, Dradin could enjoy a double image: inside, at the end of a row of three open doors—library, living room, dining room—his enormous opera singer of a mother (tall and big-boned) stuffed into the kitchen. No maid helped her, for they lived, the three of them, alone on the hill, and so she would be delicately placing mincemeats on plates, cookies on trays, splashing lemonade and punch into glasses, trying very hard to keep her hands clean and her red dress of frills and lace unstained. She would sing to herself as she worked, in an unrestrained and husky voice (it seemed she never spoke to Dradin, but only sang) so that he could hear, conducted through the various pipes, air ducts, and passageways, the words of Voss Bender's greatest opera:

Come to me in the Spring
When the rains fall hard
For you are sweet as pollen,
Sweet as fresh honeycomb.

When the hard brown branches
Of the oak sprout green leaves,
In the season of love, come to me.

Into the oven would go the annual pheasant, while outside the window Dradin could see his father, thin and meticulous in tuxedo and tails, picking his way through the puddles in the front drive, carrying a big, ragged black umbrella. Dad would *walk precisely,* as if by stepping first *here* and then *there,* he might escape the rain drops, slip between them because he knew the umbrella would do no good, riddled as it was with rips and moth holes. But, oh, what a pantomime for the guests!, while Dradin laughed and his mother sang. Apologies for the rain, the puddles, the tattered appearance of the umbrella. In later years, Dad's greetings became loutish, slurred by drink and age until they were no longer generous. But back then he would unfold his limbs like a good-natured mantis and with quick movements of his hands switch the umbrella from left to right as he gestured his apologies. All the while, the guests would be half-in, half-out of the car—Aunt Sophie and Uncle Ken, perhaps—trying hard to be polite, but meanwhile drenched to the skin. Inside, Mom would have time to steel herself, ready a greeting smile by the front door, and—one doomful eye on the soon-to-be-burnt pheasant—call for Dradin.

In a much more raging rain, Dradin had first been touched by a force akin to the spiritual. It occurred on a similarly dreary day of visiting relatives, Dradin only nine and trapped: trapped by dry pecks on the cheek; trapped by the smell of damp, sweaty bodies brought close together; trapped by the dry burn of cigars and by the alarming stares of the elderly men, eyebrows inert white slugs, moustaches wriggly, eyes enormous and watery through glasses or monocles. Trapped, too, by the ladies, even worse at that advanced age, their cavernous grouper mouths intent on devouring him whole into their bellies.

Dradin had begged his mother to invite Anthony Toliver and, against his father's wishes, she had said yes. Anthony, a fearless follower, was a wiry boy with sallow skin and dark eyes. They had met in public school, odd fellows bonded together by the simple fact that both had been beaten up by the school bully, Roger Gimmell.

As soon as Tony arrived, Dradin convinced him to escape the party. Off they snuck, through a parlor door into a backyard bounded only at the horizon by a tangled wilderness of trees. Water pelted them, splattered on shirts, and pummeled flesh, so that Dradin's ears rang with the force of it and dull aches woke him the morning after. Grass was swept away, dirt dissolving into mud.

Tony fell almost immediately and, scrabbling at Dradin, made him fall too, into the wet, grasping at weeds for support. Tony laughed at the surprised look on Dradin's face. Dradin laughed at the mud clogging Tony's left ear. Splash! Slosh! Mud in the boots, mud in the trousers, mud flecking their hair, mud coating their faces.

They grappled and giggled. The rain fell so hard it stung. It bit into their clothes, cut into the tops of their heads, attacked their eyes so they could barely open them. In the middle of the mud fight they stopped battling each other and started battling the rain. They scrambled to their feet, no longer playing, then lost touch with each other, Tony's hand slipping from Dradin's, so that Tony said only, "Come on!" and ran toward the house, never looking back at Dradin, who stood still as a frightened rabbit, utterly alone in the universe.

As Dradin stands alone in the sheets of rain, staring at the heavens that have opened up and sent the rains down, he begins to shake. The rain, like a hand on his shoulders, presses him down; the electric sensation of water on his skin rinses away mud and bits of grass, leaves him cold and sodden. He shudders convulsively, sensing the prickle of an immensity up in the sky, staring down at him. He knows from the rush and rage of blood, the magnified beat of his heart, that nothing this *alive,* this out of control, can be random.

Dradin closes his eyes and a thousand colors, a thousand images, explode inside his mind, one for each drop of rain. A rain of shooting stars, and from this conflagration the universe opening up before him. For an instant, Dradin can sense every throbbing artery and arrhythmic heart in the city below him—every darting quicksilver thought of hope, of pain, of hatred, of love. A hundred thousand sorrows and a hundred thousand joys ascending to him.

The babble of sensation so overwhelms him that he can hardly breathe, cannot feel his body except as a hollow receptacle. Then the sensations fade until, closer at hand, he feels the pinprick lives of mice in the nearby glades, the deer like graceful shadows, the foxes clever in their burrows, the ladybugs hidden on the undersides of leaves, and then nothing, and when it is gone, he says, shoulders slumped, but still on his feet, *Is this God?*

When Dradin—a husk now, his hearing deafened by the rain, his bones cleansed by it—turned back toward the house; when he finally faced the house with its shuttered windows, as common sense dictated he should, the light from within fairly burst to be let out. And Dradin saw (as he stood by the window in the hostel) not Tony, who was safely inside, but his mother. His mother. The later memory fused to the earlier seamlessly, as if they had happened together, one, of a piece. That he had turned and she was there, already leveling a blank stare toward him; that, simple as breath, the rain brought redemption and madness crashing down on both their heads, the time span no obstacle and of no importance.

. . . he turned and there was his mother, on her knees in the mud, in her red dress spattered brown. She scooped the mud up with her hands, regarded it, and began to eat, so ravenously that she bit into her little finger. The eyes on the face of stone—the face as blank as the rain—looked up at him with the most curious expression, as if trapped as Dradin had felt trapped inside the house, trapped and asking Dradin . . . to do something. And him, even then, already fourteen, not knowing what to do, calling for Dad, calling for a doctor, while the mud smudged the edges of her mouth and, unconcerned, she ate more and stared at him after each bite, until he cried and came to her and hugged her and tried to make her stop, though nothing in the world could make her stop, or make him stop trying. What unnerved him more than anything, more than the mud in her mouth, was the complete silence that surrounded her, for he had come to define her by her voice, and this she did not use, even to ask for help.

Dradin again heard the mushroom dwellers below and closed the window abruptly. He sat back on the bed. He wanted to read more of the book, except that now his thoughts floated, rose and fell like waves and, before he realized it, before he could stop it, he was, as it were, not quite dead, but merely asleep.

In the morning, Dradin rose rested and spry, his body almost certainly recovered from the jungle fever. For months he had risen to the ache of sore muscles and bruised internal organs; now he had only a fever of a different sort. Every time Dradin glanced at *The Refraction of Light in a Prison*—as he washed his face in the green-tinged basin, as he dressed, not looking at his pant legs so it took him several tries to put them on—he thought of her. What piece of glitter might catch her eye for him? For now, surely, if she had read the book, was the time to appraise her worth to him, to let her know that serious is as serious does. In just such a manner had his dad wooed his mom, Dad a rake-thin but puff-bellied proud graduate of Morrow's

University of Arts & Facts (which certainly defined Dad). She, known by the maiden name of Barsombly, the famous singer with a voice like a pit bull—almost baritone, but husky enough, Dradin admitted, to conceal a sultry sexuality. He could not remember when he had not either felt the *thrulling* vibrations of his mother's voice or heard the voice itself. Or a time when he had not watched as she applied raucous perfumes and powders to herself, after putting on the low-bodiced, gold-satin costumes that rounded her taut bulk like an impenetrable wall. He could remember her taking him into theatres and music halls through the back entrance, bepuddled and muddened, and as some helpful squire would escort him sodden to his seat, so too would she be escorted atop the stage, so that as Dradin sat, the curtain rose, simultaneous with the applause from the audience—an ovation like the crashing of waves against rock.

Then she would sing, and he would imagine the thrull of her against him, and marvel at the power of her voice, the depths and hollows of it, the way it matched the flow and melody of the orchestra only to diverge, coursing like a secret and perilous undertow, the vibration growing and growing until there was no longer any music at all, just the voice devouring the music.

Dad did not go to any of her performances and sometimes Dradin thought she sang so loud, so full of rage, that Dad might still hear her faintly, him up late reading in the study of the old house on the hill with the shutters like eyes stitched shut.

His mother would have been proud of his attempts to woo, but, alas, she had been gagged and trussed for her own good and traveled now with the Bedlam Rovers, a cruising troupe of petty psychiatrists—sailing down the Moth on a glorified houseboat under the subtitle of "Boat Bound Psychiatrists: Miracle Workers of the Mind"—to whom, finally, Dad had given over his dearest, the spiced fig of his heart, Dradin's mother—for a fee, of course; and didn't it, Dad had raged and blustered, come to the same thing? In a rest home or asylum; either situated in one place, or on the move. It was not so bad, he would say, slumping down in a damp green chair, waving his amber bottle of Smashing Ted's Finest; after all, the sights she would see, the places she would experience, and all under the wise and benevolent care of trained psychiatrists who *paid* to take that care. Surely, his father would finish with a belch or burp, there is no better arrangement.

Youngish Dradin, still smarting from the ghost of the strap of a half an hour past, dared not argue, but thought often: yes, but all such locutions of thought are reliable and reliant upon one simple supposition—to whit, that she be insane. What if not insane but sane "south by southwest" as the great Voss Bender said? What if, inside the graying but leopardesque head, the burgeoning frame, lay a wide realm of sanity, with only the outer shell susceptible to hallucinations, incantations, and inappropriate metaphors? What then? To be yanked about thus, like an animal on a chain, could this be stood by a sane individual? Might such parading and humiliation lead a person to the very insanity hitherto avoided?

And, worse thought still, that his father had driven her to it with his cruel, carefully-planned indifference.

But Dradin—remembering the awful silence of that day in the rain when Mom had stuffed her mouth full of mud—refused to dwell on it. He must find a present for his darling, this accomplished by rummaging through his pack and coming up with a necklace, the centerpiece an uncut emerald. It had been given to him by a tribal chieftain as a bribe to go away ("There is only One God," Dradin had said. "What's his name?" the chieftain asked. "God," replied Dradin. "How bloody boring," the chieftain said. "Please go away.") and he had taken it initially as a donation to the Church, although he had meant to give it to the spiced fig of his heart, the sweaty woman priest, only to have the fever overtake him first. As he held the necklace in his hand, he recognized the exceptional workmanship of the blue-and-green beads. If he were to sell it, he might pay the rent at the hostel for another week. But, more attractive, if he gave it to his love, she would understand the seriousness of his heart's desire.

With uncharacteristic grace and a touch of inspired lunacy, Dradin tore the first page from *The Refraction of Light in a Prison* and wrote his name below the name of the last monk, like so:

Brother Dradin Kashmir –
Not truly a brother, but devout
in his love for you alone

Dradin looked over his penmanship with satisfaction. There. It was done. It could not be undone.

JEFF VANDERMEER

IV

Over breakfast, his sparse needs tended to by a gaunt waiter who looked like a malaria victim, Dradin examined his dull gray map. Toast without jam for him, nothing richer like sausages frying in their own fat, or bacon with white strips of lard. The jungle climate had, from the start, made his bowels and bladder loosen up and pour forth their bile like the sludge of rain in the most deadly of monsoon seasons. Dradin had avoided rich foods ever since, saying no to such jungle delicacies as fried grasshopper, boiled pig, and a local favorite that baked huge black slugs into their shells.

From dirty gray table-clothed tables on either side, war veterans coughed and harrumphed, their bloodshot eyes perked into semi-awareness by the sight of Dradin's map. Treasure? War on two fronts? Mad, drunken charges into the eyeteeth of the enemy? No doubt. Dradin knew their type, for his father was the same, if with an academic bent. The map would be a mystery of the mind to his father.

Ignoring their stares, Dradin found the religious quarter on the map, traced over it with his index finger. It resembled a bird's eye view of a wheel with interconnecting spokes. No more a "quarter" than drawn. Cadimon Signal's mission stood near the center of the spokes, snuggled into a corner between the Church of the Fisherman and the Cult of the Seven-Edged Star. Even looking at it on the map made Dradin nervous. To meet his religious instructor after such a time. How would Cadimon have aged after seven years? Perversely, as far afield as Dradin had gone, Cadimon Signal had, in that time, come closer to the center, his home, for he had been born in Ambergris. At the religious institute Cadimon had extolled the city's virtues and, to be fair, its vices many times after lectures, in the common hall. His voice, hollow and echoing against the black marble archways, gave a raspy voice to the gossamer-thin cherubim carved into the swirl of white marble ceilings. Dradin had spent many nights along with Anthony Toliver listening to that voice, surrounded by thousands of religious texts on shelves gilded with gold leaf.

The question that most intrigued Dradin, that guided his thoughts and bedeviled his nights, was this: Would Cadimon Signal take pity on a former student and find a job for him? He hoped, of course, for a missionary position, but failing that a position which would not break his back or tie him in knots of bureaucratic red tape. Dad was an unlikely ally in this, for Dad had recommended Dradin to Cadimon and also recommended Cadimon to Dradin.

Before the fuzzy beginnings of Dradin's memory, Dad had, when still young and thin and mischievous, invited Cadimon over for tea and conversation, surrounded in Dad's study by books, books, and more books. Books on culture and civilization, religion and philosophy. They would, or so Dad told Dradin later, debate every topic imaginable, and some that were unimaginable, distasteful, or all too real until the hours struck midnight, one o'clock, two o'clock, and the lanterns dimmed to an ironic light, brackish and ill-suited to discussion. Surely this bond would be enough? Surely Cadimon would look at him and see the father in the son?

After breakfast, necklace and map in hand, Dradin wandered into the religious quarter, known by the common moniker of Pejora's Folly after Midan Pejora, the principal early architect, to whose credit or discredit could be placed the slanted walls, the jumble of Occidental and accidental, northern and southern, baroque and pure jungle, styles. Buildings battled for breath and space like centuries-slow soldiers in brick-to-brick combat. To look into the revolving spin of a kaleidoscope while heavily intoxicated, Dradin thought, would not be half so bad.

The rain from the night before took the form of sunlit droplets on plants, windowpanes, and cobblestones that wiped away the dull and dusty veneer of the city. Cats preened and tiny hop toads hopped while dead sparrows lay in furrows of water, beaten down by the storm's ferocity.

He snorted in disbelief as he observed followers of gentle Saint Solon the Decrepit placing the corpses of rain victims such as the sparrows into tiny wooden coffins for burial. In the jungle, deaths occurred in such thick numbers that one might walk a mile on the decayed carcasses, the white clean bones of deceased animals, and after a time even the most fastidious missionary gave the crunching sound not a second thought.

As he neared the mission, Dradin tried to calm himself by breathing in the acrid scent of votive candles burning from alcoves and crevices and doorways. He tried to imagine the richness of his father's conversations with Cadimon—the plethora of topics discussed, the righteous and pious denials and arguments. When his father mentioned those conversations, the man would shake off the weight of years, his voice light and his eyes moist with nostalgia. If only Cadimon remembered such encounters with similar enthusiasm.

The slap-slap of punished pilgrim feet against the stones of the street pulled him from his reverie. He stood to one side as twenty or thirty mendicants slapped on past, cleansing their sins through their calluses, on their way to one of a thousand shrines. In their calm but blank gaze, their slack mouths, Dradin saw the shadow of his mother's face, and he wondered what she had done while his father and Cadimon talked. Gone to sleep? Finished up the dishes? Sat in bed and listened through the wall?

At last, Dradin found the Mission of Cadimon Signal. Set back from the street, the mission remained almost invisible among the skyward-straining cathedrals surrounding it—remarkable only for the emptiness, the silence, and the swirl of swallows skimming through the air like weightless trapeze artists. The building that housed the mission was an old tin-roofed warehouse reinforced with mortar and brick, opened up from the inside with ragged holes for skylights, which made Dradin wonder what they did when it rained. Let it rain on them, he supposed.

Christened with fragmented mosaics that depicted saints, monks, and martyrs, the enormous doorway lay open to him. All around, acolytes frantically lifted sandbags and long pieces of timber, intent on barricading the entrance, but none challenged him as he walked up the steps and through the gateway; no one, in fact, spared him a second glance, so focused were they on their efforts.

Inside, Dradin went from sunlight to shadows, his footfalls hollow in the silence. A maze of paths wound through lush green Occidental-style gardens. The gardens centered around rock-lined pools cut through by the curving fins of corpulent carp. Next to the pools lay the eroded ruins of ancient, pagan temples, which had been reclaimed with gaily-colored paper and splashes of red, green, blue, and white paint. Among the temples and gardens and pools, unobtrusive as lamp posts, acolytes in gray habits toiled, removing dirt, planting herbs, and watering flowers. The air had a metallic color and flavor to it and Dradin heard the buzzing of bees at the many poppies, the soft *scull-skithing* as acolytes wielded their scythes against encroaching weeds.

The ragged, blue grass-fringed trail led Dradin to a raised mound of dirt on which stood a catafalque, decorated with gold leaf and the legend "Saint Philip the Philanderer" printed along its side. In the shadow of the catafalque, amid the grass, a gardener dressed in dark green robes planted lilies he had set on a nearby bench. Atop the catafalque, halting Dradin in mid-step, stood Signal. He had changed since Dradin had last seen him, for he was bald and gaunt, with white tufts of hair sprouting from his ears. A studded dog collar circled his withered neck. But most disturbing, unless one wished to count a cask of wine that dangled from his left hand—no doubt shipped in by those reliable if questionable purveyors of spirits Hoegbotton & Sons, perhaps even held, caressed, by his love—*the man was stark staring naked!* The object of no one's desire bobbed like a length of flaccid purpling sausage, held in some semblance of erectitude by the man's right hand, the hand currently engaged in an up-and-down motion that brought great pleasure to its owner.

"Ccc-Cadimon Ssss-sigggnal?"

"Yes, who is it now?" said the gardener.

"I beg your pardon."

"I said," repeated the gardener with infinite patience, as if he really would not mind saying it a third, a fourth, or a fifth time, "I said 'Yes, who is it now?'"

"It's Dradin. Dradin Kashmir. Who are you?" Dradin kept one eye on the naked man atop the catafalque.

"I'm Cadimon Signal, of course," the gardener said, patiently pulling weeds, potting lilies. *Pull, pot, pull.* "Welcome to my mission, Dradin. It's been a long time." The small, green-robed man in front of Dradin had mannerisms and features indistinguishable from any wizened beggar on Albumuth Boulevard, but looking closer Dradin thought he could see a certain resemblance to the man he had known in Morrow. Perhaps.

"Who is he, then?" Dradin pointed to the naked man, who was now ejaculating into a rose bush.

"He's a Living Saint. A professional holy man. You should remember that from your theology classes. I know I must have taught you about Living Saints. Unless, of course, I switched that with a unit on Dead Martyrs. No other kind, really. That's a joke, Dradin. Have the decency to laugh."

The Living Saint, no longer aroused, but quite tired, lay down on the smooth cool stone of the catafalque and began to snore.

"But what's a Living Saint doing here? And naked?"

"I keep him here to discomfort my creditors who come calling. Lots of upkeep to this place. My, you have changed, haven't you?"

"What?"

"I thought I had gone deaf. I said you've changed. Please, ignore my Living Saint. As I said, he's for the creditors. Just trundle him out, have him spill his seed, and they don't come back."

"I've changed?"

"Yes, I've said that already." Cadimon stopped potting lilies and stood up, examined Dradin from crown to stirrups. "You've been to the jungle. A pity, really. You were a good student."

"I have come back from the jungle, if that's what you mean. I took fever."

"No doubt. You've changed most definitely. Here, hold a lily bulb for me." Cadimon crouched down once more. *Pull, pot, pull.*

"You seem . . . you seem somehow less imposing. But healthier."

"No, no. You've grown taller, that's all. What are you now that you are no longer a missionary?"

"No longer a missionary?" Dradin said, and felt as if he were drowning, and here they had only just started to talk.

"Yes. Or no. Lily please. Thank you. Blessed things require so much dirt. Good for the lungs exercise is. Good for the soul. How is your father these days? Such a shame about your mother. But how is he?"

"I haven't seen him in over three years. He wrote me while I was in the jungle and he seemed to be doing well."

"Mmmm. I'm glad to hear it. Your father and I had the most wonderful conversations a long time ago. A very long time ago. Why, I can remember sitting up at his house—you just in a crib then, of course—and debating the aesthetic value of the Golden Spheres until—"

"I've come here looking for a job."

Silence. Then Cadimon said, "Don't you still work for—"

"I quit." Emphasis on *quit,* like the pressure on an egg to make it crack just so.

"Did you now? I told you you were no longer a missionary. I haven't changed a bit from those days at the academy, Dradin. You didn't recognize me because you've changed, not I. I'm the same. I do not change. Which is more than you can say for the weather around here."

It was time, Dradin decided, to take control of the conversation. It was not enough to counter-punch Cadimon's drifting dialogue. He bent to his knees and gently placed the rest of the lilies in Cadimon's lap.

"Sir," he said. "I need a position. I have been out of my mind with the fever for three months and now, only just recovered, I long to return to the life of a missionary."

"Determined to stick to a point, aren't you?" Cadimon said. "A point stickler. A stickler for rules. I remember you. Always the sort to be shocked by a Living Saint rather than amused. Rehearsed rather than spontaneous. Oh well."

"Cadimon . . . "

"Can you cook?"

"Cook? I can boil cabbage. I can heat water."

Cadimon patted Dradin on the side of his stomach. "So can a hedgehog, my dear. So can a hedgehog, if pressed. No, I mean cook as in the Cooks of Kalay, who can take nothing more than a cauldron of bilge water and a side of beef three days old and tough as calluses and make a dish so succulent and sweet it shames the taste buds to eat so much as a carrot for days afterwards. You can't cook, can you?"

"What does cooking have to do with missionary work?"

"Oh, ho. I'd have thought a jungle veteran would know the answer to that! Ever heard of cannibals? Eh? No, that's a joke. It has nothing to do with missionary work. There." He patted the last of the lilies and rose to sit on the bench, indicating with a wave of the hand that Dradin should join him.

Dradin sat down on the bench next to Cadimon. "Surely, you need experienced missionaries?"

Cadimon shook his head. "We don't have a job for you. I'm sorry. You've changed, Dradin."

"But you and my father . . . " Blood rose to Dradin's face. For he could woo until he turned purple, but without a job, how to fund such adventures in pocketbook as his new love would entail?

"Your father is a good man, Dradin. But this mission is not made of money. I see tough times ahead."

Pride surfaced in Dradin's mind like a particularly ugly crocodile. "I am a good missionary, sir. A very good missionary. I have been a missionary for over five years, as you know. And, as I have said, I am just now out of the jungle, having nearly died of fever. Several of my colleagues did not recover. The woman. The woman . . . "

But he trailed off, his skin goose-pimpled from a sudden chill. Layeville, Flay, Stern, Thaw, and Krug had all gone mad or died under the onslaught of green, the rain and the dysentery, and the savages with their poison arrows. Only he had crawled to safety, the mush of the jungle floor beneath his chest a-murmur with leeches and dung bugs and "molly twelve-step" centipedes. A trek into and out of hell, and he could not even now remember it all, or wanted to remember it all.

"Paugh! Dying of fever is easy. The jungle is easy, Dradin. I could survive, frail as I am. It's the city that's hard. If you'd only bother to observe, you'd see the air is overripe with missionaries. You can't defecate out a window without fouling a brace of them. The city bursts with them. They think that the festival signals opportunity, but the opportunity is not for them! No, we need a cook, and you cannot cook."

Dradin's palms slickened with sweat, his hands shaking as he examined them. What now? What to do? His thoughts circled and circled around the same unanswerable question: How could he survive on the coins he had yet on his person and still woo the woman in the window? And he must woo her; he did not feel his heart could withstand the blow of *not* pursuing her.

"I am a good missionary," Dradin repeated, looking at the ground. "What happened in the jungle was not my fault. We went out looking for converts and when I came back the compound was overrun."

Dradin's breaths came quick and shallow and his head felt light. Suffocating. He was suffocating under the weight of jungle leaves closing over his nose and mouth.

Cadimon sighed and shook his head. In a soft voice he said, "I am not unsympathetic," and held out his hands to Dradin. "How can I explain myself? Maybe I cannot, but let me try. Perhaps this way: Have you converted the Flying Squirrel People of the western hydras? Have you braved the frozen wastes of Lascia to convert the ice-cube-like Skamoo?"

"No."

"What did you say?"

"No!"

"Then we can't use you. At least not now."

Dradin's throat ached and his jaw tightened. Would he have to beg, then? Would he have to become a mendicant himself? On the catafalque, the Living Saint had begun to stir, mumbling in his half-sleep.

Cadimon rose and put his hand on Dradin's shoulder. "If it is any consolation, you were never really a missionary, not even at the religious academy. And you are definitely not a missionary now. You are . . . something else. Extraordinary, really, that I can't put my finger on it."

"You insult me," Dradin said, as if he were the gaudy figurehead on some pompous yacht sailing languid on the Moth.

"That is not my intent, my dear. Not at all."

"Perhaps you could give me money. I could repay you."

"Now *you* insult *me*. Dradin, I cannot lend you money. We have no money. All the money we collect goes to our creditors or into the houses and shelters of the poor. We have no money, nor do we covet it."

"Cadimon," Dradin said. "Cadimon, I'm desperate. I need money."

"If you are desperate, take my advice—leave Ambergris. And before the festival. It's not safe for priests to be on the streets after dark on festival night. There have been so many years of calm. Ha! I tell you, it can't last."

"It wouldn't have to be much money. Just enough to—"

Cadimon gestured toward the entrance. "Beg from your father, not from me. Leave. Leave now."

Dradin, taut muscles and clenched fists, would have obeyed Cadimon out of respect for the memory of authority, but now a vision rose into his mind like the moon rising over the valley the night before. A vision of the jungle, the dark green leaves with their veins like spines, like long, delicate bones. The jungle and the woman and all of the dead . . .

"I will not."

Cadimon frowned. "I'm sorry to hear you say that. I ask you again, leave."

Lush green, smothering, the taste of dirt in his mouth; the smell of burning, smoke curling up into a question mark.

"Cadimon, I was your student. You owe me the—"

"Living Saint!" Cadimon shouted. "Wake up, Living Saint."

The Living Saint uncurled himself from his repose atop the catafalque.

"Living Saint," Cadimon said, "dispense with him. No need to be gentle." And, turning to Dradin: "Goodbye, Dradin. I am very sorry."

The Living Saint, spouting insults, jumped from the catafalque and—his penis purpling and flaccid as a sea anemone, brandished menacingly—ran toward Dradin, who promptly took to his heels, stumbling through the ranks of the gathered acolytes and hearing directly behind him as he navigated the blue grass trail not only the Living Saint's screams of "Piss off! Piss off, you great big baboon!" but also Cadimon's distant shouts of: "I'll pray for you, Dradin. I'll pray for you." And, then, too close, much too

close, the unmistakable hot and steamy sound of a man re-
lieving himself, followed by the hands of the Living Saint
clamped down on his shoulder blades, and a much swifter
exit than he had hoped for upon his arrival, scuffing his
fundament, his pride, his dignity.

"And stay out!"

When Dradin stopped running he found himself on
the fringe of the religious quarter, next to an emaciated
macadamia salesman who cracked jokes like nuts. Out
of breath, Dradin put his hands on his hips. His lungs
strained for air. Blood rushed furiously through his chest.
He could almost persuade himself that these symptoms
were only the aftershock of exertion, not the aftershock of
anger and desperation. Actions unbecoming a missionary.
Actions unbecoming a gentleman. What might love next
drive him to?

Determined to regain his composure, Dradin straightened his shirt and collar, then continued on his way in a
manner he hoped mimicked the stately gait of a mid-level
clergy member, to whom all such earthly things were beneath and below. But the bulge of red veins at his neck, the
stiffness of fingers in claws at his sides, these clues gave
him away, and knowing this made him angrier still. How
dare Cadimon treat him as though he were practically a
stranger! How dare the man betray the bond between his
father and the church!

More disturbing, where were the agents of order when
you needed them? No doubt the city had ordinances against
public urination. Although that presupposed the existence
of a civil authority, and of this mythic beast Dradin had

yet to convince himself. He had not seen a single blue, black, or brown uniform, and certainly not filled out with a body lodged within its fabric, a man who might symbolize law and order and thus give the word flesh. What did the people of Ambergris do when thieves and molesters and murderers traversed the thoroughfares and alleyways, the underpasses and the bridges? But the thought brought him back to the mushroom dwellers and their alcove shrines, and he abandoned it, a convulsion traveling from his chin to the tips of his toes. Perhaps the jungle had not yet relinquished its grip.

Finally, shoulders bowed, eyes on the ground, in abject defeat, he admitted to himself that his methods had been grotesque. He had made a fool of himself in front of Cadimon. Cadimon was not beholden to him. Cadimon had only acted as he must when confronted with the ungodly.

Necklace still wrapped in the page from *The Refraction of Light in a Prison,* Dradin came again to Hoegbotton & Sons, only to find that his love no longer stared from the third floor window. A shock traveled up his spine, a shock that might have sent him gibbering to his mother's side aboard the psychiatrists' houseboat, if not that he was a rational and rationalizing man. How his heart drowned in a sea of fears as he tried to conjure up a thousand excuses: she was out to lunch; she had taken ill; she had moved to another part of the building. Never that she was gone for good, lost as he was lost; that he might never, ever see her face again. Now Dradin understood his father's addiction to sweet-milled mead, beer, wine and champagne, for the woman was his addiction, and he knew that if he had only seen her porcelain-perfect visage as he suffered from the jungle fevers, he would have lived for her sake alone.

The city might be savage, stray dogs might share the streets with grimy urchins whose blank eyes reflected the knowledge that they might soon be covered over, blinded forever, by the same two pennies just begged from some gentleman, and no one in all the fuming, fulminous boulevards of trade might know who actually ran Ambergris—or, if anyone ran it at all, but, like a renegade clock, it ran on and wound itself heedless, empowered by the insane weight of its own inertia, the weight of its own citizenry, stamping one, two, three hundred thousand strong; no matter this savagery in the midst of apparent civilization—still the woman in the window seemed to him more ruly, more disciplined and in control and thus, perversely, malleable to his desire, than anyone Dradin had yet met in Ambergris: this priceless part of the whale, this overbrimming stew of the sublime and the ridiculous.

It was then that his rescuer came: Dvorak, popping up from betwixt a yardstick of a butcher awaiting a hansom and a jowly furrier draped over with furs of auburn, gray, and white. Dvorak, indeed, dressed all in black, against which the red dots of his tattoo throbbed and, in his jacket pocket, a dove-white handkerchief stained red at the edges. A mysterious, feminine smile decorated his mutilated face.

"She's not at the window," Dradin said.

Dvorak's laugh forced his mouth open wide and wider still, carnivorous in its red depths. "No. She is not at the window. But have no doubt: she is inside. She is a most devout employee."

"You gave her the book?"

"I did, sir." The laugh receded into a shallow smile. "She took it from me like a lady, with hesitation, and when I told her it came from a secret admirer, she blushed."

"Blushed?" Dradin felt lighter, his blood yammering and his head a puff of smoke, a cloud, a spray of cotton candy.

"Blushed. Indeed, sir, a good sign."

Dradin took the package from his pocket and, hands trembling, gave it to the dwarf. "Now you must go back in and find her, and when you find her, give her this. You must ask her to join me at *The Drunken Boat* at twilight. You know the place?"

Dvorak nodded, his hands clasped protectively around the package.

"Good. I will have a table next to the festival parade route. Beg her if you must. Intrigue her and entreat her."

"I will do so."

"U-u-unless you think I should take this gift to her myself?"

Dvorak sneered. He shook his head so that the green of the jungles blurred before Dradin's eyes. "Think, sir. Think hard. Would you have her see you first out of breath, unkempt, and, if I may be so bold, there is a slight smell of *urine*. No, sir. Meet her first at the tavern, and there you shall appear a man of means, at your ease, inviting her to the unraveling of further mysteries."

Dradin looked away. How his inexperience must show. How foolish his suggestions. And yet, also, relief that Dvorak had thwarted his brashness.

"Sir?" Dvorak said. "Sir?"

Dradin forced himself to look at Dvorak. "You are correct, of course. I will see her at the tavern."

"Coins, sir."

"Coins?"

"I cannot live on kindness."

"Yes. Of course. Of course." Damn Dvorak! No compassion there. He stuck a hand into his pants pocket and pulled out a gold coin, which he handed to Dvorak. "Another when you return."

"As you wish. Wait here." Dvorak gave Dradin one last long look and then scurried up the steps, disappearing into the darkness of the doorway.

Dradin discovered he was bad at waiting. He sat on the curb, got up, crouched to his knees, leaned on a lamp post, scratched at a flea biting his ankle. All the while, he looked up at the blank window and thought: If I had come into the city today, I would have looked up at the third floor and seen nothing and this frustration, this impatience, this *ardor*, would not be practically bursting from me now.

Finally, Dvorak scuttled down the steps with his jacket tails floating out behind him, his grin larger, if that were possible, positively a leer.

"What did she say?" Dradin pressed. "Did she say anything? Something? Yes? No?"

"Success, sir. Success. Busy as she is, devout as she is, she said little, but only that she will meet you at *The Drunken Boat*, though perhaps not until after dusk has fallen. She looked quite favorably on the emerald and the message. She calls you, sir, a gentleman."

A gentleman. Dradin stood straighter. "Thank you," he

said. "You have been a great help to me. Here." And he passed another coin to Dvorak, who snatched it from his hand with all the swiftness of a snake.

As Dvorak murmured goodbye, Dradin heard him with but one ear, cocooned as he was in a world where the sun always shone bright and uncovered all hidden corners, allowing no shadows or dark and glimmering truths.

V

DRADIN HURRIED BACK TO THE HOSTEL. HE HARDLY SAW the flashes of red, green, and blue around him, nor sensed the expectant quality in the air, the huddled groups of people talking in animated voices, for night would bring the Festival of Freshwater Squid and the streets would hum and thrum with celebration. Already, the clean smell of fresh-baked bread, mixed with the treacly promise of sweets, began to tease noses and turn frowns into smiles. Boys let out early from school played games with hoops and marbles and bits of brick. The more adventurous imitated the grand old King Squid sinking ships with a single lash of tentacle, puddle-bound toy boats smashed against drainpipes. Still others watched the erection of scaffolding on tributary streets leading into Albumuth Boulevard. Stilt men with purpling painted faces hung candy and papiermâché heads in equal quantities from their stilts.

At last, Dradin came to his room, flung open the door, and shut it abruptly behind him. As the citizens of Ambergris prepared for the festival, so now he must prepare for his love, putting aside the distractions of joblessness and decreasing coin. He stripped and took a shower, turning the water on so hot that needles of heat tattooed his skin red, but he felt clean, and more than clean, cleansed and calm, when he came out after thirty minutes and wiped himself dry with a large green towel. Standing in front of the bathroom mirror in the nude, Dradin noted that although he had filled out since the cessation of his fever, he had not filled out into fat. Not even the shadow of a belly, and his legs thick with muscle. Hardly a family characteristic, that, for his randy father had, since the onset of Mom's river adventures, grown as pudgy as raw bread dough. Nothing for Dad to do but continue to teach ethics at the university and hope that the lithe young things populating his classes would pity him. But for his son a different fate, Dradin was sure.

Dradin shaved, running the blade across his chin and down his neck, so that he thrilled to the self-control it took to keep the blade steady; and yet, when he was done, his hand shook. There. Now various oils worked into the scalp so that his hair became a uniform black, untainted by white except at the outer provinces, where it grazed his ears. Then a spot of rouge to bring out the muddy green of his eyes—a scandalous habit, perhaps, learned from his mother of course, but Dradin knew many pale priests who used it.

For clothing, Dradin started with clean underwear and followed with fancy socks done up in muted purple and gold serpent designs. Then the trousers of gray—gray as the slits of his father's eyes in the grip of spirits, gray as his mother's listless moods after performances at the music halls. Yes, a smart gray, a deep gray, not truly conservative, followed by the shirt: large on him but not voluminous, white with purple and gold buttons, to match the socks, and a jacket over top that mixed gray and purple thread so that, from heel to head, he looked as distinguished as a debutante at some political gala. It pleased him—as much a uniform as his missionary clothes, but the goal a conversion of a more personal nature. Yes, he would do well.

Thus equipped, his pockets jingly with his last coins, his stomach wrapped in coils of nerves (an at-sea sensation of *notenoughmoney, notenoughmoney* beating inside his organs like a pulse), Dradin made his way out onto the streets.

The haze of twilight had smothered Ambergris, muffling sounds and limiting vision, but everywhere also: lights. Lights from balconies and bedrooms, signposts and horse carriages, candles held by hand and lanterns swinging on the arms of grizzled caretakers who sang out, from deep in their throats, "The dying of the light! The dying of the light! Let the Festival begin."

Wraiths riding metal bars, men on bicycles swished past, bells all a-tinkle, and children in formal attire, entow to the vast and long-suffering barges of nannies, who tottered forward on unsteady if stocky legs. Child mimes in white face approached Dradin, prancing and pirouetting, and Dradin clapped in approval and patted their heads. They reminded him of the naked boys and girls of the Nimblytod Tribe, who swung through trees and ate birds that became lost in the forest and could not find their way again into the light.

Women in the red and black of hunters' uniforms crossed his path. They rode hollow wooden horses that fit around their waists, fake wooden legs clacking to either side as their own legs cantered or galloped or pranced, but so controlled, so tight and rigid, that they never broke formation despite the random nature of their movements. The horses had each been individually painted in grotesque shades of green, red, and white: eyes wept blood, teeth snarled into black fangs. The women's lips were drawn back against the red leer of lipstick to neigh and nicker. Around them, the gathering crowd shrieked in laughter, the riders so entranced that only the whites of their eyes showed, shockingly pale against the gloom.

Dradin passed giant spits on which spun and roasted whole cows, whole pigs, and a host of smaller beasts, the spits rotated by grunting, muscular, ruddy-faced men. Everywhere, the mushroom dwellers uncurled from slumber with a yawn, picked up their red flags, and trundled off to their secret and arcane rites. Armed men mock-fought with saber and with knife while youths wrestled half-naked in the gutters—their bodies burnished with sweat, their eyes focused not on each other but on the young women who watched their battles. Impromptu dances devoid of form or unified steps spread amongst the spectators until Dradin had to struggle through their spider's webs of gyrations, inured to the laughter and chatter of conversations, the tap and stomp of feet on the rough stones. For this was the most magical night of the year in Ambergris, the Festival of the Freshwater Squid, and the city lay in trance, spellbound and difficult, and everywhere, into the apparent lull, glance met glance, eyes sliding from eyes, as if to say, "What next? What will happen next?"

At last, after passing through an archway strung with nooses, Dradin came out onto a main boulevard, *The Drunken Boat* before him. How could he miss it? It had been lit up like an ornament so that all three stories of slanted dark oak decks sparkled and glowed with good cheer.

A crowd had lined up in front of the tavern, waiting to gain entrance, but Dradin fought through the press, bribed the doorman with a gold coin, and ducked inside, climbing stairs to the second level, high enough to see far down the boulevard, although not so high that the sights would be uninvolving and distant. A tip to the waiter secured Dradin a prime table next to the railing of the deck. The table, complete with lace and embroidered tablecloth, engraved cutlery, and a quavery candle encircled by glass, lay equidistant from the parade and the musical meanderings of The Ravens, four scruffy-looking musicians who played, respectively, the mandolin, twelve-string guitar, the flute, and the drums:

In the city of lies
I spoke in nothing
but the language of spies.

In the city of my demise
I spoke in nothing
but the language of flies.

Their music reminded Dradin of high tide crashing against cliffs and, then, on the down-tempo, of the back-and-forth swell of giant waves rippling across a smooth surface of water. It soothed him and made him seasick both, and when he sat down at the table, the wood beneath him lurched, though he knew it was only the surging of his own pulse, echoed in the floorboards.

Dradin surveyed the parade route, which was lined with glittery lights rimmed with crepe paper that made a crinkly sound as the breeze hit it. A thousand lights done up in blue and green, and the crowd gathered to both sides behind them, so that the street became an iridescent replica of the Moth, not nearly as wide, but surely as deep and magical.

Around him came the sounds of laughter and polite conversation, each table its own island of charm and anticipation: ladies in white and red dresses that sparkled with sequins when the light caught them, gentlemen in dark blue suits or tuxedos, looking just as ridiculous as Dad had once looked, caught out in the rain.

Dradin ordered a mildly alcoholic drink called a Red Orchid and sipped it as he snuck glances at the couple to his immediate right: a tall, thin man with aquiline features, eyes narrow as paper cuts, and rich, gray sideburns, and his consort, a blonde woman in an emerald dress that covered her completely and yet also revealed her completely in the tightness of its fabric. Flushed in the candlelight, she laughed too loudly, smiled too quickly, and it made Dradin cringe to watch her make a fool of herself, the man a bigger fool for not putting her at ease. The man only watched her with a thin smile splayed across his face. Surely when the woman in the window, his love, came to his table, there would be only traces of this awkwardness, this ugliness in the guise of grace?

His love? Glass at his lips, Dradin realized he didn't know her name. It could be Angeline or Melanctha or Galendrace, or even—and his expression darkened as he concentrated *hard*, felt an odd tingling in his temples, finally expelled the name—"Nepenthe," the name of the sweaty woman priest in the jungles. He put down his glass. All this preparation, his nerves on edge, and he didn't even know the name of the woman in the window. A chill went through him, for did he not know her as well as he knew himself?

Soon, the procession made its way down the parade route: the vast, engulfing cloth kites with wire ribs that formed the shapes of giant squid, paper streamers for tentacles running out behind as, lit by their own inner flames, they bumped and spun against the darkened sky. Ships followed them—floats mounted on the rusted hulks of mechanized vehicles, their purpose to re-enact the same scene as the boys with their toy boats: the hunt for the mighty King Squid, which made its home in the deepest parts of the Moth, in the place where the river was wide as the sea and twice as mad with silt.

Dradin clapped and said, "Beautiful, beautiful," and, with elegant desperation, ordered another drink, for if he was to be starving and penniless anyway, what was one more expense?

On the parade route, performing wolfhounds followed the floats, then jugglers, mimes, fire-eaters, contortionists, and belly dancers. The gangrenous moon began to seep

across the sky in dark green hues. The drone of conversations grew more urgent and the cries of the people on the
street below, befouled by food, drink, and revelry, became
discordant: a fragmented roar of fragmenting desires.

Where was his love? Would she not come? Dradin's
head felt light and hollow, yet heavy as the earth spinning
up to greet him, at the possibility. No, it was not a possibility. Dradin ordered yet another Red Orchid.

She would come. Dressed in white and red she would
come, around her throat a necklace of intricate blue and
green beads, a rough emerald dangling from the center. He
would stand to greet her and she would offer her hand to
him and he would bow to kiss it. Her skin would be warm
to the touch of his lips and his lips would feel warm and
electric to her. He would say to her, "Please, take a seat,"
and pull out her chair. She would acknowledge his chivalry
with a slight leftward tip of her head. He would wait for
her to sit and then he would sit, wave to a waiter, order
her a glass of wine, and then they would talk. Circling in
toward how he had first seen her, he would ask her how she
liked the book, the necklace. Perhaps both would laugh at
the crudity of Dvorak, and at his own shyness, for surely
now she could see that he was not truly shy. The hours
would pass and with each minute and each witty comment,
she would look more deeply into his eyes and he into hers.
Their hands would creep forward across the table until,
clumsily, she jostled her wine glass and he reached out to
keep it from falling—and found her hand instead.

From there, her hand in his, their gaze so intimate
across the table, everything would be easy, because it would
all be unspoken, but no less eloquent for that. Perhaps they

≈ 70 ≈

would leave the table, the tavern, traverse the streets in the aftermath of festival. But, no matter what they did, there would be this bond between them: that they had drunk deep of the desire in each other's eyes.

Dradin wiped the sweat from his forehead, took another sip of his drink, looked into the crowd, which merged with the parade, crashing and pushing toward the lights and the performers.

War veterans were marching past: a grotesque assembly of ghost limbs, memories disassembled from the flesh, for not a one had two arms and two legs both. They clattered and shambled forward in their odd company with crutches and wheelchairs and comrades supporting them. They wore the uniforms of a hundred wars and ranged in age from seventeen to seventy; Dradin recognized a few from his hostel. Those who carried sabers waved and twirled their weapons, inciting the crowd, which now pushed and pulled and divided amongst itself like a replicating beast, to shriek and line the parade route ever more closely.

Then, with solemn precision, four men came carrying a coffin, so small as to be for a child, each lending but a single hand to the effort. On occasion, the leader would fling open the top to reveal the empty interior and the crowd would moan and stamp its feet.

Behind the coffin, in a cage, came a jungle cat that snarled and worked one enormous pitch paw through bamboo bars. Looking into the dulled but defiant eyes of the cat, Dradin gulped his Red Orchid and thought of the jungle. *The moist heat, the ferns curling into their fetid greenness, the flowers running red, the thick smell of rich black soil on the shovel, the pale gray of the woman's hand, the suddenness of coming upon a savage village, soon to be a ghost place, the savages fled or struck down by disease, the dark eyes, the questioning looks on the faces of those he disturbed, bringing his missionary word, the way the forest could be too green, so fraught with scents and tastes and sounds that one could become intoxicated by it, even become feverish within it, drowning in black water, plagued by the curse of no converts.*

Dradin shuddered again from the cold of the drink, and thought he felt the deck beneath him roll and plunge in time to the music of The Ravens. Was it possible that he had never fully recovered from the fever? Was he even now stone cold mad in the head, or was he simply woozy from Red Orchids? Or could he be, in his final distress, drunk on love? He had precious little else left, a realization accompanied by a not unwelcome thrill of fear. With no job and little money, the only element of his being he found constant and unyielding, undoubting, was the strength of his love for the woman in the window.

He smiled at the couple at the next table, though no doubt it came out as the sort of drunken leer peculiar to his father. Past relationships had been of an unfortunate nature; he could admit that to himself now. Too platonic, too strange, and always too brief. The jungle did not approve of long relationships. The jungle ate up long relationships, ground them between its teeth and spat them out. Like the relationship between himself and Nepenthe. Nepenthe. Might the woman in the window also be called Nepenthe? Would she mind if he called her that? Now the deck beneath him really did roll and list like a ship at sea, and he held himself to his chair, pushed the Red Orchid away when he had come once more to rest.

Looking out at the parade, Dradin saw Cadimon Signal and he had to laugh. Cadimon. Good old Cadimon. Was this parade to become like Dvorak's wonderfully ugly tattoo? A trip from past to present? For there indeed was Cadimon, waving to the crowds from a float of gold and white satin, the Living Saint beside him, diplomatically clothed for the occasion in messianic white robes.

"Hah!" Dradin said. "Hah!"

The parade ended with an elderly man leading a live lobster on a leash, a sight that made Dradin laugh until he cried. The lights along the boulevard began to be snuffed out, at first one by one, and then, as the mob descended, ripped out in swathes, so that whole sections were plunged into darkness at once. Beyond them, the great spits no longer turned, abandoned, the meat upon them blackened to ash, and beyond the spits bonfires roared and blazed all the more brightly, as if to make up for the death of the other lights. Now it was impossible to tell parade members from crowd members, so clotted together and at-sea were they, mixed in merriment under the green light of the moon.

Around Dradin, busboys hastily cleaned up tables, helped by barkeepers, and he heard one mutter to another, "It will be bad this year. Very bad. I can feel it." The waiter presented Dradin with the check, tapping his feet while Dradin searched his pockets for the necessary coin, and when it was finally offered, snatching it from his hand and leaving in a flurry of tails and shiny shoes.

Dradin, hollow and tired and sad, looked up at the black-and-green-tinged sky. His love had not come and would not now come, and perhaps had never planned to come, for he only had the word of Dvorak. He did not know how he should feel, for he had never considered this possibility, that he might not meet her. He looked around him—at the table fixtures, the emptying tables, the sudden lull. Now what could he do? He could take a menial job and survive on scraps until he could get a message to his father in Morrow—who then might or might not take pity on him. But for salvation? For redemption?

Fireworks wormholed into the sky and exploded in an umbrella of sparks so that the crowds screamed louder to drown out the noise. Someone jostled him from behind. Wetness dripped down his left shoulder, followed by a curse, and he turned in time to see one of the waiters scurry off with a half-spilled drink.

The smoke from the fireworks descended, mixed with the growing fog traipsing off the River Moth. It spread more quickly than Dradin would have thought possible, the night smudged with smoke, thick and dark. And who should come out of this haze and into Dradin's gloom but Dvorak, dressed now in green so that the dilute light of the moon passed invisibly over him. His head cocked curiously, like a monkey's, he approached sideways toward Dradin, an appraising look on his face. Was he poisonous like the snake, Dradin thought, or edible, like the insect? Or was he merely a bit of bark to be ignored? For so did Dvorak appraise him. A spark of anger began to smolder in Dradin, for after all Dvorak had made the arrangements and the woman was not here.

"You," Dradin said, raising his voice over the general roar. "You. What're you doing here? You're late . . . I mean, she's late. She's not coming. Where is she? *Did you lie to me, Dvorak?*"

Dvorak moved to Dradin's side and, with his muscular hands under Dradin's arms, pulled Dradin halfway to his feet with such suddenness that he would have fallen over if he hadn't caught himself.

Dradin whirled around, intending to reprimand Dvorak, but found himself speechless as he stared down into the dwarf's eyes—dark eyes, so impenetrable, the entire face set like sculpted clay, that he could only stand there and say, weakly, "You said she'd be here."

"Shut up," Dvorak said, and the stiff, coiled menace in the voice caught Dradin between anger and obedience. Dvorak filled the moment with words: "She is here. Nearby. It is Festival night. There is danger everywhere. If she had come earlier, perhaps. But now, now you must meet her elsewhere, in safety. For her safety." Dvorak put a clammy hand on Dradin's arm, but Dradin shook him off.

"Don't touch me. Where's safer than here?"

"Nearby, I tell you. The crowd, the festival. Night is upon us. She will not wait for you."

On the street below, fist fights had broken out. Through the haze, Dradin could hear the slap of flesh on flesh, the snap of bone, the moans of victims. People ran hither and thither, shadows flitting through green darkness.

"Come, sir. *Now.*" Dvorak tugged on Dradin's arm, pulled him close, whispered in Dradin's ear like an echo from another place, another time, the map of his face so inscrutable Dradin could not read it: "You must come *now*. Or not at all. If not at all, you will never see her. She will only see you now. Now! Are you so foolish that you will pass?"

Dradin hesitated, weighing the risks. Where might the dwarf lead him?

Dvorak cursed. "Then do not come. Do not. And take your chances with the Festival."

He turned to leave but Dradin reached down and grabbed his arm.

"Wait," Dradin said. "I will come," and taking a few steps found to his relief that he did not stagger.

"Your love awaits," Dvorak said, unsmiling. "Follow close, sir. You would not wish to become lost from me. It would go hard on you."

"How far—"

"No questions. No talking. Follow."

VI

DVORAK LED DRADIN AROUND THE BACK OF *THE DRUNKEN Boat* and into an alley, the stones slick with vomit, littered with sharp glass from broken beer and wine bottles, and guarded by a bum muttering an old song from the equinox. Rats waddled on fat legs to eat from half-gnawed drumsticks and soggy buns.

The rats reminded Dradin of the religious quarter and of Cadimon, and then of Cadimon's warning: *"It's not safe for priests to be on the streets after dark during Festival."* He stopped following Dvorak, his head clearer.

"I've changed my mind. I can see her tomorrow at Hoegbotton & Sons."

Dvorak's face clouded like a storm come up from the bottom of the sea as he turned and came back to Dradin. He said, "You have no choice. Follow me."

"No."

"You will never see her then."

"Are you threatening me?"

Dvorak sighed and his overcoat shivered with the blades of a hundred knives. "You will come with me."

"You've already said that."

"Then you will not come?"

"No."

Dvorak punched Dradin in the stomach. The blow felt like an iron ball. All the breath went out of Dradin. The sky spun above him. He doubled over. The side of Dvorak's shoe caught him in the temple, a deep searing pain. Dradin fell heavily on the slick slime and glass of the cobblestones. Glass cut into his palms, his legs, as he twisted and groaned. He tried, groggily, to get to his feet. Dvorak's shoe exploded against his ribs. He screamed, fell onto his side where he lay unmoving, unable to breathe except in gasps. Clammy hands put a noose of hemp around his neck, pulled it taut, brought his head up off the ground.

Dvorak held a long, slender blade to Dradin's neck and pulled at the hemp until Dradin was on his knees, looking up into the mottled face. Dradin gasped despite his pain, for it was a different face than only moments before.

Dvorak's features were a sea of conflicting emotions, his mouth twisted to express fear, jealousy, sadness, joy, hatred, as if by encompassing a map of the world he had somehow encompassed all of worldly experience, and that it had driven him mad. In Dvorak's eyes, Dradin saw the dwarf's true detachment from the world and on Dvorak's face he saw the beatific smile of the truly damned, for the face, the flesh, still held the memory of emotion, even if the mind behind the flesh had forgotten.

"In the name of God, Dvorak," Dradin said.

Dvorak's mouth opened and the tongue clacked down and the voice came, distant and thin as memory, "You are coming with me, sir. On your feet."

Dvorak pulled savagely on the rope. Dradin gurgled and forced his fingers between the rope and his neck.

"On your feet, I said."

Dradin groaned and rolled over. "I can't."

The knife jabbed into the back of his neck. "Soft! Get up, or I'll kill you here."

Dradin forced himself up, though his head was woozy and his stomach felt punctured beyond repair. He avoided looking down into Dvorak's eyes. To look would only confirm that he was dealing with a monster.

"I am a priest."

"I know you are a priest," Dvorak said.

"Your soul will burn in Hell," Dradin said.

A burst of laughter. "I was born there, sir. My face reflects its flames. Now, you will walk ahead of me. You will not run. You will not raise your voice. If you do, I shall choke you and gut you where you stand."

"I have money," Dradin said heavily, still trying to let air into his lungs. "I have gold."

"And we will take it. Walk! There is not much time."

"Where are we going?"

"You will know when we get there."

When Dradin still did not move, Dvorak shoved him forward. Dradin began to walk, Dvorak so close behind he imagined he could feel the point of the blade against the small of his back.

The green light of the moon stained everything except the bonfires the color of toads and dead grass. The bonfires called with their siren song of flame until crowds gathered at each one to dance, shout, and fight. Dradin soon saw that Dvorak's route—through alley after alley, over barricades—was intended to avoid the bonfires. There was now no cool wind in all the city, for around every corner they turned, the harsh rasp of the bonfires met them. To all sides, buildings sprang up out of the fog— dark, silent, menacing.

As they crossed a bridge, over murky water thick with sewage and the flotsam of the festivities, a man hobbled toward them. His left ear had been severed from his head. He cradled part of someone's leg in his arms. He moaned and when he saw Dradin, Dvorak masked by shadow, he shouted, "Stop them! Stop them!" only to continue on into the darkness, and Dradin helpless anyway. Soon after, following the trail of blood, a hooting mob of ten or twelve youths came a-hunting, tawny-limbed and fresh for the kill. They yelled catcalls and taunted Dradin, but when they saw that he was a prisoner they turned their attentions back to their own prey.

The buildings became black shadows tinged green, the street underfoot rough and ill hewn. A wall stood to either side.

A deep sliver of fear pulled Dradin's nerves taut. "How much further?" he asked.

"Not far. Not far at all."

The mist deepened until Dradin could not tell the difference between the world with his eyes shut and the world with his eyes open. Dradin sensed the scuffle of feet on the pavement behind and in front, and the darkness became claustrophobic, close with the scent of rot and decay.

"We are being followed," Dradin said.

"You are mistaken."

"I hear them!"

"Shut up! It's not far. Trust me."

"Trust me?" Did Dvorak realize the irony of those words? How foolish that they should converse at all, the knife at his back and the hushed breathing from behind and ahead, stalking them. Fear raised the hairs along his arms and heightened his senses, distorting and magnifying every sound.

Their journey ended where the trees were less thick and the fog had been swept aside. Walls did indeed cordon them in, gray walls that ended abruptly ten feet ahead in a welter of shadows that rustled and quivered like dead leaves lifted by the wind, but there was no wind.

Dradin's temples pounded and his breath caught in his throat. On another street, parallel but out of sight, a clock doled out the hours, one through eleven, and revelers tooted on horns or screamed out names or called to the moon in weeping, distant, fading voices.

Dvorak shoved Dradin forward until they came to an open gate, ornately filigreed, and beyond the gate, through the bars, the brooding headstones of a vast graveyard. Mausoleums and memorials, single tombs and groups, families dead together under the thick humus, the young and the old alike feeding the worms, feeding the earth.

The graveyard was overgrown with grass and weeds so that the headstones swam in a sea of green. Beyond these fading statements of life after death writ upon the fissured stones, riven and made secretive by the moonlight, lay the broken husks of trains, haphazard and strewn across the landscape. The twisted metal of engines, freight cars, and cabooses gleamed darkly green and the patina of broken glass windows, held together by moss, shone especially bright, like vast, reflective eyes. Eyes that still held a glimmer of the past when coal had coursed through their engines like blood and brimstone, and their compartments had been busy with the footsteps of those same people who now lay beneath the earth.

The industrial district. Dradin was in the industrial district and now he knew that due south was his hostel and southwest was Hoegbotton & Sons, and the River Moth beyond it.

"I do not see her," Dradin said, to avoid looking ahead to the squirming shadows.

Dvorak's face as the dwarf turned to him was a sickly green and his mouth a cruel slit of darkness. "Should you see her, do you think? I am leading you to a graveyard, missionary. Pray, if you wish."

At those words, Dradin would have run, would have taken off into the mist, not caring if Dvorak found him and gutted him, such was his terror. But then the creeping tread of the creatures resolved itself. The sound grew louder, coming up behind and ahead of him. As he watched, the shadows became shapes and then figures, until he could see the glinty eyes and glinty knives of a legion of silent, waiting mushroom dwellers. Behind them, hopping and rustling, came toads and rats, their eyes bright with darkness. The sky thickened with the swooping shapes of bats.

"Surely," Dradin said, "surely there has been a mistake."

In a sad voice, his face strangely mournful and moonlike, Dvorak said, "There have indeed been mistakes, but they are yours. Take off your clothes."

Dradin backed away, into the arms of the leathery, stretched, musty folk behind. Cringing from their touch, he leapt forward.

"I have money," Dradin said to Dvorak. "I will give you money. My father has money."

Dvorak's smile turned sadly sweeter and sweetly sadder. "How you waste words when you have so few words left to waste. Remove your clothes or they will do it for you," and he motioned to the mushroom dwellers. A hiss of menace rose from their assembled ranks as they pressed closer, closer still, until he could not escape the dry, piercing rot of them, nor the sound of their shambling gait.

He took off his shoes, his socks, his trousers, his shirt, his underwear, folding each item carefully, until his pale body gleamed and he saw himself in his mind's eye as switching positions with the Living Saint. How he would have loved to see the hoary ejaculator now, coming to his rescue, but there was no hope of that. Despite the chill, Dradin held his hands over his penis rather than his chest. What did modesty matter, and yet still he did it.

Dvorak hunched nearer, hand taut on the rope, and used his knife to pull the clothes over to him. He went through the pockets, took the remaining coins, and then put the clothes over his shoulder.

"Please, let me go," Dradin said. "I beg you." There was a tremor in his voice but, he marveled, only a tremor, only a hint of fear.

Who would have guessed that so close to his own murder he could be so calm?

"I cannot let you go. You no longer belong to me. You are a priest, are you not? They pay well for the blood of priests."

"My friends will come for me."

"You have no friends in this city."

"Where is the woman from the window?"

Dvorak smiled with a smugness that turned Dradin's stomach. A spark of anger spread all up and down his back and made his teeth grind together. The graveyard gate was open. He had run through graveyards once, with Anthony—graveyards redolent with the stink of old metal and ancient technologies—but was that not where they wished him to go?

"In the name of God, what have you done with her?"

"You are too clever by half," Dvorak said. "She is still in Hoegbotton & Sons."

"At this hour?"

"Yes."

"W-w-why is she there?" His fear for her, deeper into him than his own anger, made his voice quiver.

Dvorak's mask cracked. He giggled and cackled and stomped his foot. "Because, because, sir, sir, I have taken her to pieces. I have dismembered her!" And from behind and in front and all around, the horrible, galumphing, har-rumphing laughter of the mushroom dwellers.

Dismembered her.

The laughter, mocking and cruel, set him free from his inertia. Clear and cold he was now, made of ice, always keeping the face of his beloved before him. He could not die until he had seen her body.

Dradin yanked on the rope and, as Dvorak fell forward, wrenched free the noose. He kicked the dwarf in the head and heard a satisfying howl of pain, but did not wait, did not watch—he was already running through the gate before the mushroom dwellers could stop him. His legs felt like cold metal, like the churning pistons of the old coal-chewing trains. He ran as he had never run in all his life, even with Tony. He ran like a man possessed, recklessly dodging tombstones and high grass, while behind came the angry screams of Dvorak, the slithery swiftness of the mushroom dwellers. And still Dradin laughed as he went—bellowing as he jumped atop a catacomb of mausoleums and leapt between monuments, trapped for an instant by abutting tombstones, and then up and running again, across the top of yet another broad sepulcher. He found his voice and shouted to his pursuers, "Catch me! Catch me!", and cackled his own mad cackle, for he was as naked as the day he had entered the world and his beloved was dead and he had nothing left in the world to lose. Lost as he might be, lost as he might always be, yet the feeling of freedom was heady. It made him giddy and drunk with his own power. He crowed to his pursuers, he needled them, only to pop up elsewhere, thrilling to the hardness of his muscles, the toughness gained in the jungle where all else had been lost.

Finally, he came to the line of old trains, byzantine and convoluted and dark, surrounded by the smell of dank, rusting metal. One backward glance before entering the maze revealed that the mushroom dwellers, led by Dvorak, had reached the last line of tombstones, fifty feet away.

—but a glance only before he swung himself into the side door of an engine, walked on the balls of his feet into the cool darkness. Hushed quiet. This was what he needed now. Quiet and stealth in equal measures so that he could reach the relative safety of the street beyond the trains. His senses heightened, he could hear *them* coming, the whispers between them as they spread out to search the compartments.

Spider-like, Dradin moved as he heard them move, shadowing them but out of sight—into their clutches and out again with a finesse he had not known he possessed— always working his way farther into the jungle of metal. Train tracks. Dining cars. Engines split open by the years, so that he hid among their most secret parts and came out again when danger had passed him by, a pale figure flecked with rust.

Ahead, when he dared to take his gaze from his pursuers, Dradin could see the uniform darkness of the wall and, from beyond, the red flashes of a bonfire. Two rows of cars lay between him and the wall. He crept forward through the gaping doorway of a dining car—

—just as, cloaked by shadow, Dvorak entered the car from the opposite end. Dradin considered backing out of the car, but no: Dvorak would hear him. Instead, he crouched down, hidden from view by an overturned table, a salt-and-pepper shaker still nailed to it.

Dvorak's footsteps came closer, accompanied by raspy breathing and the shivery threat of the knives beneath his coat. A single shout from Dvorak and the mushroom dwellers would find him.

Dvorak stopped in front of the overturned table. Dradin could smell him now, the *must* of mushroom dweller, the *tang* of Moth silt.

Dradin sprang up and slapped his left hand across Dvorak's mouth, spun him around as he grunted, and grappled for Dvorak's knife. Dvorak opened his mouth to bite Dradin. Dradin stuck his fist in Dvorak's mouth, muffling his own scream as the teeth bit down. Now Dvorak could make no sound and the dwarf frantically tried to expel Dradin's fist. Dradin did not let him. The knife seesawed from Dvorak's side up to Dradin's clavicle and back again. Dvorak thrashed about, trying to dislodge Dradin's hold on him, trying to face his enemy. Dradin, muscles straining, entangled Dvorak's legs in his and managed to keep him in the center of the compartment. If they banged up against the sides, it would be as loud as a word from Dvorak's mouth. But the knife was coming too close to Dradin's throat. He smashed Dvorak's hand against a railing, a sound that sent up an echo Dradin thought the mushroom dwellers must surely hear. No one came as the knife fell from Dvorak's hand. Dvorak tried to grasp inside his jacket for another. Dradin pulled a knife from within the jacket first. As Dvorak withdrew his own weapon, Dradin's blade was already buried deep in his throat.

Dradin felt the dwarf's body go taut and then lose its rigidity, while the mouth came loose of his fist and a thick, viscous liquid dribbled down his knife arm.

Dradin turned to catch the body as it fell, so that as he held it and lowered it to the ground, his hand throbbing and bloody, he could see Dvorak's eyes as the life left them. The tattoo, in that light, became all undone, the red dots of cities like wounds, sliding off to become merely a crisscross of lines. Dark blood coated the front of his shirt.

Dradin mumbled a prayer under his breath from reflex alone, for some part of him—the part of him that had laughed to watch the followers of Saint Solon placing sparrows in coffins—insisted that death was unremarkable, undistinguished, and, ultimately, unimportant, for it happened every day, everywhere. Unlike the jungle, Nepenthe's severed hand, here there was no amnesia, no fugue. There was only the body beneath him and an echo in his ears, the memory of his mother's voice as she *thrulled* from deep in her throat a death march, a funeral veil stitched of words and music. How could he feel hatred? He could not. He felt only emptiness.

He heard, with newly preternatural senses, the movement of mushroom dwellers nearby and, resting Dvorak's head against the cold metal floor, he left the compartment, a shadow against the deeper shadow of the wrecked and rotted wheels.

Now it was easy for Dradin, slipping between tracks, huddling in dining compartments, the mushroom dwellers blind to his actions. The two rows of cars between him and the wall became one row and then he was at the wall. He climbed it tortuously, the rough stone cutting into his hands and feet. When he reached the top, he swung up and over to the other side.

Ah, the boulevard beyond, for now Dradin wondered if he should return to the graveyard and hide there. Strewn across the boulevard were scaffolds and from the scaffolds men and women had been hung so that they lolled and, limp, had the semblance of rag dolls. Rag dolls in tatters, the flesh pulled from hindquarters, groins, chests, the red meeting the green of the moon and turning black. Eyes stared sightless. The harsh wind carried the smell of offal. Dogs bit at the feet, the legs, the bodies so thick that as Dradin walked forward, keen for the sound of mushroom dwellers behind him, he had to push aside and duck under the limbs of the dead. Blood splashed his shoulders and he breathed in gasps and held his side, as if something pained him, though it was only the sight of the bodies that pained him. When he realized that he still wore a noose of his own, he pulled it over his head with such speed that it cut him and left a burn.

Past the hanging bodies and burning buildings and flamed out motored vehicles, only to see . . . stilt men carrying severed heads, which they threw to the waiting crowds, who kicked and tossed them . . . a man disemboweled, his intestines streaming out into the gutter as his attackers continued to hack him apart and he clutched at their legs . . . a woman assaulted against a brick wall by ten men who held her down as they cut and raped her . . . fountains full of floating, bloated bodies, the waters turned red-black with blood . . . glimpses of the bonfires, bodies stacked for burning in the dozens . . . a man and woman decapitated, still caught in an embrace, on their knees in the murk of rising mist . . . the unearthly screams, the taste of blood rising in the air, the smell of fire and burning flesh . . . and the female riders on their wooden horses, riding over the bodies of the dead, their eyes still turned inward, that they might not know the horrors of the night.

Oh, that he could rip his own eyes from his sockets! He did not wish to see and yet could not help but see if he wished to live. In the face of such carnage, his killing of Dvorak became the gentlest of mercies. Bile rose in his throat and, sick with grief and horror, he vomited beside an abandoned horse buggy. When the sickness had passed, he gathered his wits, found a landmark he recognized, and by passing through lesser alleys and climbing over the rooftops of one-story houses set close together, came once again to his hostel.

The hostel was empty and silent. Dradin crept, limping from glass in his foot and the ache in his muscles, up to the second floor and his room. Once inside, he did not even try to wash off the blood, the dirt, the filth, did not put on clothes, but stumbled to his belongings and stuffed his pictures, *The Refraction of Light in a Prison,* and his certificate from the religious college into the knapsack. He stood in the center of the room, knapsack over his left shoulder, the machete held in his right hand, breathing heavily, trying to remember who he might be and where he might be and what he should do next. He shuffled over to the window and looked down on the valley. What he saw made him laugh, a high-pitched sound so repugnant to him that he closed his mouth immediately.

The valley lay under a darkness broken by soft, warm lights. No bonfires raged in the valley below. No one hung from scaffolding, tongues blue and purpling. No one bathed in the blood of the dead.

Seeing the valley so calm, Dradin remembered when he had wondered if, perhaps, his beloved lived there, amid the peace where there were no missionaries. No Living Saints. No Cadimons. No Dvoraks. He looked toward the door. It was a perilous door, a deceitful door, for the world lay beyond it in all its brutality. He stood there for several beats of his heart, thinking of how beautiful the woman had looked in the third story window, how he had thrilled to see her there. What a beautiful place the world had been then, so long ago.

Machete held ready, Dradin walked to the door and out into the night.

VII

WHEN DRADIN HAD AT LAST FOUGHT HIS WAY BACK TO Hoegbotton & Sons, Albumuth Boulevard was deserted except for a girl in a ragged flower print dress. She listened to a tattered phonograph that played Voss Bender tunes.

In the deep of winter:
Snatches of song
Through the branches
Brittle as bone.

You'll not see my face
But there I'll be,
Frost in my hair,
My hunger hollowing me.

The sky had cleared and the cold, white pricks of stars shone through the black of night, the green-tinge of moon. The black in which moon and stars floated was absolute; it ate the light of the city, muted everything but the shadows, which multiplied and rippled outward. Behind Dradin, sounds of destruction grew nearer, but here the stores were ghostly but whole. And yet here too men, women, and children hung from the lamp posts and looked down with lost, vacant, and wondering stares.

The girl sat on her knees in front of the phonograph. Over her lay the shadow of the great lambent eye, shiny and saucepan blind, of one of the colorful cloth squid, its tentacles rippling in the breeze. Bodies were caught in its fake coils, sprawled and sitting upright in the maw and craw of the beast, as if they had drowned amid the tentacles, washed ashore still entangled and stiffening.

Dradin walked up to the girl. She had brown hair and dark, unreadable eyes with long lashes. She was crying, although her face had long ago been wiped clean of sorrow and of joy. She watched the phonograph as if it were the last thing in the world that made sense to her.

He nudged her. "Go. Go on! Get off the street. You're not safe here."

She did not move, and he looked at her with a mixture of sadness and exasperation. There was nothing he could do. Events were flowing away from him, caught in an undertow stronger than that of the Moth. It was all he could do to preserve his own life, his bloody machete proof of the dangers of the bureaucratic district by which he had come again to Albumuth. The same languid, nostalgic streets of daylight had become killing grounds, a thousand steely-

eyed murderers hiding amongst the vetch and honeysuckle. It was there that he had rediscovered the white-faced
mimes, entangled in the ivy, features still in death.

Dradin walked past the girl until Hoegbotton & Sons
lay before him. The dull red brick seemed brighter in the
night, as if it reflected the fires burning throughout the
city.

And so it ends where it began, Dradin thought. In
front of the very same Hoegbotton & Sons building. Were
he not such a coward, he should have ended it there much
sooner.

Dradin stole up the stairs to the door. He smashed the
glass of the door with his already mangled fist, grunting
with pain. The pain pulsed far away, disconnected from
him in his splendid nakedness. *Pinpricks on the souls of distant sinners.* Dradin swung the door open and shut it with
such a clatter that he was sure someone had heard him and
would come loping down the boulevard after him. But no
one came and his feet, naked and dirty and cut, continued
to slap the steps inside so loudly that surely she would run
away if she was still alive, thinking him an intruder. But
where to run? He could hear his own labored breathing
as he navigated the stairs: the sound filled the landing; it
filled the spaces between the steps; and it filled him with
determination, for it was the most vital sign that he still
lived, despite every misfortune.

Dradin laughed, but it came out ragged around the
edges. His mind sagged under the weight of carnage: the
cries of looting, begging; the sound of men swinging by
their necks or their feet. Swinging all across a city grown
suddenly wise and quiet in their deaths.

But that was out there, in the city. In here, Dradin promised, he would not lose himself to such images. He would not lose the thread.

Curious, but on reaching the door to the third floor, Dradin paused, halted, did not yet grasp the iron knob. For this door led to the window. He had engraved her position so perfectly on the interstices of his memory that he knew exactly where she must be . . . One moment more of hesitation, and then Dradin entered her.

A room. Darkened. The smell of sawdust packing and boxes. Not the right room. Not her room. The antechamber only, for receiving visitors, perhaps, the walls lined with decadent art objects, and beyond that, an open doorway, leading to . . .

The next room was lined with Occidental shadow puppets that looked like black scars, seared and shaped into human forms: bodies entwined in lust and devout in prayer, bodies engaged in murder and in business. Harlequins and pierrots with bashful red eyes and sharp teeth lay on their backs, feet up in the air. Jungle plants trellised and cat's cradled the interior, freed from terrariums, while a clutter of other things hidden by the shadows beckoned him with their strange, angular shapes. The smell of moist rot mixed with the stench of mushroom dweller and the sweet bitter of sweat, as if the very walls labored for the creation of such wonderful monstrosities.

She still faced the window, but set back from it, in a wooden chair, so that the curling curious fires ravaging the city beyond could not sear her face. The light from these fires created a zone of blackness and Dradin could see only her black hair draped across the chair.

It seemed to Dradin as he looked at the woman sitting in the chair that he had not seen her in a hundred, a thousand, years; that he saw her across some great becalmed ocean or desert, she only a shape like the shadow puppets. He moved closer.

His woman, the woman of his dreams, gazed off into the charred red-black air, the opposite street, or even toward the hidden River Moth beyond. He thought he saw a hint of movement as he approached her—a slight uplifting of one arm—she no longer concerned with the short view, but with the long view, the perspective that nothing of the moment mattered or would ever matter. It had been Dvorak's view, with the map that had taken over his body. It was Cadimon's view, not allowing the priest to take pity on a former student.

"My love," Dradin said, and again, "My love," as he walked around so he could see the profile of her face. A white sheet covered her body, but her face, oh, her face . . . her eyebrows were thin and dark, her eyes like twin blue flames, her nose small, unobtrusive, her skin white, white, white, but with a touch of color that drew him down to the sumptuous curve of her mouth, the bead of sweat upon the upper lip, the fine hairs placed to seduce, to trick; the way in which the clothes clung to her body and made it seem to curve, the arms placed upon the arms of the chair, so naturally that there was no artifice in having done so. Might she . . . could she . . . still be . . . alive?

Dradin pulled aside the white sheet—and screamed, for there lay the torso, the legs severed and in pieces beneath, but placed cleverly for the illusion of life, the head balanced atop the torso, dripping neither blood nor precious humors, but as dry and slick and perfect as if it had never known a body. Which it had not. From head to toe, Dradin's beloved was a mannequin, an artifice, a deception. *Hoegbotton & Sons, specialists in all manner of profane and Occidental technologies. . .*

Dradin's mouth opened and closed but no sound came from him. Now he could see the glassy finish of her features, the innate breakability of a creature made of papier-mâché and metal and porcelain and clay, mixed and beaten and blown and sandpapered and engraved and made up like any other woman. A testimony to the clockmaker's craft, for at the hinges and joints of the creature dangled broken filaments and wires and gimshaw circuitry. Fool. He was thrice a fool.

Dradin circled the woman, his body shivering, his hands reaching out to caress the curve of cheekbone, only to pull back before he touched skin. The jungle fever beat within him, fell away in *decrescendo,* then again *crescendo.* Twice more around and his arm darted out against his will and he touched her cheek. Cold. So cold. So monstrously cold against the warmth of his body. Cold and dead in her beauty despite the heat and the bonfires roaring outside. Dead. Not alive. Never alive.

As he touched her, as he saw all of her severed parts and how they fit together, something small and essential broke inside him; broke so he couldn't ever fix it. Now he saw Nepenthe in his mind's eye in all of her darkness and grace. Now he could see her as a person, not an idea. Now he could see her nakedness, remember the way she had felt under him—smooth and moist and warm—never moving as he made love to her. As he took her though she did not want to be taken. If ever he had lost his faith it was then, as he lost himself in the arms of a woman indifferent to him, indifferent to the world. He saw again the flash of small hand, severed and gray, and saw again his own hand, holding the blade. Her severed hand. His hand holding the blade. Coming to in the burning missionary station, severed of his memory, severed from his faith, severed from his senses by the fever. Her severed gray hand in his and in the other the machete.

Dradin dropped the machete and it landed with a clang next to the mannequin's feet.

Feverish, he had crawled back from his jungle expedition, the sole survivor, only to find that the people he had gone out to convert had come to the station and burned it to the ground . . . fallen unconscious, and come to with the hand in his, Nepenthe naked and dead next to him. Betrayal.

The shattered pieces within came loose in an exhalation of breath. He could not contain himself any longer, and he sobbed there, at the mannequin's feet. As he hugged her to him, the fragile balance came undone and her body scattered into pieces all around him, the head staring up at him from the floor.

"I killed her I did I killed her I didn't kill her I didn't mean to I meant to I didn't mean to she made me I let her I wanted her I couldn't have her I never wanted her I wanted her not the way I wanted I couldn't I meant to I couldn't have meant to but I did it I don't know if I did it—*I can't remember!*"

Dradin slid to the floor and lay there for a long while, exhausted, gasping for breath, his mouth tight, his jaw unfamiliar to him. He welcomed the pain from the splinters that cut into his flesh from the floorboards. He felt hollow inside, indifferent, so fatigued, so despairing that he did not know if he could ever regain his feet.

But, after a time, Dradin looked full into the woman's eyes and a grim smile spread across his face. He thought he could hear his mother's voice mixed with the sound of rain thrumming across a roof. He thought he could hear his father reading the adventures of Juliette and Justine to him. He knelt beside the head and caressed its cheek. He lay beside the head and admired its features.

He heard himself say it.

"I love you."

He still loved her. He could not deny it. Could not. It was a love that might last a minute or a day, an hour or a month, but for the moment, in his need, it seemed as permanent as the moon and the stars, and as cold.

It did not matter that she was in pieces, that she was not real, for he could see now that she was his salvation. Had he not been in love with what he saw in the third story window, and had what he had seen through that window changed in its essential nature? Wasn't she better suited to him than if she had been real, with all the avarices and hungers and needs and awkwardnesses that create disappointment? He had invented an entire history for this woman and now his expectations of her would never change and she would never age, never criticize him, never tell him he was too fat or too sloppy or too neat, and he would never have to raise his voice to her.

It struck Dradin as he basked in the glow of such feelings, as he watched the porcelain lines of the head while shouts grew louder and the gallows jerked and swung merrily all across the city. It struck him that he could not betray this woman. There would be no decaying, severed hand. No flowers sprayed red with blood. No crucial misunderstandings. The thought blossomed bright and blinding in his head. He could not betray her. Even if he set her head upon the mantel and took a lover there, in front of her, as his father might once have done to his mother, those eyes would not register the sin. This seemed to him, in that moment, to be a form of wisdom beyond even Cadimon, a wisdom akin to the vision that had struck him as he stood in the backyard of the old house in Morrow.

Dradin embraced the pieces of his lover, luxuriating in the smooth and shiny feel of her, the precision of her skin. He rose to a knee, cradling his beloved's head in his shaking arms. Was he moaning now? Was he screaming now? Who could tell?

With careful deliberateness, Dradin took his lover's head and walked into the antechamber, and then out the door. The third floor landing was dark and quiet. He began to walk down the stairs, descending slowly at first, taking pains to slap his feet against each step. But when he reached the second floor landing, he became more frantic, as if to escape what lay behind him, until by the time he reached the first floor and burst out from the shattered front door, he was running hard, knapsack bobbing against his back.

Down the boulevard, seen through the folds of the squid float, a mob approached, holding candles and torches and lanterns. Stores flared and burned behind them . . .

Dradin spared them not a glance, but continued to run—past the girl and her phonograph, still playing Voss

Bender, and past *Borges Bookstore,* in the shadow of which prowled the black panther from the parade, and then beyond, into the unknown. Sidestepping mushroom dwellers at their dark harvest, their hands full of mushrooms from which spores broke off like dandelion tufts, and the last of the revelers of the Festival of the Freshwater Squid, their trajectories those of pendulums and their tongues blue if not black, arms slack at their sides. Through viscera and the limbs of babies stacked in neat piles. Amongst the heehaws and gimgobs, the drunken dead and the lolly lashers with their dark whips. Weeping now, tears without end. Mumbling and whispering endearments to his beloved, running strong under the mad, mad light of the moon—headed forever and always for the docks and the muscular waters of the River Moth, which would take him and his lover as far as he might wish, though perhaps not far enough. ❧

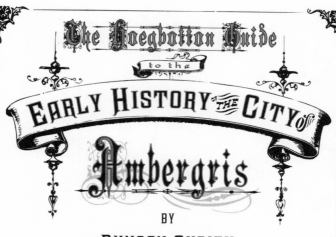

The Hoegbotton Guide

to the

EARLY HISTORY of THE CITY of

Ambergris

BY

DUNCAN SHRIEK

I

HE HISTORY OF AMBERGRIS, FOR OUR
purposes, begins with the legendary ex-
ploits of the whaler-cum-pirate Cappan
John Manzikert,[1,2,3] who, in the Year of
Fire—so called for the catastrophic vol-
canic activity in the Southern Hemisphere that season—
led his fleet of 30 whaling ships up the Moth River Delta
into the River Moth proper. Although not the first

1. By Manzikert's time, the rough southern accent of his people
had permanently changed the designation "Captain" to "Cappan."
"Captain" referred not only to Manzikert's command of a fleet of
ships, but also to the old Imperial titles given by the Saphants to the
commander of a *see* of islands; thus, the title had both religious and
military connotations. Its use, this late in history, reflects how perva-
sive the Saphant Empire's influence was: 200 years after its fall, its
titles were still being used by clans that had only known of the Empire
secondhand.
2. A footnote on the purpose of these footnotes: This text is rich
with footnotes to avoid inflicting upon you, the idle tourist, so much
knowledge that, bloated with it, you can no longer proceed to the
delights of the city with your customary mindless abandon. In order to
hamstring your predictable attempts—once having discovered a topic
of interest in this narrative—to skip ahead, I have weeded out all of
those cross references to other Hoegbotton publications that litter the
rest of this pamphlet series like a plague of fungi.
3. I should add to footnote 2 that the most interesting information will be included only in footnote form, and I will endeavor to include as many footnotes as possible. Indeed, information alluded to in

foot-reported incursion of Aan whaling clans into the region, it is the first incursion of any importance.

Manzikert's purpose was to escape the wrath of his clansman Michael Brueghel, who had decimated Manzikert's once-proud 100-ship fleet off the coast of the Isle of Aandalay. Brueghel meant to finish off Manzikert for good, and so pursued him some 40 miles upriver, near the current port of Stockton, before finally giving up the chase. The reason for this conflict between potential allies is unclear—our historical sources are few and often inaccurate; indeed, one of the most infuriating aspects of early Ambergrisian history is the regularity with which truth and legend pursue separate courses—but the result is clear: in late summer of the Year of Fire, Manzikert found himself a full 70 miles upriver, at the place where the Moth forms an inverted "L" before straightening out both north and south. Here, for the first time, he found that the fresh water flowing south had completely cleansed the salt water seeping north.[4]

Manzikert anchored his ships at the joint of the "L," which formed a natural harbor, at dusk of the day of their arrival. The banks were covered in a lush undergrowth very

---

footnote form will later be expanded upon in the main text, thus confusing any of you who have decided not to read the footnotes. This is the price to be paid by those who would rouse an elderly historian from his slumber behind a desk in order to coerce him to write for a common travel guide series.

4. Today, the salinity of the river changes to fresh water a mere 25 miles upriver; the reason for this change is unknown, but may be linked to the build-up of silt at the river's mouth, which acts as a natural filter.

familiar to the Aan, as it would have approximated the vegetation of their own native southern islands.[5] They had, encouragingly enough, seen no signs of possibly hostile habitation, but could not muster the energy, as dusk approached, to launch an expedition. However, that night the watchmen on the ships were startled to see the lights of campfires clearly visible through the trees and, as more than one keen-eared whaler noticed, the sound of a high and distant chanting. Manzikert immediately ordered a military force to land under cover of darkness, but the Truffidian monk Samuel Tonsure persuaded him to rescind the order and await the dawn.

Tonsure—who, following his capture from Nicea (near the mouth of the Moth River Delta), had persuaded the Cappan to convert to Truffidism and thus gained influence over him—plays a major role, perhaps the major role, in our understanding of Ambergris' early history.[6] It is from

5. Almost 500 years later, the Petularch Dray Mikal would order the uprooting of native flora around the city in favor of the northern species of his youth, surely among the most strikingly arrogant responses to homesickness on record. The Petularch would be dead for 50 years before the transplantation could be ruled a success.

6. And yet, what is our understanding of the monk's early history? Obscure at best. The records at Nicea contain no mention of a Samuel Tonsure, and it is possible he was just passing through the city on his way elsewhere and so did not actively preach there. "Samuel Tonsure" may also be a name that Tonsure created to disguise his true identity. A handful of scholars, in particular the truculent Mary Sabon, argue that Tonsure was none other than the Patriarch of Nicea himself, a man who is known to have disappeared at roughly the same time Tonsure appeared with Manzikert. Sabon offers as circumstantial evidence the oft repeated story that the Patriarch sometimes traversed his city incognito, dressed as a simple monk to spy on his

Tonsure that most histories descend—both from the discredited (and incomplete) *Biography of John Manzikert I of Aan and Ambergris*,[7] obviously written to please the Cappan, and from his secret journal, which he kept on his person at all times and which we may assume Manzikert never saw since otherwise he would have had Tonsure put to death.

The journal contains a most intricate account of Manzikert, his exploits, and subsequent events. That this journal appeared (or, rather, reappeared) under somewhat dubious circumstances should not detract from its overall

---

subordinates. He could easily have been captured without knowledge of his rank—which, if revealed, would have given Manzikert such leverage over Nicea that he might well have been able to take the city and settle behind its walls, safe from Brueghel. If so, however, why didn't the Patriarch make any attempt to escape once he had gained Manzikert's trust? The case, despite some of Sabon's other evidence, seems wrong-headed from its inception. My own research, corroborated by the Autarch of Nunk, indicates that the Patriarch's disappearance coincides with that of the priestess Caroline of the Church of the Seven Pointed Star, and that the Patriarch and Caroline eloped together, the ceremony performed by a traveling juggler hastily ordained as a priest.

7. For reasons which will become clear, Tonsure could no longer complete it; therefore, 10 years later, Manzikert's son had another Truffidian monk summoned from Nicea for this purpose. Unfortunately, this monk, whose name is lost to us, believed in wearing hair shirts, daily flagellation, and preaching "the abomination of the written word." He did indeed complete the biography, but he might as well have spared himself the effort. Although edited by Manzikert II himself, it contains such prose as "And his highly exhulted majesty set foot on land like a swaggorin conquor from daes of your." Clearly this abominator's abominations against the Written Word far outweigh any crimes It may have perpetrated upon him.

validity, and does not explain the derision directed at it from certain quarters, possibly because the name "Samuel Tonsure" sounds like a joke to a few small-minded scholars. It certainly was not a joke to Samuel Tonsure.[8]

At daybreak, Manzikert ordered the boats lowered and with 100 men, including Tonsure, set off on a reconnaissance mission to the shore. It must have been a somewhat ridiculous sight, for as Tonsure writes of Manzikert, a man possessed of a cruel and mercurial temper, "he must occupy one boat himself, save for the oarsman, such a large man was he and the boat beneath him a child's toy."[9] Here, as Manzikert is rowed toward the site of the city he will found, it is appropriate to quote in full Tonsure's famous appraisal of the Cappan:

> I myself marveled at the man; for nature had combined in his person all the qualities necessary for a military commander. He stood at the height of almost seven feet, so that to look at him men would tilt back their heads as if toward the top of a hill or a high mountain. Possessed of startling blue eyes and furrowed brows, his countenance was neither gentle nor pleasing, but put one in mind of a tempest; his voice

8. If the careful historian needs further proof that Sabon is wrong, he need look no further than the inscription on the monk's journal: "Samuel Tonsure." Why would he bother to maintain the pretense since the contents of the journal itself would condemn him to death? And why would he, if indeed the Patriarch (a learned and clever man by all accounts), choose such a clumsy and obvious pseudonym?

9. All quotes without attribution are from Tonsure's journal, not the biography.

was like thunder and his hands seemed made for tearing down walls or for smashing doors of bronze. He could spring like a lion and his frown was terrible. Those who saw him for the first time discovered that every description that they had heard of him was an understatement.[10]

Alas, the Cappan possessed no corresponding wisdom or quality of mercy. Tonsure obviously feared his master's mood on this occasion, for he tried to persuade Manzikert to remain onboard his flagship and allow the more reasonable of his lieutenants—perhaps even his son John Manzikert II,[11] who would one day govern his people brilliantly—to lead the landing party, but Manzikert, Truffidian though he was, would have none of it. The Cappan also actively encouraged his wife, Sophia, to accompany them. Unfortunately, Tonsure tells us little about Sophia Manzikert in either the biography or the journal (her own biography has not survived), but from the little we do know Tonsure's description of her husband might fit her equally well; the two often waxed romantic on the pleasures of being able to pillage together.

---

10. Quote taken from the biography. One wonders: if the Cappan was so fierce, how much more fearsome must Michael Brueghel have been to make him flee the south?

11. The Cappan's appending "II" to his son's name gives us an early indication that he meant to settle on land and found a dynasty. The Aan clan would have thought the idea of a dynasty odd, for usually cappans were chosen from among the ablest sailors, with hereditary claims a secondary consideration.

And so, Manzikert, Sophia, Tonsure, and the Cappan's men landed on the site of what would soon be Ambergris. At the moment, however, it was occupied by a people Tonsure christened "gray caps," known today as "mushroom dwellers."

Tonsure reports that they had advanced hardly a hundred paces into the underbrush before they came upon the first inhabitant, standing outside of his "rounded and domed single-story house, built low to the ground and seamless, from which issued a road made of smooth, shiny stones cleverly mortared together." The building might have once served as a sentinel post, but was now used as living quarters.

Clearly Tonsure found the building more impressive than the native standing outside of it, for he spends three pages on its every minute detail and gives us only this short paragraph on the building's inhabitant:

Stout and short, he came only to the Cappan's shoulder: swathed from head to foot in a gray cloak that covered his tunic and trousers, these made from lighter gray swatches of animal skin stitched together. Upon his head lay a hat the color of an Oliphaunt's skin: a tall, wide contrivance that covered his face from the sun. His features, what could be seen of them, were thick, sallow, innocent of knowledge. When the Cappan inquired as to the nature and name of the place, this unattractive creature could not answer except in a series of clicks, grunts, and whistles that appeared to imitate the song of the cricket and locust. It could not be considered speech or language. It was, as with insects, a warning or curious sound, devoid of other meaning.[12]

We can take a farcical delight from imagining the scene: the giant leaning down to communicate with the dwarf, the dwarf speaking a language so subtle and sophisticated that it has resisted translation to the present day,

12. I find it necessary to interject three observations here. First, that the paragraph on the gray caps written for the Cappan's biography is far worse, describing as it does "small, piglike eyes, a jowly jagged crease for a mouth, and a nose like an ape." The gray caps actually looked much like the mushroom dwellers of today—which is to say, like smaller versions of ourselves—but the Cappan was already attempting to dehumanize them, and thus create a justification, a rationalization, for depriving them of life and property. Second, and surprisingly, evidence suggests that the gray caps wove their clothing from the cured pelts of field mice. Third, Tonsure appears to have given away a secret—if, in fact, the gray cap they met came "only to the Cappan's shoulder" and the gray caps averaged, by Tonsure's own admission, three and one-half feet in height (as do the modern mushroom dwellers), then the Cappan could only have stood four and one-half feet to five feet in height, something of a midget himself. (Is it of import that in a letter concerning future trade relations written to the Kalif, Brueghel calls Manzikert "my insignificant enemy," since "insignificant" in the Kalif's language doubles as a noun meaning "dwarf" and Brueghel, who wrote his own letters of state, loved word play?) Perhaps Tonsure's description of Manzikert in the biography was dictated by the Cappan, who wished to conceal his slight stature from History. Unfortunately, the Cappan's height, or lack thereof, remains an ambiguous subject, and thus I will stay true to the orthodox version of the story as related by Tonsure. Still, it is delicious to speculate. (If indeed Manzikert was short, we might have hoped he would look upon the gray caps as long-lost cousins twice removed. Alas, he did not do so.)

while the giant spits out a series of crude consonants and vowels that must have seemed to the gray cap a sudden bout of apoplexy.

Manzikert found the gray cap repellent, resembling as it did, he is quoted as saying, "both child and mushroom,"[13] and if not for his fear of retaliation from a presumed ruling body of unknown strength, the Cappan would have run the native through with his sword. Instead, he left the gray cap to its incomprehensible vigil, still clicking and whistling to their backs,[14] and proceeded along the silvery road until they reached the city.

Although Tonsure has, criminally, neglected to provide us with the reactions of Manzikert and Sophia upon their first glimpse of the city proper—and, from the monk's description of aqueducts, almost certainly the future site of Albumuth Boulevard—we can imagine that they were as impressed as Tonsure himself, who wrote:

13. We can only speculate as to why Manzikert should find children and mushrooms repulsive. He certainly ate mushrooms and had had a child with Sophia. Perhaps, if indeed undertall, his nickname growing up had been "little mushroom"?

14. As this is the first and last time the gray caps actively attempted to communicate with the Aan, one wonders just what the gray cap was saying to Manzikert. A friendly greeting? A warning? The very loquaciousness of this particular gray cap in relation to the others they were to encounter has led more than one historian to assume that he (or she—contrary to popular opinion, there are as many female gray caps as male; the robes tend to make them all look unisexual) had been assigned to greet the landing party. What opportunities did Manzikert miss by not trying harder to understand the gray cap's intent? What tragedies might have been averted?

The buildings visible beyond the increasingly scanty tree cover were decorated throughout by golden stars, like the very vault of heaven, but whereas heaven has its stars only at intervals, here the surfaces were entirely covered with gold, issuing forth from the center in a never-ending stream. Surrounding the main building were other, smaller buildings, themselves surrounded completely or in part by cloisters. Structures of breathtaking complexity stretched as far as the eye could see. Then came a second circle of buildings, larger than the first, with lawns covered in mushrooms of every possible size and color—from gigantic growths as large as the Oliphaunt[15] to delicate, glassy nodules no larger than a child's fingernail. These mushrooms—red capped and blue capped, their undersides dusted with streaks of silver or emerald or obsidian—gave off spores of the most varied and remarkable fragrances, while the gray caps themselves

15. Tonsure was criminally fond of Oliphaunts. References to them, usually preceded by mundanea like "as large as" or "as gray as," occur 30 times in the journal. Possessed of infinite mercy, I shall spare you 28 of these comparisons.

16. Tonsure's description in the biography also includes a series of mushroom drawings by Manzikert—an attempt to "appear sensitive," Tonsure sneers in his journal—from which I provide three samples for the half dozen of you who are curious as to the Cappan's illustrative skills:

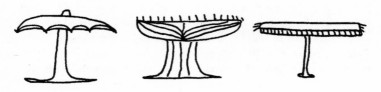

tended their charges with, in this one instance, admirable delicacy and loving concern . . . [16] There were also fountains which filled basins of water; gardens, some of them hanging, full of exotic mosses, lichens, and ferns, others sloping down to the level ground; and a bath of pure gold that was beautiful beyond description.[17]

We can only imagine the slavering delight of Manzikert and his wife upon seeing all that gold; unfortunately, as they would soon find out, much of the "gold" covering the buildings was actually a living organism similar to lichen that the gray caps had trained to create decorative patterns; *not* only was it not gold, it wasn't even edible.

Nonetheless, Manzikert and his men began to explore the city. The most elemental details about the buildings they ignored, instead remarking upon the abundance of tame rats as large as cats,[18] the plethora of exotic birds, and, of course, the large quantities of fungus, which the gray caps appeared to harvest, eat, and store against future famine.[19]

---

17. Apparently, since Tonsure fails to describe it.

18. The mammologist Xaver Daffed maintains that these were "actually cababari, a stunted relation of the pig that resembles a rat." (Quote taken from *The Hoegbotton Guide to Small, Indigenous Mammals*.) If so, then, as subsequent events will show, the rats of Ambergris have managed something of a public relations coup; the poor cababari are today extinct in the southern climes.

19. James Lacond has suggested that the fungus had hallucinogenic qualities. Tonsure, for his part, sampled a "fungus that

While Manzikert explores, I shall pass the time by relating a few facts about the city. According to the scant gray cap records that have been found and, if not translated, then haltingly understood, they called the city "Cinsorium," although the meaning of the word has been lost, or, more accurately, never been found. It is estimated by those who have studied the ruins lying beneath Ambergris[20] that at one time Cinsorium could have housed 250,000 souls, making it among the largest of all ancient cities. Cinsorium also boasted highly advanced plumbing and water distribution systems that would be the envy of many a city today.[21]

---

resembled an artichoke" and found it tasted like unleavened bread; he reports no side effects, although Lacond claims that the rest of Tonsure's account must be considered a drug-induced dream. Lacond further claims that Tonsure's later account of Manzikert's men glutting themselves on the fungi—some of which tasted like honey and some like chicken—explains their sudden mercilessness. But Lacond contradicts himself: if the rest of Tonsure's account is a fever dream, then so is his description of the men eating the fungus. As always when discussing the gray caps, debate tends to describe the same circles as their buildings. (A similar circularity drove a subdivided Lacond, late in his life, to declare that the world as we know it is actually a product of the dream dreamt by Tonsure. Since our knowledge of our identity as Ambergrisians, where we came from, is so dependent on Tonsure's journal, this is close to the heresy of madness.)

20. Admittedly, a perilous and notoriously inaccurate undertaking; the mushroom dwellers tend to look unkindly upon intrusions into their territory.

21. The question of where the gray caps came from and why they were concentrated only in Cinsorium remains a mystery. The subject has frustrated many a historian and, to avoid a similar fate, I shall pass over it entirely.

However, at the time Manzikert stumbled upon Cinsorium, Tonsure argued, it was well past its glory years. He based this conclusion on rather shaky evidence: the "undeniable decadence" of its inhabitants. Surely Tonsure is prejudicial beyond reason, for the city appeared fully functional—the high domed buildings in sparkling good repair, the streets swept constantly, the amphitheaters looking as if they might, within minutes, play host to innumerable entertainments.

Tonsure ignored these signs of a healthy culture, perhaps fearing to admit that an almost certainly heretical people might be superior. Instead, he argued, in the biography especially, but also in his journal, that the current inhabitants—numbering no more, he estimates, than 700—had no claim to any greatness once possessed by their ancestors, for they were "clearly the last generations of a dying race," unable to understand the processes of the city, unable to work its machines, unable to farm, "reduced to hunting and gathering."[22] Their watch fires scorched the interiors of great halls, whole clans wetly bickering with one another within a territory marked by the walls of a single building. They did not a one of them, according to Tonsure, comprehend the legacy of their heritage.

Tonsure's greatest argument for the gray caps' degeneracy may also be his weakest. That first day, Manzikert and Sophia entered what the monk described as a library, a structure "more immense than all but the most

22. But surely they farmed the fungus?

revered ecclesiastical institutions I have studied within." The shelves of this library had rotted away before the onslaught of a startling profusion of small dark purple mushrooms with white stems. The books, made from palm frond pulp in a process lost to us, had all spilled out upon the main floor—thousands of books, many ornately engraved with strange letters[23] and overlaid by the now familiar golden lichen. The use the current gray caps had made of these books was as firewood, for as Manzikert watched in disbelief, gray caps came and went, collecting the books and condemning them to their cooking fires.

Did Tonsure correctly interpret what he saw in the "library"? I think not, and have published my doubts in a monograph entitled "An Argument for the Gray Caps and Against the Evidence of Tonsure's Eyes."[24] I believe the "library" was actually a place for religious worship, the "books" prayer rolls. Prayer rolls in some cultures, particularly in the far Occident, are consigned to the flames in a holy ritual. The "shelves" were rotted wooden planks *specifically* inserted into the walls to foster the growth of the special purple mushrooms, which grew nowhere else in

---

23. Tonsure reports the following symbol showed up repeatedly:

24. Volume XX, Issue 2, of *The Real History Newsletter,* published by the Ambergrisians For The Original Inhabitants Society.

Cinsorium and may well have had religious significance.[25] Another clue lay in the large, mushroom-shaped stone erected just beyond the library's front steps, since determined to have been an altar.

Sophia chose this moment to remark upon what she termed the "primitivism" of the natives, chiding her husband for his "cowardice." Faced with such a rebuke, Manzikert became more aggressive and free of any moral restraints. Fortunately, it took several days for this new attitude to manifest itself, during which time Manzikert moved more and more of his people off the ships and onto the lip of the bay, where he commenced building docks. He also appropriated several of the round, squat structures on the fringes as living quarters, evicting the native inhabitants who, burbling to themselves, complacently walked into the city proper.

Not only were Manzikert's clan members glad to stretch their legs, but the land that awaited them proved, upon exploration, to be ideal. Abundant springs and natural aquifers fed off of the Moth, while game, from pigs to deer to a flightless bird called a "grout," provided an ample food source. The curve of the river accentuated the breeze that blew from the west, generally cooling the savage climate, and with the breeze came birds, swallows in particular, to swoop down at dusk and devour the vast clouds of insects that hovered over the water.

---

25. In a city otherwise so pristine, such blatant "disorder" should have made Tonsure suspicious. Was he now so completely set, as was his master, on the goal of discrediting and dehumanizing the gray caps, that he could see it no other way?

Tonsure spent these five or six days wandering the city, which he still found a marvel. He had, he wrote in his journal, "squandered" much of his early life in the realm of the Kalif, where architectural marvels crowded every city, but never had he seen anything like Cinsorium.[26] First of all, the city had no corners, only curves. Its architects had built circles within circles, domes within domes, and circles within domes. Tonsure found the effect soothing to the eye, and more importantly to the spirit: "This lack of edges, of conflicting lines, makes of the mind a plateau both serene and calm." The possible truth of this observation has been confirmed by modern-day architects who, on review of the reconstructed blueprint of Cinsorium, have described it as the structural equivalent of a tuning fork, a vibration in the soul.

Just as delightful were the huge, festive mosaics lining the walls, most of which depicted battles or mushroom harvesting, while a few consisted of abstract shiftings of red and black; these last gave Tonsure as much unease as the lack of corners had given him comfort, although again he could not say why. The mosaics were made from lichen and fungus skillfully placed and trained to achieve the desired effect. Sometimes fruits, vegetables, or seeds were also used to form decorative patterns—cauliflower to depict a sheep-like creature called the "lunger," for example—with the gray caps replacing these weekly. If Tonsure can be believed, one mosaic used the eggs of a native

26. Unfortunately, this claim strengthens Sabon's assertion with regard to the Patriarch of Nicea—see footnote 6.

thrush to depict the eyes of a gray cap; when the eggs hatched, the eyes appeared to be opening.

The library yielded the most magnificent of Tonsure's discoveries: a mechanized golden tree, its branches festooned with intricate jeweled shrikes and parrots, while on the circular dais by which it moved equally intricate deer, stalked by lions, pawed the golden ground. By use of a winding key, the birds would burst simultaneously into song while the lions roared beneath them. The gray caps maintained it in perfect working condition, but had no appreciation for its beauty, as if they "were themselves clockwork parts in some vast machine, fated to retrace the same movements year after year."

Yet, as Tonsure's appreciation for the city grew, so to did his loathing of its inhabitants. Runts, he calls them—cripples. In their ignorance of the beauty of their own city, he wrote (in the biography), they "had become unfit to rule over it, or even to live within its boundaries." Their "pallor, the sickly moistness of their skin, even the rheumy discharge from their eyes," all pointed to the "abomination of their existence, mocking the memory of what they once had been."[27]

27. Poor Tonsure. Just preceding this diatribe, the monk describes a kind of hard mushroom, about seven inches tall, with a stem as thick as its head. When squeezed, this mushroom suddenly throbs to an even greater size. While walking innocently between the "library" and the amphitheater, Tonsure came across a group of gray cap women using these mushrooms in what he calls a "lascivious way." So perhaps we should forgive him his hyperbole. Still, shocked or not—and he was a more worldly monk than many—Tonsure should have noticed that for every such "perversion," the gray caps had developed a dozen

Why the normally tolerant Tonsure came to espouse such ideas we may never know; certainly, there is none of the element of pity that marks his journal comments about Manzikert, whom he calls "a seething mass of emotions, a pincushion of feelings who would surely be locked away if he were not already a leader of men." Although Tonsure's disparaging comments in his journal seem overwrought, similar comments in the biography are easily attributed to Manzikert himself, for if the monk reviled the natives, the Cappan hated them with an intensity that can have no rational explanation. Tonsure records that whenever Manzikert had cause to walk through the city, he would casually murder any gray cap in his path. Perhaps even more chilling, other gray caps in the vicinity ignored such unprovoked murder, and the mortally wounded themselves expired without a struggle.[28]

---

more useful wonders. For example, another type of mushroom stood two feet tall and had a long, thin stem with a wide hood that, when plucked, could be used as an umbrella; the hood even collapsed into the stem for easy storage.

28. Here Lacond proves useful. He puts forth two theories for the gray caps' passivity: first, that Manzikert had landed in the midst of a religious festival during which the gray caps were forbidden to take part in any aggressive acts, even to defend themselves; second, that the gray cap society resembled that of bees or ants, and thus none of the "units" in the city had free will, being extensions of some hive intellect. This second theory by Lacond seems extreme to some historians, but the idea of passivity being bred into particular classes of gray cap society cannot be ruled out. This would support my own theory that the entire city of Cinsorium was a religious artifact, a temple, if you will, in which violence was not permitted to be inflicted by its keepers. Were Manzikert's actions tantamount to desecration?

At the end of the first week, Manzikert and Sophia held a festival not only to celebrate the completion of the docks, but also "this new beginning as dwellers on the land." Due to its timing, this celebration must be considered the forerunner of the Festival of the Freshwater Squid.[29] During the festivities, Manzikert christened the new settlement "Ambergris," after the "most secret and valuable part of the whale"[30]—over Sophia's objections, who, predictably enough, wanted to call the settlement "Sophia."

The next morning, Manzikert, groggy from grog the night before, got up to relieve himself and, about to do so beside one of the gray caps' round dwellings, noticed on the wall a small, flesh-colored lichen that bore a striking resemblance to the Lepress Saint Kristina of Malfour, a major icon in the Truffidian religion. Menacing the Saint was a lichen that looked uncannily like a gray cap. Manzikert fell into a religious rage, gathered his people and told them of

29. Typically, Sabon cannot bite her tongue and disagrees, citing the Calabrian Calendar used by the Aan as schismatic—most definitely *not* synchronized with the modern calendar. However, Sabon fails to take into account that *Tonsure*, as the non-Aan author of the biography and the journal, would have used the Kalif's calendar, which is identical to our own.

30. Cynically, Tonsure reports, "Better to name a city after the nether parts of a whale than to actually go whaling, for Manzikert, lazy as he is, finds piracy much easier than whaling: when you harpoon an honest sailor, he is less likely to drag you 300 miles across open water and then, turning, casually devour you and drown your companions." Other names Manzikert considered include "Aanville," "Aanapolis," and "Aanburg," so we may be fairly certain that Tonsure suggested "Ambergris," despite his ridicule of the name.

his vision. In the biography Tonsure dutifully reports the jubilant reaction of Manzikert's men upon learning they were going to war because of a maliciously-shaped fungus,[31] but neglects to mention this reaction in his journal, presumably out of shame.[32]

Late in the afternoon, Sophia and Tonsure at his side, Cappan Manzikert I of Aan and Ambergris led a force of 200 men into the city. The sun, Tonsure writes, shone blood red, and the streets of Cinsorium soon reflected red independent of the sun, for at Manzikert's order, his men began to slaughter the gray caps. It was a horribly mute affair. The gray caps offered no resistance, but only stared up at their attackers as they were cut down.[33] Perhaps if they had resisted, Manzikert might have shown them mercy, but their silence, their utter willingness to die rather

31. Or, as Sabon put it, "how cunning a fungus."

32. Tonsure does, in his journal, write that the lichen in question "more closely resembled one blob rutting with another blob, but who is to doubt the vision of cappans?" Are we to believe that the carnage to come was all the result of two unfortunately-shaped lichen? Sabon points to the Holy Visitation of Stockton (alternately known by historians as the Sham Involving Jam), where a stain of blueberry jam resembling the heretic Ibonof Ibonof sparked seven days of riots. Lacond, in agreement with Sabon, relates the story that the Kalif's order to attack the Menite town of Richter was the direct result of a Richter lemon squirting him in the eye when he cut it open. Unfortunately, Sabon and Lacond have joined forces to support an idea that lacks merit given the context. It is my opinion that, lichen or no lichen, Manzikert would have attacked the gray caps.

33. Tonsure never indicates what he did during the massacre—whether to participate or intervene; later circumstantial evidence indicates he may have tried to intervene. Nonetheless, Tonsure's description of the massacre has a disturbingly cold, disinterested edge

than fight back, infuriated the Cappan, and the massacre continued unabated until dusk. By this time "the newly-christened city had become indistinguishable from a charnel house, so much blood had been spilled upon the streets; the smell of the slaughter gathered in the humid air, and the blood itself clung to us like sweat." The bodies were so numerous that they had to be stacked in piles so that Manzikert and his men could navigate the streets back to the docks.

Except that Manzikert, as the sunset finally bled into night and his men lit their torches, did *not* return to the docks.

For, as they passed the great "library" and the inert shapes sprawled on its front steps, Manzikert espied a gray cap dressed in purple robes standing by the red-stained altar. This gray cap not only clicked and whistled at the Cappan, but, after making an unmistakably rude gesture, fled up the stairs. At first shocked, Manzikert pursued with a select group of men,[34] shouting out to Sophia to lead the rest back to the ships; he would follow shortly. Then he and his men—including, for some reason, Tonsure, journal in his pocket—disappeared into the "library." Sophia, always a good soldier, followed orders and returned to the docks.

---

to it. Predictably, the biography account speaks of Manzikert's bravery as, surrounded by "dangerous gray caps armed to the teeth," (read: "wide-eyed, weaponless midgets") he managed to cut his way through them to safety.

34. The bersar, an honorary title peculiar to the Aan and awarded only to men who had shown great bravery in combat.

The night passed without event—except that Manzikert did not return. At first light, Sophia immediately re-entered the city with a force of 300 men, larger by a half than the small army that had slaughtered the gray caps the evening before.

It must have been an odd sight for Sophia and the young Manzikert II.[35] The morning sun shone down upon an empty city. The birds called out from the trees, the bees buzzed around their flowers, but nowhere could be found a dead gray cap, a living man—not even a trace of blood, as if the massacre had never happened and Manzikert himself had never walked the earth. As they walked through the silent streets, fear so overcame them that by the time they had reached the library, which lay near the city's center, more than half the men had broken ranks and headed back to the docks. Although Sophia and Manzikert II did not lose their nerve, it was a close thing. Manzikert II writes that:

Not only had I not seen my Mother so afrightened before, I had never thought to see the day; and yet it was undeniable: she shook with fear as we went up the library steps. Her hands whitest white, her eyes nervous in her head, that something might any moment leap out of bluest sky, the gentle air, the unshadowed dwellings, and set upon her. Seeing my

35. All the information we have about the events that follow comes from Manzikert II, who is not nearly as entertaining as Tonsure, lacking both his wit and powers of description. Manzikert II was serious and 17—a disastrous combination for historical writing, as I can attest—and I have resisted direct quotation for the most part.

Mother so afeared, I thought myself no coward for my own fear.

Within the library, which had been emptied of its books, its mushrooms, its "shelves," they found only a single chair,[36] and sitting in that chair, Manzikert,[37] who wept and covered his face with his hands. Behind him, in the far wall: a gaping hole with stairs that led down into Cinsorium's extensive network of underground tunnels. Into this hole the night before, Manzikert I would later divulge, he, Tonsure, and his bersar had entered in pursuit of the fleeing gray cap.

But at the moment, all Manzikert I could do was weep, and when Sophia finally managed to pry his hands from his face, she could see that there were no tears, for his "eyes had been plucked from their sockets so cleanly, so expertly, that to look at him, this pitiable man, one might think he had been born that way." Of Tonsure, of the Cappan's men, there was no sign, and no sign of any except for the monk would ever turn up. They had effectively vanished for all time.

Manzikert I remained incoherent for several days, screaming out in the night, vomiting, and subject to fits that appear to have been epileptic in nature. He also had

36. The gray caps must also have taken the fabulous golden tree, for there is no mention of it in Manzikert II's account, or in any future chronicle. It defies the laws of probability that such a remarkable invention would *not* be mentioned somewhere, in some account, had it not already been taken back by the gray caps.

37. I will call him Manzikert I from this point on, so as to avoid confusing him with his son.

lost his bearings, for he claimed to have been underground for more than a month, when clearly he had only just gone underground the night before.

During this difficult time—her husband incapacitated, her son stricken with immobility by the double trauma of his father's condition and Tonsure's disappearance—Sophia's grief and fear turned into rage. On the third day after discovering her husband in the library, she reached a decision that has divided historians throughout the ages: she put Cinsorium to the torch.[38]

The conflagration began in the library, and she is said to have expressed great regret that no "books" remained to feed to the fire. The city burned for three days, during which time, due to a miscalculation, the Aan were forced to work long hours protecting the docks which, when the winds shifted, were in serious danger of going up in flame as well. Finally, though, the city burned to the ground, leaving behind only the fleeting descriptions in Tonsure's journal, a few other scattered accounts from Manzikert I's clan, and a handful of buildings that proved resistant to the blaze.[39] Chief among these were the walls of the library itself, which proved to have been made of a fire-repellent

38. Lacond: "An act of utter barbarism, destroying the finest artifacts of a culture that has never been found anywhere else in the known world and destroying a people both peaceful and advanced. Genocide is too kind a word." Sabon: "Without Sophia's bravery, the new-born city of Ambergris would soon have perished, undone by the treachery of the gray caps."

39. Sophia, in the biography, would have us believe that she destroyed all of the buildings, but since we find Manzikert II, 10 years later, using several of them for defensive and storage purposes, this seems unlikely.

stone, the aqueducts, and the altar outside of the library (these last two still stand today). Sophia realized the futility, not to mention the economic consequences, of dismantling the aqueducts, and so took out her frustrations on the altar and the library. The altar was made of a stone so strong they could not crack it with their hammers and other tools. When they tried to dig it out, they discovered it was a pillar that descended at least 100 feet, if not farther, and thus impregnable. The library, however, she had taken apart until "not one stone stood upon another stone." As for the entrances to the underground sections of the ancient city, Sophia had these blocked up with several layers of burned stones from the demolished buildings, and then topped this off with a crude cement fashioned from mortar, pebbles, and dirt. This layer was reinforced with wooden planks stripped from the ships. Finally, Sophia posted sentries, in groups of ten, at each site, and five years later we find a description of these sentries in Manzikert II's journal, still manning their posts.

By this time, Sophia's husband had regained his senses—or, rather, had regained as much of them as he ever would . . .

Manzikert I refused to discuss what had occurred underground, so we will never know whether he even remembered the events that led up to his blinding. He would talk of nothing but the sleek, fat rats that, hiding from the carnage and the fires, had re-emerged to wander the cindered city, no doubt puzzled by the changes. Manzikert I claimed the rats were the reincarnated spirits of saints and martyrs, and as such must be worshipped, groomed, fed, and housed to the extent that they had known such comforts in their former lives.[40] These claims drove Sophia to distraction, and many were the screaming matches aboard the flagship over the next few weeks. However, when she realized that her husband had not recovered, but had, in a sense, died underground, she installed him near the docks, in the very building beside which he had met his first gray cap. There she allowed him to indulge his mania to his heart's content.

Although no longer a fearsome sight, short or tall, Manzikert I lived out his remaining years in a state of perpetual happiness, his gap-toothed grin as prominent as his frown had been in previous years. It was common to see him, with the help of a walking stick, blindly leading his huge charges—sleek, well-fed, and increasingly tame—around the city he had named. At night, the rats all crowded into his new house, and to his son's embarrassment, slept by his side, or even on his bed. Such reverence as he showed the rats, whether the result of insanity or genuine religious epiphany, greatly impressed many of the Aan, especially those who still worshipped the old icons and those who had participated in the slaughter of the gray caps. Soon, he had many helpers.[41] One morning, eight years after the fires, these helpers found Manzikert in his bed, gnawed to death by his "saints and martyrs," and yet, if Manzikert II is to be believed, "with a smile upon his eyeless face."

40. We begin to wonder if Manzikert did believe in his heart of hearts that he should massacre the gray caps because of two oddly-shaped lichens.

41. So many that Manzikert II had to ban the feeding of rats during a time of famine.

Thus ended the oddly poignant life of Ambergris' first ruler—a man who thoroughly deserved to be gnawed to death by rats, as a year had not gone by before his blinding when he had not personally murdered at least a dozen people. Brave but cruel, a tactical genius at war but a failure at peace, and an enigma in terms of his height, Manzikert I is today remembered less as the founder of Ambergris, than as the founder of a religion which still has its adherents today in the city's Religious Quarter and which is still known as "Manziism."[42]

II[43]

To Manzikert I's son, Cappan Manzikert II, would fall the monumental task of converting a pirate/whaling fleet into a viable land-based culture that could supplement fishing with extensive farming and trade with other communities.[44] Luckily, Manzikert II possessed virtues his

42. Much to the disgust of Truffidians everywhere, Manziists often claim to be the Brothers and Sisters of Truff, a claim that has led to riots—and dozens of rats cooked on spits—in the Religious Quarter.
43. The impatient, feckless reader, possessed of no glimmer of intellectual or historical curiosity, should do an old historian a favor and skip the next few pages, proceeding directly to the Silence itself (Part III). I would assume that, in these horrid modern times, that will include most of you. Of course, those readers least likely to read these footnotes, and thus least likely to appreciate the next few pages, will skip this note and bore themselves upon the ennui of history . . .
44. Sophia was never the same after Manzikert I returned to her blinded and deranged—she died soon after him and while alive

father lacked, and although never the military leader his father had been, neither did he have the impulsive nature that had led to their exile in the first place.[45] He also had the ghost of Samuel Tonsure at his disposal, for he had taken the monk's teachings to heart.

Above all else, Manzikert II proved to be a builder—whether it was establishing a permanent town within the old city of Cinsorium or creating friendships with nearby tribes.[46] When peace proved impossible—with, for example, the western tribe known as the Dogghe—Manzikert II showed no reluctance to use force. Twice in the first ten years, he abandoned his rebuilding efforts to battle the Dogghe, until, in a decisive encounter on the outskirts of Ambergris itself, he put to flight and decimated a large tribal army and, using his naval strength to its best effect, annihilated the rest as they took to their canoes. The chieftain of the Dogghe died of extreme gout during the

---

expressed little or no interest in governing, although she did on at least two occasions, at her son's insistence and with great success, lead punitive expeditions against the southern tribes. Sophia had truly loved her brute of a man, although not in the maudlin terms described by Voss Bender in his first and least successful opera, *The Tragedy of John and Sophia*; it is difficult not to laugh while John dances with a man in a rat suit, which he has mistaken in his madness for Sophia, toward the end of Act III.

45. He was, by all accounts, a handsome man, if not possessed of the swarthy, thick handsomeness of his father; he had a slender frame and a head topped with a tangle of black hair, beneath which his green eyes shone with a cunning fierceness.

46. For a long time, these tribes avoided the city and accorded the new settlement an undue measure of respect—until they began to realize the gray caps had left, apparently for good, after which a vigorous contempt for the Aan became the norm.

fighting and with his death the Dogghe had no choice but to come to terms.

Thus, in Manzikert II's eleventh year of rule, he was finally able to focus exclusively on building roads, promoting trade, and, most importantly, designing the layers of efficient bureaucracy necessary to govern a large area. He himself never conquered much territory, but he laid the groundwork for the system that would reach its apogee 300 years later during the reign of Trillian the Great Banker.[47]

Manzikert II also laid the groundwork for Ambergris' unique religious flavor by building churches in what would become the Religious Quarter—and, less to his credit, by active plundering of other cities. Obsessed with relics, Manzikert II was forever sending agents to the south and west to buy or steal the body parts of saints, until by the end of his reign he had amassed a huge collection of some 70 mummified noses, eyelids, feet, kneecaps, fingers, hearts, and livers.[48] Housed in the various churches, these relics attracted thousands of pilgrims (along with their

47. For a thorough overview of the early political and economic systems, as well as particulars on crops, etc., see Richard Mandible's excellent "Early Ambergrisian Finance and Society," recently published in Vol. XXXII, Issue 3, of *Historian's Quarterly*. Such detailed information lies beyond the brief of this particular essay, not to mention the patience of the reader and the endurance of an old historian with creaky joints.

48. A catalog kept during Manzikert II's reign indicates that at least two of these relics were taken from saintly men while still living, and that although the Cappan's agents bargained long and hard for the purchase from the Kalif of the "penis and left testicle of Saint George of Assuf," they managed only to procure the testicle. (We can

money), some of whom stayed in the city, thus helping to spark the rapid growth that made Ambergris a thriving metropolis only 20 years after its foundation. Remarkably, Manzikert II's astute diplomacy averted catastrophe in at least four instances where his thievery of relics so infuriated the plundered cities that they were ready to invade Ambergris.

On the architectural front, Manzikert II built many remarkable structures with the help of his chief architect Midan Pejora, but none so well-known as the Cappan's Palace, which would exist intact until, 350 years later, the Kalif's Grand Vizir, upon his temporary occupation of Ambergris, dismantled much of it.[49] The palace was, by all accounts, a rather peculiar building. The exterior inspired the noted traveler Alan Busker to write:

---

only imagine the bizarre sight of the testicle's triumphant entrance to the city, borne upon a perfumed, gold-embroidered pillow held high by a senior Truffidian priest while the crowds cheered wildly.) At the height of the religious frenzy, the Church of the Seven Pointed Star even put together an array of different saints' body parts—a head here, an ear there—to make a creature they called the "The Saint of Saints," a sort of super saint. This was put on display for 20 years until several other churches, on the verge of bankruptcy due to their own lack of relics, launched a joint raid and "dismembered" this early golem.

49. The rebuilt palace elicited neither condemnation nor praise; indeed, its most interesting features were its many interior murals and portraits, several of which commemorate victories against the Kalif created out of thin air by Ambergrisian historians. Worse, the first two portraits in the Great Hall depict cappans who never existed, to gloss over the Occupation, a period when the city was under the Kalif's control. To this day, Ambergrisian school children are taught the exploits of Cappan Skinder and Cappan Bartine. Braver if less substantial leaders have rarely trod upon the earth . . .

The walls, the columns rise until, at last, as if in ecstasy, the crests of the arches break into a marble foam, and toss themselves far into the blue sky in flashes and wreaths of sculptured spray, as if the breakers on the shore had been frost bound before they fell, and the river nymphs had inlaid them with diamonds and amethyst.

However, the interior prompted him to write: "We shall find that the work is at least pure in its insipidity, and subtle in its vice; but this monument is remarkable as showing the refuse of one style encumbering the embryo of another, and all principles of life entangled either in diapers or the shroud." The actual bust of Manzikert II pleased Busker even less: "A huge, gross, bony clown's face, with the peculiar sodden and sensual cunning in it which is seen so often in the countenances of the worst Truffidian priests; a face part of iron and part of clay. I blame the sculptor, not the subject."

Manzikert II ruled for 43 years and sired a son on his sickly wife Isobel when he was already a gray beard of 45 years. During his reign, he had managed the impossible task of both consolidating his position and preparing for future growth. If his religious fervor led him to bad decisions, then at least his gift for diplomacy saved him from the consequences of those decisions.

Following the death of Manzikert II,[50] Manzikert III duly took his place as ruler of lands that now stretched

50. Evidence suggests he may have been poisoned by his ambitious son, whom he was always careful to bring on campaign

some 40 miles south of Ambergris and 50 miles north.[51] Manzikert III suffered from mild oliphauntitus[52] that apparently affected his internal organs, yet oddly enough he died, after six tumultuous years, of jungle rot[53] received while on a southern expedition to procure lemur eyelids and kidneys for an exotic meat pie. The Cappan's condition was not immediately diagnosed, perhaps due to his

---

with him, so as to keep the boy under a watchful eye. Manzikert II died suddenly, with no apparent symptoms, his body quickly cremated on his son's order. If there was little protest, this may have been because he had never been a popular leader, despite his excellent record. He lacked the necessary charisma for men to follow him unthinkingly.

51. In the north, the Cappandom of Ambergris, as it was now officially known, encountered implacable resistance from the Menites, adherents to a religion that saw Truffid as heresy. The Menites would subsequently establish a vast northern commercial empire, based in the city of Morrow, some 85 miles upriver from Ambergris.

52. Sabon insists it was leprosy, while others believe it was epilepsy. Regardless, we can choose from three spectacular diseases with very different symptoms.

53. Jungle rot can have various manifestations, but, according to an anonymous observer, Manzikert III's jungle rot was among the nastiest ever recorded: "Suddenly an abscess appeared in his privy parts then a deep-seated fistular ulcer; these could not be cured and ate their way into the very midst of his entrails. Hence there sprang an innumerable multitude of worms, and a deadly stench was given off, since the entire bulk of his members had, through gluttony, even before the disease, been changed into an excessive quantity of soft fat, which then became putrid and presented an intolerable and most fearful sight to those who came near it. As for the physicians, some of them were wholly unable to endure the exceeding and unearthly stench, while those who still attended his side could not be of any assistance, since the whole mass had swollen and reached a point where there was no hope of recovery."

oliphauntitus, and by the time doctors had discovered the nature of his condition, it was too late. Displaying a fine disregard for mercy, Manzikert III's last order before he died was for every last member of the Institute of Medicine to be boiled alive in an eel broth; evidently, he had thought up a new recipe.[54]

Manzikert III had not been a good cappan.[55] During his reign, he had launched numerous futile assaults on the Menites, and although no one ever doubted his personal bravery, he had all of his grandfather's impatience and impulsiveness, but none of that man's charisma or shrewdness. A grotesque gastronome, he put on decadent banquets even during the famine that struck in the third year of his reign.[56] About all that can be said in Manzikert III's defense is that he provided monies for research that

54. Although Manzikert III's order (rescinded after his death) was extreme, his charge that the city's doctors knew little of their craft is, unfortunately, true. In an attempt to upgrade its service, the Institute sent representatives to the Kalif's court, as well as to the witchdoctors of native tribes. The Kalif's physicians refused to reveal their methodology, but the witchdoctors proved very helpful. The Institute incorporated such native procedures as applying the freshwater electric flounder as a local anesthetic during surgery. Another procedure, perhaps even more ingenious, solved the problem of infection during the stitching up of intestines. Large senegrosa ants, placed along the opening, clamped the wounds shut with their jaws; the witchdoctor then cut away the bodies, leaving only the heads. After replacing the intestines in the stomach, the witchdoctor would sew up the abdomen. As the wound healed, the ant heads would gradually dissolve.

55. Although I have certainly devoted enough footnotes to him.

56. One menu for such a banquet included calf's brain custard, roast hedgehog, and a dish rather cruelly known as Oliphaunt's

resulted in refinements of the mariner's compass and the invention of the double-ruddered ship (useful for maneuvering in narrow tributaries). However, Manzikert III is best remembered for his poor treatment of the poet Maximillian Sharp. Sharp came to Ambergris as an emissary of the Menites, and when it came time for him to leave, Manzikert III would not allow him safe passage by the most convenient route. He was consequently obliged to make his way back through malarial swampland as a result of which this greatest of all ancient masters caught a fever and died.[57] Manzikert III, when brought news of Sharp's death, is said to have joked, "Consider this my con-

---

Delight, the incomplete recipe for which was uncovered by the Ambergrisian Gastronomic Association just last year:

    1 scooped out oliphaunt's skull
    1 pureed oliphaunt's brain
    1 gallon of brandy
    6 oysters
    2 very clean pigs' bladders
    24 eggs
    salt, pepper, and a sprig of parsley

I am unhappy to report that the search is on for the missing ingredients.

57. In all fairness to Manzikert III, Sharp had an insufferable ego. His autobiography, published from the unedited manuscript found on his body, contains such gems as, "From East and West alike my reputation brings them flocking to Morrow. The Moth may water the lands of the Kalif, but it is my golden words that nourish their spirit. Ask the Brueghelites or the followers of Stretcher Jones: they will tell you that they know me, that they admire me and seek me out. Only recently there arrived an Ambergrisian, impelled by an insurmountable desire to drink at the fountain of my eloquence."

tribution to the Arts."[58] Another year and Manzikert III might have exhausted both the treasury and his people's patience. As it was, he managed little permanent damage and all of this was put right by his successor: Manzikert II's illegitimate son by a distant third cousin, the handsome and intelligent Michael Aquelus, arguably the greatest of the Manzikert cappans.[59] If not for Aquelus' firm hand, Ambergris, cappandom and city, might well have crumbled to dust within a generation.

58. The Scathadian novelist George Leopran had an experience almost as bad, returning to Scatha only after much tribulation: "I boarded my vessel and left the city that I had thought to be so rich and prosperous but is actually a starveling, a city full of lies, tricks, perjury and greed, a city rapacious, avaricious and vainglorious. My guide was with me, and after 49 days of ass-riding, walking, horse-riding, fasting, thirsting, sighing, weeping, and groaning, I arrived at the Kalif's court. Even this was not the end of my sufferings, for upon setting out for the final stretch of my journey, I was delayed by contrary winds at Paust, deserted by my ship's crew at Latras, unkindly received by a eunuch bishop and half-starved on Lukas and subjected to three consecutive earthquakes on Dominon, where I subsequently fell in among thieves. Only after another 60 days did I finally return to my home, never again to leave it." If he had known that an arthritic Ambergrisian historian would some day find his account hilarious, he might have cheered up. Or perhaps not. In any event, we can certainly understand historical novelists' tendency to vilify Manzikert III beyond even his due.

59. We will never know why Aquelus was accepted so readily, unless Manzikert III had proclaimed him ruler on his deathbed or Manzikert II, knowing his son's sickly nature, had already decreed that if Manzikert III died, Aquelus should take his place. The story that, in his childhood, a golden eagle alighted at Aquelus' bedroom window and told him he would one day be cappan is almost certainly apocryphal.

❧❦

We now stand on the threshold of the event known as the Silence. Almost 70 years have passed since the massacre of the gray caps and the destruction of the ancient city of Cinsorium. The new Cappandom of Ambergris has begun to thrive over its ruins and no gray caps have been seen since the day of the massacre. An initial population that may well have flinched in anticipation of some terrible reprisal for genocide has given way to people who have never seen a gray cap, many of them Aan clans folk from the south who also wish to resettle on land. Manzikert II has already, during an exceedingly long reign, overseen the painful transition to a permanent settlement—already, too, a prosperous middle class of merchants, shopkeepers, and bankers has sprung up, supplemented by farmers who have settled in Ambergris and the outlying minor towns.[60] River trade is booming, and has made the city rich in a short period of time. Compulsory two-year military service has proven a success—the army is strong but civic-minded while Ambergris' enemies appear few and impotent. Units of barter based on a gold standard have been introduced and these coins form the principal form of currency, followed closely by the southern Aan sel, which will gradually be phased out. All of Ambergris' rulers—including Manzikert III—have successfully foiled attempts by the

60. Three centuries later, city mayors all along the Moth would cast off the yoke of cappans and kings and create a league of city-states based on trade alliances—eventually plunging Ambergris into its current state of "functional anarchy."

upper classes (mostly descendants of Manzikert I's lieutenants) to form a ruling aristocracy by parceling out most of the land to small farmers. Thus, there are no serious internal threats to the succession. Finally, we are on the cusp of a period of inspired building and invention known as the Aquelus Age.

Everywhere, new ideas take root. The refurbished whaling fleet has focused its efforts on the giant freshwater squid, with great success. Aquelus will not just make freshwater squid products a national industry, but part of the national identity, inadvertently introducing the Festival of the Freshwater Squid, which will remain a peaceful event throughout the rule of the Manzikerts.[61] The old aqueducts have been made functional again and extensive settlement has occurred in the valley beyond the city

---

61. The first festival, held by Manzikert I, had been a simple affair: a two-course feast attended by an elderly swordswallower who managed to impale himself. More elaborate entertainments would mark the reign of Aquelus in particular. Such celebrations included a representation of the Gardens of Nicea, 300 yards across, built on rafts between the two banks of the Moth, complete with flowers, trees of brightly-colored crystal, and an artificial lake stocked with fish, from which guests were to choose their dinner before retiring to a banquet. In the year after the Silence, at a touch from the Cappaness' hand, an outsized artificial owl sped around the public courtyard, sparking off a hundred torches as it, finally, came to rest on an 80-foot high replica of the Kalif's Arch of Tarbut. But perhaps the most audacious presentation occurred during the reign of Manzikert VII, who resurrected the gray caps' old coliseum, sealed it off, had the arena flooded with water, and recreated famous naval battles using ships built to 2/3 scale. All this pomp and circumstance served as genuine celebration, but also, in later years, to hide the city's growing poverty and military weakness.

proper, creating a separate town of craftspeople. Every day a new house goes up and a new street is dedicated, and by the time of Aquelus there are over 30,000 permanent residents in Ambergris: approximately 13,000 men and 17,000 women and children.[62]

And yet, as Aquelus enters his sixth year in power, there is something *dreadfully wrong*, and although no one knows the source of this wrongness, perhaps a few suspect, at least a little. First, there is the sinister way in which the gray caps have entered the collective consciousness of the city: parents tell tales of the old inhabitants of Cinsorium to children at bedtime—that the gray caps will creep up out of the ground on their clammy pale hands and feet, crawl in through an open window, and *grab you* if you don't go to sleep.

Or, more frequently now, the term "mushroom dweller" is used instead of "gray cap," no doubt become more common because, rather disturbingly, the only major failure of the civil government and private citizens has been the war against the fungus that has overgrown many areas of Ambergris: cascades of dark and bright mushrooms, gaily festooned with red and green, or somber in jackets of gray or brown, sometimes as thick as the very grass. Public complaints proliferate, for certain types exude a slick poison which, when it comes into contact with legs, feet, arms, hands, leaves the victim in extreme pain and covered with purple splotches for up to a week. More alarmingly, a new type of mushroom with a stem as thick as an oak and four or five feet tall, begins to spring up in the middle of

62. Fourth Census—on file in the old bureaucratic quarter.

certain streets, wrenching free from the cobblestones. These blue-tinged "white whales,"[63] as some wag nicknamed them, have to be chopped down by either fire emergency workers or the civil police department, causing hours of inconvenience and lost work time. They also smell so strongly of rotten eggs that whole neighborhoods have to be evacuated, sometimes for days.

Certainly the afflicted areas had grown more numerous in those last years before the Silence, almost as if the fungi formed a vast, nonsentient advance guard . . . but for what? At least one prominent citizen, the inventor Stephen Bacilus[64]—the great-great-great grandfather of the influential statistician Gort—appears to have known what for, and to have recognized a potential danger. As he put it to the Home Council, a body created to address issues of citywide security:

The very fact that we cannot stop their proliferation, that every poison only makes them thrive the more,

63. Lacond's most delicious "theory" according to most historians (and therefore well worth relating) postulates that some mushroom dwellers actually gestated within such mushrooms. This explains both why the axe blows to fell them caused the mushrooms to shriek and why their centers often proved to be composed of a dark, watery mass reminiscent of afterbirth or amniotic fluid. I myself now believe they "shrieked" because this is the sound a certain rubbery consistency of fungi flesh makes when an axe cleaves it; as for the "afterbirth," many fungi contain a nutrient sac. We could wish that Lacond had done more research on the subject before venturing an opinion, but then we would be bereft of this marvelous conjecture.

64. By now in his late sixties, Bacilus was a fiery old man with a smoking white beard who must have made quite a spectacle in public.

should alarm us. For it indicates the presence of another, superior, force determined that these fungi should live. The further observation, made by many in this room tonight, that some fungi, after we have uprooted them and placed them in the appointed garbage heaps for burning, mysteriously find their way back to their former location—this should also shock us into action . . . and, finally, I need not remind you, except that so many of us today have short memories, that several of these mushrooms are purple in hue. Until a few years ago, a purple mushroom could not be found in all the city. Somehow, I find this fact more sinister than any other . . .

Unfortunately, the Council dismissed his evidence as based on old wives' tales, and placed an edict on Bacilus that forbid him to speak about "mushrooms, fungi, lichen, moss, or related plants so as not to unwittingly and unnecessarily cause a general panic amongst the populace."[65] After all, the Home Council was responsible for security in the city.

65. In the Council's defense, Bacilus had a rather checkered reputation in Ambergris. We have, today, the luxury of distance, but the Council had had no time to expunge from memory such Bacilus innovations as artificial legs for snakes, mittens for fish, or the infamous Flying Jacket. Bacilus reasoned that if trapped air will make an object float upon the water, then trapped air might also allow an object, in this case a man, to float upon the air. Therefore, Bacilus created a special body suit he called the Flying Jacket. Made from hollowed out pig and cow stomachs, it consisted of three dozen air sacs sewn together. Without prior testing, Bacilus persuaded his

But did Bacilus have cause for alarm? Perhaps so. According to police reports, three years before the Silence the city experienced 76 unexplained or unsolved break-ins, up from only 30 the previous year. Two years before the Silence this figure rose to 99 break-ins, and in the year before the Silence, almost 150 unexplained break-ins occurred within the city limits. No doubt some of these burglaries can be attributed to the large number of unassimilated immigrant adventurers flooding into Ambergris, and no doubt the authorities' failure to show undue concern means they had reached a similar conclusion. However, the victims in an astonishing number of these cases claim, when they saw anyone at all, that the intruder was a *small person*, usually hidden by shadow and almost always *wearing a large felt hat*. These mystery burglars most often made off with cutlery, jewelry, and food items.[66]

---

cousin Brandon Map to don the Flying Jacket and, in front of some of Aquelus' foremost ministers, to jump from the top of the new Truffidian Cathedral. After the poor man had plummeted to his death, it was generally observed within Bacilus' earshot, if only to make the loss appear not completely pointless, that yes, perhaps his cousin *had* flown a little bit before the end. Another minister, less kindly, remarked that if Bacilus himself, surely a natural windbag if ever he'd seen one, had donned the jacket, the results might have been different, for it was obvious that Brandon had no air within him anymore, nor blood, nor bones . . . The Truffidians were, of course, horrified that their new cathedral had been christened with such a splatter of blood—and even more upset when they discovered Brandon had been an atheist. (I should note, however, that Truffidians have spent the last seven centuries being horrified by some event or other.)

66. This police report filed by Richard Krokus provides a typical example: "I woke in the middle of the night to a humming sound from

It is unfortunate indeed that the urban legend of the mushroom dwellers had spread so widely, because, reduced to stories to scare children, no one took them seriously. The police passed off such accounts as hysterical or as bald-faced lies, while criminals complicated the situation

---

the kitchen. It must have been two in the morning and my wife was by my side, and we have no children, so I knew no one who was supposed to be in the house was fixing themselves a midnight snack. So I go into the kitchen real quiet-like, having picked up a plank of wood for a weapon that I was going to use to reinforce the mantel, but hadn't gotten around to on account of my bad back—I served like everyone in the army and messed up my back when I fell during training exercises and even got disability payments for awhile, until they found out I'd slipped on a tomato—and my wife had been nagging me to fix the mantel so I picked up the wood—from the store, first, I mean, and then that night I picked it up, but not so as to fix the mantel, you know, but to defend myself. Where was I? Oh, yes. So I go into the kitchen and I'm already thinking about making myself a sandwich with the left-over bread, so maybe I'm not paying as much attention as I should to the situation, and I'll be f— if there isn't this little person, this wee little person in a great big felt hat just sitting on the counter-top, stuffing its face with the missus' chocolate cake. I looked at it and it looked at me, and I didn't move and it didn't move. It had great big eyes in its head, and a small nose, and a grin like all get out, only it had teeth, too, real big teeth, so it kind of spoiled the cheerfulness. Of course, it had already spoiled my wife's cake, so I was going to hit it with my plank of wood, only then it threw a mushroom at me and next thing I know it's morning and not only is the cake completely gone, but my wife is slapping my face and telling me to get up have I been drinking again don't I know I'm late for work. And later that day, when I'm setting the plates for dinner, I can't find any of the knives or forks. They're all gone. Oh, yes, and I almost forgot—I couldn't find the mushroom that hit me, either, but I'm telling you, it was heavier than it looked because it left this great big bump on top of me head. See?"

by disguising themselves in gray cap "garb" when committing burglaries.[67]

Worse still, the efficient government and the network of peace treaties Manzikert II and Aquelus had created proved to be built on a fragile foundation.

At the time of the Silence, it would have seemed that Ambergris was not only secure but richer than ever before. Indeed, Aquelus had just formed an even stronger alliance with the Menites[68]—and took the first step toward the continuation of his bloodline by marrying the old Menite

67. A few local souvenir shops, hoping to cash in on the pilgrim business, had begun to sell small statues and dolls of the mushroom dwellers, as well as potpourris made from mushrooms; a singular tavern called "The Spore of the Gray Cap" even sprouted up. (This tavern still exists today and serves some of the best cold beer in the city.)

68. Aquelus, in a brilliant maneuver, sent, along with his ambassador suggesting marriage, a bevy of Truffidian monks to Morrow, to negotiate a religious compromise that would allow the Menite kingdom and the Truffidian cappandom to reconcile their differences. Many of the arguments were extremely obscure. For example, the Menites believed God was to be found in all creatures, while the Truffidians, in their attempts to disassociate themselves from Manziism, believed rats were "of the Devil"; after weeks of ridiculous testimony on the merits ("their fur is pleasant to stroke") and deficiencies ("they spread disease") of rats, the compromise was that "of the Devil" should be struck from the Truffidian literature and replaced with the language "not of God" (originally changed to "made of God, but perhaps strayed from His teachings," but the Truffidians would not accept this). After a tortuous year of negotiation, and possibly more from exhaustion and boredom than because anyone actually *believed* in it, a settlement was reached, much to the relief of both rulers (who, although religious, had a strong streak of pragmatism). This agreement would last for 70 years, until made void by the Great Schism, and even then the dissolution of the contract transpired

King's daughter Irene,[69] who by all accounts was not only beautiful but intelligent and could be expected to rule jointly with Aquelus, much as had, in their fashion, Sophia and Manzikert I.[70]

The same year, Aquelus secured his western borders against possible attacks by the Kalif[71] with the signing of a treaty in which Ambergrisian merchants would receive preferential treatment (especially the waiver of export taxes) and in return Aquelus promised to hold Ambergris in vassalage to the Kalif.[72]

---

through the offices of the main Truffidian Church in the lands of the Kalif.

69. Chroniclers of the period call the marriage one of convenience, as evidence suggests Aquelus was a homosexual. But if begun in convenience, it soon deepened into mutual love. Certainly nothing rules out the possibility of Aquelus being bisexual, much as the homosexual scholar cappan of Ambergris, Meriad, writing two centuries later, would have us believe Aquelus was as bent as a broken bow.

70. Given Sophia and Manzikert I's example, it is not surprising that, until the fall of Trillian the Great Banker and his Banker Warriors, women served in the army, many of them attaining the highest ranks. Irene herself excelled as a hunter, could outrun and outfight the fastest of her five brothers, and had studied strategy with no less a personage than the Kalif's brilliant general, Masouf.

71. Please note that in these several references to the Kalif over the past 60 years, I have been referring to more than one ruler. The Kalif was chosen by secret ballot, and his identity never revealed, so as to protect against assassination attempts. Each Kalif was called simply "the Kalif." It is little wonder that the position of Royal Genealogist has so few rewards and so many frustrations.

72. If this arrangement seems extreme, we should consider that in effect the vassalage meant nothing—the Kalif was far too busy consolidating his recent eastern conquests (rebellions in these lands secretly funded by Aquelus, who left nothing to chance) to exact tribute or even send his own administrators to oversee the Cappandom.

The depth of Aquelus' deviousness is best illustrated by his response when the Kalif asked Aquelus to help suppress the southern rebellion of Stretcher Jones in return for further trade concessions. The Kalif, a devious man himself, also wrote that Aquelus' two half-brothers, closest successors to the cappanship, had been awarded the honor of studying in the Kalif's court, under the tutelage of his most able instructors, "amongst the most learned men in the civilized world." Aquelus, who had remained neutral in the conflict, replied that a Brueghelite armada of 100 sail already threatened Ambergris—a fleet actually some 200 miles away, contentedly plundering the southern islands— and he could not spare any ships to attack a friendly Truffidian power in the west; nonetheless, he gratefully accepted the privileges so generously offered by the Kalif. As for the invitation to his half-brothers, Aquelus returned his "devout and immense thanks," but they never went. Had they gone, the Kalif would almost certainly have kept them as hostages.[73]

However pleased Aquelus may have been at the adroit deflection of these potential threats, he still, as the annual fresh water squid expedition came ever closer, had two

---

However, the Kalif may have outmaneuvered Aquelus in this regard, since in later centuries his successors would claim that the Cappandom of Ambergris belonged by right to them and would wage war to "liberate" it.

73. When Stretcher Jones was finally defeated, in a bloody battle that consolidated the Kalif's western supremacy for 300 years, Aquelus responded with the following words: "Being a friend of both sovereigns, I can only say, with God: I rejoice with them that do rejoice and weep with them that weep."

other dangerous situations that required swift resolution. First, the clear shortfall in the spring crops, combined with the influx of new settlers (which he had no wish to see slacken) meant the possibility of famine. Second, the Haragck, a warlike clan of nomads who rode sturdy mountain ponies into battle, had begun to make inroads on his western borders.[74] Aquelus had no cavalry, but the Haragck had no fleet, and if it came to armed confrontation, Aquelus must have been confident—now that Morrow, in firm control of the northern Moth, was an ally—that he could stop the barbarians from crossing the river in force.

If the Haragck had been Aquelus' only enemy, he would still have had cause to thank his good fortune, but to the south an old adversary chose this moment to re-assert itself: the Aan descendants of the same Brueghel who had chased Manzikert I upriver. Drawn by the Aan exodus to the rich suburbs of Ambergris, these Brueghe-lites, as they called themselves, had begun to make trouble in the south. Understandably, they resented the loss of so much potential manpower when they found themselves beset by the still more southerly Gray Tribes. Most dam-aging, in light of the famine, the Brueghelites waged a trade war instead of a military war, which might at least

74. Even before Stretcher Jones' fall these fierce warriors had been driven east by the slowly-advancing armies of the Kalif, who most cer-tainly wished for them to weaken Ambergris. They have since passed out of history in a manner both shocking and absurd, but tangential to the concerns of this essay; suffice it to say that exploding ponies do not a pretty sight make, and that no one knows who was responsible for the worms.

have been resolved quickly. Some of their weapons included transit dues on Ambergrisian goods, heavy tolls on produce bound for the southern islands, and customs houses (backed by large, well-armed garrisons) along the Moth.[75]

Eventually, Aquelus would find a way to set the Haragck against the Brueghelites, eliminating both as a threat to Ambergris,[76] but as the freshwater squid season approached, Aquelus could not know that his bribes and political maneuverings would bear fruit. Thus, he made the fateful decree that three times as many ships would participate in the hunt as usual. His purpose was to offset the shortfall of crops with squid meat and byproducts, and to provide enough extra food to withstand a siege by either the Brueghelites or the Haragck.[77] In the event there was no siege, these provisions could accommodate the continuing flow of immigrants. The maneuvers to catch the squid, coincidentally, required a prowess and skill level far greater

75. With access to the sea blocked in this way, it is hardly surprising that Ambergris did not become the dominant naval power in the region until the days of Manzikert V, who established the Factory: a world-renowned shipbuilding center that could produce a galley in 12 hours, a fully-armed warship in two days.

76. And, coincidentally, providing Aquelus with an excellent example of what happens when an army with a strong cavalry fights a primarily naval force: nothing.

77. To this end, Aquelus built land walls to protect against an assault from the north, south, or east. He also set out defensive fortifications on the river side that included provisions for converting ships into floating barricades. Very little remains of any of these structures, as the contractor who won the bid, purportedly a former Brueghelite, used inferior materials; the extreme eastern side of the Religious Quarter still abuts the last nub of the land walls.

than necessary during an actual war, and so Aquelus also looked to toughen up his navy.

At the appointed time, Aquelus, at the head of nearly 5,000 men and women, took to the river in his 100 ships.[78] They would be gone for two weeks, the longest period of time Aquelus thought he could safely remain away from the capital. His new wife stayed behind. No two turns of fate—Irene's choice to stay at home and the enormity of the fleet that set off for the southern hunting grounds— would have a more profound effect on Ambergris during its early history.

III

ANY HISTORIAN MUST TAKE EXTREME CARE WHEN DIS- cussing the Silence, for the enormity of the event demands respect. But when the historian in question, myself, explains the Silence for a paltry pamphlet series, he must display a degree of solemnity in direct inverse proportion to the frivolity of the surrounding information. I find it unacceptable that you, the reader, should flip—a most dis- agreeably shallow word—from this pamphlet to the next, which may concern Best Masquerade Festivals or Where to Procure a Prostitute, without being made to grasp the awful ramifications of the Event. This requires no melo-

---

78. Even if there had been no famine, Aquelus would have been obliged to take nearly as many ships with him, for they would have to pass through the outer edge of Brueghelite waters in order to hunt the squid.

dramatic folderol on my part, for the facts themselves should suffice: *upon Aquelus' return, the city of Ambergris lay empty, not a single living soul to be found upon any of its boulevards, alleyways, and avenues, nor within its many homes, public buildings, and courtyards.*

Aquelus' ships landed at docks where the only sound was the lapping of water against wood. Arrived in the early morning, having raced home to meet the self-imposed two-week deadline, the Cappan found the city cast in a weak light, wreathed in mist come off the river. It must have been an ethereal scene—perhaps even a terrifying one.

At first, no one noticed the severity of the silence, but as the fleet weighed anchor and the crews walked out onto the docks, many thought it odd no one had come out to greet them. Soon, they noticed that the river defenses lay unmanned, and that the boats in the harbor around them, as they came clear of the mist, drifted, under no one's control.

When Aquelus noticed these anomalies, he feared the worst—an invasion by the Brueghelites during his absence—and ordered the crews back onto the ships. All ships but his own sailed back out into the middle of the River Moth, where they remained, laden with squid, at battle readiness.

Then Aquelus, anxious to find his new bride, personally led an expedition of 50 men into the city.[79] His fears

79. Aquelus' one weakness was a penchant for taking personal command of military expeditions. Such bravery often helped him win the day, but it would also be the cause of his death a few days shy of his

of invasion seemed unfounded, for everywhere they
went, Ambergris was as empty of enemies as it was of
friends.

We are lucky indeed that among the leaders of the
expedition was one Simon Jersak, a common soldier who
would one day serve as the chief tax collector for the western provinces. Jersak left us with a full account of the
expedition's journey into Ambergris, and I quote liberally
from it here:

> As the mist, which had hidden the true extent of the
> city's emptiness from us, dissipated, and as every
> street, every building, every shop on every corner,
> proved to have been abandoned, the Cappan himself
> trembled and drew his cloak about him. Men from
> among our ranks were sent randomly through the
> neighborhoods, only to return with the news that
> more silence lay ahead: meals lay on tables ready to
> eat, and carts with horses stood placidly by the sides of
> avenues that, even at the early hour, would normally
> have been abustle. But nowhere could we find a soul:
> the banks were unlocked and empty, while in the
> Religious Quarter, the flags still weakly fluttered, and
> the giant rats meandered about the courtyards, but,

67th birthday, when, although incapacitated as we shall see, he
insisted in riding a specially-trained horse into battle against the
Skamoo, who had come down from the frozen tundra to attack
Morrow. Aquelus never saw the northern giant who felled him with a
battle axe.

again, no people; even the fungi that had been our scourge had gone away. We quickly searched through the public baths, the granaries, the porticos, the schools—nothing. When we reached the Cappan's palace and found no one there—not his bride, not the least retainer—the Cappan openly wept, and yet underneath the tears his face was set as if for war. He was not the only man reduced to tears, for it soon became clear that our wives, our children, had all disappeared, and yet left behind all the signs of their presence, so we knew we had not been dreaming our lives away—they had existed, they had lived, but they were no longer in the city . . . And so, disconsolate, robbed of all power to act against an enemy whose identity he did not know, my Cappan sat upon the steps of the palace and stared out across the city . . . until such time as one of the men who had been sent out discovered certain items on the old altar of the gray caps. At this news, the Cappan donned his cloak once more, wiped the tears from his face, drew his sword and sped to the site with all haste. As we followed behind our Cappan, through that city once so full of lives and now as empty as a tomb, there were none among us who did not, in our heart of hearts, fear what we would find upon the old altar . . .

What did they find upon the altar? An old weathered journal and two human eyeballs preserved by some unknown process in a solid square made of an unknown clear metal. Between journal and squared eyeballs blood had been used to draw a symbol:[80]

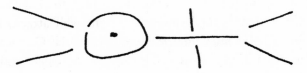

More ominous still, the legendary entrance, once blocked up, boarded over, lay wide open, the same stairs that had enticed Manzikert I beckoning now to Aquelus.

The journal was, of course, the one that had disappeared with Samuel Tonsure 60 years before. The eyes, a fierce blue, could belong to no one but Manzikert I. Who the blood had come from, no one cared to guess, but Aquelus, finally confronted with an enemy—for who could now doubt the return of the gray caps and their implication in the disappearance of the city's citizens?[81]—acted decisively.

Those commanders who argued that a military force should attack the underground found themselves overruled by Aquelus, who, in the face of almost overwhelming opposition, ordered all of his military commanders back to the ships, there to speed up the disembarkation so as to

80. Note the difference between this symbol and the one accompanying footnote 23. No one has yet deciphered the original symbol, nor the meaning of its "dismemberment."

81. Who but Sabon, of course. Sabon claims the Menites herded up the city's residents, massacred them some fifty miles from the city, and then left behind evidence to implicate the gray caps. She supports this ridiculous theory by pointing out the Cappaness' fate (soon to be revealed).

simultaneously process the squid, which otherwise would have rotted, and take up defensive positions throughout the city. Aquelus knew that the Haragck, upon hearing of the developments in Ambergris, might well attack, followed by the Brueghelites. Worse still, if the Cappaness could not be found, the political consequences—regardless of his love for her—would be disastrous. Might not the King of the Menites blame Aquelus for the death of his daughter?

Once the commanders had taken their leave, Aquelus transferred power to his minister of finance, one Thomas Nadal,[82] and announced that he intended to go down below himself.[83] The Cappan's decision horrified his

82. Aquelus' lover for many years. What Irene thought of this arrangement we do not know, but we do know that she treated Nadal with much more kindness and respect than he treated her. Later, he would lose his position for it.

83. The reason for this decision appears to have been both political and personal. Although Aquelus never commented on the decision either in public or private, Nadal wrote after the Cappan's death that (much to Nadal's distress) the Cappan truly loved Irene and, in the madness of his grief, was convinced she still lived underground. However, Nadal's account must be considered somewhat disingenuous, for if Aquelus believed his wife was alive, surely he would have allowed the military to send a large force after her? No, his sacrifice served several other purposes: if *he* did not go, then in the current state of anger and anguish, these men would surely take their own actions, possibly overthrowing him if he tried to stop them again. (Further, if his descent was seen as taken on behalf of Irene, perhaps the Menite king would look more kindly upon the Cappan.) Most importantly, Aquelus was an ardent student of history and must have known the details of the gray cap massacre and the subsequent burning of Cinsorium. No doubt he interpreted the gray caps' actions as revenge, and what must be avoided at all costs were reprisals against them,

ministers.[84] In addition to their personal affection for Aquelus, they feared losing their Cappan after all else that had been taken from them. Many, Nadal included, also feared the Haragck and the Brueghlites, but Aquelus countered these arguments by pointing out, truthfully enough, that his military commanders could easily lead any defense of the city—after all, they had drawn up a plan for just such a situation months ago. However, when Nadal then asked, "Yes, but who other than you can lead us to rebuild the morale of this shattered city?" Aquelus ignored him. Clearly, only he or his disappeared wife could make Ambergris a viable, living metropolis again. Still, down below he went, and down below he stayed for three days.[85]

---

which would only lead to further retaliation on both sides, permanently destabilizing the city and making it impossible to rule. For, if the gray caps could make 25,000 people disappear without a trace, then Aquelus had only two choices: to leave the city forever, or reach some sort of accommodation. Perhaps perceiving that, having taken their revenge, the gray caps might be persuaded to negotiate, knowing also that *some* action must be taken, and even now hoping against hope to rescue his wife, he must have felt he had no choice. If Aquelus saw the situation in this light, then he was among the most selfless leaders Ambergris would ever have; such selflessness would carry a heavy price.

84. In the unlikely event that you are wondering how so many ministers survived the Silence, let me draw aside the veils of ignorance: Ministers were in no way exempted from periodic military service—in fact, their positions demanded it, since Aquelus was determined to keep the army as "civilian" as possible. Therefore, at least seven major ministers or their designees had sailed with the fleet.

85. Peter Copper, in his biography *Aquelus*, provides a poignant account of the Cappan's departure for the nether regions. Copper writes: "And so down he went, down into the dark, not as Manzikert

Above ground, Aquelus' military commanders might well have staged a coup if not for the arrival that first night of Irene, only 12 hours after Aquelus' descent into the domains of the mushroom dwellers. By a quirk of chance both cruel and kind, she had left the capital for a two-day hunting trip in the surrounding countryside.[86]

Faced with the double-edged horror of the Silence and her husband's underground sojourn, Cappaness Irene never faltered, taking quick, decisive action. The rebellious commanders—Seymour, Nialson, and Rayne—she had thrown in prison. Simultaneously, she sent a fast boat to Morrow with a message for her father, asking for his immediate military support.[87] The Cappaness might have thought this ended her immediate problems, but she had severely under-estimated the mood of the men and women who had returned to the city. The soldiers guarding the rebel commanders freed their prisoners[88] and led a drunken mob of naval cadets to the front steps of the palace.

Inside, the Cappan's ministers had succumbed to panic—burning documents, stripping murals for their gold

---

I had done, for blood sport, but after much thought and in the belief that no other action could deliver his city from annihilation physical and spiritual. As the darkness swallowed him up and his footsteps became an ever fainter echo, his ministers truly believed they would never see him again."

86. Near Baudux, where the old ruins of Alfar still stand; grouse and wild pigs are plentiful in the region.

87. At the time she meant for such help to strengthen her internal position, not to defend the city from external threats.

88. That the Cappaness even managed to have the commanders imprisoned is testimony not only to Irene's strength of character, but to the civil service system put into place by Manzikert II. Most

thread, and preparing to abandon the city under cover of darkness. When they came to the Cappaness with news of the insurrection and told her she must flee too, she refused and, as reported by Nadal, said to them:

> Every man who is born into the light of day must sooner or later die; and how could I allow myself the luxury of such cowardice when my husband took all our sins upon himself and went underground? May I never willingly shed the colors of Ambergris, nor see the day when I am no longer addressed by my title. If you, my noble ministers, wish to save your skins, you will have little difficulty in doing so. You have plundered the palace's riches and with luck you can reach the river and your boats moored there. But consider first whether when you reach safety you will not regret that you did not choose death. For those who remain,

---

survivors of the Silence, when the Cappan's decision and the rumor of the mushroom dwellers' involvement became common knowledge, were for an all-out assault on the underground areas of the city. Indeed, despite the Cappaness' reiteration of Aquelus' orders, Red Martigan, a lieutenant on the Cappan's flagship, *did* lead a clandestine operation against the mushroom dwellers while the Cappan was still below ground. He took some 50 men to the city's extreme southeastern corner and entered the sewer system through an open culvert. Some days later, a friend who had not joined Martigan's expedition went down to the culvert to check on them. He found, neatly set out across the top of the culvert, the heads of Red Martigan and his 50 men, their eyes scooped out, their mouths to a one set in a kind of "grimacy" smile that was more frightening than the sight of the heads themselves. As to whether this action on Martigan's part hurt Aquelus' efforts underground, I can only offer the by now familiar, and irritating, refrain of "alas, we shall never know."

I shall ask only that you contain your fear, for we must present a brave face if we are to survive this night.

Shamed by these words, Nadal and his colleagues had no choice but to follow the Cappaness out to the front steps of the palace. What followed must be considered the crowning achievement of early Ambergrisian nationalism—a moment that even today sends "chills down the spine" of the least patriotic city dweller. This daughter of Menites, this Cappaness without a Cappan, made her famous speech in which she called upon the mob to lay down its arms "in the service of a greater good, for the greater glory of a city unique in the history of the world. For if we can overcome this strife now, we shall never fear ourselves ever again."[89] She then detailed in cold-blooded fashion exactly who the rebels would have to kill to gain power and the full extent of the repercussions for a severely divided Ambergris: instant assimilation by the Brueghelites.[90] Further, she promised to strengthen the elected position of city mayor[91] and not to pursue reprisals against the mob itself, only its leaders.

Such was the magnetism of her personality and the passion of her speech that the mob turned on its leaders and brought them to the Cappaness in chains. Thus was

89. While we can trust Nadal on the contents of the speech, he is a less trustworthy reporter of the actual verbiage: in his mouth, even the word "nausea" becomes both vainglorious and tediously melodramatic. He is, however, our only source.

90. In reality, the Haragck were the greater threat.

91. With the result that in later years, under weak cappans, the mayor actually had equal status.

the most severe internal crisis in the cappandom's short history diffused by Irene—the daughter of a foreign state with a heretical (to the Truffidians) religion. The people would not soon forget her.

But the Cappaness and her people had no time to draw breath, for on the second day of Aquelus' disappearance, 7,000 Haragck crossed the Moth and attacked Ambergris.[92] The Cappaness' forces, although taken by surprise, managed to keep the Haragck pinned down in the region of the docks, except for a contingent of 2,000, whom Irene allowed to break through to the city proper; she rightly

92. How did the Haragck cross over in such numbers? Atrocious swimmers, they somehow managed to make 7,000 inflatable animal skins—not, as rumor has it, made from their ponies, which they loved—and, fully armed, floated/dog paddled across the Moth. The reliefs that depict this event are among the only surviving examples of Haragck artwork:

The more perplexing question is: How did the Haragck know to attack so soon? Until recent times, it remained a mystery. Even a good rider could not have reached Ambergris' western borders in less than three days, and it would take three days to return after receiving the news—to say nothing of crossing the Moth itself. Five years ago, a carpenter in the western city of Nysimia accidentally unearthed a series of stone tablets carved with Haragck folk legends, and among

sought to split the Haragck army in two, and in the labyrinthine streets of Ambergris, her own troops had a distinct advantage.[93]

Outflanked by the Ambergrisian ships behind them, which they had neglected to secure before establishing their beach head, the rest of the Haragck floundered; bereft of their ponies, they fought hand-to-hand on the shore while the Ambergrisian sailors assaulted them from behind with arrows and burning faggots. If the Haragck had managed to fire the ships, they might still have won the day, but instead they tried to capture them (rightly perceiving that without a navy they would never be able to conquer the region). Even so, the defenders barely managed to hold their positions through the night. But at dawn of the third day an advance guard of light horsemen arrived from Morrow and turned the fortunes of the defenders, who, tired and disheartened by all they had lost, would soon have given way to Haragck pressure.

By nightfall, the surviving Haragck had either tried to bob back over the Moth on their inflated animal skins or

---

these is one, dating from the right time period, that tells of a mushroom that sprang suddenly from the ground, and from which emerged an old man who told them to attack their "eastern enemies." Could it be that the mushroom dwellers managed to coordinate the Haragck attack with their Silence? And could the old man have been Tonsure himself?

93. Seeking to redeem themselves, some rebel Ambergrisian commanders asked to be put in charge of the dangerous street-to-street fighting, and accounted themselves well enough that although they were deprived of their rank and returned to civilian life after the emergency, their lands were not confiscated, and neither were their lives.

run north or south. Those who swam were slaughtered by the navy (the inflated animal skins were neither maneuverable nor inflammable);[94] those who fled south ended up as slaves to the Arch Duke of Malid[95] (who, in his turn, would be enslaved by the encroaching Brueghelites); those who fled north managed to evade the Menite army marching south, but then ran into the ferocious Skamoo with their spears made of ice.[96]

That night, Cappan Aquelus made his way back to the surface on his hands and knees, his hair a shocking white

94. Worse still, whatever animal they had made their floats from had wide pores and the skins, hastily prepared, suffered slow leakage; although the vast majority had survived the initial crossing, many sank upon the return trip.

95. A notorious cannibal with a taste for the western tribes; that Aquelus kept him on retainer as a buffer against the Brueghelites may have been a political necessity, but it was still morally reprehensible.

96. The only reason the Haragck regrouped so quickly—they would pose a threat to Ambergris again a mere three years later—is that their great general Heckira Blgkkydks escaped the Skamoo with seven of his men and, his anger fearsome to behold (more fearsome than that of Manzikert I), eventually reached the fortress of Gelis, where the Haragck Khan Grnnck (who had ordered the amphibious attack on Ambergris) had taken refuge. Starving, shoeless, his clothes in tatters, Blgkkydks burst into the Khan's court, reportedly roared out, *"Inflatable animal skins?!"*, cut off his ruler's head with a single blow of his sword, and promptly proclaimed himself Khan; he would remain Khan for 20 years before the destruction of the Haragck as a political/cultural entity. Luckily, he spent the next three years annihilating the Skamoo, for he had suffered terribly at their hands, and by the time he refocused on Ambergris, the city had sufficiently recovered to defend itself. (One long-term effect on the Haragck as a consequence of their failed attack on Ambergris was a crucial lack of good translators, almost all of whom had been killed by the burning faggots of Ambergris. Thus, when Blgkkydks issued a formal demand for Ambergrisian surrender as a pretense for declaring war, the threat

and his eyes plucked from him;[97] they would never, even posthumously, be returned to him.[98] Weak with hunger and delirium, Aquelus soon recovered under the personal ministrations of his wife, who was also a noted surgeon. Like Manzikert I, he would never discuss what had happened to him. Unlike Manzikert I, he would rule again, but in the three days of his absence, the dynamics of power

---

which accompanied the demand read, "I will put fried eggs up your armpits," when the old Haragck saying *should* have read, "I will tear you armpit to armpit like a chicken.")

97. Some horticulturists—none of the ones consulted for this travel guide—have pointed out that the tissue in eyeballs provides excellent nutrient value for fungi.

98. We cannot forget the late Voss Bender's opera about the Silence, *The King Underground*, which—although it contains a patently idiotic wish fulfillment sequence in which the Cappan single-handedly slays two dozen midgets dressed as mushroom dwellers, after which "all quaver before him"—has a rather profound and singular beauty to it, especially in the scene where the Cappan crawls back up the steps to the surface, hears the voice of his Irene, and, his hand upon her cheek (aft, not nether), sings:

My fingers are not blind,
and they hunger still
for the sight of you;
and you, not seen but seeing,
can you bear the sight of me?

As Bender's opera is more popular than any history book, his vision has become the popular conception of the event, conveniently ignoring the unfortunate Nadal's passion for the Cappan. Luckily, many subjects—including the Haragck's use of floating animal skins—Bender thought to be unsuitable for opera, and it is in such low domains, far below the public eye, that creatures such as myself are still allowed to crawl about while muttering our "expert" opinions.

had undergone a radical shift. His Cappaness had proven herself quite capable of governing and had demonstrated remarkable toughness in the face of catastrophe. The Cappandom was also indebted to the Menite King for his help.

Finally, not only had Aquelus been blinded, but even many of his own ministers concluded that his underground adventure had been an act of rashness and/or cowardice. Never again would Aquelus be the sole ruling authority; from now on it would be his wife who, backed by her father, ruled in matters of defense and foreign diplomacy. More and more, Aquelus would oversee building projects and provide valuable advice to his wife. That she ever intended to usurp the cappanship is unlikely,[99] but once she had it, the people would not let her abdicate it.[100]

The problem went deeper than this, however. Although Aquelus had sacrificed his sight for them—indeed, many have speculated that Aquelus reached a pact with the mushroom dwellers that saved the city—the people no longer trusted him, and would never regain their former love for him. That he had gone below and survived when so many had not was proof enough for the common naval cadet that their Cappan had conspired with the enemy. Tales circulated that he snuck out at midnight to seek

99. Although the Menite king did pressure her to annex Ambergris for Morrow; already firmly committed to her adopted people, she put him off by invoking the specter of intervention by the Kalif should the Cappandom fall into Menite hands.

100. That Aquelus still loved her is undeniable, and he himself made no complaint, although many of his ministers, who effectively lost power as a result, did complain—vociferously.

council with the mushroom dwellers. It was said that a tunnel had been dug from his private chambers to the mushroom dwellers' underground lair. Most ridiculous of all, some claimed that Aquelus was actually a doppelganger, made of fungus, under the mushroom dwellers' control; he had, after all, forbidden anyone from attacking them.[101]

The latter part of Aquelus' "reign" was marked by increasingly desperate attempts to regain the respect of his subjects. To this end, he would have himself led out into the city disguised as a blind beggar and listen to the common laborers and merchants as they walked by his huddled form. He also gave away huge sums of money to the poor, so seriously draining the treasury that Irene was forced to order a halt to his largesse. Aquelus' spending, combined with the promises made to entice people to settle in Ambergris, led to the selling of titles and, in later years, a landed aristocracy that would prove a constant source of treasonous ambition.

Despite these failings, Aquelus managed partial redemption by having four children with Irene, although surely the irony of the Cappaness being the instrument of his salvation was not lost on him. These children— Mandrel, Tiphony, Cyril, and Samantha—became Aquelus' delight and main reason for living. While Irene ruled, he doted on them, and the people doted on them

---

101. Nadal, who had stuck by Aquelus through all of this, reports to us a conversation in which the Cappan chastised Nadal for his anger at the many slurs, saying, "They have suffered a terrible loss. If to heal they must remake me in the image of the villain, let them."

too. In Aquelus' love for his children, Ambergrisians saw the shadow of their former love for him, and many forgave him his involvement with the mushroom dwellers—a charge almost certainly false anyway.

Thus, although in many ways tragic, the partnership of Cappaness and Cappan would define and redefine Ambergris—both internally and in the world beyond—for another 30 years.[102] They would be haunted years, however, for the legacy of the Silence would permeate Ambergris for generations—in the sudden muting of the voices of children, of women, of those men who had stayed behind. For those inhabitants who had lost their families, their friends, the city was nothing more than a giant morgue, and no matter how they might console one another, no matter how they might set to their tasks with almost superhuman intensity, the better to block out the memories, they could never really escape the Silence, for the "City of Remembrance and Memorial," as one poet called it, was all around them.[103] It was common in those early, horrible years—still scarred by famine, despite the reduction in the population—for men and women to break down on the street in a sudden flux of tears.

102. It is outside the scope of this essay to tell of the continuation of the Manzikert line or of the mushroom dwellers; suffice it to say, the mushroom dwellers are still with us, while the Manzikerts exist only as a borderline religion and as a rather obnoxious model of black, beetle-like motored vehicle.

103. Little wonder that many moved away, to other cities, and that their places were taken by settlers from the southern Aan islands and, north, from Morrow. Additional bodies were drummed up amongst the tribes neighboring the city; Irene offered them jobs and reduced taxation in return for their relocation. The influx of these foreign cul-

The Truffidian priest Michael Nysman came to the city as part of a humanitarian mission the year after the Silence and was shocked by what he found there. In a letter to his diocese back in Nicea, he wrote:

The buildings are gray and their windows often like sad, empty eyes. The only sound in the street is that of weeping. Truly, there is a great emptiness to the city, as if its heart had stopped beating, and its people are a grim, suspicious folk. They will hardly open their doors to you, and have as many locks as can be imagined . . . Few of them sleep more than two or three hours at a time, and then only when someone else is available to watch over them. They abhor basements, and have blocked up all the dirt floors with rocks. Nor will they suffer the slightest section of wall to harbor fungus of any kind, but will scrape it off immediately, or preferably, burn it. Some neighborhoods have formed Watches during the night that go from home to home with torches, making sure that all within are safe. Most eerie and discomfiting, the

---

tures into the predominantly Aan city forever diversified and rejuvenated the local culture . . . We might well ask why so many people were willing to reinhabit a place where 25,000 souls had disappeared, but, in fact, the government deliberately spread misinformation, blaming the invading Haragck and the Brueghelites for the loss of life. In the confusion of the times, it appears many outside of the city did not even hear the real story. Others chose not to believe it, for it was not, after all, a very believable story. Thus, for several centuries, historians who should have known better promulgated false stories of plague and civil war.

JEFF VANDERMEER

citizens of this bleak city leave lanterns burning all through the night, and in such proliferation that the city, in such a hard, all-seeing light, cannot fail to seem already enveloped in the flames of Hell, it only remaining for the Lord of the Nether World to take up his throne and scepter and walk out upon its streets. Just yesterday some unfortunate soul tried to rob a watchmaker and was torn to pieces before it was discovered he was not a gray cap . . . Worst of all: no children; the schools have closed down and their radiant, innocent voices are no longer heard in the church choirs. The city is childless, barren—it has only visions of the happy past, and what parent will bring a child into a city that contains the ghosts of so many children? Some parents—although usually only one parent has survived—believe that their children will return, and some tried to unblock the hole by the old altar before the Cappaness made it a hanging offense. Still others wait by the door at dinner, certain that a familiar small shape will walk by. It breaks my heart to see this. Can such a city ever now lose a certain touch of cruelty, of melancholy, a lingering hint of the macabre? Is this, then, the grief of the gray caps 70 years later given palpable form? I fear I can do little more here at this time; I am caught up in their sadness, and thus cannot give them solace for it, although unscrupulous priests sell "dispensations" which they say will protect the user from the mushroom dwellers while simultaneously absolving the disappeared of their sins.

CITY OF SAINTS AND MADMEN

What are we, in this modern era, to make of the assertion that 25,000 people simply disappeared, leaving no trace of any struggle? Can it be believed? If the number were 1,000 could we believe it? The answer the honest historian reluctantly comes to is that the tale must be believed, because it happened. Not a single person escaped from the mushroom dwellers. More hurtful still, it left behind a generation known simply as the Dispossessed.[104] The city recovered, as all cities do, and yet for at least 100 years,[105] this absence, this silence, insinuated itself into the happiest of events: the coronations and weddings of cappans, the extraordinarily high birthrate (and low mortality rate), the victories over both Haragck and Brueghelite. The survivors retook their homes uneasily, if at all, and some areas, some houses, stood abandoned for a generation, never re-entered, so that dinners set out before the Silence rotted, moldered, and eventually fossilized.[106] There remained the terrible convic-

104. Given the magnitude of the loss, remarkably few survivors killed themselves. We must credit the industriousness of Irene and Aquelus—the example they set and the work they provided.

105. For, at the 100-year mark, the mushroom dwellers first began to integrate themselves with Ambergrisian society, albeit as garbage collectors.

106. As recently as 50 years ago, a few homes were found in this state: they had been boarded up and then built over, and were discovered by accident during a survey expedition to install street lamps. The surveyors found the atmosphere within these rooms (the dust over everything, the plates and kitchen implements corroded, the smell dry as death, the dried flowers set out as a memorial) so oppressive that after a brief reconnaissance, they not only boarded

tion among the survivors that they had brought this upon themselves through Manzikert I's massacre of the gray caps and Sophia's torching of Cinsorium. It was hard not to feel that it was God's judgment to see Ambergris destroyed soul by soul.[107]

Worst of all, there was never any clue as to the fate of the Disappeared, and in the absence of information, imaginations, as always, imagined the worst. Soon, in the popular folklore of the times, the Disappeared had not only been killed, but had been subjected to terrible tortures and defilements. Although some still claimed the Brueghelites had carried off the 25,000, most people truly believed the mushroom dwellers had been responsible. Theories as to *how* cropped up much more frequently than *why* because, short of revenge, no one could fathom *why*. It was said that the ever-present fungus had released spores that, inhaled, put all of the city's inhabitants to sleep, after which the mushroom dwellers had come out and dragged them underground. Others claimed that the spores had not put the Disappeared to sleep, but had actually, in chemical combination, formed a mist that corroded human flesh, so that the inhabitants had slowly melted into nothing. The truth is, we shall never know unless the mushroom dwellers deign to tell us.

---

them back up, but filled them in, despite a vigorous protest from myself and various other old farts at the Ambergrisian Historical Society.

107. If so, then the Devil has saved it several times over.

IV[108]

BUT WHAT OF SAMUEL TONSURE'S JOURNAL? WHAT,
after all these years, did it contain? Aquelus wisely had it
placed in the care of the librarians at the Manzikert
Memorial Library.[109] In effect, the book disappeared again,
as—hidden and known by only a few—it was not part of
the public discourse.[110] Aquelus made the librarians swear
not to reveal the contents of the journal, or even hint at its
existence to anyone, on pain of death. The journal was kept
in a locked strong box, which was then put inside another
box. We can certainly understand why Aquelus kept it a

---

108. At this point in the narrative I begin to make my formal
farewells, for those of you who ever even noticed my marginal existence. By now the blind mechanism of the story has surpassed me, and
I shall jump out of its way in order to let it roll on, unimpeded by my
frantic gesticulations for attention. The time-bound history is done:
there is only the matter of sweeping the floors, taking out the garbage,
and turning off the lights. Meanwhile, I shall retire once more to the
anonymity of my little apartment overlooking the Voss Bender
Memorial Square. This is the fate of historians: to fade ever more into
the fabric of their history, until they no longer exist outside of it.
Remember this while you navigate the afternoon crowd in the
Religious Quarter, your guidebook held limply in your pudgy left
hand as your right hand struggles to balance a half-pint of bitter.

109. The library already housed a number of unique manuscripts,
including the anonymous Dictionary of Foreplay, Stretcher Jones'
Memories, a few sheets of palm-pulp paper with mushroom dweller
scrawls on them, and 69 texts on preserving flesh, stolen from the
Kalif, that had been of great use to Manzikert II while conducting his
body parts shopping spree among the saints.

110. As it is, when copies were made available 50 years later, it
forced Cappan Manzikert VI to abdicate and join a monastery.

secret, for the journal tells a tale both macabre and frightening. If the general populace had, at the time, known of its contents, they would no longer have had anything to fear from their imaginations—only to have their worst nightmares given validation. The burden on Aquelus and Irene of not releasing this information was terrible—Nadal, who was privy to most state secrets, reports that the two frequently fought over whether the journal should be made public, often switching sides in mid-argument.

To head librarian Michael Abrasis fell the task of examining the journal, and luckily he kept notes. Abrasis describes the journal as:

> . . . leather-bound, 6 x 9, with at least 300 pages, of which almost all have been used. The leather has been contaminated by a green fungus that, ironically, has helped to preserve the book; indeed, were the lichen to be removed, the covers would disintegrate, so ingrained and so uniform are these green "shingles." Of the ink, it would appear that the first 75 pages are of a black ink easily recognizable as distilled from whale's oil. However, the sections thereafter are written using a purple ink that, after careful study, appears to have been distilled from some sort of fungus. These sections exude a distinctly sweet odor.[111]

Abrasis had copies of the journal made and secreted them away—which accounts for the existence of the text in

---

111. Alas, Abrasis never commented on the consistency of the handwriting!

the city to this day—but, unfortunately, the original was pawned to the Kalif during the tragic last days of Trillian.

We have already discussed the early days of Ambergris as recounted in Tonsure's journal, but what of the last portion of the journal? The first entry Tonsure managed to make following his descent[112] reads:

Dark and darker for three days. We are lost and cannot find our way to the light. The Cappan still pursues the gray caps, but they remain flitting shadows against the pale, dead glow of the fungus, the mushrooms that stink and writhe and even seem to speak a little. We have run out of food and are reduced to eating from the mushrooms that rise so tall in these caverns we must seek sustenance from the stem alone—maddeningly aware of succulent leathery lobes too high to reach. We know we are being watched, and this has unnerved all but the strongest men. We can no longer afford to sleep except in shifts, for too often we have woken to find another of our party missing. Early yesterday I woke to find a stealthy gray cap about to murder the Cappan himself, and when I gave the alarm, this creature smiled most chillingly, made a chirping sound, and ran down the passageway. We gave chase, the Cappan and I and some 20 others. The gray cap escaped, and when we returned our supplies were gone, as were the 15 men who had remained behind. The gray caps' behavior here is as different as

112. With the exception of his entry describing the massacre and Manzikert I's decision to go underground.

night is to day—here they are fast and crafty and we hardly catch sight of them before they strike. I do not believe we will make it to the surface alive.

Tonsure's composure is admirable, although his sense of time is certainly faulty—he writes that three days had passed, when it must still have been but a single night, for Manzikert I was found in the library the very next morning.[113] Another entry, dated just a few "days" later, is more disjointed and, one feels, soaked through with terror:

Three more gone—taken. In the night. Morning now. What do we find arranged around us like puppet actors? We find arranged around us the heads of those who have been taken from us. Ramkin, Starkin, Weatherby, and all the rest. Staring. But they cannot stare. They have no eyes. I wish I had no eyes. Cappan long ago gave up on all but the idea of escape. And it eludes us. We can taste it—the air sometimes fresher, so we know we are near the surface, and yet we might as well be a hundred miles underground! We must escape these blind staring heads. We eat the fungus, but I feel it eats us instead. Cappan near despair. Never seen him this way. Seven of us. Trapped. Cappan just stares at the heads. Talks to them, calls

113. No less a skeptic than Sabon half-heartedly documents the folktale that the Manzikert I who reappeared in the library was actually a construct, a doppelganger, created out of fungus. Although ridiculous on the face of it, we must remember how often tales of doppelgangers intertwine with the history of the mushroom dwellers.

them by name. He's not mad. He's not mad. He has it easier in these tunnels than I.[114] And still they watch us . . .

Tonsure then describes the deaths of the men still with the Cappan and Tonsure—two by poisoned mushrooms, two by blow dart, and one by a trap set into the ground that cut the man's legs off and left him to bleed to death. Now it is just the Cappan and Tonsure, and, somehow, Tonsure has recovered his nerve:

We wonder now if there ever were such a dream as above ground, or if this place has always been the reality and we simply deluding ourselves. We shamble through this darkness, through the foul emanations of the fungus, like lost souls in the Nether World . . . Today, we beseeched them to end it, for we could hear their laughter all around us, could glimpse the shadows of their passage, and we are past fear. End it, do not toy with us. It is clear enough now that here, on their territory, they are our Masters. I looked over my notes last night and giggled at my innocence. "Degenerate traces of a once-great civilization" indeed. We have passed through so many queer and ominous chambers, filled with otherworldly buildings, otherworldly sights—the wonders I have seen! Luminous purple mushrooms pulsing in the darkness. Creatures that can only be seen when they smile, for their skin reflects their surroundings. Eyeless, pul-

114.   Another indication Manzikert was a little man.

sating, blind salamanders that slowly ponder the dead darkness through other senses. Winged animals that speak in voices. Headless things that whisper our names. And ever and always, the gray caps. We have even spied upon them at play, although only because they disdain us so, and seen the monuments carved from solid rock that beggar the buildings above ground. What I would give for a single breath of fresh air. Manzikert resists even these fancies; he has become sullen, responding to my words with grunts and clicks and whistles . . . More disturbing still, we have yet to retrace our steps; thus, this underground land must be several times larger than the above ground city, much as the submerged portion of an iceberg is larger than the part visible to a sailor.

Clearly, however, Tonsure never regained his timesense, for on this day, marked by him as the sixth, Manzikert would already have been five days above ground, eyeless but alive. Perhaps Tonsure deluded himself that Manzikert remained by his side to strengthen his own resolve, or perhaps the fringe-historians have for once been too conservative: instead of a golem Manzikert being returned to the surface, perhaps the underground Manzikert was replaced with a golem. Tonsure certainly never tells us what happened to Manzikert; his entries simply do not mention him after approximately the ninth day. By the twelfth day, the entries become somewhat disjointed, and the last coherent entry, before the journal dissolves into fragments, is this pathetic paragraph:

They're coming for me. They've had their fun—now they'll finish me. To my mother: I have always tried to be your obedient son. To my illegitimate son and his mother: I have always loved you, although I didn't always know it. To the world that may read this: know that I was a decent man, that I meant no harm, that I lived a life far less pious than I should have, but far better than many. May God have mercy on my soul.[115]

And yet, apparently, they did not "finish" him,[116] for another 150 pages of writing follow this entry. Of these 150 pages, the first two are full of weird scribbles punctuated by a few coherent passages,[117] all written using the strange purple ink described by Abrasis as having been distilled from fungus. These pages provide damning evidence of a mind gone rapidly deranged, and yet they are followed by 148 lucid pages of essays on Truffidian religious rituals, broken infrequently by glimpses into Tonsure's captivity. The essays have proven invaluable to present-day Truffidians who wish to read an "eyewitness" account of the

115. Then as now, bastards were a sel-a-dozen amongst the clergy; how much more interesting to know where this mother and child resided—Nicea, perhaps?

116. Sabon dryly writes, "Tonsure was already the most finished man in the history of the world. How then could they improve upon perfection?"

117. Most of the scribbles are erotic in nature and superfluous. Of the writings, the following lines appear in no known religious text and are accompanied by the notation "d.t.," meaning "dictated to." Scholars believe that the lines are an example of mushroom dweller poetry translated by Tonsure.

early church, but baffle those of us who naturally want answers to the mysteries inherent in the Silence and the journal itself. The most obvious question is, why did the mushroom dwellers suffer Tonsure to live? On this subject, Tonsure at least provides his own theory, the explanation inserted into the middle of a paragraph on the Truffidian position on circumcision:[118]

> Gradually, as they come to me time after time and rub my bald head, it has struck me why I have been spared. It is such a simple thing that it makes me laugh even to contemplate it: I look like a mushroom. Quick! Alert the authorities! I must send a message aboveground—tell them all to shave their heads! I can hardly contain my laughter even now, which startles my captors and makes it hard to write legibly.

Later, stuck between a discussion on the divine properties of frogs and a diatribe against inter-species marriages,

---

We are old.
We have no teeth.
We swallow what we chew.
We chew up all the swallows.
Then we excrete the swallows.
Poor swallows—they do not fly
once they are out of us.

If this is indeed mushroom dweller poetry, then we must conclude that either the translator—under stress and with insufficient light—did a less than superlative job, or that the mushroom dwellers had a spectactular lack of poetic talent.

118. They're for it, by the way.

Tonsure provides us with another glimpse into the mush-room dwellers' world that entices the reader like a flash of gold:

> They have led me to a vast chamber unlike any place I have ever seen, above or below. There stands before me a palace of shimmering silver built entirely of interlocking mushrooms, and festooned with lichen and moss of green and blue. A sweet, sweet perfume hangs pungent in the air. The columns that support this dwelling are, it appears, made of living tissue, for they recoil at the touch . . . from the doorway steps the ruler of the province, who is herself but a foot soldier compared to the mightiest ranks that can be found here. All glows with an unearthly splendor and suppli-cant after supplicant kneels before the ruler and begs for her blessing. I am made to understand that I must come forward and allow the ruler to rub my head for luck. I must go.

Other entries hint that Tonsure made at least two attempts to escape, each followed by harsh punishment, the second of which may have been partial blinding,[119] and at least one sentence suggests that afterwards he was led

---

119. Lacond's pet theory, sneered at by Sabon: the two shall con-tinue to make war, history itself their battlefield, hands caressing each other's necks, legs entwined for all eternity, and yet neither shall ever win in such a subjective area as theoretical history. (Although my pet theory is that Lacond and Sabon are the conflicting sides of the same hopelessly divided historian. If only they could reach some under-standing?)

secretly to the surface: "Oh, such torture, to be able to hear the river chuckling below me, to feel the night wind upon my face, to smell the briny silt, but to see *nothing*." However, Tonsure may have been blindfolded or been so old and have existed in darkness for so long that his eyes could not adapt to the outside, day or night. Tonsure's sense of time being suspect, we can only guess as to his age when he wrote that entry.

Finally, toward the end of the journal, Tonsure relates a series of what surely must be waking dreams, created by his long diet of fungus and the attendant fumes thereof:

> They wheeled me into a steel chamber and suddenly a window appeared in the side of the wall and I saw before me a vision of the city that frightened me more than anything I have yet seen below ground. As I watched, the city grew from just the docks built by my poor lost Cappan to such immense structures that half the sky was blotted out by them, and the sky itself fluxed light, dark, and light again in rapid succession, clouds moving across it in a flurry. I saw a great palace erected in a few minutes. I saw carts that moved without horses. I saw battles fought in the city and without. And, in the end, I saw the river flood the streets, and the gray caps came out once again into the light and rebuilt their old city and everything was as before. The one I call my Keeper wept at this vision, so surely he must have seen it too?[120]

___

120. Sabon has suggested that the mushroom dwellers had a form of zoetrope or "magic lantern" that could project images on a wall. As

Then follow the last 10 pages of the journal, filled with so concrete and frenzied a description of Truffidian religious practices that we can only conclude that he wrote these passages as a bulwark against insanity and that, ultimately, when he ran out of paper, he ran out of hope—either writing on the walls[121] or succumbing to the despair that must have been a tangible part of every one of his days below ground. Indeed, the last line of the journal reads: "An inordinate love of ritual can be harmful to the soul, unless, of course, in times of great crisis, when ritual can protect the soul from fracture."

Thus passes into silence one of the most influential and mysterious characters in the entire history of Ambergris. Because of Tonsure, Truffidianism and the Cappandom cannot, to this day, be separated from each other. His tutorials informed the administrative genius of Manzikert II, while his counsel both inflamed and restrained Manzikert I. Aquelus studied his journal endlessly, perhaps seeking some clue to which only he, with his own experience below ground, was privy. Tonsure's biography of Manzikert I (never out of print) and his journal remain the sources his-

---

for the reference to a "Keeper," it appears nowhere else in the text and thus is frustratingly enigmatic. Many a historian has ended his career dashed to pieces on the rocks of Tonsure's journal; I refuse to follow false beacons, myself.

121. I have a certain affection for Lacond's theory that Tonsure's journal is merely the introduction to a vast piece of fiction/nonfiction scrawled on the walls of the underground sewer system, and that this work, if revealed to the world above ground, would utterly change our conception of the universe. Myself, I believe such a work might, at best, change our conception of Lacond—for, if it existed, at least one of his theories might be accepted by mainstream historians.

torians turn to for information about early Ambergris and early Truffidianism.

If the journal proves anything it is that another city exists below the city proper, for Cinsorium was not truly destroyed when Sophia razed its above ground manifestation. Unfortunately, all attempts to explore the under ground have met with disaster,[122] and now that the city has no central government, it is unlikely that there will be further attempts—especially since such authority as does exist would prefer the mysteries remain mysteries for the sake of tourism.[123] It would seem that two separate and very different societies shall continue to evolve side by side, separated by a few vertical feet of cement. In our world, we see their red flags and how thoroughly they clean the city, but we are allowed no similar impact on their world except through the refuse that goes down our sewer pipes.

The validity of the journal has been called into question several times over the years—lately by the noted writer Sirin, who claims that the journal is actually a forgery based on Manzikert I's biography. He points to the writer Maxwell Glaring, who lived in Ambergris some 40 years after the Silence. Glaring, Sirin says, carefully studied

---

122. The most recent, 30 years ago, resulting in the loss of the entire membership of the Ambergrisian Historical Society, and two of its dog mascots.

123. Until recently you could take an ostensible tour of the mushroom dwellers' tunnels run by a certain Guido Zardoz. After tourists had imbibed refreshments laced with hallucinogens, Zardoz would lead them down into his basement, where several dwarfs in felt hats awaited the signal to leap out from hiding and say "Boo!" Reluctantly, the district councilor shut the establishment down after an old lady from Stockton had a heart attack.

the biography written by Tonsure, incorporated elements of it into his fake, invented the underground accounts, used an odd purple ink distilled from the freshwater squid[124] for the last half, and then "produced" the "journal" via a friend in the administrative quarter who spread the rumor that Aquelus had suppressed it for 50 years. Sirin's theory has its attractions—Glaring, after all, forged a number of state documents to help his friends embezzle money from the treasury, and his novels often contain an amount of desperate derring-do in keeping with the fragments of reason found in the latter portion of the journal.[125] Adding to the controversy, Glaring was murdered—his throat cut as he crossed a back alley on his way to the post office—shortly after the release of the journal.

Sabon prefers the alternate theory that, yes, Glaring *did* forge parts of the journal, but only the sections on obscure Truffidian religious practices[126]—these pages inserted to replace pages removed by the government for national security reasons. Glaring was then killed by the Cappan's operatives to preserve the secret. Unfortunately, a fire gutted part of the palace's administrative core, destroying the records that might have provided a clue as to

124. And since discontinued—too runny.

125. A passage from his *Midnight for Munfroe* reads "It was in this cloying darkness, the lights from Krotch's house stabbing at me from beyond the grave, that I could no longer hold onto the idea that I was going to be all right. I would have to kill the bastard. I would have to do it before he did it to me. Because if he did it to me, there would be no way for me to do it to him."

126. Certainly possible—Glaring could have interviewed any number of Truffid monks or read any number of books, few now surviving, on the subject.

whether Glaring was on the national payroll. Sabon further speculates that Glaring's embezzlement had been discovered and was used as leverage to make him forge the journal pages, for otherwise, some of his relatives having disappeared in the Silence, he would have been disinclined to suppress evidence as to mushroom dweller involvement.[127] Sabon explains away the few paragraphs dealing with Tonsure's captivity as Glaring's genius in knowing that a good forgery must address issues of its authenticity—the journal must therefore contain some evidence of Tonsure's underground experiences. These paragraphs, meanwhile, *Lacond* claims are genuine, pulled from the real journal.[128]

Another claim, which has taken on the status of popular myth, suggests that the mushroom dwellers skillfully rewrote and replaced many pages, to keep inviolate their secrets, but this theory is rendered ridiculous by the fact that the journal was left on the altar—a fact confirmed by Nadal, the then minister of finance. This eyewitness account also nixes the first of Sabon's theories: that the entire journal is a forgery.[129]

127. Sabon notes that Glaring kept copies of his forgeries. Further, that a letter Glaring wrote to a friend mentions "a rather unusual memoir of sorts I've been told to duplicate." Sabon believes Glaring made a true copy of the original pages. If so, no one has found this true copy.

128. It is perhaps too cruel to think of Tonsure not only struggling to express himself, to communicate, underground, but also struggling above ground to be heard as Glaring tries equally hard to snuff him out.

129. Although Sabon, predictably, claims Nadal's eyewitness account could also have been forged by Glaring.

To further complicate matters, an obscure sect of Truffidians who inhabit the ruined fortress of Zamilon near the eastern approaches to the Kalif's empire claim to possess the last true page of Tonsure's journal. According to legend, Trillian's men once stayed at the fortress on their way to the Kalif, bearing the journal that, the careful reader will remember, was hocked by the Cappandom. A monk crept into the room where the journal was kept and stole the last page, apparently as revenge for the left femur of their leader having been spirited away by agents of Cappan Manzikert II 300 years before.

The front of the page consists of more early Truffidian religious ritual, but the back of the page reads as follows:

We have traveled through a series of rooms. The first rooms were tiny—I had to crawl into them, and even then barely squeezed through, banging my head on the ceiling. These rooms had the delicate yet ornate qualities of an illuminated manuscript, or one of the miniature paintings so beloved by the Kalif. Golden lichen covered the walls in intricate patterns, crossed through with a royal red fungus that formed star shapes. Strangely, in these rooms I felt as if I had unlimited space in which to move and breathe. Each room we entered was larger and more elaborate than its predecessor—although never did I have the sense that anyone had ever lived in the rooms, despite the presence of chairs, tables, and bookshelves—so that I found myself bedazzled by the light, the flourishes, the engraved ceilings. And yet, oddly enough, as the curious rooms expanded, my sense of claustrophobia

expanded too, so that it took over all my thoughts . . .
This continued for days and days, until I had become
numb to the glamour and dulled to the claustrophobia. When hungry, we broke off pieces of the walls
and ate of them. When thirsty, we squeezed the chair
arms and greedily drank the drops of mossy elixir that
came from them. Eventually, we would push open the
now immense doors leading to the next room and see
only distantly the far wall . . . Then, just when I
thought this journey might never end—and yet surely
could not continue—I was brought through one final
door (as large as many of the rooms we had passed
through). Beyond this door, it was night, lit vaguely by
the stars, and we had come out upon a hill of massive
columns, through which I could see, below us, a vast
city that looked uncannily like Cinsorium, surrounded
by a forest. A sweet, sweet breeze blew through the
trees and lifted the grass along the hill. Above, the
immense sky—and I thought, I thought, that I had
been brought above ground, for the entire world
seemed to spread out before me. But no, I realized
with sinking heart, for far above me I could see,
when I squinted, that, luminous blue against the
blackness, the lines of strange constellations had been
set out there, using some instrument more precise
than known of above ground. And yet the stars themselves *moved* in phosphorescent patterns of blue,
green, red, yellow, and purple, and after a moment
I discovered that these "stars" were actually huge
moths gliding across the upper darkness . . . My
captors intend to leave me here; I am given to under-

stand that I have reached the end of my journey—
they are done with me, and I am free. I have but a few
more minutes to write in this journal before they take
it from me. What now to do? I shall not follow the
light of the moths, for it is a false light and wanders
where it will. But, in the lands that spread out before
me, a light beckons in the distance. It is a clear light,
an even light, and because light still, to me, means the
surface, I have decided to walk toward it in hopes,
after all this time, of regaining the world I have lost. I
may well simply find another door when I find the
source of the light, but perhaps not. In any event, God
speed say I.

Surely, *surely*, such visions indicate Tonsure's advanced
delirium or, more probably, monkish forgery, but one is
almost convinced by the holy reverence in which the
inhabitants of Zamilon hold their page, for it means more
to them than any other of their possessions, and even now,
after many a reading, it moves more than one monk to
tears.[130]

To attempt to put the controversy to rest[131]—after all,
Tonsure has become a saint to the Truffidians by virtue of
his faith in the face of adversity—a delegation from the
Morrow-based Institute of Religiosity,[132] led by the

130. I myself have journeyed to Zamilon to see the page, and am
cagey enough at this stage of my bizarre career to decline comment on
its authenticity or fakery.
131. Admittedly confined to the pages of obscure history journals
and religious pamphlets.
132. Then called the Morrow Religious Institute.

distinguished Head Instructor Cadimon Signal,[133] journeyed 20 years ago to the lands of the Kalif, under guar-
antee of safe passage, to examine the journal in its place of
honor in Lepo.

The conditions under which the delegation could view
the journal—conditions set after their arrival—could not
have been more rigid: they could examine the book for an
hour, but, due to the book's fragile condition, they themselves could not touch it; they must allow an attendant to
do so for them. Further, the attendant would flip through
all of the pages once, and then the delegation would be
able to study up to 10 individual pages, but no more than
10—and they must name the page numbers in question on
the basis of the first flip through.[134] The delegation had no
alternative but to accept the ridiculous conditions,[135] and
resolved to make the most of their time. After half an hour,
they found it appeared parts of the book *had* been replaced
with different paper, and that the penmanship appeared, in

133. Cadimon Signal was a friend of mine and so, to avoid a
conflict of interest, I shall not expound upon his many virtues—his
strength of character, his fine sense of humor, the pedigree of the
wines hidden in his basement.

134. The Kalif had had golden page numbers added for his convenience.

135. Signal reports that the attendant "flipped through the pages at
such incredible speed that we could hardly see them. When it came
time for us to present the 10 page numbers, which we simply chose at
random, a great ceremony was made of taking them to the attendant,
who made an equally great show of finding the right page, during
which we were made to wait outside, for fear we might see a forbidden
page. By the time the first page was located and presented to us some
20 minutes had elapsed, and it turned out to be blank, except for the
words 'see next page.'"

places, somewhat different from Tonsure's own (as compared against the biography). Alas, at the half-hour mark, news reached the Kalif by carrier pigeon that the then mayor of Ambergris had tendered a major personal insult to the Kalif, and he immediately expelled the delegation from the reading room and sent them via fast horses to his borders, where they were unceremoniously dumped with their belongings. Their notes had been taken from them, and they could not remember any useful particulars about the page they had seen. No further examination has been allowed as of the date of this writing.

Thus, although we have copies of the journal, we may never know why pages were replaced in this invaluable primary source of history. We are left with the difficult task of either repudiating the entire document or, as I believe, embracing it all. If you do believe in Samuel Tonsure's journal, in its validity, then your pleasure will be enhanced as you pass the equestrian statue of Manzikert I[136] in the

---

136. Suitably tall, although the statue's torso and legs (and the horse itself—Manzikert never saw a horse, let alone rode on one) are not of Manzikert I, but the remains of an equestrian statue dating from the period of the Kalif's brief occupation of the city—onto which someone has rather crudely attached Manzikert's head. The original statue of Manzikert I was of an unknown height and showed Manzikert I surrounded by his beloved rats, rendered in bronze. An enterprising but none too bright bureaucrat sold the statue, sans head, for scrap to the Arch Duke of Banfours a century before the Kalif's invasion; the Arch Duke promptly recast the statue as a cannon affectionately christened "Old Manzikert" and bombarded the stuffing out of Ambergris with it. As for the rats, they now decorate a small altar near the aqueduct, and if they look more like cats than rats, this is because the sculptor's models died half way through the commission and he had to use his tabby to complete it.

Banker's Courtyard and as you survey the ruined aqueducts on Albumuth Boulevard that are, besides the
mushroom dwellers themselves, the only remaining sign of
Cinsorium, the city *before* Ambergris.[137] &

137. Surely, after all, it is more comforting to believe that the
sources on which this account is based are truthful, that this has not
all, in fact, been one huge, monstrous lie? And with that pleasant
thought, O Tourist, I take my leave for good.

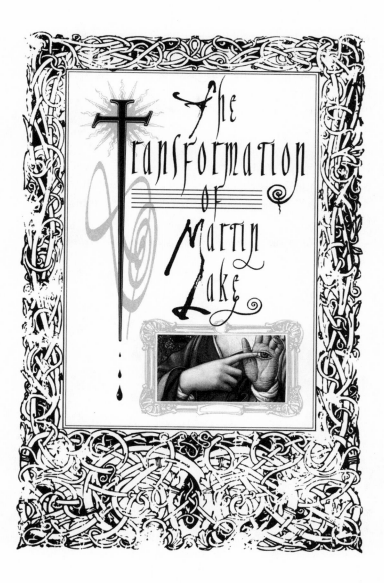

The Transformation of Martin Lake

A fresh river in a beautiful meadow
Imagined in his mind
The good Painter, who would some day paint it
—*Comanimi*

If I was strange, and strange was my art,
Such strangeness is a source of grace and strength;
And whoever adds strangeness here and there to his style,
Gives life, force and spirit to his paintings . . .
—*Engraved at Lake's request on his memorial in Trillian Square*

EW PAINTERS HAVE RISEN WITH SUCH speed from such obscurity as Martin Lake, and fewer still are so closely identified with a single painting, a single city. What remains obscure, even to those of us who knew him, is how and why Lake managed the extraordinary transformation from pleasing but facile collages and acrylics, to the luminous oils—both fantastical and dark, moody and playful—that would come to define both the artist and Ambergris.

Information about Lake's childhood has a husk-like quality to it, as if someone had already scooped out the meat within the shell. At the age of six he contracted a rare bone disease in his left leg that, exacerbated by a hit-and-run accident with a Manzikert motored vehicle at age 12, made it necessary for him to use a cane. We have no other information about his childhood except for a quick glimpse of his parents: Theodore and Catherine Lake. His father worked as an insect catcher outside of the town of Stockton, where the family lived in a simple rented apartment. There is some evidence, from comments Lake made to me prior to his fame, and from hints in subsequent interviews, that a tension existed between Lake and his father, created by Lake's desire to pursue art and his father's desire that the boy take up the profession of insect catcher.

Of Lake's mother there is no record, and Lake never spoke of her in any of his few interviews. The mock-historian Samuel Gorge has put forth the theory that Lake's mother was a folk artist of considerable talent and also a fierce proponent of Truffidianism—that she instilled in Lake an appreciation for mysticism. Gorge believes the magnificent murals that line the walls of the Truffidian cathedral in Stockton are the anonymous work of Lake's mother. No one has yet confirmed Gorge's theory, but if true it might account for the streak of the occult, the macabre, that runs through Lake's art—stripped, of course, of the underlying religious aspect.

Lake's mother almost certainly gave him his first art lesson, and urged him to pursue lessons at the local school, under the tutelage of a Mr. Shores, who unfortunately passed away without ever being asked to recall the work of his most famous (indeed, *only* famous) student. Lake also took several anatomy classes when young; even in his most surreal paintings the figures often seem hyper-real—as if there are layers of paint unseen, beneath which exist veins, arteries, muscles, nerves, tendons. This hyper-reality creates tension by playing against Lake's assertion that the "great artist swallows up the world that surrounds him until his whole environment has been absorbed in his own self."

We may think of the Lake who arrived in Ambergris from Stockton as a contradictory creature: steeped in the technical world of anatomy and yet well-versed in the miraculous and ur-rational by his mother—a contradiction further enriched by his guilt over not following his father into the family trade. These are the elements Lake brought to Ambergris. In return, Ambergris gave Lake the freedom to be an artist while also opening his eyes to the possibilities of color.

Of the three years Lake lived in Ambergris prior to the startling change in his work, we know only that he befriended a number of artists whom he would champion, with mixed results, once he became famous. Chief among these artists was Jonathan Merrimount, a life-long friend. He also met Raffe Constance, who many believe was his life-long romantic companion. Together, Lake, Merrimount, and Constance would prove to be the most visible and influential artists of their generation. Unfortunately, neither Merrimount nor Constance has been willing to shed any illumination on the subject of Lake's life—his inspiration, his disappointments, his triumphs. Or, more importantly, how such a middle class individual could have created such sorrowful, nightmarish art.

Thus, I must attempt to fill in details from my own experience of Lake. It is with some hesitancy that I reveal Lake first showed his work at my own Gallery of Hidden Fascinations, prior to his transformation into an artist of the first rank. Although I cannot personally bear witness to that transformation, I can at least give the reader a pre-fame portrait of a very private artist who was rarely seen in public.

Lake was a tall man who appeared to be of average height because, in using his cane, he had become stooped—an aspect that always gave him the impression of listening intently to you, although in reality he was a terrible listener and never hesitated to rudely interrupt when bored by what I said to him.

His face had a severe quality to it, offset by a firm chin, a perfect set of lips, and eyes that seemed to change color but which were, at base, a fierce, arresting green. In either anger or humor, his face was a weapon—for the narrowness became even more narrow in his anger and the eyes lanced you, while in laughter his face widened and the eyes admitted you to their compelling company. Mostly, though, he remained in a mode between laughter and anger, a mood which aped that of the "tortured artist" while at the same time keeping a distance between himself and any such passion. He was shy and clever, sly and arrogant—in other words, no different from many of the other artists I handled at my gallery. —From Janice Shriek's *A Short Overview of The Art of Martin Lake and His Invitation to a Beheading*, for the *Hoegbotton Guide to Ambergris*, 5th edition.

కు

One blustery spring day in the legendary metropolis of Ambergris, the artist Martin Lake received an invitation to a beheading.

It was not an auspicious day to receive such an invitation and Lake was nursing several grudges as he made his way to the post office. First and foremost, the Reds and Greens were at war; already, a number of nasty skirmishes had spread disease-like up and down the streets, even infecting portions of Albumuth Boulevard itself.

The Reds and Greens as a phenomenon simultaneously fascinated and repulsed Lake. In short, the Greens saw the recent death of the (great) composer Voss Bender as a tragedy while the Reds thought the recent death of the (despotic) composer Voss Bender a blessing. They had taken their names from Bender's favorite and least favorite colors: the green of a youth spent in the forests of Morrow; the red flags of the indigenous mushroom dwellers who he believed had abducted his cousin.

No doubt these two political factions would vanish as quickly as they had appeared, but in the meantime Lake kept a Green flag in his right pocket and a Red flag in his left pocket, the better to express the correct patriotic fervor. (On a purely aural level, Lake sympathized with the Reds, if only because the Greens polluted the air with a thousand Bender tunes morning, noon, and night. Lake had hardly listened to Bender while the man was alive; he resented having to change his habits now the man was dead.)

Confronted by such dogma, Lake suspected his commitment to his weekly walk to the post office indicated a fatal character flaw, a fatal artistic curiosity. For he knew he would pull the wrong flag from the right pocket before the day was done. And yet, he thought, as he limped down Truff Avenue—even the blood-clot clusters of dog lilies, in their neat sidewalk rows, reminding him of the conflict— how else was he to exercise his crippled left leg? Besides, no vehicle for hire would deliver him through the disputed areas to his objective.

Lake scowled as a youth bejeweled in red buttons and waving a huge red flag ran into the street. In the wake of the flag, Lake could see the distant edges of the post office, suffused with the extraordinary morning light, which came down in sheets of gold.

The secondary tier of Reasons Why I Should Have Stayed At Home concerned, much to Lake's irritation, the post office itself. He had no sympathy for its archaic architecture and only moderate respect for its function; the quality of a monopolistic private postal service being poor, most of his commissions arrived via courier. He also found distasteful the morbid nature of the building's history, its stacks of "corpse cases" as he called the postal boxes. These boxes, piled atop each other down the length and breadth of the great hall, climbed all the way to the ceiling. Surely any of the children previously shelved there had, on their ascent to heaven, found themselves trapped by that ugly yellow ceiling and to this day were banging their tiny ectoplasmic heads against it.

But, as the post office rounded into view—looming and guttering like some monstrous, senile great aunt—none of these objections registered as strongly as the recent change of name to the "Voss Bender Memorial Post Office." A shockingly *rushed* development, as the (great, despotic) composer and politician had died only three days before—rumors as to cause ranging from heart attack to poison—his body sequestered secretly, yet to be cremated and the ashes cast into the River Moth per Bender's request. (Not to mention that a splinter faction of the Greens, in a flurry of pamphlets and broadsheets, had advertised the resurrection of their beloved Bender: he would reappear in the form of the first child born after midnight in one year's time. Would the child be born with arias bursting forth from his mouth like nightingales, Lake wondered.)

The renaming alone made Lake's teeth grind together. It seemed, to his absurdly envious eye—he *knew* how absurd he was, but could not control his feelings—that every third building of any importance had had the composer's name rudely slapped over old assignations, with no sense of decorum or perspective. Was it not enough that while alive Bender had been a virtual tyrant of the arts, squashing all opera, all theater, that did not fit his outdated melodramatic sensibilities? Was it not enough that he had come to be the de facto ruler of a city that simultaneously abhorred and embraced the cult of personality? Did he now have to usurp the *entire* city—every last stone of it—forever and always as his mausoleum? Apparently so. Apparently everyone soon would be permanently lost, for every avenue, alley, boulevard, dead end, and cul de sac would be renamed "Bender." "Bender" would be the name given to all new-borns; or, for variety's sake, "Voss." And a whole generation of Benders or Vosses would trip and tangle their way through a city which from every street corner threw back their name at them like an impersonal insult.

Why—Lake warmed to his own vitriol—if another Manzikert flattened him as he crossed this very street, he would be lucky to have his own name adorn his own gravestone! No doubt, he mused sourly—but with satisfaction—as he tested the post office's front steps with his cane, his final resting place would display the legend, "Voss Bender Memorial Gravestone" with the words "(occupied by Martin Lake)" etched in tiny letters below.

Inside the post office, at the threshold of the great hall, Lake walked through the gloomy light cast by the far windows and presented himself to the attendant, a man with a face like a knife; Lake had never bothered to learn his name.

JEFF VANDERMEER

Lake held out his key. "Number 7768, please."

The attendant, legs propped against his desk, looked up from the broadsheet he was reading, scowled, and said, "I'm busy."

Lake, startled, paused for a moment. Then, showing his cane, he tossed his key onto the desk.

The attendant looked at it as if it were a dead cockroach. "That, sir, is your key, sir. Yes it is. Go to it, sir. And all good luck to you." He ruffled the broadsheet as he held it up to block out Lake.

Lake stared at the fingers holding the broadsheet and wondered if there would be a place for the man's sour features in his latest commission—if he could immortalize the unhelpfulness that was as blunt as the man's knuckles. After the long, grueling walk through hostile territory, this was really too much.

Lake peered over the broadsheet, using his cane to pull it down a little. "You *are* the attendant, aren't you? I haven't been giving you my key all these months only to now discover that you are merely a conscientious volunteer?"

The man blinked and put down his broadsheet to reveal a crooked smile.

"I *am* the attendant. That *is* your key. You *are* crippled. Sir."

"Then what is the problem?"

The man looked Lake up and down. "Your attire, sir. You are dressed somewhat . . . ambiguously."

Lake wasn't sure if the answer or the comfortable use of the word "ambiguously" surprised him more. Nonetheless, he examined his clothes. He had thrown on a blue vest over a white shirt, blue trousers with black shoes and socks.

The attendant wore clothes the color of overripe tomatoes.

Lake burst out laughing. The attendant smirked.

"True, true," Lake managed. "I've not *declared* myself, have I? I must have a coming out party. What am I? Vegetable or mineral?"

In clipped tones, his eyes cold and empty, the attendant asked, "Red or Green: which is it, sir."

Lake stopped laughing. The buffoon was serious. This same pleasant if distant man he had seen every week for over two years had succumbed to the dark allure of Voss Bender's death. Lake stared at the attendant and saw a stranger.

Slowly, carefully, Lake said, "I am green on the outside, being as yet youthful in my chosen profession, and red on the inside, being, as is everyone, a mere mortal." He produced both flags. "I have your flag—and the flag of the other side." He dangled them in front of the attendant. "Did I dislike Voss Bender and abhor his stranglehold on the city? Yes. Did I wish him dead? No. Is this not enough? Why must I declare myself when all I wish is to toss these silly flags in the River Moth and stand aside while you and your cohorts barrel through bent on butchery? I am neutral, sir." (Lake thought this a particularly fine speech.)

"Because, sir," the attendant said, as he rose with a great show of exertion and snatched up Lake's key, "Voss Bender is not dead."

He gave Lake a stare that made the little hairs on the back of his neck rise, then walked over to the boxes while Lake smoldered like a badly-lit candle. Was the whole city going to play such games? Next time he went to the grocery store would the old lady behind the counter demand he sing a Bender aria before she would sell him a loaf of bread?

The attendant climbed one of the many ladders that leaned against the stacks like odd wooden insects. Lake hoped his journey had not been in vain—let there at least be a missive from his mother which might stave off the specter of homesickness. His father was, no doubt, still encased in the tight-lipped silence that covered him like a cicada's exoskeleton.

The attendant pulled Lake's box out, retrieved something from it, and climbed back down with an envelope.

"Here," the attendant said, glaring, and handed it to Lake, who took both it and his key with unintended gentleness, his anger losing out to bewilderment.

Bare of place and time, the maroon envelope displayed neither a return address nor his own address. More mysterious, he could find no trace of a postmark, which could only mean someone had hand-delivered it. On the back, Lake discovered a curious seal imprinted in an orange-gold wax that smelled of honey. The seal formed an owl-like mask which, when Lake turned it upside down, became transformed into a human face. The intricate pattern reminded Lake of Trillian the Great Banker's many signature casts for coins.

"Do you know how this letter got here?" Lake started to say, turning toward the desk, but the attendant had vanished, leaving only the silence and shadows of the great hall, the close air filtering the dust of one hundred years through its coppery sheen, the open door a rectangle of golden light.

From the broadsheet on the desk the name "Voss Bender," in vermilion ink, winked up at him like some infernal, recurring joke.

❧

With only this feeble skeleton of a biography as our background material, we must now approach the work that has *become* Martin Lake: "Invitation to a Beheading." The piece marks the beginning of the grotesqueries, the controlled savagery of his oils—the slashes of emerald slitting open the sky, the deft, tinted green of the windows looking in, the moss green of the exterior walls: all are vintage Lake.

The subject is, of course, the Voss Bender Memorial Post Office, truly among the most imposing of Ambergris' many eccentric buildings. If we can trust the words of Bronet Raden, the noted art critic, when he writes

> The marvelous is not the same in every period of history—it partakes in some obscure way of a sort of general revelation only the fragments of which come down to us: they are the romantic ruins, the modern mannequins, or any other symbol capable of affecting the human sensibility for a period of time,

then the first of Lake's many accomplishments was to break the post office down into its fragments and recreate it from "romantic ruins" into the dream-edifice that, for 30 years, has horrified and delighted visitors to the post office.

JEFF VANDERMEER

The astute observer will note that the post office walls in Lake's painting are created with careful crosshatching brushstrokes layered over a dampened whiteness. This whiteness, upon close examination, is composed of hundreds of bones—skulls, femurs, ribs—all compressed and rendered with a pathetic delicacy that astounds the eye.

On a surface level, this imagery surely functions as a symbolic nod to the building's former usage. Conceived to house the Cappan and his family, the brooding structure that would become the Voss Bender Memorial Post Office was abandoned following the dissolution of the Cappandom and then converted into a repository for the corpses of mushroom dwellers and indigent children. After a time, it fell into disuse—as Lake effectively shows with his surfaces beneath surfaces: the white columns slowly turning gray-green, the snarling gargoyles blackened from disrepair, the building's entire skin pocked by lichen and mold.

Lake frequently visited the post office and must have been familiar with its former function. When the old post office burned down and relocated to its present location in what was little better than an abandoned morgue, it is rumored that the first patrons of the new service eagerly opened their post boxes only to find within them old and strangely delicate bones—the bones Lake has "woven" into the "fabric" of his painting.

Lake's interpretation of the building is superior in its ability to convey the post office's psychic or spiritual self. As the noted painter and instructor Leonard Venturi has written:

Take two pictures representing the same subject; one may be dismissed as illustration if it is dominated by the subject and has no other justification but the subject, the other may be called painting if the subject is completely absorbed in the style, which is its own justification, whatever the subject, and has an intrinsic value.

Lake's representation of the post office is clearly a painting in Venturi's sense, for the subject is riddled through with wormholes of style, with layers of meaning. —From Janice Shriek's *A Short Overview of The Art of Martin Lake and His Invitation to a Beheading,* for the *Hoegbotton Guide to Ambergris,* 5th edition.

∽∾∾

Lake lived farthest from the docks and the River Moth, at the eastern end of Albumuth Boulevard, where it merged with the warren of middle class streets that laboriously, some thought treacherously, descended into the valley below. The neighborhood, its narrow mews crowded with cheap apartments and cafes, was filthy with writers, artists, architects, actors, and performers of every kind. Two years ago it had been resplendently fresh and on the cutting edge of the New Art. Street parties had lasted until six in the morning, and shocking conversations about the New Art, often destined for the pages of influential journals, had permeated the coffee-and-mint flavored air surrounding every eatery. By now, however, the sycophants and hangers-on had caught wind of the little miracle and begun to masticate it into a safe, stable "community." Eventually, the smell of rot—rotting ideas, rotting relationships, rotting art—would force the real artists out, to settle new frontiers. Lake hoped he would be going with them.

Lake's apartment, on the third floor of an old bee-hive-like tenement run by a legendary landlord known alternately as "Dame Tuff" or "Dame Truff," depending on one's religious beliefs, was a small studio cluttered with the salmon, saffron, and sapphire bluster of his art: easels made from stripped birch branches, the blank canvases upon them flap-flapping for attention; paint-splattered stools; a chair smothered in a tangle of shirts that stank of turpentine; and in the middle of all this, like a besieged island, his cot, covered with watercolor sketches curled at the edges and brushes stiff from lazy washings. The sense of a furious mess pleased him; it always looked like he had just finished attacking some new work of art. Sometimes he added to the confusion just before the arrival of visitors, not so self-deluded that he couldn't laugh at himself as he did it.

Once back in his apartment, Lake locked the door, discarded his cane, threw the shirts from his chair, and sat down to contemplate the letter. Faces cut from various magazines stared at him from across the room, waiting to be turned into collages for an as-yet-untitled autobiography in the third person written (and self-published) by a Mr. Dradin Kashmir. The collages represented a month's rent and he was late completing them. He avoided the faces as if they all wore his father's scowl.

Did the envelope contain a commission? He took it out of his pocket, weighed it in his hand. Not heavy. A single sheet of paper? The indifferent light of his apartment made the maroon envelope almost black. The seal still scintillated so beautifully in his artist's imagination that he hesitated to break it. Reluctantly—his fingers must be coerced into such an action—he broke the seal, opened the flap, and pulled out a sheet of parchment paper shot through with crimson threads. Words had been printed on the paper in a gold-orange ink, followed by the same mask symbol found on the seal. He skimmed the words several times, as if by rapid review he might discover some hidden message, some hint of closure. But the words only deepened the mystery:

Invitation To A Beheading
You Are Invited to Attend:
45 Archmont Lane
7:30 in the evening
25th Day of This Month
Please arrive in costume

Lake stared at the message. A masquerade, but to what purpose? He suppressed an impulse to laugh and instead walked over to the balcony and opened the windows, letting in fresh air. The sudden chaos of voices from below, the rough sounds of street traffic—on foot, on horses, or in motored vehicles—gave Lake a comforting sense of community, as if he were debating the mystery of the message with the world.

From his balcony window he could see, on the right, a green-tinged slice of the valley, while straight ahead the spires and domes of the Religious Quarter burned white, gold, and silver. To the left, the solid red brick and orange marble of more apartment buildings.

Lake liked the view. It reminded him that he had survived three years in a city notorious for devouring innocents whole. Not famous, true, but not dead or defeated either. Indeed, he took a perverse pleasure from enduring and withstanding the city's countless petty cruelties, for he believed it made him stronger. One day he might rule the city, for certainly it had not ruled him.

And now this—this letter that seemed to have come from the city itself. Surely it was the work of one of his artist friends—Kinsky, Raffe, or that ruinous old scoundrel, Sonter? A practical joke, perhaps even Merrimount's doing? "Invitation To A Beheading." What could it mean? He vaguely remembered a book, a fiction, with that title, written by Sirin, wasn't it? Sirin, whose pseudonyms spread through the pages of literary journals like some mad yet strangely wonderful disease.

But perhaps it meant nothing at all and "they" intended that he waste so much time studying it that he would be late finishing his commissions.

Lake walked back to his chair and sat down. Gold ink was expensive, and the envelope, on closer inspection, was flecked with gold as well, while the paper for the invitation itself had gold threads. The paper even smelled of orange peel cologne. Lake frowned, his gaze lingering on the shimmery architecture of the Religious Quarter. The cost of such an invitation came to a sum equal to a week's commissions. Would his friends spend so much on a joke?

His frown deepened. Perhaps, merriest joke of all, the letter had been misdelivered, the sender having used the wrong address. Only, it *had no* address on it. Which made him suspect his friends again. And might the attendant, if he went back to the post office, recall who had slipped the letter through the front slot of his box? He sighed. It was hopeless; such speculations only fed the—

A pebble sailed through the open window and fell onto his lap. He started, then smiled and rose, the pebble falling to the floor. At the window, he looked down. Raffe stared up at him from the street: daring Raffe in her sarcastic red-and-green jacket.

"Good shot," he called down. He studied her face for any hint of complicity in a plot, found no mischief there, realized it meant nothing.

"We're headed for the Calf for the evening," Raffe shouted up at him. "Are you coming?"

Lake nodded. "Go on ahead. I'll be there soon."

Raffe smiled, waved, and continued on down the street.

Lake retreated into his room, put the letter back in its envelope, stuffed it all into an inner pocket, and retired to the bathroom down the hall, the better to freshen up for the night's festivities. As he washed his face and looked into the moss-tinged mirror, he considered whether he should remain mum or share the invitation. He had still not decided when he walked out onto the street and into the harsh light of late afternoon.

By the time he reached the Cafe of the Ruby-Throated Calf, Lake found that his fellow artists had, aided by large quantities of alcohol, adopted a cavalier attitude toward the War of the Reds and the Greens. As a gang of Reds ran by,

dressed in their patchwork crimson robes, his friends rose together, produced their red flags and cheered as boisterously
as if at some sporting event. Lake had just taken a seat, generally ignored in the hubbub, when a gang of Greens trotted
by in pursuit, and once again his friends rose, green flags in
hand this time, and let out a roar of approval.

Lake smiled, Raffe giving him a quick elbow to the
ribs before she turned back to her conversation, and he
let the smell of coffee and chocolate work its magic. His
leg ached, as it did sometimes when he was under stress,
but otherwise, he had no complaints. The weather had
remained pleasant, neither too warm nor too cold, and a
breeze ruffled the branches of the potted zindel trees with
their jade leaves. The trees formed miniature forests around
groups of tables, effectively blocking out rival conversations
without blocking the street from view. Artists lounged in
their iron latticework chairs or slouched over the black-
framed round glass tables while imbibing a succession of
exotic drinks and coffees. The night lanterns had just been
turned on and the glow lent a cozy warmth to their own
group, cocooned as they were by the foliage and the soothing murmur of conversations.

The four sitting with Lake he counted as his closest friends: Raffe, Sonter, Kinsky, and Merrimount. The
rest had become as interchangeable as the bricks of
Hoegbotton & Sons' many trading outposts, and about as
interesting. At the moment, X, Y, and Z claimed the outer
tables like petty island tyrants, their faces peering pale
and glinty-eyed in at Lake's group, one ear to the inner
conversation while at the same time trying to maintain an
uneasy autonomy.

Merrimount, a handsome man with long, dark lashes and wide blue eyes, combined elements of painting and performance art in his work, his life itself a kind of performance art. Merrimount was Lake's on-again, off-again lover, and Lake shot him a raffish grin to let him know that, surely, they would be on-again soon? Merrimount ignored him. Last time they had seen each other, Lake had made Merri cry. "You want too much," Merri had said. "No one can give you that much love, not and still be human. Or sane." Raffe had told Lake to stay away from Merri but, painful as it was to admit, Lake knew Raffe meant *he* was bad for Merri.

Raffe, who sat next to Merrimount—a buffer between him and Lake—was a tall woman with long black hair and dark, expressive eyebrows that lent a needed intensity to her light green eyes. Raffe and Lake had become friends the day he arrived in Ambergris. She had found him on Albumuth Boulevard, watching the crowds, an overwhelmed, almost defeated, look on his face. Raffe had let him stay with her for the three months it had taken him to find his city legs. She painted huge, swirling, passionate city scapes in which the people all seemed caught in midstep of some intricate and unbearably graceful dance. They sold well, and not just to tourists.

Lake said to Raffe, "Do you think it wise to be so . . . careless?"

"Why, whatever do you mean, Martin?" Raffe had a deep, distinctly feminine voice that he never tired of hearing.

The strong, gravely tones of Michael Kinsky, sitting on the other side of Merrimount, rumbled through Lake's answer: "He means, aren't we afraid of the donkey asses known as the Reds and the monkey butts known as the Greens."

Kinsky had a wiry frame and a sparse red beard. He made mosaics from discarded bits of stone, jewelry, and other gimcracks discovered on the city's streets. Kinsky had been well-liked by Voss Bender and Lake imagined the composer's death had dealt Kinsky's career a serious blow—although, as always, Kinsky's laconic demeanor appeared unruffled by catastrophe.

"We're not afraid of anything," Raffe said, raising her chin and putting her hands on her sides in mock bravado.

Edward Sonter, to Kinsky's right and Lake's immediate left, giggled. He had a horrible tendency to produce a high-pitched squeal of amusement, in total contrast to the sensuality of his art. Sonter made abstract pottery and sculptures, vaguely obscene in nature. His gangly frame and his face, in which the eyes floated unsteadily, could often be seen in the Religious Quarter, where his work enjoyed unusually brisk sales.

As if Sonter's giggle had been a signal, they began to talk careers, gauge the day's fortunes and misfortunes. They had tame material this time: a gallery owner—no one Lake knew—had been discovered selling wall space in return for sexual favors. Lake ordered a cup of coffee, with a chocolate chaser, and listened without enthusiasm.

Lake sensed familiar undercurrents of tension, as each artist sought to ferret out information about his or her fellows—weasels, bright-eyed and eager for the kill, that their own weasel selves might burn all the brighter. These tensions had eaten more than one conversation, leaving the table silent with barely suppressed hatred born of envy. Such a cruel and cutting silence had even eaten an artist or two. Personally, Lake enjoyed the tension because it rarely centered around him; he was by far the most obscure member of the inner circle, kept there by the strength of Raffe's patronage. Now, though, he felt a different tension, centered around the letter. It lay in a pocket against his chest like a second heart in his awareness of it.

As the shadows deepened into early dusk and the buttery light of the lanterns on their delightfully curled bronze posts held back the night, the conversation, lubricated by wine, became to Lake's ears tantalizingly anonymous, as will happen in the company of people one is comfortable with, so that Lake could never remember exactly who had said what, or who had argued for what position. Lake later wondered if anything had been said, or if they had sat there, beautifully mute, while inside his head a conversation took place between Martin and Lake.

He spent the time contemplating the pleasures of reconciliation with Merri—drank in the twinned marvels of the man's perfect mouth, the compact, sinuous body. But Lake could not forget the letter. This, and his growing ennui, led him to direct the conversation toward a more timely subject:

"I've heard it said that the Greens are disemboweling innocent folk near the docks, just off of Albumuth. If they bleed red, they are denounced as sympathizers against Voss Bender; if they bleed green, then their attackers apologize for the inconvenience and try to patch them up. Of course, if they bleed green, they're likely headed for the columbarium anyhow."

"Are you trying to disgust us?"

"It wouldn't surprise me if it *were* true—it seems in keeping with the man himself: self-proclaimed Dictator of Art, with heavy emphasis on 'Dic.' We all know he was a genius, but it's a good thing he's dead . . . unless one of you is a Green with a dagger . . . "

"Very funny."

"Certainly it is rare for a single artist to so thoroughly dominate the city's cultural life—"

"—Not to mention politics—"

("Who started the Reds and the Greens anyhow?")

"And to be discussed so thoroughly, in so many cafes—"

("It started as an argument about the worth of Bender's music, between two professors of musicology on Trotten Street. Leave it to musicians to start a war over music; now that you're caught up, listen for God's sake!")

"—Not to mention politics, you say. And isn't it a warning to us all that Art and Politics are like oil and water? To comment—"

"—'oil and water'? Now we understand why you're a painter."

"How clever."

"—as I said, to comment on it, perhaps, if forced to, but not to participate?"

"But if not Bender, then some bureaucratic businessman like Trillian. Trillian, the Great Banker. Sounds like an advertisement, not a leader. Surely, Merrimount, we're damned either way. And why not let the city run itself?"

"Oh—and it's done such a good job of that so far—"

"Off topic. We're bloody well off topic—again!"

"Ah, but what you two *don't* see is that it is precisely his audience's passionate connection to his *art*—the fact that people believe the operas are the man—that has created the crisis!"

"Depends. I thought his *death* caused the crisis?"

At that moment, a group of Greens ran by. Lake, Merrimount, Kinsky, and Sonter all raised their green flags with a curious mixture of derision and drunken fervor. Raffe sat up and shouted after them, "He's dead! He's dead! He's dead!" Her face was flushed, her hair furiously tangled.

The last of the Greens turned at the sound of Raffe's voice, his face ghastly pale under the lamps. Lake saw that the man's hands dripped red. He forced Raffe to sit down: "Hush now, hush!" The man's gaze swept across their table, and then he was running after his comrades, soon out of sight.

"Yes, not so obvious, that's all."

"Their spies are everywhere."

"Why, I found one in my nose this morning while blowing it."

"The morning or the nose?"

Laughter, and then a voice from beyond the inner circle, muffled by the dense shrubbery, offered, "It's not certain Bender is dead. The Greens claim he is alive."

"Ah yes." The inner circle deftly appropriated the topic, slamming like a rude, massive door on the outer circle.

"Yes, he's alive."

"—or he's dead and coming back in a fortnight, just a bit rotted for the decay. Delay?"

"—no one's actually seen the body."

"—hush hush secrecy. Even his friends didn't see—"

"—and what we're witnessing is actually a *coup*."

"Coo coo."

"Shut up, you bloody pigeon."

"I'm not a pigeon—I'm a cuckoo."

"Bender hated pigeons."

"He hated cuckoos too."

"He was a cuckoo."

"Boo! Boo!"

"As if *anyone* really controls this city, anyway?"

"O fecund grand mother matron, Ambergris, bathed in the blood of versions under the gangrenous moon." Merrimount's melodramatic lilt was unmistakable, and Lake roused himself.

"Did I hear right?" Lake rubbed his ears. "Is this *poetry*? Verse? But what is this gristle: bathed in the blood of *versions*? Surely, my merry mount, you mean *virgins*. We all were one once—or had one once."

A roar of approval from the gallery.

But Merrimount countered: "No, no, my dear Lake, I *meant* versions—I protest. I meant versions: Bathed in the blood of the city's many *versions* of itself."

"A nice recovery"—Sonter again—"but I still think you're drunk."

At which point, Sonter and Merrimount fell out of the conversation, the two locked in an orbit of "version"/ "virgin" that, in all likelihood, would continue until the sun and moon fell out of the sky. Lake felt a twinge of jealousy.

Kinsky offered a smug smile, stood, stretched, and said, "I'm going to the opera. Anyone with me?"

A chorus of boos, accompanied by a series of "Fuck off's!"

Kinsky, face ruddy, guffawed, threw down some coins for his bill, and stumbled off down the street which, despite the late hour, twitched and rustled with foot traffic.

"Watch out for the Reds, the Greens, and the Blues," Raffe shouted after him.

"The Blues?" Lake said, turning to Raffe.

"Yes. The Blues—you know. The sads."

"Funny. I think the Blues are more dangerous than the Greens and the Reds put together."

"Only the Browns are more deadly."

Lake laughed, stared after Kinsky. "He's not serious, is he?"

"No," Raffe said. "After all, if there is to be a massacre, it will be at the opera. You'd think the theater owners, or even the actors, would have more sense and close down for a month."

"Shouldn't we leave the city? Just the two of us—and maybe Merrimount?"

Raffe snorted. "And maybe Merrimount? And where would we go? Morrow? The Court of the Kalif? Excuse me for saying so, but I'm broke."

Lake smirked. "Then why are you drinking so much."

"Seriously. Do you mean you'd pay for a trip?"

"No—I'm just as poor as you." Lake put down the drink. "But, I would pay for some advice."

"Eat healthy foods. Do your commissions on time. Don't let Merrimount back into your life."

"No, no. Not that kind of advice. More specific."

"About what?"

He leaned forward, said softly, "Have you ever received an anonymous commission?"

"How do you mean?"

"A letter appears in your post office box. It has no return address. Your address isn't on it. It's clearly from someone wealthy. It tells you to go to a certain place at a certain time. It mentions a masquerade."

Raffe frowned, the corners of her eyes narrowing. "You're serious."

"Yes."

"I've never gotten a commission like that. You have?"

"Yes. I think. I mean, I think it's a commission."

"May I see the letter."

Lake looked at her, his best friend, and somehow he couldn't share it with her.

"I don't have it with me."

"Liar!"

As he started to protest, she took his hand and said, "No, no—it's all right. I understand. I won't take an advantage from you. But you want advice on whether you should go?"

Lake nodded, too ashamed to look at her.

"It might be your big break—a major collector who wants to remain anonymous until he's cornered the market in Lake originals. Or . . . "

She paused and a great fear settled over Lake, a fear he knew could only overwhelm him so quickly because it had been there all along.

"Or?"

"It could be a . . . special assignation."

"A *what*?"

"You don't know what I mean?"

He took a sip of his drink, set it down again, said, "I'll admit it. I've no idea what you're talking about."

"Naive, naive Martin," she said, and leaned forward to ruffle his hair.

Blushing, he drew back, said, "Just tell me, Raffe."

Raffe smiled. "Sometimes, Martin, a wealthy person will get a filthy little idea in a filthy little part of their mind—and that idea is to have personalized pornography done by an artist."

"Oh."

Quickly, she said, "But I'm probably wrong. Even if so, that kind of work pays very well. Maybe even enough to let you take time off from commissions to do your own work."

"So I should go?"

"You only become successful by taking chances . . . I've been meaning to tell you, Martin, as a friend and fellow artist—"

"What? What have you been meaning to tell me?"

Lake was acutely aware that Sonter and Merrimount had fallen silent.

She took his hand in hers. "Your work is small."

"Miniatures?" Lake said incredulously.

"No. How do I say this? Small in ambition. Your art treads carefully. You need to take bigger steps. You need to paint a bigger world."

Lake looked up at the clouds, trying to disguise the hurt in his voice, the ache in his throat: *"You're saying I'm no good."*

"I'm only saying *you* don't think you're any good. Why else do you waste such a talent on facile portraits, on a thousand lesser disciplines that *require* no discipline. You, Martin, could be the Voss Bender of artists."

"And look what happened to him—he's dead."

"Martin!"

Suddenly he felt very tired, very . . . small. His father's voice rang in his head unpleasantly.

"There's something about the quality of the light in this city that I cannot capture in paint," he mumbled.

"What?"

"The quality of light is deadly."

"I don't understand. Are you angry with me?"

He managed a thin smile. "Raffe, how could I be angry with you? I need time to think about what you've said. It's not something I can just agree with. But in the meantime, I'll take your advice—I'll go."

Raffe's face brightened. "Good! Now escort me home. I need my sleep."

"Merrimount will be jealous."

"No I won't," Merrimount said, with a look that was half scowl, half grin. "You just *wish* I'd be jealous."

Raffe squeezed his arm and said, "After all, no matter what the commission is, you can always say no."

❧ ❦

However, once we have explored Lake's own exploration of the post office as building and metaphor, how much closer are we to the truth? Not very close at all. If biography is too slim to help us and the post office itself too superficial, then we must turn to other sources—specifically Lake's other paintings of note, for in the differences and similarities to "Invitation" we may uncover a kind of truth.

We can first, and most generally, discuss Lake's work in terms of architecture, in terms of his love for his adopted home. If "Invitation to a Beheading" marked Lake's emergence into maturity, it also inaugurated his fascination with Ambergris. The city is often the sole subject of Lake's art—and in almost every case the city encloses, crowds, or enmazes the people sharing the canvas. Further, the city has a palpable *presence* in Lake's work. It almost *intercedes* in the lives of its citizens.

Lake's well-known "Albumuth Boulevard" trip-tyche consists of panels that ostensibly show, at dawn, noon and dusk, the scene from a fourth story window, looking down over a block of apartment buildings beyond which lie the domes of the Religious Quarter (shiny with the transcendent quality of light that Lake first perfected in "Invitation to a Beheading"). The painting is quite massive, the predominant colors yellow, red, and green. The one human constant to the three panels is a man standing on the boulevard below, surrounded by pedestrians. At first, the architecture appears identical, but on closer inspection, the streets, the buildings, clearly change or shift in each scene, in each panel further encroaching on the man. By dusk, the buildings have grown gargoyles where once perched pigeons. The people surrounding the man have become progressively more animal-like, their heads angular, their noses snouts, their teeth fangs. The expressions on the faces of these people become progressively sadder, more melancholy and tragic, while the man, impassive, with his back to us, has no face. The buildings themselves come to resemble sad faces, so that the overall effect of the final panel is overwhelming . . . and yet, oddly, we feel sad not for the people or the buildings, but for the one immutable element of the series—the faceless man who stands with his back to the viewer.

This, then, is where Lake parts company with such symbolists as the great Darcimbaldo—Lake refuses to lose himself in his grotesque structures, or to abandon himself solely to an imagination under no causal restraints. All of his mature paintings possess a sense of overwhelming *sorrow*. This sorrow lifts his work above that of his contemporaries and provides the depth, the mystery, that so captivates the general public. —From Janice Shriek's *A Short Overview of The Art of Martin Lake and His Invitation to a Beheading*, for the *Hoegbotton Guide to Ambergris*, 5th edition.

≈≫≪

Lake slept fitfully that moonless night, but when he woke the moon blossomed obscenely bright and red beyond his bed. His sheets had become, in that crimson light, violet waves of rippled fabric slick with his sweat. He smelled blood. The walls stank of it. A man stood in front of the open balcony windows, almost eclipsed by the weight of the moon at his back. Lake could not see the man's face. Lake sat up in bed.

"Merrimount? Merrimount? You've returned to me after all."

The man stood at the side of the bed. Lake stood by the balcony window. The man lay in the bed. Lake walked to the balcony. The man and Lake stood a foot apart in the middle of the room, the moon crepuscular and blood-engorged behind Lake. The moon was breathing its scarlet breath upon his back. He could not see the man's face. He was standing right in front of the man and could not see his face. The apartment, fixed in the perfect clarity of the bleeding light cried out to him in the sharpness of its detail, so that his eyes cut themselves upon such precision. Every bristle on his dried out brushes surrendered to him its slightest imperfection. Every canvas became porous with the numbing roughness of its gesso.

"You're not Merrimount," he said to the man.

The man's eyes were closed.

Lake stood facing the moon. The man stood facing Lake.

The man opened his eyes and the ferruginous light of the moon shot through them and formed two rusty spots on Lake's neck, as if the man's eyes were just holes that pierced his skull from back to front.

The moon blinked out. The light still streamed from the man's eyes. The man smiled a half-moon smile and the light trickled out from between his teeth.

The man held Lake's left hand, palm up.

The knife sliced into the middle of Lake's palm. He felt the knife tear through the skin, and into the palmar fascia muscle, and beneath that, into the tendons, vessels, and nerves. The skin peeled back until his entire hand was flayed and open. He saw the knife sever the muscle from the lower margin of the annular ligament, then felt, almost heard, the lesser muscles snap back from the bones as they were cut—six for the middle finger, three for the ring finger—the knife now grinding up against the os magnum as the man guided it into the area near Lake's wrist—slicing through extensor tendons, through the nerves, through the farthest outposts of the radial and ulnar arteries. He could see it all—the yellow of the thin fat layer, the white of bone obscured by the dull red of muscle, the gray of tendons, as surely as if his hand had been labeled and diagrammed for his own benefit. The blood came thick and heavy, draining from all of his extremities until he only had feeling in his chest. The pain was infinite, so infinite that he did not try to escape it, but tried only to escape the red gaze of the man who was butchering him while he just stood there and let him do it. The thought went through his head like a dirge, like an epitaph, *I will never paint again.*

He could not get away. He could not get away.

Lake's hand began to mutter, to mumble . . .

In response, the man sang to Lake's hand, the words incomprehensible, strange, sad.

Lake's hand began to scream—a long, drawn out scream, ever higher in pitch, the wound become a mouth into which the man continued to plunge the knife.

Lake woke up shrieking. He was drowning in sweat, his right hand clenched around his left wrist. He tried to control his breathing—he sucked in great gulps of air—but found it was impossible. Panicked, he looked toward the window. There was no moon. No one stood there. He forced his gaze down to his left hand (he had done nothing, nothing, nothing while the man cut him apart) and found it whole.

He was still shrieking.

❧❦

In "Invitation to a Beheading," the sorrow takes the form of two figures: the insect catcher outside the building and the man highlighted in the upper window of the post office itself. (If it seems that I have kept these two figures a secret in order to make of them a revelation, it is because they *are* a revelation to the viewer—due to the mass of detail around them, they are generally the last seen, and then, in a tribute to their intensity, the *only* things seen.)

The insect catcher, his light dimmed but for a single orange spark, hurries off down the front steps, one hand held up behind him, as if to ward off the man in the window. Is this figure literally Lake's father, or does it represent some mythical insect catcher—*the* Insect Catcher? Or did Lake see his father as a mythic figure? From my conversations with Lake, the latter interpretation strikes me as most plausible.

But to what can we attribute the single clear window in the building's upper story, through which we see a man who stands in utter anguish, his head thrown back to the sky? In one hand, the man holds a letter, while the other is held palm up by a vaguely stork-like shadow that has driven a knife through it. The scene derives all of its energy from this view through the window: the greens radiate outward from the pulsing crimson spot that marks where the knife has penetrated flesh. Adding to the effect, Lake has so layered and built up his oils that a trick of perspective is created by which the figure simultaneously exists inside and outside the window.

Although the building that houses this intricate scene lends itself to fantastical interpretation, and Lake might be thought to have recreated some historical event in phantasmagorical fashion, the figure with the pierced palm is clearly a man, not a child or mushroom dweller, and the letter held in the man's right hand indicates an admission of the building's use as a post office rather than as a morgue (unless, under duress, we are forced to acknowledge the weak black humor of "dead letter office").

Further examination of the man's face reveals two disturbing elements: (1) it bears a striking resemblance to Lake's own face, and (2) under close scrutiny with a magnifying glass, there is a second, almost translucent set of features transposed over the first. This "mask," its existence disputed by some critics, mimics, like a mold made from life, the features of the first, except in two particulars: this man has teeth made of broken glass and he, unlike his counterpart, smiles with unnerving brutality. Is this the face of the faceless man from "Albumuth Boulevard?" Is this the face of Death?

Regardless of Lake's intent, all of these elements combine to create in the viewer—even the viewer who only subconsciously notes certain of the more hidden elements—a true sense of unease and dread, as well as the release of this dread through the anguished, voiceless cry of the man in the window. The man in the window provides us with the only movement in the painting, for the insect catcher, hurrying away, is already in the past, and the bones of the post office are also in the past. Only the forlorn figure in the window is still alive, caught forever in the present. Further, although foresaken by the insect catcher and pierced by a shadow that may be a manifestation of his own fear, the *light* never forsakes or betrays him. Lake's tones are, as Venturi has noted, "resonant rather than bright, and the light contained in them is not so much a physical as a psychological illumination." —From Janice Shriek's *A Short Overview of The Art of Martin Lake and His Invitation to a Beheading*, for the *Hoegbotton Guide to Ambergris*, 5th edition.

৵৹

Lake spent the next day trying to forget his nightmare. To rid himself of its cloying atmosphere, he left his apartment—but not before receiving a stern lecture from Dame Truff on how loud noises after midnight showed no consideration for other tenants, while behind her a few neighbors, who had not come to his aid but obviously had heard his screams, gave him curious stares.

Then, punishment over, he made his way through the crowded streets to the Gallery of Hidden Fascinations, portfolio under one arm. The portfolio contained two new paintings, both of his father's hands, as he remembered them, open wide like wings as a cornucopia of insects—velvet ants, cicadas, moths, butterflies, walking sticks, praying mantises—crawled over them. It was a study he had been working on for years. His father had beautifully ruined hands, bitten and stung countless times, but as polished, as smooth, as white marble.

The gallery owner, Janice Shriek, greeted him at the door; she was a severe, hunched woman with calculating, cold blue eyes. This morning she had thrown on foppishly male trousers, and a jacket over a white shirt, the sleeves of which ended in cuffs that looked as if they had been made from doilies. Shriek rose up on tip-toe to plant a ceremonial kiss on his cheek while explaining that the short, portly gentleman currently casting his round shadow over the far end of the gallery had expressed interest in one of Lake's pieces, how fortunate that he had stopped by, and that while she continued to enflame that interest—she actually said "enflamed," much to Lake's amazement; was he to be some artistic gigolo now?—Lake should set down his portfolio and, after a decent interval, walk over and introduce himself, that was a dear—and back she scamper-lurched to the potential customer, leaving Lake rather breathless on her behalf. No one could ever say Janice Shriek lacked energy.

Lake placed his portfolio on a nearby table, the art of his countless rivals glaring down at him from the walls. The only good art (besides Lake's, of course) was a miniature entitled "Amber in the City" by Shriek's great find, Roger Mandible, who, unbeknownst to Shriek, had created his subtle amber shades from the earwax of a well-known diva who had had the misfortune to fall asleep at a cafe table where Mandible was mixing his paints. It made Lake snicker every time he saw it.

After a moment, Lake walked over to Shriek and the gentleman and engaged in the kind of obsequious small talk that nauseated him.

"Yes, I'm the artist."

"Maxwell Bibble. A pleasure to meet you."

"Likewise . . . Bibble. It is exceedingly rare to meet a true lover of art."

Bibble stank of beets. Lake could not get over it. Bibble stank of beets. He had difficulty not saying *Bibble imbibes bottled beets beautifully* . . .

"Well, you do . . . you do so well with, er, *colors*," Bibble said.

"How discerning you are. Did you hear what he said, Janice," Lake said.

Shriek nodded nervously, said, "Mr. Bibble's a business-man, but he has always wanted to be a—" *Beet?* thought Lake; but no: " . . . a critic of the arts," Shriek finished.

"Yes, marvelous colors," Bibble said, this time with more confidence.

"It is nothing. The *true artiste* can bend even the most stubborn light to his will," Lake said.

"I imagine so. I thought this piece might look good in the kitchen, next to the wife's needlepoint."

" 'In the kitchen, next to the wife's needlepoint,' " Lake echoed blankly, and then put on a frozen smile.

"But I'm wondering if maybe it is too big . . . "

"It's smaller than it looks," Shriek offered, somewhat pathetically, Lake thought.

"Perhaps I could have it altered, cut down to size," Lake said, glaring at Shriek.

Bibble nodded, putting a hand to his chin in rapt contemplation of the possibilities.

"Or maybe I should just saw it in fourths and you can take the fourth you like best," Lake said. "Or maybe eighths would be more to your liking?"

Bibble stared blankly at him for a moment, before Shriek stepped in with, "Artists! Always joking! You know, I really don't think it will be too large. You could always buy it and if it doesn't fit, return it—not that I could refund your money, but you could pick something else."

Enough! Lake thought, and disengaged himself from the conversation. Leaving Shriek to ramble on convincingly about the cunning strength of his brushstrokes, a slick blather of nonsense that Lake despised and admired all at once. He could not complain that Shriek neglected to promote him—she was the only one who would take his work—but he hated the way she appropriated his art, speaking at times almost as if she herself had created it. A failed painter and a budding art historian, Shriek had started the gallery through the largesse of her famous brother, the historian Duncan Shriek, who had also procured for her many of her first and best clients. Lake felt that her drive to push, push, push was linked to a certain guilt at not having had to start at the bottom like everyone else.

Eventually, as Lake gave a thin-lipped smile, Bibble, still reeking of beets, announced that he couldn't possibly commit at the moment, but would come back later. Definitely, he would be back—and what a pleasure to meet the artist.

To which Lake said, and was sorry even as the words left his mouth, "It is a pleasure to *be* the artist."

A nervous laugh from Shriek. An unpleasant laugh from the almost-buyer, whose hand Lake tried his best to crush as they shook goodbye.

After Bibble had left, Shriek turned to him and said, "That was wonderful!"

"What was wonderful?"

Shriek's eyes became colder than usual. "That smug, arrogant, better-than-thou artist's demeanor. They like that, you know—it makes them feel they've bought the work of a budding genius."

"Well haven't they?" Lake said. Was she being sarcastic? He'd pretend otherwise.

Shriek patted him on the back. "Whatever it is, keep it up. Now, let's take a look at the new paintings."

Lake bit his lip to stop himself from committing career suicide, walked over to the table, and retrieved the two canvases. He spread them out with an awkward flourish.

Shriek stared at them, a quizzical look on her face.

"Well?" Lake finally said, Raffe's words from the night before buzzing in his ears. "Do you like them?"

"Hmm?" Shriek said, looking up from the paintings as if her thoughts had been far away.

Lake experienced a truth viscerally in that moment which he had only ever realized intellectually before: he was the least of Shriek's many prospects, and he was boring her.

Nonetheless, he pressed on, braced for further humiliation: "Do you like them?"

"Oh! The paintings?"

"No—the . . . " *The ear wax on your walls?* he thought. *The beets?* "Yes, the paintings."

Shriek's brows furrowed and she put a hand to her chin in unconscious mimicry of the departed Bibble. "They're very . . . interesting."

Interesting.

"They're of my father's hands," Lake said, aware that he was about to launch into a confession both unseemly and useless, as if he could help make the paintings more appealing to her by saying *this happened,* this is a person *I know*, it is *real* therefore it is *good*. But he had no choice—he plunged forward: "He is a startlingly nonverbal man, my father, as most insect catchers are, but there was one way he felt comfortable communicating with me, Janice—by coming home with his hands closed—and when he'd open them, there would be some living jewel, some rare wonder of the insect world—sparkling black, red, or green—and his eyes would sparkle too. He'd name them all for me in his soft, stumbling voice—lovingly so; how they were all so very different from one another, how although he killed them and we often ate them in hard times, how it must be with respect and out of knowledge." Lake looked at the floor. "He wanted me to be an insect catcher too, but I wouldn't. I couldn't. I had to become an artist." He remembered the way the joy had shriveled up inside his father when he realized his son would not be following in his footsteps. It had hurt Lake to see his father so alone, trapped by his reticence and his solitary profession, but he knew it hurt his father more. He missed his father; it was an ache in his chest.

"That's a lovely story, Martin. A lovely story."

"So you'll take them?"

"No. But it is a lovely story."

"But see how perfectly I've rendered the insects," Lake said, pointing to them.

"Yes, you have. But it's a slow season and I don't have the space. Maybe when your other work sells." Her tone as much as said not to press her too far.

With a great effort of will, Lake said, "I understand. I'll come visit again in a few months."

The invitation to a beheading was looking better to Lake all the time.

When Lake returned to his apartment to work on Mr. Kashmir's commission, he was decidedly out of sorts. In addition to his disappointing trip to the gallery, he had spent money on greasy sausage that now sat in his belly like an extra coil of intestines. It did not help that the image of the man from his nightmares blinked on and off in his head no matter how hard he tried to suppress it.

Nevertheless, he dutifully picked up the pages of illustrations he had torn from discarded books bought cheap at the back door of the Borges Bookstore. He set about cutting them out with his rusty paint-speckled scissors. Ideas for his commissions came to him not in flashes from his muse but as calm re-creations of past work. Lately, he knew, he had become lazy, providing literal "translations" for his commissions, while suppressing any hint of his own imagination.

Still, this did not explain why, following a period of work during which he stared at the envelope and the invitation where it lay on his easel, he looked down to find that after carefully cutting out a trio of etched dancing girls, he had just as carefully sliced off their heads and then cut star designs out of their torsos.

In disgust, Lake tossed the scissors aside and let the ruins of the dancing girls flutter to the floor like exotic confetti. Obviously, Mr. Kashmir's assignment would have to await a spark of inspiration. In the meantime, the afternoon still young, he would take Raffe's advice and work on something for himself.

Lake walked over to the crowded easel, emptied it by placing four or five canvases on the already chaotic bed, pulled his stool over, retrieved a blank canvas, and pinned it up. Slowly, he began to brushstroke oils onto the canvas. Despite three years of endless commissions, the familiar smell of fresh paint excited his senses and, even better, the light behind him was sharp, clear, so he did not have to resort to borrowing Dame Truff's lantern.

As he progressed, Lake did not know the painting's subject, or even how best to apply the oils, but he continued to create layers of paint, sensitive to the pressure of the brush against canvas. Raffe had forced the oils upon him months ago. At the time, he had given her a superior, doubtful look, since her last gift had been special paints created from a mixture of natural pigments and freshwater squid ink. Lake had used them for a week before his first paintings began to fade; soon his canvases were as blank as before. Raffe, always trying to find the good in the bad, had told him, when next they met at a cafe, that he could become famous selling "disappearing paintings." He had thrown the paint set at her. Fortunately, it missed and hit a stranger—a startled and startlingly handsome man named Merrimount.

This time, however, Raffe's idea appeared to be a good one. It had been several years since he had used oils and he had forgotten the ease of creating texture with them, how the paint built upon itself. He especially liked how he could blend colors for gradations of shadow. Assuming the current troubles were temporary—and that a drop cloth would suffice until that time—and even now giving a quick look over his shoulder, he worked on building color: emerald, jade, moss, lime, verdigris. He mixed all the shades in, until he had a luminous, shining background. Then, in dark green, he began to paint a face . . .

Only the Religious Quarter's evening call to prayer—the solemn tolling of the bell five times from the old Truffidian cathedral—roused Lake from his trance. He blinked, turned toward the window, then looked back at his canvas. In shock and horror, he let the brush fall from his hand.

The head had a brutish mouth of broken glass teeth through which it smiled cruelly, while above the ruined nose, the eyes shone like twin flames. Lake stared at the face from his nightmare.

For a long time, Lake examined his work. His first impulse, to paint over it and start fresh, gradually gave way to a second, deeper impulse: to finish it. Far better, he thought, that the face should remain in the painting than, erased, once more take up residence in his mind. A little thrill ran through him as he realized it was totally unlike anything he had done before.

"I've trapped you," he said to it, gloating.

It stared at him with its unearthly eyes and said nothing. On the canvas it might still smile, but it could not smile only at him. Now it smiled at the world.

He worked on it for a few more minutes, adding definition to the eyelids and narrowing the cheekbones, relieved, for now that he had come around to the idea that the face *belonged* in the world, that perhaps it had always been in the world, he wanted it perfect in every detail, that no trace of it should ever haunt him again.

As the shadows lengthened and deepened, falling across his canvas, he put aside his palette, cleaned his brushes with turpentine, washed them in the sink across the hall, and quickly dressed to the sounds of a busker on the street below. After he had put on his jacket, he stuck his sketchbook and two sharpened pencils into his breast pocket—in case his mysterious host should need an immediate demonstration of his skills—and, running his fingers over the ornate seal, deposited the invitation there as well.

A few moments of rummaging under his bed and he had fished out a collapsible rubber frog head he had worn to the Festival of the Freshwater Squid a year before—it would have to do for a costume. He stuffed it in a side pocket, one bulbous yellow eye staring up at him absurdly. Further rummaging uncovered his map. Every wise citizen of Ambergris carried a map of the city, for its alleys were legion and seemed to change course of their own accord.

He spent a nervous moment adjusting his tie, then locked his apartment door behind him. He took a deep breath, descended the stairs, and set off down Albumuth Boulevard as the sky melted into the orange-green hue peculiar to Ambergris and Ambergris alone.

❧❧

We find this quality of illumination in almost all of Lake's paintings, but nowhere more strikingly than in the incendiary "The Burning House," where it is meshed to a comment on his fear of birds—the only painting with any hint of birds in it besides "Invitation to a Beheading" and "Through His Eyes" (which I will discuss shortly). "The Burning House" blends reds, yellows, and oranges much as "Invitation" blends greens, but for a different effect. The painting shows a house with its roof and front wall torn away—to expose an owl, a stork, and a raven that are burning alive, while the totality of the flames themselves form the shadow of a fire bird, done in a style similar to Lagach. Clearly, this is as close to pure fantasy as Lake ever came, a wish fulfillment work in which his fear of birds is washed away by fire. As Venturi wrote, "The charm of the picture lies in its mysteriously suggestive power—the sigh of fatality that blows over the strangely contorted figures." Here we may hold another piece of the puzzle that describes the process of Lake's transformation. If so, we do not know quite where to place it—and whether it should be placed near or far away from the puzzle piece that is "Invitation to a Beheading."

A less ambiguous link to "Invitation" can be found in the person of Voss Bender, the famous opera composer nee politician, and the tumult following his death—a death that occurred only three days before Lake began "Invitation." In later interviews, the usually taciturn Lake professed to hold Voss Bender in the highest regard, even as an inspiration (although, when I knew him, I cannot recall him ever mentioning Bender). More than one art historian, noting the repetition of Bender themes in Lake's work, has wondered if Lake obsessed over the dead composer. Perhaps "Invitation" represents a memorial to Voss Bender. If so, it is the first in a trilogy of such paintings, the last two, "Through His Eyes" and "Aria to the Brittle Bones of Winter," clear homages to Bender. —From Janice Shriek's *A Short Overview of The Art of Martin Lake and His Invitation to a Beheading*, for the *Hoegbotton Guide to Ambergris*, 5th edition.

❧

The dusk had a mingled blood-and-orange-peel scent, and the light as it faded left behind a faint golden residue on the brass doorknobs of bank entrances, on the coppery flagpoles outside the embassies of foreign dignitaries, and on the Fountain of Trillian, with its obelisk at the top of which perched a sad rose-marble cherub, one elbow propped atop a leering black skull. Crowds had gathered at the surrounding lantern-lit square to hear poets declaim their verse while standing on wooden crates. Nearby taverns shed music and light in equal quantities, the light breaking against the cobblestones in thick shafts, while sidewalk vendors plied passersby with all manner of refreshments, from Lake's ill-starred sausages to flagrantly sinful pastries. Few outside of Ambergris realized that the great artist Darcimbaldo had created his fruit and seafood portraits from life—stolen from the vendors, who arranged oranges, apples, figs, and melons into faces with black grapes for eyes, or layered crayfish, trout, crabs, and the lesser squid into the imperious visage of the mayor; these vendors were almost as popular as the sidewalk poets, and had taken to hanging wide-angle lanterns in front of their stalls so that passersby could appreciate their ephemeral art. Through this tightly-packed throng, occasional horse-and-carriages and motored vehicles lurched through like lighthouses for the drunk and disorderly, who would push and rock them at every opportunity.

Here, then, in the flushed faces, in the mixing of dark and light, in the swirling, shadowy facades of buildings, were a thousand scenes that lent themselves to the artist's eye, but Lake, intent on his map, saw them only as hindrances now.

And more than hindrances, for the difficulty of circumnavigating the crowds with his cane convinced Lake to flag down a for-hire motored vehicle. An old, sumptuous model, nicer than his apartment and prudently festooned with red and green flags, it had only two drawbacks: the shakes—almost certainly from watered down petrol—and a large, very dirty sheep with which he was forced to share the back seat. Man and sheep contemplated each other with equal unease while the driver smiled and shrugged apologetically (to him or the sheep?), his vehicle racing through the narrow streets. Nonetheless, Lake left the vehicle first, deposited at the edge of the requested neighborhood. The nervous driver sped off at top speed as soon as Lake had paid him. No doubt the detour to deliver Lake had made the sheep late for an appointment.

As for the neighborhood, located on the southeastern flank of the Religious Quarter, Lake had rarely seen one grimmer. The buildings, four and five stories high, had a scarcity of windows that made them appear to face away from him—inward, toward the maze of houses and apartments that contained his destination. Such stark edifices gave Lake a glimpse of the future, of the decay into which his own apartment building might fall when the New Art moved on and left behind only remnants of unkept promises. The walls were awash in fire burns, the ground level doors rotted or broken open, the balconies that hung precariously over them black with rust. In some places, Lake could see bones worked into the mortar, for there had been a time when the dead were buried in the walls of their own homes.

Lake took out his invitation, ran his hand across the maroon-gold threads. Perhaps it *was* all a practical joke. Or perhaps his host just wanted to be discreet. He wavered, hesitated, but then his conversation with Raffe came back to him, followed by the irritating image of Shriek's face as she said, "Interesting." He sighed, trembled, and began to walk between two of the buildings, uncomfortable in the shadow of their height, under the blank or cracked windows whose dust-covered panes were somehow predatory. His cane clacked against rocks, a plaintive sound in that place.

Eventually, he emerged from the alleyway onto a larger street, strewn with rubbish. A few babarusa pigs, all grunts and curved tusks, fought with anemic-looking mushroom dwellers for the offal. The light had faded to a deep blue colder in its way than the temperature. The distant calls to prayer from the Religious Quarter sounded like the cries of men drowning fifty feet underwater.

By the guttering light of a public lamp, Lake made out the name of the street—Salamander—but could not locate it on his map. For a long time, the darkness broken by irregularly-posted lamps, he walked alone, examining signs, finding none of the streets on his map. He kept himself from thinking *lost!* by trying to decide how best the surrounding shadows could be captured on canvas.

Gradually, he realized that the darkness, which at least had been broken by the lamps, had taken on a hazy quality through which he could see nothing at all. Fog, come off the River Moth. He cursed his luck. First, the stars went out, occluded by the weight of the shadows and by the dull, creeping rage of the fog. It was an angry fog, a sneering fog that ate its way through the sky, through the spaces between things, and it obscured the night. It smelled of the river: of silt and brackish water, of fish and mangroves. It rolled through Lake as if he did not exist. And because of this, the fog made Lake ethereal, for he could no longer see his arms or legs, could feel nothing but the cloying moisture of the fog as it clung to and settled over him. He was a ghost. He was free. There could be no reality to this fog-ridden world. There could be no reality to him while in it.

Lost and lost again, turning in the whiteness, not sure if he had walked forward or retraced his steps. The freedom he had felt turned to fear—fear of the unknown, fear that he might be late. So when he became aware of a dimly bobbing light ahead, he began to fast walk toward it, heedless of obstacles that might make him turn an ankle or fall on his face.

A block later, he came upon the source of the light: the tall, green-hooded, green-robed figure of an insect catcher, his great, circular slab of glass attached to a round, buoy-shaped lantern that swung below it. As with most insect catchers, who are products of famine, this one was thin, with bony but strong arms. The glass was so large that the man had to hold onto it with both gloved hands, while grasshoppers, moths, beetles, and ant queens smacked up against it, trying to get to the light.

The glass functioned like a sticky lens inserted into a circular brass frame; when filled with insects, the lens would be removed and placed in a bag. The insect catcher would then insert a new lens and repeat the process. Once home, the new catch would be carefully plucked off the lens, then boiled or baked and salted, after which the insects would hang from his belt on strings for sale the next day. Many times Lake had spent his evening tying insects into strings, using a special knot taught to him by his father.

Steeped in such memories and in the fog, his first thought was that this man *was* his father. Why couldn't it be his father? They would be ghosts together, sailing through the night.

His first words to the insect catcher were tentative, respectful of his own past.

"Excuse me? Excuse me, sir?"

The man turned with a slow grace to peer down at this latest catch. The folds of the insect catcher's robes covered his face, but for a jutting nose like a scythe.

"Yes?" The man had a deep, sonorous voice.

"Do you know which way to Archmont Lane? My map is no help at all."

The insect catcher raised one bony finger and pointed upward.

Lake looked up. There, above the insect catcher's light, was a sign for Archmont Lane. Lake stood on Archmont Lane.

"Oh," he said. "Thank you."

But the insect catcher had already shambled on into the fog, little more than a shadow under a lantern that had already begun to fade . . .

From there, it was relatively easy to find 45 Archmont Lane—unlike the other entrances to left and right, it suffered few signs of disrepair and a lamp blazed above the doorway. The numerals "4" and "5" were rendered in glossy gold, the door painted maroon, the steps swept clean, the door knocker a twin to the seal on the envelope—all permeated by a sudsy smell.

Reassured by such cleanliness, Raffe's advice still whispering in his ear, Lake raised the doorknocker and lowered it—once, twice, thrice.

The door opened a crack, light flooded out, and Lake caught sight of a wild, staring eye, rimmed with crusted red. It was an animal's eye, the reflection in its black pupil his own distorted face. Lake took a quick step back.

The voice, when it came, sounded unreal, falsified: "What do you want?"

Lake held up the invitation. "I have this."

A blink of the horrible eye. "What does it say?"

"An invitation to a—"

"Quick! Put on your mask!" hissed the voice.

"My mask?"

"Your mask for the masquerade!"

"Oh! Yes. Sorry. Just a moment."

Lake pulled the rubber frog mask out of his pocket and put it over his head. It felt like slick jelly. He did not want it next to his skin. As he adjusted the mask so he could see out of the eyeholes that jutted from the frog's nostrils, the door opened, revealing a splendid foyer and the outstretched arm of the man with the false voice. The man himself stood to one side and Lake, his vision restricted to what he could see directly in front of him, had to make do with the beckoning white-gloved hand and a whispered, *Enter now!* He walked forward. The man slammed the door behind him and locked it.

JEFF VANDERMEER

Ahead, through glass paneled doors, Lake saw a staircase of burnished rosewood and, at the foot of the stairs, a globe of the world upon a polished mahogany table with lion paws for feet. Candles guttered in their slots, the wavery light somehow religious. On the left he glimpsed tightly stacked bookcases hemmed in by generous tables, while to the right the house opened up onto a sitting room, flanked by portraits. Black drop clothes covered the name plate and face of each portrait: a line of necks and shoulders greeted him from down the hall. The smell of soap had faded, replaced by a faint trace of rot, of mildew.

Lake turned toward the front door and the person who had opened it—a butler, he presumed—only to find himself confronted by a man with a stork head. The red-ringed eyes, the cruel beak, the dull white of the feathered face, merged with a startlingly pale neck atop a gaunt body clothed in a black-and-white suit.

"I see that you are dressed already," Lake managed, although badly shaken. "And, unfortunately, as the natural predator of the frog. Ha ha. Perhaps, though, you can now tell me why I've been summoned here, Mister . . . ?"

The joke failed miserably. The attempt to discover the man's name failed with it. The Stork stared at him as if he came from a foreign, barbaric land. The Stork said, "Your jacket and your cane."

Lake disliked relinquishing his cane, which had driven off more than one potential assailant in its day, but handed both it and his jacket to the Stork. After placing them in a closet, the Stork said, "Follow me," and led Lake past the stairs, past the library, and into a study with a decorative fireplace, several upholstered chairs, a handful of glossy black wooden tables and, adorning the walls, eight paintings by masters of the last century: hunting scenes, city scapes, still lifes—all genuine and all completely banal.

The Stork beckoned Lake to a couch farthest from the door. The couch was bounded by a magnificent, if unwieldy, rectangular box of a table that extended some six feet down the width of the room. It had decorative handles, but no drawers.

As Lake sat, making certain not to bang his gimp leg against the table, he said, "Who owns this house?" to the Stork's retreating back.

The Stork spun around, put a finger to its beak, and said, "Don't speak! Don't speak!"

Lake nodded in a gesture of apology. The master of the house obviously valued his privacy.

The Stork stared at Lake a moment longer, as if afraid he might say something more, then turned on his heel.

Leaving Lake alone in his frog mask, which had become uncomfortably hot and scratchy. It smelled of a familiar cologne—Merri must have worn it since the festival and not cleaned it out.

Claustrophobia battled with a pleasing sense of anonymity. Behind the mask he felt as if he would be capable of actions forbidden to the arrogant but staid Martin Lake. Very well, then, the new Martin Lake would undertake an examination of the room for more clues as to his host's taste—or lack thereof.

A bust of Trillian stared back at him from a far table, its white marble infiltrated by veins of some cerise stone. Also on this table lay a book entitled *The Architect of Ruins,* above which stood the stuffed and bejeweled carcass of a tortoise. Across from it, upon a dais, stood a tele-scope which, in quite a clever whimsy, faced a map of the world upon the wall. Atlases and other maps were strewn across the tables, but Lake had the sense that these had been placed haphazardly as the result of cold calculation. Indeed, the room conveyed an aura of artificiality, from the burgundy walls to the globe-shaped fixtures that spread a pleasant, if pinkish, light. Such a light was not conducive to reading or conversation. Despite this, the study had a rich warmth to it, both relaxing and com-fortable.

Lake sat back, content. Who would have thought to find such refinement in the midst of such desolation? It ap-peared Raffe had been right: some wealthy patron wished to commission him, perhaps even to collect his art. He began to work out in his head an asking price that would be high enough, even if eventually knocked down by hard bargaining, to satisfy him. He could buy new canvases, replace his old, weary brushes, perhaps even convince an important gallery to carry his work.

Gradually, however, as if the opening notes of a music so subtle that the listener could not at first hear it, a tap-tap-tapping intruded upon his pleasant daydream. It trav-eled around the room and into his ears with an apologetic urgency.

He sat up and tried to identify the source. It came neither from the walls nor the door. But it definitely origi-nated from *inside* the room . . . and, although muffled, as if underground, from somewhere close to him. Such a gentle sound—not loud enough to startle him, just this cautious, moderate *tap*, this minor key *rap*.

He listened carefully—and a smile lit his face. Why, it was coming from the table in front of him! Someone or something was *inside* the table, gently rapping. What a splendid disguise for the masquerade. Lake tapped back. Whatever was inside the table tapped back twice. Lake tapped twice, answered by three taps. Lake tapped thrice.

A frenzied rapping and *smashing* erupted from the table. Lake sucked in his breath and pulled his fist back abruptly. A frisson of dread traveled up his spine. It had just occurred to him that the playful game might not be a playful game after all. The black table, on which he had laid his invitation, was not actually a table but an unadorned coffin from which someone desperately wanted to get out!

Lake rose with an "Uh!" of horror—and at that moment, the Stork returned, accompanied by two other men.

The Stork's companions were both of considerable weight and height, and from a certain weakness underlying the ponderous nature of their movements, which he remembered from his days of sketching models, Lake realized both were of advancing years. Both wore dark suits identical to that worn by the Stork, but the resemblance ended there. The larger of the two men—not fat but merely broad—wore a resplendent raven's head over his own, the glossy black feathers plucked from a real raven (there was no mistaking the distinctive sheen). The eyes shone sharp and hard and heavy. The beak, made of a silvery metal, caught the subdued light and glimmered like a distant reflection in a pool of still water.

The third man wore a mask that replicated both the doorknocker and the seal on Lake's invitation: the owl, brown-gold feathers once again genuine, the curved beak a dull gray, the human eyes peering out from the shadow of the fabricated orbits. Unfortunately, the Owl's extreme girth extended to his neck and the owl mask was a tight fit, covering his chins, but constricting the flesh around the neck into a jowly collar. This last detail made him hideous beyond belief, for it looked as if he had been denuded of feathers, revealing the plucked skin beneath.

The three stood opposite Lake across the coffin—the top of which had begun to shudder upwards as whatever was inside smashed itself against the lid.

"What . . . what is in there?" Lake asked. "Is this part of the masquerade? Is this a joke? Did Merrimount send you?"

The Owl said, "A very nice disguise," and still staring at Lake, rapped his fist so hard against the coffin lid that black paint rubbed off on his white glove. The thrashing inside the coffin subsided. "A good disguise for this masquerade. The frog, who is equally at home on land as in the water." The Owl's voice, like that of the Stork, came out distorted, as if the man had stuffed cotton or pebbles in his mouth.

"What," Lake said again, pointing a tremulous finger at the coffin, "is in there?"

The Owl laughed—a horrid coughing sound. "Our other guest will be released shortly, but first we must discuss your commission."

"My commission?" A thought flashed across his mind like heat lightning, leaving no impression behind: *Raffe was right. I am to paint their sex games for them.*

"It is an unusual commission and before I give you the details, you must resign yourself to it with all your heart.

You have no choice. Now that you are here, you are our instrument."

Raffe had never suggested that he must *become* part of the pornography, and he rebelled against the notion: this was too far to take a commission, even for all the money in the world.

"Sirs," Lake said, standing, "I think there has been a misunderstanding. I am a painter and a painter only—"

"A painter," the Owl echoed, as if it were an irrelevant detail.

"—and I am going to leave now. Please forgive me. I mean no offense."

He began to sidle out from behind the coffin, but stopped when the Raven blocked his path, a long gutting knife held in one gloved hand. It shone like the twin to the Raven's beak. The sight of it paralyzed Lake. Slowly, he sidled back to the middle of the couch, the coffin between him and these predators. His hands shook. The frog mask was awash in sweat.

"What do you want?" Lake said, guarding unsuccessfully against the quaver in his voice.

The Owl rubbed his hands together and cocked his head to regard Lake with one steel-gray eye. "Simply put, your commission shall be its own reward. We shall not pay you, unless you consider allowing you to live payment. Once you have left this house, your life will be as before, except that you shall be a hero: the anonymous citizen of the city who righted a grievous wrong."

"What do you want?" Lake asked again, more terror-stricken than before.

"A murder," croaked the Raven.

"An execution," corrected the Stork.

"A beheading," specified the Owl.

"*A murder?*" Lake shouted. "A murder! Are you mad?"

The Owl ruffled its feathers, said, "Let me tell you what your response will be, and then perhaps you can move past it to your destiny all the quicker. First, you will moan. You will shriek. You will even try to escape. You will say 'No!' emphatically even after we subdue you. We will threaten you. You will weaken. Then you will say 'No' again, but this time we will be able to tell from the questioning tone of your voice that you are closer to the reality, closer to the deed. And then the cycle will repeat itself. And then, finally, whether it takes an hour or a week, you will find yourself carrying out your task, because even the most wretched dog wants to feel the sun on its face one more day.

"It would save us all some time if you just accepted the situation without all the attendant fuss."

"I will not."

"Open the coffin."

"No!"

Lake, his leg encumbering him, leapt over the coffin table. He made it as far as the bust of Trillian before the Stork and the Raven knocked him to the floor. He twisted and kicked in their grasp, but his leg was as supple as a wooden club and they were much too strong. They wrestled him back to the coffin. The Stork held him face-down on the couch, the frog mask cutting so painfully into his mouth that he could hardly draw breath. The Raven yanked his head up and held the knife to his throat. In such a position, his eyeholes askew, he could see only the interior of the mask and a portion of the maroon-gold leaf ceiling.

From somewhere above him, the Owl said, with almost sensual sloth, "Accept the commission, my dear frog, or we shall kill you and choose another citizen."

The Stork, sitting on Lake, jabbed his kidneys, then punched in the same spot—hard. Lake grunted with pain. The Raven bent Lake's left arm back behind him until it felt as if his bones would break.

He shrieked. Suddenly, they were both off of him. He flipped over on his back, adjusted his mask, and looked up—to find all three men staring down at him.

"What is your answer?" the Owl asked. "We must have your answer now."

Lake groaned and rolled over onto his side.

"Answer!"

What did a word mean? Did a single word really mean . . . anything? Could it exile whole worlds of action, of possibility?

"Yes," he said, and the word sounded like a death rattle in his throat.

"Good," said the Owl. "Now open the coffin."

They moved back so that he would have enough space. He sat up on the couch, his leg throbbing. He grappled with the locks on the side of the coffin, determined to speed up the nightmare, that it might end all the more swiftly.

Finally, the latches came free. With a grunt, he opened the lid . . . and stared down at familiar, unmistakably patrician features. The famous shock of gray hair disheveled, the sharp cheekbones bruised violet, the intelligent blue eyes bulging with fear, the fine mouth, the sensual lips, obstructed by a red cloth gag that cut into the face and left a line of blood. Blood trickled from his hairline where he had banged his head against the coffin lid. Strange symbols had been carved into his arms as if he were an offering to some cruel god.

Lake staggered backward, fell against the edge of the couch, unable to face this final, dislocating revelation—unable to comprehend that indeed the Greens were right: *Voss Bender was alive.* What game had he entered all unwitting?

For his part, Bender tried to get up as soon as he saw Lake, even bound as he was in coils of rope that must cruelly constrict his circulation, then thrashed about again when it became clear Lake would not help him.

The Raven stuck his head into Bender's field of vision and caw, caw, cawed like his namesake. The action sent Bender into a hysterical spasm of fear. The Raven dealt him a cracking blow across the face. Bender slumped back down into the coffin. His eyelids fluttered; the smell of urine came from the coffin. Lake couldn't tear his gaze away. This was Voss Bender, savior and destroyer of careers, politicians, theaters. Voss Bender, who had been dead for two days.

"Why? Why have you done this to him?" Lake said, though he had not meant to speak.

The Stork sneered, said, "He did it to *himself*. He brought everything on himself."

"He's no good," the Raven said.

"He is," the Owl added, "the very epitome of Evil."

Voss Bender moved a little. The eyes under the imperious gray eyebrows opened wide. Bender wasn't deaf or stupid—Lake had never thought him stupid—and the man followed their conversation with an intense if weary interest. Those eyes demanded that Lake save him. Lake looked away.

"The Raven here will give you his knife," the Owl said, "but do not think that just because you have a weapon you can escape." As if to prove this, the Owl produced a *gun*, one of those sleek, dangerous-looking models newly invented by the Kalif's scientists.

The Raven held out his knife.

Senses stretched and redefined, Lake glanced at Voss Bender, then at the knife. A thin line of light played over the metal and the grainy whorls of the hilt. He could read the words etched into the blade, the name of the knife's maker: *Hoegbotton & Sons*. That the knife should have a history, a pedigree, that he should know more about the knife than about the three men struck him as absurd, as horrible. As he stared at the blade, at the words engraved there, the full, terrible weight of the deed struck him. To take a life. To snuff out a life, and with it a vast network of love and admiration. To create a hole in the world. It was no small thing to take a life, no small thing at all. He saw his father smiling at him, palms opened up to reveal the shiny, sleek bodies of dead insects.

"For God's sake, don't make me kill him!"

The burst of laughter from the Owl, the Raven, the Stork, surprised him so much that he laughed with them. He shook with laughter, his jaw, his shoulders, relaxed in anticipation of the revelation that it was all a joke . . . before he understood that their laughter was throaty, fey, cruel. Slowly, his laughter turned to sobs.

The Raven's hilarity subsided before that of the Owl and the Stork. He said to Lake, "He is already dead. The whole city *knows* he's dead. You cannot kill someone who is already dead."

Voss Bender began to moan, and redoubled his efforts to break free of his bonds. The three men ignored him.

"I won't do it. I won't do it." His words sounded weak, susceptible to influence. He knew that faced with his own extinction he would do *anything* to stay alive, even if it meant corrupting, perverting, destroying, everything that made him Martin Lake. And yet his father's face still hovered in his head, and with that image everything his father had ever said about the sanctity of life.

The Owl said, with remorseless precision, "Then we will flay your face until it is only strips of flesh hanging from your head. We will lop off your fingers, your toes, as if they were carrots for the pot. You, sir, will become a bloody red riddle for some dog to solve in an alley somewhere. And Bender will still be dead."

Lake stared at the Owl and the Owl stared back, the owl mask betraying not a hint of weakness.

The eyes were cold wrinkled stones, implacable and ancient.

When the Raven offered Lake the knife, he took it. The lacquered wooden hilt had a satisfying weight to it, a smoothness that spoke of practiced ease in the arts of killing.

"A swift stroke across the throat and it will be done," the Raven said, while the Stork took a white length of cloth and tucked it over Bender's body, leaving exposed only his head and neck. How many times had he drawn his brush across a painted throat, the model before him fatally disinterested? He wished he had not taken so many anatomy classes. He found himself counting and naming the muscles in Bender's neck, cataloging arteries and veins, bones and tendons.

The Raven and the Stork withdrew to beyond the coffin. The divide between them and Lake was enormous, the knife cold and heavy in his hand. Lake could see that tiny flakes of rust had infected the center of each engraved letter of *Hoegbotton & Sons*.

He looked down at Voss Bender. Bender's eyes bulged, bloodshot, watery. The man pleaded with Lake through his gag, words Lake could only half understand. *"Don't . . . Don't . . . what have I . . . Help . . ."* Lake admired Bender's strength and yet, as he stood over his intended victim, Lake found he *enjoyed* the power he wielded over the composer. To have such *control*. This was the man he had only the other day been cursing, the man who had so changed the city that his death had polarized it, splintered it.

Voss Bender began to thrash about and, as if the movement had broken a spell, Lake's sense of triumph turned to disgust, buttressed by nausea. He let out a broken little laugh.

"I can't do it. I *won't* do it."

Lake tried to drop the knife, but the Raven's hand covered his and, turning into a fist, forced his own hand into a fist that guided the knife down into the coffin, making Lake stoop as it turned toward Bender's throat. The Stork held Bender's head straight, caressing the doomed man's temples with an odd gentleness. The Owl stood aloof, watching as an owl will the passion play beneath its perch. Lake grunted, struggling against the Raven's inexorable downward pressure. Just when it seemed he must succumb, he went limp. The knife descended at a hopeless angle, aided by Bender's mighty flinch. The blade did only half the job—laying open a flap of skin to the left of the jugular. Blood welled up truculently.

As if the stroke had been a signal, the Raven and the Stork stood back, breathing heavily. Bender made a choking gurgle; he sounded as if he might suffocate in his own blood.

Lake rocked back and forth on his knees.

The Owl said to his companions, "You lost your heads. Do you want his blood on our hands?"

Lake stared at the knife and at Voss Bender's incompetently cut throat, and back at the knife.

Blood had obscured all but the "Hoeg" in "Hoegbotton." Blood had speckled his left hand. It looked nothing like paint: it was too bright. It itched where it had begun to dry.

He closed his eyes and felt the walls of the study rush away from him until he stood at the edge of an infinite darkness. From a great distance, the Owl said, "He will die now. But slowly. Very slowly. Weaker and weaker until, having suffered considerable pain, he will succumb some hours or days hence. And we will not lift a feather or finger to help him. We will just watch. *Your* choice remains the same—finish him and live; don't and die with him. It is a mercy killing now."

Lake looked up at the Owl. "Why me?"

"How do you know you are the first? How do you know you were chosen?"

"That is your answer?"

"That is the only answer I shall ever give you."

"What could he have done to you for you to be so merciless?"

The Owl looked to the Raven, the Raven to the Stork, and in the sudden quaver, the slight shiver, that passed between them, Lake thought he knew the answer. He had seen the same look pass between artists in the cafes along Albumuth Boulevard as they verbally dissected some new young genius.

Lake laughed bitterly. "You're afraid of him, aren't you? You're envious and you want his power, but most of all, you fear him. You're too afraid to kill him yourself."

The Owl said, "Make your choice."

"And the hilarious thing," Lake said. "The hilarious thing is, you see, that once he's dead, you'll have made him *immortal.*" Was he weeping? His face was wet under the mask. Lake watched, in the silence, the blood seeping from the wound in Bender's throat. He watched Bender's hands trembling as if with palsy.

What did the genius composer see in those final moments? Lake wondered later. Did he see the knife, the arm that held it, descending, or did he see himself back in Morrow, by the river, walking through a green field and humming to himself? Did he see a lover's face contorted with passion? Did he see a moment from before the creation of the fame that had devoured him? Perhaps he saw nothing, awash in the crescendo of his most powerful symphony, still thundering across his brain in a wave of blood.

As Lake bent over Voss Bender, he saw reflected in the man's eyes the black mask of the Raven, who had stepped nearer to watch the killing.

"Back away!" Lake hissed, stabbing out with the knife. The Raven jumped back.

Lake remembered how the man in his nightmare had cut his hand apart so methodically, so completely. He remembered his father's hands opening to reveal bright treasures, Shriek's response to his painting of his father's hands. Ah, but Shriek knew nothing. Even Raffe knew nothing. None of them knew as much as he knew now.

Then, cursing and weeping, his lips pulled back in a terrible snarl, he drew the blade across the throat, pushed down with his full weight, and watched as the life drained out of the world's most famous composer. He had never seen so much blood before, but worse still there was a moment, a single instant he would carry with him forever, when Bender's eyes met his and the dullness of death crept in, extinguishing the brightness, the spark, that had once been a life.

❧ ❧

"Through His Eyes" has an attitude toward perspective unique among Lake's works, for it is painted from the vantage point of the dead Voss Bender in an open coffin (an apocryphal event—Bender was cremated), looking up at the people who are looking down, while perspective gradually becomes meaningless, so that beyond the people looking down, we see the River Moth superimposed against the sky and mourners lining its banks. Of the people who stare down at Bender, one is Lake, one is a hooded insect catcher, and three are wearing masks—in fact, a reprisal of the owl, raven, and stork from "The Burning House." Four other figures stare as well, but they are faceless. The scenes in the background of this monstrously huge canvas exist in a world which has curved back on itself, and the details conspire to convince us that we see the sky, green fields, a city of wood, and the river banks simultaneously.

As Venturi writes, "The colors deepen the mystery: evening is about to fall and the river is growing dim; reds are intense or sullen, yellows and greens are deep-dyed; the sinister greenish sky is a cosmetic reflection of earthly death." The entirety of the painting is ringed by a thin line of red that bleeds about a quarter of an inch inward. This unique frame suggests a freshness out of keeping with the coffin, while the background scenes are thought to depict Lake's ideal of Bender's youth, when he roamed the natural world of field and river. Why did Lake choose to show Bender in a coffin? Why did he choose to use montage? Why the red line? Some experts suggest that we ignore the coffin and focus on the red line and the swirl of images, but even then can offer no coherent explanation.

Even more daring, and certainly unique, "Aria for the Brittle Bones of Winter" creates an equivalence between sounds and colors: a musical scale based on the pictorial intensity of colors in which "color is taken to speak a mute language." The "hero" rides through a crumbling graveyard to a frozen lake. The sky is dark, but the reflection of the moon, which is also a reflection of Voss Bender's face, glides across the lake's surface. The reeds which line the lake's shore are composed of musical notes, so cleverly interwoven that their identity as notes is not at first evident. Snow is falling, and the flakes are also musical notes—fading notes against the blue-black sky, almost as if Bender's aria is disintegrating even as it is being performed.

In this most ambitious of all his paintings, Lake uses subtle gradations of white, gray, and blue to mimic the progression of the aria itself—indeed, his brushstrokes, short or long, rough or smooth, duplicate the aria's movement as if we were reading a sheet of music.

All of this motion in the midst of apparent motionlessness flows in the direction of the rider, who rides against the destiny of the aria as a counterpoint, a dissenting voice. The light of the moon shines upon the face of the rider, but, again, this is the light of the *reflection* so that the rider's features are illuminated from *below*, not above. The rider, haggard and sagging in the saddle, is unmistakably Lake. (Venturi describes the rider as "a rhythmic throb of inarticulate grief.") The rider's expression is abstract, fluid, especially in relation to the starkly realistic mode of the rest of the painting. Thus, he appears ambivalent, undecided, almost unfinished—and, certainly, at the time of the painting, and in relation to Voss Bender, Lake *was* unfinished.

If "Aria for the Brittle Bones of Winter" is not as popular as even the experimental "Through His Eyes," it may be because Lake has employed too personal an iconography, the painting meaningful only to him. Whereas in "Invitation" or "Burning House," the viewer feels empowered—welcomed—to share in the personal revelation, "Aria . . . " feels like a closed system, the artist's eye looking too far inward. Even the doubling of image and name, the weak pun implicit in the painting's lake and the painter Lake, cannot help us to understand the underpinnings of such a work. As Venturi wrote, "While Lake's canvases do not generally inflict a new language upon us, when they do, we have no guide to translate for us." The controversial art critic Bibble has gone so far as to write, in reference to "Aria," "[Lake's] paintings are so many tombstones, so many little deaths—on canvases too big for the wall in their barely suppressed violence."

Be this as it may, there are linked themes, linked reson-ances, between "Invitation," "Through His Eyes," and "Aria . . . " These are tenuous connections, even mysterious connections, but I cannot fail to make them.

Lake appears in all three paintings—and only these three paintings. Only in the second painting, "Through His Eyes," do the insect catcher and Bender appear to-gether. The insect catcher does appear in "Invitation" but not in "Aria . . . " (where, admittedly, he would be a bizarre and unwelcome intrusion). Bender appears in "Aria" and is implied in "Through His Eyes," but does not appear, im-plied or otherwise, in "Invitation." The question becomes: Does the insect catcher inhabit "Aria" unbeknownst to the casual observer—perhaps even in the frozen graveyard? And, more importantly, does the spirit of Voss Bender in some way haunt the canvas that is "Invitation to a Behead-ing"? —From Janice Shriek's *A Short Overview of The Art of Martin Lake and His Invitation to a Beheading*, for the *Hoegbotton Guide to Ambergris*, 5th edition.

❧❧

Afterwards, Lake stumbled out into the night. The fog had dissipated and the stars hung like pale wounds in the sky.

He flung off his frog mask, retched in the gutter, and staggered to a brackish public fountain, where he washed his hands and arms to no avail: the blood would not come off. When he looked up from his frantic efforts, he found the mushroom dwellers had abandoned their battle with the pigs to watch him with wide, knowing eyes.

"Go away!" he screamed. "Don't look at me!"

Further on, headed at first without direction, then with the vague idea of reaching his apartment, he washed his hands in public restrooms. He sanded his hands with gravel. He gnawed at them. None of it helped: the stench of blood only grew thicker. He was being destroyed by something larger than himself that was still somehow trapped inside him.

He haunted the streets, alleys, and mews through the tail end of the bureaucratic district, and down a ways into the greenery of the valley, until a snarling whippet drove him back up and into the merchant districts. The shops were closed, the lanterns and lamps turned low. The streets, in the glimmering light, seemed slick, wet, but were dry as chalk. He saw no one except for once, when a group of Reds and Greens burst past him, fighting each other as they ran, their faces contorted in a righteous anger.

"It doesn't mean *anything*!" Lake shouted after them. "He's *dead*!"

But they ignored him and soon, like some chaotic beast battling itself, moved out of sight down the street.

Over everything, as he wept and burned, Lake saw the image of Voss Bender's face as the life left it: the eyes gazing heavenward as if seeking absolution, the body taking one last full breath, the hands suddenly clutching at the ropes that bound, the legs vibrating against the coffin floor ... and then *stillness*. Ambergris, cruel, hard city, would not let him forget the deed, for on every street corner Voss Bender's face stared at him—on posters, on markers, on signs.

Eventually, his crippled leg tense with a gnawing ache, Lake fell down on the scarlet doorstep of a bawdy house. There he slept under the indifferent canopy of the night, beneath the horrible emptiness of the stars, for an hour or two—until the Madame, brandishing curses and a broom, drove him off.

As the sun's wan light infiltrated the city, exposing Red and Green alike, Lake found himself in a place he no longer understood, the streets crowded with faces he did not want to see, for surely they all stared at him: from the sidewalk sandwich vendors in their pointy orange hats and orange-striped aprons, to the bankers with their dark tortoise-shell portfolios, their maroon suits; from the white-faced, well-fed nannies of the rich to the bravura youths encrusted in crimson make up that had outgrown them.

With this awareness of others came once again an awareness of himself. He noticed the stubble on his cheek, the grit between his teeth, the sour smell of his dirty clothes. Looking around him at the secular traffic of the city, Lake discovered a great hunger in him for the Religious Quarter, all thoughts of a return to his apartment having long since left his head.

His steps began to have purpose and speed until, arrived at his destination, he walked among the devotees, the pilgrims, the priests—stared speechless at the endless permutations of devotional grottos, spires, domes, arches of the cathedrals of the myriad faiths, as if he had never seen them before. The Reds and Greens made no trouble here, and so refugees from the fury of their convictions flooded the streets.

The Church of the Seven Pointed Star had an actual confessional box for sinners. For a long time Lake stood outside the church's modest wooden doors (above which rose an equally modest dome), torn between the need to confess, the fear of reprisal should he confess, and the conviction that he should not be forgiven. Finally, he moved on, accompanied by the horrid, gnawing sensation in his stomach that would be his burden for years. There was no one he could tell. No one. Now the Religious Quarter too confounded him, for it provided no answers, no relief. He wandered it as aimlessly as he had the city proper the night before. He thirsted, he starved, his leg tremulous with fatigue.

At last, on the Religious Quarter's outskirts, where it kissed the feet of the Bureaucratic District, Lake walked through a glade of trees and was confronted by the enormous marble head of Voss Bender. The head had been ravaged by fire and overgrown by vines, and yet the lines of the mouth, the nose, stood out more heroically than ever, the righteous eyes staring at him. Under the weight of such a gaze, Lake could walk no further. He fell against the soft grass and lay there, motionless in the shadow of the marble head.

It was not until late in the afternoon that Raffe found him there and helped him home to his apartment.

She spoke words at him, but he did not understand them. She pleaded with him. She cried and hugged him.

He found her concern so tragically funny that he could not stop laughing. But he refused to tell her anything and, after she had forced food and water on him, she left him to find Merrimount.

As soon as he was alone again, Lake tore apart his half-finished commissions. Their smug fatuousness infuriated him. He spared only the paintings of his father's hands and the oil painting he had started the day before. He found himself still entranced by the greens against which the head of the man from nightmare jutted threateningly. The painting seemed to contain the soul of the city in all its wretched depravity, for of course the man with the knife was himself, the smile a grimace. He could not let the painting go, just as he could not bring himself to finish it.

Sometimes what the painter chooses *not* to paint can be as important as what he does paint. Sometimes an absence can leave an echo all its own. Does Bender cry out to us by his absence? Many art critics have supposed that Lake must have met Bender during his first three years in Ambergris, but no evidence for this meeting exists; certainly, if he did meet with Bender, he failed to inform any of his friends or colleagues, which seems highly unlikely. Circumstantial evidence points to the stork-like shadow in "Invitation . . .", as Bender had a well-known pathological fear of birds, but since Lake *also* had a pathological fear of birds, I cannot agree. (Some also find it significant that it is Lake's apparent wish, upon his death, to be cremated in similar fashion to Bender, his ashes spread over the River Moth.)

In the absence of more complete biographical information about Lake following this period, one must rely on such scanty information as exists in the history books. As is common knowledge, Bender's death was followed by a period of civil strife between the Reds and the Greens, culminating in a siege of the Voss Bender Memorial Post Office, which the Reds took by force only to be bloodily expelled by the Greens a short time later.

Could this, then, as some critics believe, be the message of "Invitation"? The screaming face of the man, the knife blade through the palm, which is wielded by Death, who has just claimed Voss Bender's life? Perhaps. But I believe in a more personal interpretation. Given what I know about Lake's relationship with his father, this personal meaning is all too clear. For in these three paintings, beginning with "Invitation," we see the repudiation of Lake by his natural father (the insect catcher) and Lake's embrace of Bender as his real, artistic father.

What, then, does "Invitation" tell us? It shows Lake's father metaphorically leaving his son. It shows his son, distraught, with a letter sent by his father—a letter which contains written confirmation of that repudiation. The "beheading" in "Invitation to a Beheading" is the dethroning of the king—his father . . . and yet, when a king is beheaded, a new king always takes his place.

Within days of this spiritual rejection, Voss Bender dies and for Lake the two events—the rejection by his father, the death of a great artist—are forever linked, and the only recourse open to him is worship of the dead artist, a path made possible through his upbringing by a mystical, religious mother. Thus, "Through His Eyes" is about the death and life of Bender, and the metaphorical death of his real father. "Aria . . . " gives Bender a resurrected face, a resurrected life, as the force, the light, behind the success of the haggard rider, who is grief-stricken because he has buried his real father in the frozen graveyard—has allowed his natural father to be eclipsed by the myth, the potency, of his new father, the moon, the reflection of himself: Bender.

In the end, these paintings are about Lake's yearning for a father he never had. Bender makes a safe father because, being dead, he can never repudiate the son who has adopted him. If the paintings discussed become increasingly more inaccessible, it is because their meaning becomes ever more personal. —From Janice Shriek's *A Short Overview of The Art of Martin Lake and His Invitation to a Beheading,* for the *Hoegbotton Guide to Ambergris,* 5th edition.

The days continued on at their normal pace, but Lake existed outside of their influence. Time could not touch him. He sat for long hours on his balcony, staring out at the clouds, at the sly swallows that cut the air like silver-blue scissors. The sun did not heat him. The breeze did not make him cold. He felt hollowed out inside, he told Raffe when she asked how he was doing. And yet, "felt" was the wrong word, because he couldn't feel anything. He was unreal. He had no soul—would never love again, never *connect* with anyone, he was sure, and because he did not experience these emotions, he did not miss their fulfillment. They were extraneous, unimportant. Much better that he simply *be* as if he were no better, no worse, than a dead twig, a clod of dirt, a lump of coal. (Raffe: "You don't mean that, Martin! You can't mean that . . . ") So he didn't paint. He didn't do much of anything, and he realized later that if not for the twinned love of Raffe and Merrimount, a love that he need not return, he might have died within a month. While they were helping him, he detested their help. He didn't deserve help. They must *leave him alone.* But they ignored his stares of hatred, his tantrums. Worst of all, they demanded no explanations. Raffe provided him with food and paid his rent. Merrimount shared his bed and comforted him when his nights, in stark and terrifying contrast to the dull, dead, uneventful days, were full of nightmares, detailed and hideous: the white of exposed throat, the sheen of sweat across the shadow of the chin, the lithe hairs that parted before the knife's path . . .

The week after Raffe had found him, Lake forced himself to attend Bender's funeral, Raffe and Merrimount insistent on attending with him even though he wanted to go alone.

The funeral was a splendid affair that traveled down to the docks via Albumuth Boulevard, confetti raining all the way. The bulk of the procession formed a virtual advertisement for Hoegbotton & Sons, the import/export business that had, in recent years, grabbed the major share of Ambergris trade. Ostensibly held in honor of Bender's operas, the display centered around a springtime motif, and in addition to the twigs, stuffed birds, and oversized bumblebees attached to the participants like odd extra appendages, the music was being played by a ridiculous full orchestra pulled along on a platform drawn by draft horses.

This display was followed by the senior Hoegbotton, his

eyes two shiny black tears in an immense pale face, waving from the back of a topless Manzikert and looking for all the world as if he were running for political office. Which he was: Hoegbotton, of all the city's inhabitants, stood the best chance of replacing Bender as unofficial ruler of the city . . .

In the back seat of Hoegbotton's Manzikert sat two rather reptilian-looking men, with slitted eyes and cruel, sensual mouths. Between them stood the urn with Bender's ashes: a pompous, gold-plated monstrosity. It was their number—three—and Hoegbotton's mannerisms that first roused Lake's suspicions, but suspicions they remained, for he had *no proof.* No tell-tale feathers ensnarled for a week to now slowly spin and drift down from the guilty parties to Lake's feet.

The rest of the ceremony was a blur for Lake. At the docks, community leaders including Kinsky, Hoegbotton conspicuously absent, mouthed comforting platitudes to memorialize the man, then took the urn from its platform, pried open the lid, and cast the ashes of the world's greatest composer into the blue-brown waters of the Moth.

Voss Bender was dead.

✺✺

Is my interpretation correct? I would like to think so, but one of the great challenges, the great allures, of a true work of art is that it either defies analysis or provides multiple theories for its existence. Further, I cannot fully explain the presence of the three birds, nor certain aspects of "Through His Eyes" with regard to the ring of red and the montage format.

Whatever the origin of and the statement made by "Invitation to a Beheading," it marked the beginning of Lake's illustrious career. Before, he had been an obscure painter. After, he would be classed among the greatest artists of the southern cities, his popularity as a painter soon to rival that of Bender as a composer. Lake would design wildly inventive sets for Bender operas and thus be responsible for an interpretive revival of those operas. He would be commissioned, albeit disastrously, to do commemorative work for Henry Hoegbotton, de facto ruler of Ambergris after Bender's death. His illustrations for the Truffidians' famous *Journal of Samuel Tonsure* would be revered as minor miracles of the engraver's art. Exhibitions of his work would even grace the Court of Kalif himself, while nearly every year publishers would release a new book of his popular prints and drawings. In a hundred ways, he would rejuvenate Ambergris' cultural life and make it the wonder of the south. (In spite of which, he always seemed oddly annoyed, even stricken, by his success.) These facts are beyond doubt.

What, finally, was the mystery behind the letter held in the screaming man's hand, the mystery of "Invitation to a Beheading," we may never know. —From Janice Shriek's *A Short Overview of The Art of Martin Lake and His Invitation to a Beheading*, for the *Hoegbotton Guide to Ambergris*, 5th edition.

৵৽

A year passed, during which, as Raffe and many of his other friends remarked to Lake, he appeared to be doing penance for some esoteric crime. He spent long hours in the Religious Quarter, haunting back alleys and narrow streets, searching in the dirty, antique light for those scenes, and those scenes alone which best embodied his grief and the cruelty, the dispassionate passion, of the city he had adopted as his home. He heard the whispers behind his back, the rumors that he had gone mad, that he was no longer a painter but a priest of an as yet unnamed religion, that he had participated in some unspeakable mushroom dweller ritual, but he ignored such talk; or, rather, it did not register with him.

Six months after Bender's funeral, Lake visited 45 Archmont Lane, new cane trembling in his hand. He found it a burnt out husk, the only recognizable object amidst the ruins the bust of Trillian, blackened but intact. At first he picked it up, meaning to salvage it for his apartment, but as he wandered the wreckage for some sign of what had occurred there, the idea became distasteful, and he left the head in the rubble, its laconic eyes staring up at the formless sky. Nothing remained but the faint smell of carrion and smoke, rubbing against his nostrils. It might as well have been a dream.

Later that month, Lake asked Merrimount—lovely Merrimount, precious Merrimount—to move in with him permanently. He did not know he was going to ask Merri, but as the words left his lips they felt like the right words and Merri, tears in his eyes, said yes, smiling for the first time since before Lake's ordeal. They celebrated at a cafe, Raffe giving her guarded approval, Sonter and Kinsky bringing gifts and good cheer.

Things went better for Lake after that. Although the

nightmares still afflicted him, he found that Merrimount's very presence helped him to forget, or at least disremember. He went by Shriek's gallery and took all of his paintings back, burning them in a barrel behind his apartment building. He began to frequent the Ruby Throated Calf again. His father even visited in late winter, a meeting which went better than expected, even after the guarded old man realized the nature of his son's relationship with Merrimount. He seemed genuinely touched when Lake presented him with the twin paintings of his own hands covered with insects, and with that approval Lake felt himself awakening even more. There were cracks in the ice. A light amid the shadows.

Yet Ambergris—city of versions and virgins both—did its best to remind him of the darkness. Everywhere, new tributes to Bender sprang up, for Bender's popularity had never been so high. It could be said with confidence that the man might never fade from memory. Under the vengeful eyes of Bender statues, posters, and memorial buildings, the Reds and Greens gradually lost their focus and exhausted themselves. Some merged with traditional political factions, but many died in a final confrontation at the Voss Bender Memorial Post Office. By spring, Ambergris seemed much as it had before Bender's death.

It was in the spring, one chilly morning, that Lake sat down in front of the unfinished painting of the man from his nightmare. The man smiled with his broken teeth, as if in warning, but he wasn't fearsome anymore. He was lonely and sad, trapped by the green paint surrounding his face.

Lake had snuck out of bed, so as not to disturb his still-sleeping lover, but now he felt Merri's eyes upon his back. Gingerly, he picked up a brush and a new tube of moss-green paint. The brush handle felt rough, grainy, the paint bottle smooth and sleek. His grasp on the brush was tentative but strong. The paint smelled good to him and he could feel his senses awakening to its promise. The sun from the balcony embraced him with its warmth.

"What are you doing?" Merrimount mumbled.

Lake turned, the light streaming from the window almost unbearable, and said, with a wry, haunted grin, "I'm painting." ∾

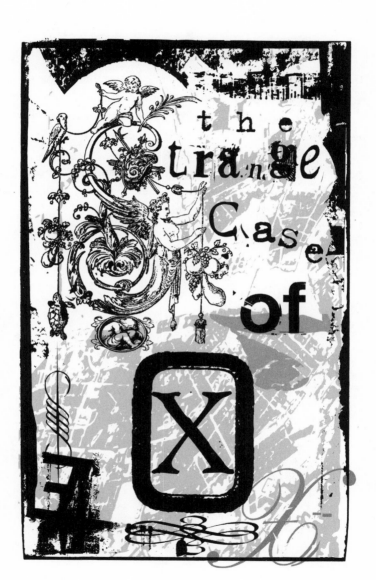

the Strange Case of X

The objects that are being summoned assemble, draw near from different spots; in doing so, some of them have to overcome not only the distance of space but that of time: which named, you may wonder, is more bothersome to cope with, this one or that, the young poplar, say, that once grew in the vicinity but was cut down long ago, or the singled-out court-yard which still exists today but is situated far away from here?
—*Vladimir Nabokov, "The Leonardo"*

 T WAS DAMP AND UNPLEASANT THAT morning, a methodical drizzle drifting down out of a dull gray sky. An ephemeral rain he might have thought, and yet the buildings, discolored and blackened in their sooty ranks, steeped in the smell of gasoline and hay mixed with dung, seemed to have been contoured and worn down by it, or at least *resigned* to it. The few passersby on the street, shivering against the cold, were subdued, anonymous, sickly; their shoes made wet *splacking* noises in the puddles. The sound, startling in the silence, depressed him and he was glad to reach his destination, glad when the glass doors closed behind him, shutting out the smell of the rain.

Inside, the ironic smell of mold and a sickly sweet sterility. He sneezed and put down his briefcase. He took off his galoshes, placed them by the door. Removed his raincoat, which looked as if the rain had worn grooves into it, and hooked it on the absurdly sinister coat rack with its seething gargoyle heads. He shook himself, stray water drops spraying in all directions, straightened his tie, and smoothed back his hair. Bemoaned the lack of coffee. Took a slip of paper from his jacket pocket. Room 54. Downstairs. Down many stairs.

He stared across the empty hall. White and gray tile. Anonymous doors. Sheets of dull lighting from above, most of it aflicker with abnormalities. And clocks—clocks created for bureaucrats so that they formed innocuous gray circles every few yards, their dull hands clucking quietly. He could only hear them because most of the staff was away for the holidays. The emptiness lent a certain ease to his task. He meant to take his time.

He picked up his briefcase and walked up the hall, shoes squeaking against the shiny tile floor; amazingly enough, the janitorial staff had recently waxed it.

He passed a trio of coat racks, all three banal in their repetition of gargoyles, and not at all in keeping with the dream of a modern facility dreamt by his superiors. Ahead, a lone security guard stood at attention in a doorway. The man, gaunt to the point of starvation, looked neither right nor left. He nodded as he passed but the guard did not even blink. Was the guard dead? The man smelled of old leather and tar. Would he smell of old leather and tar if he was dead? Somehow the thought amused him.

He turned left onto another colorless, musty corridor, this time lit reluctantly by oval light bulbs in ancient fixtures that might once have been brass-colored but were now a gunky black.

As he walked, he made a note of the water dripping from the ceiling; better that the janitors fix leaks than wax floors. Before you knew it, mold would be clotting the walls and mushrooms sprouting from the most unexpected places.

He approached a length of corridor where so much mud had been tracked in by way of footprints that a detective (which, strictly speaking, he was not) would have assumed a scuffle had broken out among a large group of untidy, rather frenzied and determined, individuals. Perhaps it had; patients often did not like being labeled patients.

The mud smell thickened the air, but entwined around it, rooted within it, another smell called to him: a fragrance both fresh and unexpected. He stopped, frowned, and sniffed once, twice. He turned to his left and looked down. In the crack between the wall and the floor, amid a patch of what could only be dirt, a tiny rose blossomed, defiantly blood-red.

He bent over the flower. How rare. How lovely. He blinked, took a quick look down the corridor to his right and left. No one.

Deftly, he plucked the rose, avoiding the thorns on the stem. Straightening up, he stuck the flower through the second buttonhole of his jacket, patted his jacket back into place, and continued down the corridor.

Soon he came to a junction, with three corridors radiating out to left, right, and center. Without hesitation, he chose the left, which slanted downward. The air quickly became colder, mustier, and overlaid with the faint scent of . . . *trout?* (Were cats hoarding fish down here?) The light grew correspondingly dimmer. He had hoped to review the files on "X" before reaching Room 54, but found it an impossible task in the gloom. (Another note to the janitors? Perhaps not. They were an unruly lot, unaccustomed to reprimand, and they might make it difficult for him. No matter: the words of his colleagues still reverberated in his head: "X is trapped between the hemispheres of his own brain"; "X is a tough nut to crack"; "X will make an excellent thesis on guilt.")

No matter. And although he appreciated the position of those who believed the building should be renovated to modern standards, he did enjoy the walk, for it created a sense of mystery, an atmosphere conducive to exploration and discovery. He had always thought that, in a sense, he shed irrelevant parts of himself on the long walk, that he became very much *functional* in his splendid efficiency.

He turned left, then right, always descending. He had the sensation of *things flitting* through the air, just on the verge of brushing his skin. A coppery taste suffused the air, as if he were licking doorknobs or bed posts. The bulbs became irregular, three burnt out for each buttery round glow. His shoes scraped against unlikely things in the darkness that lay beneath his feet.

Finally, he reached the black spiral staircase that led to Room 54. A true baroque monstrosity, in the spirit of the gargoyle coat racks, it twisted and turned crankily, almost spitefully, into a well of darkness dispelled only by the occasional glimmer of railing as it caught the light of the single, dull bulb hanging above it. Of all the building's eccentricities, he found the staircase the most delightful. He descended slowly, savoring the feel of the wrought-iron railings, the roughness of the black paint where it had chipped and weathered to form lichen-shaped patterns. The staircase smelled of history, of ancestors, of another world.

By the time he had reached the bottom, he had shed the last of his delight, his self-interest, his selfishness, his petty irritations, his past. All that remained were curiosity, compassion, instinct, and the rose: a bit of color; a bit of misdirection.

He fumbled for the light switch, found it, and flooded the small space beneath the stairs with stale yellow. He took out his keys. Opened the door. Entered. Closed it behind him.

Inside, he blinked and shaded his eyes against the brightness of superior lighting. Smell of sour clothes. Faint musk of urine. Had X been marking his territory?

When his eyes adjusted, he saw a desk, a typewriter, a bed, a small provision of canned goods, and a separate room for the toilet. Windows—square, of a thick, syrupy glass—lined the walls at eye level, but all that lay beyond them was the blankness of dirt, of mortar, of cement.

The writer sat behind the desk, on a rickety chair. But he wasn't writing. He was staring at me.

I smiled, put down my briefcase. I took off my jacket, careful not to disturb the rose, and laid it over the arm of the nearest chair.

"Good morning," I said, still smiling.

He continued to observe me. Very well, then, I would observe him back. We circled each other with our eyes.

From the looseness of his skin, I deduced that he had once been fat, but no longer; he had attained the only thinness possible for him: a condition which suggests thinness, which *alludes to* thinness, but is only a pale facsimile at best. He had too much skin, and broad shoulders with a barrel chest. His mouth had fixed itself half-way between a laconic grin and a melancholy frown. A new beard had sprouted upon his chin (it was not unkind to him) while above a slight, almost feminine, nose, his blue eyes pierced the light from behind the golden frames of his glasses. He wore what we had given him: a nondescript pair of slacks, a white shirt, and a brown sweater over the shirt.

What did he smell of? A strangeness I could not identify. A hint of lilacs in the spring. The waft of rain-soaked air on a fishing boat, out on the river. The draft from a door opening onto a room full of old books.

Finally, he spoke: "You are here to question me. Again. I've already answered all the questions. Numerous times." A quaver in the voice. Frustration barely held in check.

"You must answer them one more time," I said. Briefcase again in hand, I walked forward until I stood in front of his desk.

He leaned back in his chair, put his hands behind his head. "What will that accomplish?"

I did not like his ease. I did not like his comfort. I decided to break him of it.

"I'll not mislead you: I am here to decide your final disposition. Should we lock you away for five or ten years, or should we find some other solution? But do not think you can lie your way into my good graces. You have, after all, answered these questions several times. We must reach an understanding, you and I, based solely on your current state of mind. I can smell lies, you know. They may look like treacle, but they smell like poison."

I had given this speech, or a variant of it, so many times that it came all too easily to me.

"Let me not mislead you," he replied, no longer leaning back in his chair, "I am now firmly of the belief that Ambergris, and all that is associated with Ambergris, is a figment of my imagination. I no longer believe it exists."

"I see. This information does not in any way mean I will now pack up my briefcase and set you free. I must question you."

He looked as if he were about to argue with me. Instead, he said, "Then let me clear the desk. Would you like me to give you a statement first?"

"No. My questions shall provide you with the means to make a statement." I smiled as I said it, for although he need not hope too much, neither did I wish to drive him to despair.

X was not a strong man and I had to help him lift the typewriter off the desk; it was an old, clunky model and its keys made a metallic protest when we set it on the floor.

When we had sat down, I took out a pen and pad of paper. "Now, then, do you know where you are and why?"

"I am in a Chicago psychiatric ward because I have been hallucinating that a world of my creation is actually real."

"When and where were you born?"

"Belfont, Pennsylvania. In 1968."

"Where did you grow up?"

"My parents were in the Peace Corps—are you going to write all of this down again? The scribbling irritates me. It sounds like cockroaches scuttling."

"You don't like cockroaches?"

He scowled at me.

"As you like."

I pulled his file out of my briefcase. I arranged the transcripts in front of me. A few words flashed out at me: *fire . . . Trial . . . of course I loved her . . . control . . . the reality . . . It was in the room with me . . .*

"I shall simply check off on these previous interrogatories duplications of answers. I shall only write down your answers when they are new or stray from the previous truths you have been so kind as to provide us with. Now: Where did you grow up?"

"In the Fiji Islands."

"Where is that?"

"In the South Pacific."

"Ah . . . What was your family like? Any brothers or sisters?"

"Extremely dysfunctional. My parents fought a lot. One sister—Vanessa."

"Did you get along with your sister? How dysfunctional?"

"I got along with my sister better than Mom and Dad. Very dysfunctional. I'd rather not talk about that—it's all in the transcripts. Besides, it only helps explain why I write, not why I'm delusional."

In the transcripts he'd called it the "ten year divorce." Constant fighting. Verbal and some physical abuse. Nasty, but not all that unusual. It is popular to analyze a patient's childhood these days to discover that one trauma, that one unforgivable incident, which has shaped or ruined the life. But I did not care if his childhood had been a bedsore of misery, a canker of sadness. I was here to determine what he believed *now*, at this moment. I would ask him the requisite questions about that past, for such inquiries seemed to calm most patients, but let him tell or not tell. It was all the same to me.

"Any visions or hallucinations as a child?"

"No."

"None?"

"None."

"In the transcripts, you mention a hallucination you had,

when you thought you saw two hummingbirds mating on the wing from a hotel room window. You were sick, and you said, rather melodramatically, 'I thought if I could only hold them, suspended, with my stare, I could forever feast upon their beauty. But finally I had to call to my sister and parents, took my eyes from the window, and even as I turned back, the light had changed again, the world had changed, and I knew they were gone. There I lay, at altitude, on oxygen—'"

"—But that's not a hallucination—"

"—Please don't interrupt. I'm not finished: 'on oxygen and, suddenly, at my most vulnerable, the world had revealed the very extremity of its grace. For me, the moment had been Divine, as fantastical as if those hummingbirds had flown out of my mouth, my eyes, my thoughts.' That is not a hallucination?"

"No. It's a statement on beauty. I really did see them—the hummingbirds."

"Is beauty important to you?"

"Yes. Very important."

"Do you think you entered another world when you saw those hummingbirds?"

"Only figuratively. I'm very balanced, you know, between my logical father and my illogical mother. I know what's real and what's not."

"That is not for you to determine. And what do your parents do? No one seems to have asked that question."

"My dad's an entomologist—studies bugs, not words. My mom's an artist. And an author. She's done a book on graveyard art."

"Ah!" I took out two items that had been on his person when he had been brought here: a book entitled *City of*

Saints and Madmen and a page of *cartoon* images. "So you are a writer. You take after your mother."

"No. Yes. Maybe."

"I guess that would explain why we gave you a type-writer: you're a writer. I'm being funny. Have the decency to laugh. Now, what have you been writing?"

"'I will not believe in hallucinations' one thousand times."

"It's my turn to be rude and not laugh." I held up *City of Saints and Madmen.* "You wrote this book."

"Yes. It's sold over one million copies worldwide."

"Funny. I'd never heard of it until I saw this copy."

"Lucky you. I wish *I'd* never heard of it."

"But then, I rarely read modern authors, and when I do it is always thrillers. A straight diet of thrillers. None of the poetics for me, although I do dabble in writing my-self . . . I did read this one, though, when I was assigned to your case. Don't you want to hear what I thought about it?"

X snorted. "No. I get—got—over a hundred fan letters a day. After awhile, you just want to retire to a deserted island."

"Which is exactly what you have done, I suppose. Metaphorically." Only the island had turned out to be inhabited. All the worse for him.

He ignored my probing, said, "Do you think I *wanted* to write that stuff? When the book came out, all anyone wanted were more Ambergris stories. I couldn't *sell* any-thing *not* set in Ambergris. And then, after the initial clamor died down, I *couldn't* write anything else. It was horrible. I'd spend ten hours a day at the typewriter just making this world I'd created more and more real in this world. I felt like a sorcerer summoning up a demon."

"And this? What is this?" I held up the sheet of cartoons:

"Sample drawings from Disney—no doubt destined to become a collector's item—for the animated movie of my novella 'Dradin, In Love.' It should be coming out next month. Surely you've heard of it?"

"I don't go to the movies."

"What do you do then?"

"Question sick people about their sicknesses. It would be good to think of me as a blank slate, that I know nothing. This will make it easier for you to avoid leaving out important elements in your answers . . . I take it your books are grossly popular then?"

"Yes," he said, with obvious pride. "There are Dwarf & Missionary role-playing games, Giant Squid screen savers, a 'greatest hits' CD of Voss Bender arias sung by the Three Tenors, plastic action figures of the mushroom dwellers, even Ambergris conventions. All pretty silly."

"You made a lot of money in a relatively condensed period of time."

"I went from an income of $15,000 a year to something close to $500,000 a year, after taxes."

"And you were continually surrounded by the products of your imagination, often given physical form by other people?"

"Yes."

Razor-sharp interrogator's talons at the ready, I zeroed in, no longer anything but a series of questions in human guise, as elegant as a logarithm. I'd tear the truth right out of him, be it bright or bloody.

INTERROGATOR: When did you begin to sense something was amiss?

X: The day I was born. A bit of fetal tissue didn't form right and, presto!, a cyst, which I had to have removed from the base of my spine twenty-four years later.

I: Let me remind you that if I leave this room prematurely, *you* may never leave this room.

X: Don't threaten me. I don't respond well to threats.

I: Who does? Begin again, but please leave out the sarcasm.

X: . . . It started on a day when I was thinking out a plot line—the story for what would become "The Transformation of Martin Lake." I was walking in downtown Tallahassee, where I used to live, past some old brick buildings. The streets are all narrow and claustrophobic, and I was trying to imagine what it might be like to *live* in Ambergris. This was a year after the U.S. publication of *City of Saints and Madmen*, and they wanted more stories to flesh out a second book. I was pretty deep into my own thoughts. So I turn a corner and I look up, and there, for about six seconds—too long for a mirage, too short for me to be certain—I saw, clotted with passersby—the Borges Bookstore, the Aqueduct, and, in the distance, the masts of ships at the docks: all elements from my book. I could smell the briny silt of the river and the people were so close I could have reached out and touched them. But when I started to walk forward, it all snapped back into reality. It just snapped . . .

I: So you thought it was real.

X: I could smell the street—piss and spice and horse. I could smell the savory aroma of chicken cooking in the outdoor stoves of the sidewalk vendors. I could feel the breeze off the river against my face. The light—the light was *different*.

I: How so?

X: Just different. Better. Cleaner. *Different.* I found myself saying, "I cannot capture the quality of this light in paint," and I knew I had the central problem, the central question, of my character's—Martin Lake's—life.

I: Your character, you will pardon me, does not interest me. I want to know why you started to walk forward. In at least three transcripts, you say you walked forward.

X: I don't know why.

I: How did you feel after you saw this . . . image?

X: Confused, obviously. And then horrified because I realized I must have some kind of illness—a brain tumor or something.

I stared at him and frowned until he could not meet my gaze.

"You know where we are headed," I said. "You know where we are going. You may not like it, but you must face it." I gestured to the transcripts. "There are things you have not said here. I will indulge you by teasing around the edges for awhile longer, but you must prepare yourself for a more blunt approach."

X picked up my copy of *City of Saints and Madmen*, began to flip through it. "You know," he said, "I am so thoroughly sick of this book. I kept waiting for the inevitable backlash from the critics, the trickling off of interest from readers. I really wanted that. I didn't see how such success could come so . . . effortlessly. Imagine my distress to find this world I had grown sick of, waiting for me around the corner."

"Liar!" I shouted, rising and bending forward, so my face was inches from his face. "Liar! You walked toward that vision because it fascinated you! Because you found it irresistible. Because you saw something of the real world there! And afterwards, you weren't sorry. You weren't sorry you'd taken those steps. Those steps seemed like the only sane thing to do. You didn't even tell your wife . . . your wife"—he looked at me like I'd become a living embodiment of the coat rack gargoyles while I rummaged through the papers—"your wife Hannah that you had had a vision, that you were worried about having a brain tumor. You *told* us that already. Didn't I tell you *not* to lie to me?"

This speech, too, I had given many times, in many different forms. X looked shaken to the core by it.

X: Haven't you ever . . . Wouldn't you like to live in a place with more mystery, with more color, with more life? *Here* we know everything, we can do everything. Me, I worked for five years as a technical editor putting together city ordinances in book form. I didn't even have a window in my office. Sometimes, as I was codifying my fiftieth, my seventy-fifth, my one hundredth wastewater ordinance, I just wanted to get up, smash my computer, set my office on fire, and burn the whole rotten, horrible place down . . . The world is so small. Don't you ever want—need—more mystery in your life?

I: Not at the expense of my sanity. When did you begin to realize that, as you put it, "I had not created Ambergris, but was merely describing a place that already existed, that was real"?

X: You're a bastard, you know that?

I: It's my function. Tell me what happened next.

X: For six months, everything was normal. The second book came out and was a bigger success than the first. I was flying high. I'd almost forgotten those six seconds in Tallahassee . . . Then we took a vacation to New Orleans, my wife and me—partly to visit our friend and writer Nathan Rogers, and partly for a writers' convention. We usually go to as many bookstores as we can when we visit other cities—there are so many out-of-print books I want to get hold of, and Hannah, of course, likes to see how many of the new bookstores carry her magazine, and if they don't, get them to carry it. So I was in an old bookstore with Hannah—in the French Quarter, a real maze to get there. A real maze, which is half the fun. And once there, I was anxious to buy something, to make the effort worthwhile. But I couldn't find anything to buy, which was killing me, because sometimes I just have a compulsion to buy books. I guess it's a security blanket of sorts.

But when I rummaged through the guy's discard cart—the owner was a timid old man without any eyebrows—I found a paperback of Frederick Prokosch's *The Seven Who Fled* so I bought that.

I: And it included a description of Ambergris?

X: No, but the newspaper he had wrapped it in was a weathered broadsheet published by Hoegbotton & Sons, the exporter/importer in my novel.

I: They do travel guides, too?

X: Yes. You have a good memory . . . We didn't even notice the broadsheet until we got back to the hotel. Hannah was the one who noticed it.

I: Hannah noticed it.

X: Yeah. She thought it was a prank I was playing on her, that I'd put it together for her. I'll admit I've done that sort of thing before, but not this time.

I: You must have been ecstatic that she found it.

X: Wildly so. It meant I had physical proof, and an independent witness. It meant I wasn't crazy.

I: Alas, you never found that particular bookstore again.

X: More accurately, it never found us.

I: But Hannah believed you.

X: She at least knew something odd had happened.

I: You no longer possess the broadsheet, however.

X: It burned up with the house later on.

I: Yes, the much alluded to fire, which also conveniently devoured all of the other evidence. What was the other evidence?

X: Useless to discuss it—it doesn't exist anymore.

I: Discuss it briefly anyway—for my sake.

X: Okay. For example, later we visited the British Museum in London. There was an ancient, very small, almost miniature altar in a glass case in a forgotten corner of the Egyptian exhibits. Behind a sarcophagus. The piece wasn't labeled, but it certainly didn't look Egyptian. Mushroom designs were carved into it. I saw a symbol that I'd written about in a story. In short, I thought it was a mushroom dweller religious object. You remember the mushroom dwellers from *City of Saints and Madmen*?

I: I am familiar with them.

X: There were two tiny red flags rising from what would normally be considered incense holders. It was encrusted with gems showing a scene that could only be a mushroom dweller blood sacrifice. I took pictures. I asked an attendant what it was. He didn't know. And when we came back the next day, it was gone. Couldn't find the attendant, either. That's a pretty typical example.

I: You *wanted* to believe in Ambergris.

X: Perhaps. At the time.

I: Let us return to the question of the broadsheet. Did you believe it was real?

X: Yes.

I: What was the subject of the broadsheet?

X: Purportedly, it was put out by Hoegbotton on behalf of a group called the "Greens," denouncing the "Reds" for having somehow caused the death of the composer Voss Bender.

I: You had already written about Voss Bender in your book, correct?

X: Yes, but I'd never heard of the Greens and the Reds. That was the lucky thing—I'd put my story "The Transformation of Martin Lake" aside because

I was stuck, and that broadsheet unstuck me. The Reds and Greens became an integral part of the story.

I: Nothing about the broadsheet, on first glance, struck you as familiar?

X: I'm not sure I follow you. What do you mean by "familiar"?

I: Nothing inside you, a voice perhaps, told you that you had seen it before?

X: You think I created the broadsheet and then blocked the memory of having done so? That I somehow then planted it in that bookstore?

I: No. I mean simply that sometimes one part of the brain will send a message to another part of the brain—a warning, a sign, a symbol. Sometimes there is a . . . division.

X: I don't even know how to respond to such a suggestion.

I sighed, got up from my chair, walked to the opposite end of the room, and stared back at the writer. He had his head in his hands. His breathing made his head bob slowly up and down. Was he weeping?

"Of course this process is stressful," I said, "but I must have definitive answers to reach the correct decision. I cannot spare your feelings."

"I haven't seen my wife in over a week, you know," he said in a small voice. "Isn't it against the law to deny me visitors?"

"You'll see whomever chooses to see you after we finish, no matter the outcome. *That* I can promise you."

"I want to see Hannah."

"Yes, you talk a great deal about Hannah in the transcripts. It seems to reassure you to think of her."

"If she's not real, I'm not real," he muttered. "And I know she's real."

"You loved her, didn't you?"

"I *still* love my wife."

"And yet you persisted in following your delusions?"

"Do you think I wanted it to be real?" he said, looking up at me. His eyes were red. I could smell the salt of his tears. "I thought I'd dug it all out of my imagination, and so I have, but at the time . . . I've lost the thread of what I wanted to say . . . "

Somehow, his confusion, his distress, touched me. I could tell that a part of him *was* sane, that he truly struggled with two separate versions of reality, but just as I could see this, I could also see that he would probably always remain in this limbo where, in someone else, the madness would have won out long ago . . . or the sanity.

But, unfortunately, it is the nature of the writer to question the validity of his world and yet to rely on his senses to describe it. From what other tension can great literature be born? And thus, he was trapped, condemned by his nature, those gifts and talents he had honed and perfected in pursuit of his craft. Was he a good writer? The answer meant nothing: even the worst writer sometimes sees the world in this light.

"Do you need an intermission?" I asked him. "Do you want me to come back in half an hour?"

"No," he said, suddenly stubborn and composed. "No break."

I: After the broadsheet incident, you began to see Ambergris quite often.

X: Yes. I was in New York City three weeks after New Orleans, on business—this is before we actually moved north—and I stayed at my agent's house. I took a shower one morning and as I was washing my hair, I closed my eyes. When I opened them, rain was coming down and I was naked in a dirty side alley in the Religious Quarter.

I: Of New York?

X: No—of Ambergris, of course. The rain was fresh and cold on my skin. A group of boys stared at me and giggled. The cobblestones were rough against my feet. My hair was still thick with shampoo . . . I spent five minutes huddled in that alley while the boys called to passersby beyond the alley mouth. I was an exhibit. A curiosity. They thought I was a Living Saint, you see, who had escaped from a church, and they kept asking me which church I belonged to. They threw coins and books—books!—at me as payment for my blessings while I shouted at them to go away. Finally, I ran out of the alley and hid at a public altar. I was crowded together with a thousand mendicants, many wearing only a loin cloth, who were all chanting what sounded like obscure obscenities as loudly as they could. At some point, I closed my eyes again, wondering if I could possibly be dreaming, and when I opened them, I was back in the shower.

I: Was there any evidence that you'd been "away," as it were?

X: My feet were muddy. I could swear my feet were muddy.

I: You took something with you out of Ambergris?

X: Not that I knew of at the time. Later, I realized something had come with me . . .

I: You sound as if you were terrified.

X: I *was* terrified! It was one thing to see Ambergris from afar, to glean information from book wrappings, totally different to be deposited naked into that world.

I: You found it more frightening than New York?

X: What do you mean by that?

I: A joke, I guess. Tell me more about New York. I've never been there.

X: What's to tell? It's dirty and gray and yet more alive than any city except—

I: Ambergris?

X: I didn't say that. I may have thought it, but then a city out of one's imagination would have to be more alive, wouldn't it?

I: Not necessarily. I would have liked to have heard more about New York from your unique perspective, but you seem agitated and—

X: And it's completely irrelevant.

I: No doubt. What did you do after the incident in New York?

X: I flew back to Tallahassee without finishing my business . . . what did I say? You look startled.

I: Nothing. It's nothing. Continue. You flew back without finishing your business.

X: And I told Hannah we were going on vacation *right now* for two weeks. We flew to Corfu and had a great time with my Greek publisher—no one recognized me there, see? Hannah's daughter Sarah loved the snorkeling. The water was incredible. This clear blue. You could see to the bottom.

I: What did Sarah think of Ambergris?

X: She never read the books. She was really too young, and she always made a great show of being unimpressed by my success. I can't blame her for that—she did the same thing to Hannah with her magazine.

I: Did the vacation make a difference?

X: It seemed to. No more visions for a long time. Besides, I'd reached a decision—I wasn't going to write about Ambergris ever again.

I: Did Hannah agree with your decision?

X: Without a doubt. She saw how shaken I'd been after getting back from New York. She just wanted whatever I thought was best.

I: Did it work out?

X: Obviously not. I'm sitting here talking to you, aren't I? But at first, it did work. I really thought that Ambergris would cease to exist if I just stopped writing about it. But my sickness went deeper than that.

I: I'm afraid we have reached a point where I must probe deeper. Tell me about the fire.

X: I don't want to.

I: Then tell me about the thing in your work room first.

X: Can't it wait? For a little while?

The dripping of water had become a constant irritation for me. If it had become an irritation, then I had failed to concentrate hard enough. I had not left enough of myself outside the room. I wondered how long the session would last—more specifically, how long my patience would last. If we are to be honest, the members of my profession, then we must recognize that our judgments are based on our own endurance. How long can we go on before we simply cannot stand to hear more and leave the room? Often the subject, the patient, has nothing to do with the decision.

"I hear music down here sometimes," X said, staring at the ceiling. "It comes from above. It sounds like some infernal opera. Is there an opera house nearby, or does someone in this building play opera?"

I stared at him. This part was always difficult. How could it fail to be?

"You are avoiding the matter at hand."

"What did you think of my book?" X asked. "One writer to another," he added, not quite able to banish the condescension from his voice.

Oddly enough, the first novella in the book, 'Dradin, In Love,' had struck me, on a very primitive level, as evidence of an underlying sanity, for X clearly had conceptualized Dradin as a madman. No delusions there, for Dradin *was* a madman. I had even theorized that X saw Dradin as his alter ego, but dismissed the idea on the basis that it is unwise to match events in a work of fiction with events in the writer's life.

Of course, I did not think it useful to share any of these thoughts with X, so I shrugged and said, "It was fanciful in its way and yet some of its aspects were as realistic as any hard-boiled thriller. I thought 'Dradin, In Love' moved slowly. You devote an entire chapter to Dradin's walk back to his hostel."

"No, no, no! That's foreshadowing. That's symbolism. That's showing you the beginning of the carnage, in the form of the sleeping mushroom dwellers."

"Well, perhaps it did not speak to me as forcefully as you wanted it to. But you must remember, I was reading it for clues."

"As to my mental state? Isn't that dangerous?"

"Of course. To both questions. And I must also determine whether you most identify with Dradin, or the dwarf Dvorak, or the priest Cadimon, or even the Living Saint."

"A dead end. I identify with none of them. And all of them contain a part of me."

I shrugged. "I must gather clues where I can."

"You mean if I don't give you enough information."

"Some give me information without meaning to."

"I am not sure I can give you what you want."

"Actually," I said, picking up *City of Saints and Madmen*, "there was a passage in here that I found quite interesting.

Not from 'Dradin, In Love,' but from this other story, 'Learning to Leave the Flesh.' You make a distinction in the introduction to that tale—you call it a forerunner to the Ambergris stories, and yet in your response to the other interrogatories, you say the story was written quite recently."

"Surely you know that a writer can create a precursor tale after he has written the tales which come after, just as he can write the final tale in a series before he has finished writing the others."

The agitation had returned to X's features, almost as if he knew I was steering the conversation back toward my original objective.

"True, true," I said as I turned pages, "but there is one passage—about the dwarf, Davy Jones, that interests me most. Ah, here it is—where Jones haunts the main character. Why don't you read it for me?" I handed it to him and he took it with a certain eagerness. He had a good reading voice, neither too shrill nor too professional.

"Then he stands at the foot of my bed, staring at me. A cold blue tint dyes his flesh, as if the TV's glow has burnt him. The marble cast of his face is as perfect as the most perfect sentence I have ever written. His eyes are so sad that I cannot meet his gaze; his face holds so many years of pain, of wanting to leave the flesh. He speaks to me and although I cannot hear him, I know what he is saying. I am crying again, but softly, softly. The voices on the street are louder and the tinkling of bells so very light."

I: A very nice passage from a rather eccentric story. Whence came the dwarf? Did he walk out of your imagination or out of your life?

X: From life, at first. When I was going to college at the University of Florida, I had a classmate named David Wilson who was a dwarf. We took statistics together. He tutored me past the rough bits. He was poor but couldn't get enough financial aid and his overall grades weren't good enough for scholarships, so he rented himself out for dwarf-tossing contests at local bars. He had a talent for math, but here he was renting himself out to bars, and sometimes to the county fair when it came by. One day, he stopped coming to class and the next week I learned from a rather lurid article in the local paper that he had drunk himself to death.

I: Did he visit *you* at the foot of your bed?

X: You will remember I had resolved not to write about Ambergris ever again, but at first I resolved not to write at all. So I didn't. For five months I quit writing. It was hell. I had to turn a part of myself off. It was like a relentless itching in my brain. I had to unlearn taking notes on little pieces of paper. I had to unlearn making observations. Or, rather, I had to ignore these urges. And I was thinking about David Wilson because I had always wanted to write about him and couldn't. I guess I figured that if I thought about a story I couldn't write, I'd scratch the itch in a harmless way . . . And it was then that the dwarf—or what I thought was the dwarf—began to haunt me. He'd stand at the foot of the bed and . . . well, you read the story. To stop him from haunting me, I relented and sat down to write what became "Learning to Leave the Flesh."

I: But he was already Dvorak.

X: No. Dvorak was just a dwarf. He had nothing of David Wilson in him. David Wilson was a kind and gentle soul.

I: The story mentions Albumuth Boulevard.

X: Yes, it does. I had not only broken my vow not to write, but Ambergris had, in somewhat distorted form, crept back into my work.

I: Did you see the dwarf again?

X: One last time. When he became the manta ray. That was when I realized that I had brought something back from Ambergris with me. It scared the shit out of me.

I: The manta ray is mentioned in the transcripts, but never described. What is a manta ray?

X: You've never heard of a manta ray?

I: Perhaps under another name. What is it, please?

X: A big, black, saltwater . . . fish, I guess, but wide, with flaps like huge, graceful wings. Sleek. Smooth. Like a very large skate or flounder.

I: Ah! A flounder! You'll forgive my ignorance.

X: Clearly you devote too much time to your job.

I: You may be right, but to return to our topic: you were given *this fish* by the apparition of the dwarf. It is important that we get the symbolism correct.

X: No. The "fish" was the dwarf all along, leading me astray. The dwarf *became* the manta ray.

I: How did this happen?

X: I wish I could say Hannah saw it too, but she had fallen asleep. It was a cold night and I was wide awake, every muscle in my body tense. Suddenly, as before, Wilson stood at the foot of my bed. He just watched me for a long time, a smile upon his face . . . and then, as I watched him, he became like a pen-and-ink drawing of himself— only lines, with the rest of him translucent. And then this drawing began to fill up with cloudy black ink—like from a squid; do you know what a squid is?

I: Yes.

X: And when he was completely black with ink, the blackness oozed out from his body, until his body was eclipsed by the creature that looked exactly like a manta ray. It had tiny red eyes and it swam through the air. It terrified me. It horrified me. For the creature *was* Ambergris, come to reclaim me. The blackness of it was diffused by flashes of light through which I could see scenes of the city, of Ambergris, tattooed into its flesh—and they were *moving*. I hid under the covers, and when I looked again, in the morning, it was gone.

I: Did you tell your wife?

X: No! I should have, but I didn't. I felt as if I were going mad. I couldn't sleep. I could hardly eat.

I: This is when you lost all the weight?

X: Yes.

I: What, specifically, did you think this black creature was? Surely not "Ambergris," as you say?

X: I thought I'd brought it back with me from Ambergris—that it was a physical manifestation of my psychosis.

I: You thought it was a part of you. I know you were terrified by it, but did you ever, for a moment, consider that it might have been benevolent?

X: No!

I: I see. It has been my experience—and my experience is substantial—that some men learn to master their madness, so that even if all manner of horrific hallucinations surround them, they do not react. They live in a world where they cannot trust their senses, and yet no one would guess this from their outward composure.

X: I am not one of those men. It terrified me to my soul.

I: And yet such men find such hallucinations a blessing, for they give warning of a skewed reality. How much worse to slip—to just *slip*, as if slouching in your chair, as if blinking—into madness with no immediate sign that you had done so. So I call your visitation a helper, not a destroyer.

X: You may call it what you will. I did not think to call it anything.

I: What did you do to reestablish your equilibrium after this incident?

X: I began to write again. I spent eight to ten hours in my work room, scribbling away. Now I felt my only salvation *was* to write—and I wrote children's stories. "Sarah and the Land of Sighs" was the first one, and it went well. My agent liked it. It sold.

Eventually, it won an honorable mention for the Caldecott. So I wrote more stories, except that at some point—and I still can't recall when exactly—the manta ray reappeared.

I: What was your reaction?

X: Fear. Pure, unadulterated fear.

I: Tell me what happened.

X: I will not discuss what happened. But I have written about it—a story fragment you could call it.

X reached under the desk and handed me a thin sheaf of papers. I took them with barely disguised reluctance.

"Fiction lies."

X snorted. "So do people."

"I will read with reservations."

"Yes, and if you'll excuse me . . . " He trotted off to use the bathroom.

Leaving me with the manuscript. The title was "The Strange Case of X."

I began to read.

The man sat in the room and wrote on a legal sheet. The room was small, with insufficient light, but the man had good pens so he did not care. The man was a writer. This is why he wrote. Because he was a writer. He sat alone in the room which had no windows and he wrote a story. Sometimes he listened to music while he wrote because music inspired him to write. The story he wrote was called "Sarah and the Land of Sighs" and it was his attempt to befriend the daughter of his wife, who was not his own daughter. His children were his stories, and they were not always particularly well-behaved. "Sarah and the Land of Sighs" was not particularly well-behaved. It had nothing at all to do with the world of Ambergris, which was the world he wrote about for adults (all writers have separate worlds they write about, even those writers who think they do not have separate worlds they write about). And yet, when he had finished writing for the day and reread what he had written, he found that bits and pieces of Ambergris were in his story. He did not know how they had gotten into his story but because he was a writer and therefore a god—a tiny god, a tiny, insignificant god, but a god nonetheless—he took his pen and he slew the bits and pieces of Ambergris he found in his children's story. By this time, it was dusk. He knew it was dusk because he could feel the dusk inside of him, choking his lungs, moving across that part of him which housed his imagination. He coughed up a little darkness, but thought nothing of it. There is a little darkness in every writer. And so he sat down to dinner with his wife and her daughter and they asked him how the writing had gone that day and he said, "Rotten! Horrible! I am not a writer. I am a baker. A carpenter. A truck driver. I am not a writer." And they laughed because they knew he was a writer, and writers lie. And when he coughed up a little more darkness, they ignored it because they knew that there is a little more darkness in a writer than in other souls.

All night the writer coughed up bits of darkness—shiny darkness, rough darkness, slick darkness, dull darkness—so that by dawn all of the darkness had left him. He awoke refreshed. He smiled. He yawned. He ate breakfast and brushed his teeth. He kissed his wife and his wife's daughter as they left for work and for school. He had forgotten the darkness. Only when he entered his work room did he remember the darkness, and how much of it had left him. For his darkness had taken shape and taken wing, and had flown up to a corner of the wall where it met the ceiling and flattened itself against the stone, the tips of its wings fluttering slightly. The writer considered the creature for a moment before he sat down to write. It was dark. It was beautiful. It looked like a sleek, black manta ray with cat-like amber-red eyes. It looked like a stealth bomber given flesh. It looked like the most elegant, the wisest creature in the world. And it had come out of him, out of his darkness. The writer had been fearful, but now he decided to be flattered, to be glad, that he had helped to create such a gorgeous apparition. Besides, he no longer coughed. His lungs were free of darkness. He was a writer. He would write. And so he did—all day.

Weeks passed. He finished "Sarah and the Land of Sighs" and moved on to other stories. The writer kept the lights ever dimmer so that when his wife entered his work room she would not see the vast shadow clinging to the part of the wall where it met the ceiling. But she never saw it, no matter how bright the room was, so the writer stopped dimming the room. It did not matter. She could not see the gorgeous darkness. It glowed black, pulsed black, while he wrote below it. And although the creature had done him no harm, and he found it fascinating, the writer began to end his evenings early and take the work he had done for the day out into the living room. There he would reread it. He was a writer. Writers write. But writers also edit. And it was as he sat there one day, lips pursed, eyebrows knit, absorbed in the birth of his latest creation, that he noticed a very disturbing fact. Some of the lines were not his own. That one, for instance. The writer distinctly remembered writing, "Silly Sarah didn't question the weeping turtle, but, trusting its wise old eyes, followed it cheerfully into the unknown city." But what the writer read on the page was, "Silly Sarah didn't question the mushroom dweller, and when she had turned her back on it, it snatched her up cheerfully and took her back into Ambergris." There were others—a facet of character, a stray description, a place name or two. The story had been taken over by Ambergris. The story had been usurped by the city. How could this have happened? Writers work hard, sometimes too hard. Perhaps he had been working too hard. That must be it. The writer thought only fleetingly of the beautiful, sleek manta ray. All writers had a little darkness. And even though this darkness had become externalized, it was still a little darkness, and now it did not clot his lungs so. The writer thought of the calming silence of the creature, unmoving but for the slight rippling of its massive wings. The writer frowned as he sat in his chair and corrected the story. Could a thing his wife could not see impact upon the world? On him?

The next day, as the writer wrote, he felt the weight of the dark creature on his shoulder, but when he looked up, it still hugged the wall where it met the ceiling. He returned to his work, but found himself overcome by thoughts of Ambergris.

Surely, these thoughts said, he had abandoned Ambergris for too long. Surely, it was time to come home to the city. His pen, almost against his will, began to write of the city: the tendrils of vines against the sides of buildings in the burnt out bureaucratic district; the sad, lonely faces on the statues in Trillian Square; the rough lapping of water at the docks. The pen was a black pen. Writers write with black pens. He dropped the pen, picked up the blue pens he used for editing, but the best he could do when he tried to run a line through what he had written was to correct his poor spelling. Writers may write, writers may edit, but writers are lousy spellers. He looked up again at the manta ray. He looked up at the little darkness and he said, "You are dark, and all writers have a little darkness inside them, but not all writers have a little darkness outside them. What are you? Who are you?" But the darkness did not answer. The darkness could only write. And edit. As if it too were a writer.

Within a short time, the writer wrote only about Ambergris. He described every detail of its glistening spires as the morning light hit them. He described the inner workings of the Truffidian religion that so dominated the city's spiritual life. He described houses and orphans, furniture and social customs. He wrote stories and he wrote essays. He wrote stories disguised as essays. A part of him delighted in the speed with which the pen sped effortlessly, like a talented figure skater, across the ice of his pages. A part of him pompously scorned the children's stories he had worked on before his transformation. A part of him was so frightened that it could not articulate its fear. A part of him screamed and gibbered and raged against the darkness. It seemed that Ambergris was intent on becoming real in the world that the writer knew as real, that it meant to seduce him, to trick him into believing it existed without him. But a writer writes, even when he doesn't want to write, and so he wrote, but not without pain. Not without fear. For days he ate nothing and fed the creature on the wall everything, hoping it would reveal more of

Ambergris to him. His wife began to worry, but he impatiently told her everything was fine, was fine, was fine. He began to carry a notebook everywhere and write notes at embarrassing times during social events. Soon, he stopped attending social events. Soon, he slept in his work room, with the bright darkness above him as a night light. Being a writer is addictive. Being a writer is an addiction. All those words, all those words. The act of writing is addictive. But the writer didn't feel like a writer anymore. He felt like a drug addict. He felt like a drug addict in constant need of a fix. Could he be fixed? His fingers and his wrist were constantly sore and arthritic from over-use. His mind was a soaring, wheeling roller coaster of exhilaration and fear. When the creature held back information or he was forced away from his desk by his wife, or even the need to perform bodily functions, he had the shakes, the sweats. He vomited. He was sick with Ambergris. It was a virus within him, attacking his red and white blood cells. It was a cancer, eating away at corpuscles. It was a great, black darkness in the corner of his mind. He was drunk on another world. And the thing on the wall, always growing larger, stared down at him and rippled its wings and mewled for more food, which, of course, consisted of pieces of the writer's soul. His whole life had become a quest for Ambergris, to make Ambergris more real. He would find notes on the city that he did not remember writing scattered around the house, even the manuscripts of librettos by Bender, stories by Sirin. His wife thought he had written them, but he knew better. He knew that the creature on the wall had written them, and then left them, like bread crumbs, for him to follow, to the gingerbread house, to the witch, to death.

Finally, one wan autumn day, when the leaves outside the house had turned golden brown and distributed themselves across the lawn, the writer knew he must destroy the creature or be destroyed by it. He was sad that he must destroy it, for he knew that he was destroying a part of himself. It had come out of him. He had created it. But he was a writer. All writers write. All writers edit. All writers, surely must, on occasion, destroy their creations before their creations turn stale and destroy them. The writer had no love for the creature any more, only hatred, but he did love his wife and his wife's daughter, and he thought that such love was the greatest justification he could ever have for his actions. And so he entered his work room and attacked the darkness. His wife heard terrible sounds coming from the work room—a man crying, a man screaming, a man pounding on the walls; and was that the smell of fire?—but before she could come to his rescue, he stumbled out of the room, his features stricken with fear and failure. She asked what was wrong and held him tight. "All writers write," he whispered. "All writers edit," he muttered. "All writers have a little darkness in them," he sobbed. "All writers must sometimes destroy their creations," he shouted. But only one writer has a darkness that cannot be destroyed, he thought to himself as he clutched his wife to him and kissed her and sought comfort in her, for she was the most precious thing in his life and he was afraid—afraid of loss, afraid of the darkness, and, most of all, afraid of himself.

❧❧

After I had finished reading, I turned to the writer and I said gently, "This is an interesting allegory in its way, although the ending seems a little . . . melodramatic? And a most valuable document as well. I can see how people would like your writing."

The writer again sat behind the desk. "It's not an allegory. It's my life." He seemed defeated, as if he had reread the tale over my shoulder.

"Don't you think it is time to discuss the fire?" I asked him. "Isn't this all leading to the fire?"

He turned his head to one side, as if he were a horse resisting a bit. "Maybe. Maybe it is. When can I see my wife?"

"Not until we're done," I said. Who knew when he would see his wife? It has been my experience that I must lie, or half-lie, in order to preserve a certain equilibrium in the patient. I do not enjoy it. I do not relish it. But I do it.

"You have to understand," X said, "that I don't fully understand what happened. I can only guess."

"I will gladly accept your best guess."

But, despite my control, a grim smile played across my lips. I could smell his desperation: it smelled like yellow grass, like stale biscuits, like sour milk.

X: Gradually, the manta ray grew in size until it covered more than ten feet of the wall. As it grew, it began to change the room. Not visual changes, at first, but I began to smell the jungle, and then auto exhaust, and then to hear noises as of a bustling but far away city. Gradually, the manta ray fit itself into its corner and shaped itself to the wall like a second skin. It also began to smell—not a pleasant smell: like fruit rotting, I guess.

I: And this continued until . . . ?

X: Until one day I woke up early from a terrible nightmare: I was being stabbed in the palm by a man with no face, and I didn't even try to pull away while he was doing it . . . I walked into my work room and there was an intense light coming from the corner where the creature had been—just a creature-shaped hole through which Ambergris peeked through. It was the Religious Quarter—endless calls to prayer and lots of icons and pilgrims.

I: What did you feel?

X: Anger. I wanted to tear Ambergris apart stone by stone. I wanted to lead a great army and batter down its gates and kill its people and raze the city. Anger would be too weak a word.

I: And do you believe this was the manta ray's purpose when it gave you the gift of returning to Ambergris?

X: "Gift"? It was *not* a gift, unless you consider madness a gift.

I: Forgive me. I did not mean to upset you. Do you believe the curse visited upon you by the manta ray was given so you could destroy Ambergris?

X: No. I was always, deep down, at cross purposes with the creature. It destroyed my life.

I: What did you do when confronted by the sight of Ambergris? Or what do you think you did?

X: I climbed up the wall and over into the other world.

I: And this, according to the transcripts, is where your memory grows uncertain. Would it still be accurate to say your memory is "hazy"?

X: Yes.

I: Then I will redirect my questioning and come back to that later. Tell me about Janice Shriek.

X: I've already—never mind. She was a fan of my work, and Hannah and I both liked her, so we had let her stay with us—she was on sabbatical. She painted, but made her living as an art historian. Her brother Duncan was a famous historian—had made his fortune writing about the Byzantine Empire. Duncan was in Istanbul doing research at the time, or he would have come to see us too. He didn't get to see his sister much.

I: And you wrote them into your stories?

X: Yes, I'd given them both "parts" in stories of mine, and they'd been delighted. Janice even helped me to smooth out the art history portions of "The Transformation of Martin Lake."

I: Did you feel any animosity toward Janice Shriek or her brother?

X: No. Why would I?

I: Describe Janice Shriek for me.

X: She was a small woman, not as small as, for example, the actress Linda Hunt, but getting there. She was a bit stooped. A comfortable weight. About fifty-four years old. Her forehead had many, many worry wrinkles. She liked to wear women's business suits and she smoked these horrible cigars she got from Syria. She had a presence about her, and a wit. She was a polyglot, too.

I: You said in an earlier interrogation that "sometimes I had the feeling she existed in two places at once, and I wondered if one of those worlds wasn't Ambergris." What did you mean?

X: I wondered if I hadn't so much written her into Ambergris as she'd already had a life in Ambergris. What it came down to was this: Were my stories verbatim truths about the city, including its inhabitants, or were only the settings true, and the characters out of my head?

I: I ask you again: Did you feel any animosity toward Janice Shriek?

X: No!

I: You did not resent her teasing you about the reality of Ambergris?

X: Yes, but that's no motive for . . .

I: You did not feel envy that, if she indeed existed in both worlds, she seemed so self-possessed, so in control. You wanted that kind of control, didn't you?

X: Envy is not animosity. And, again, not a motive for . . . for what you are suggesting.

I: Had you any empirical evidence—such as it might be—that she existed in both worlds?

X: She hinted at it through jokes—you're right about that. She'd read all of my books, of course, and she would make references to Ambergris as if it were real. She said to me once that the reason she'd wanted to meet me was because I'd written about the real world. And once she gave me a peculiar birthday gift.

I: Which was?

X: *The Hoegbotton Travel Guide to Ambergris.* She said it was real. That she'd just ducked into the Borges Bookstore in Ambergris and bought it, and here it was. I got quite pissed off, but she wouldn't say it was a lie. Hannah said the woman was a fanatic. That of course she had created it, and that I'd better either take it as a compliment or start asking lawyers about copyright infringement.

I: Why did you doubt your wife?

X: The guidebook was so *complete*, so perfect. So detailed. How could it be a fake?

I: Surely a polyglot art historian like Janice Shriek could create such a work?

X: I don't know. Maybe. Anyway, that's where I got the idea about her.

I: Let us return to your foray into Ambergris. The manta ray had become an opening to that world. I know your memory is confused, but what do you recall finding there?

X: I was walking down Albumuth Boulevard. It was very chilly. The street was crowded with pedestrians and motor vehicles. I wasn't nude this time, of course, for which I was very appreciative, and I just . . . I just lost myself in the crowds. I didn't think. I didn't analyze. I just walked. I walked down to the docks to see the ships. Took in a parade near Trillian Square. Then I explored the food markets and, after awhile, I went into the Bureaucratic District.

I: Where exactly did it happen?

X: I don't . . . I can't . . .

I: I'll spare you the recall. It's all down here in the transcripts anyway. You say you saw a woman crossing the street. A vehicle bore down on her at a great speed, and you say you pushed her out of harm's way. Would that be accurate?

X: Yes.

I: What did the woman look like?

X: I only saw her from behind. She was shortish. Older than middle aged. Kind of shuffled as she walked. I *think* she was carrying a briefcase or port-folio or something . . .

I: What color was the vehicle?

X: Red.

I: And after you pushed the woman, what happened?

X: The van passed between me and the woman, and I was back in the real world. I felt a great heat on my face, searing my eyebrows. I had collapsed outside of my writing room, which I had set on fire. Soon the whole house would be on fire. Hannah had already taken Sarah outside and now she was trying to drag me away from it when I "woke up." She was screaming in my ear, "Why did you do it? Why did you do it?"

I: And what had you done?

X: I had pushed Janice Shriek into the flames of the fire I had set.

I: You had murdered her.

X: I had pushed her into the fire.

We faced each other across the desk in that small, barren room and I could see from his expression that he still did not understand the crux of the matter, that he did not understand what had truly happened to Janice Shriek. How much would I tell him? Very little. For his sake. Merciless, I continued with my questioning, aware that he now saw me as the darkness, as his betrayer.

I: How happy do you feel having saved the life of the woman in Ambergris in relation to the sadness you feel for having killed Janice Shriek?

X: It's not that simple.

I: But it is that simple. Do you feel guilt, remorse, for having murdered Janice Shriek?

X: Of course!

I: Did you feel responsible for your actions?

X: No, not at first.

I: But now?

X: Yes.

I: Did you feel responsible for saving the woman in Ambergris?

X: No. How could I? Ambergris isn't *real*.

I: And yet, you say in these transcripts that in the trial that resulted from Shriek's death, you claimed Ambergris was real! Which is it? Is Ambergris real or isn't it?

X: That was then.

I: You seem inordinately proud that, as you say, the first jury came back hung. That it took two juries to convict. Indecently proud, I'd say.

X: That's just a writer's pride at the beautiful trickery of my fabrication.

I: "That's just a writer's pride at the beautiful trickery of my fabrication." Listen to yourself. Your pride is ghastly. A human being had been murdered. You were on trial for that murder. Or did you think that Janice Shriek led a more real existence in Ambergris? That you had, in essence, killed only an echo of her true self?

X: No! I didn't think Ambergris was more real. *Nothing* was real to me at that point. The arrogance, the pride, was a wall—a way for me to cope. A way for me not to think.

I: How did you get certain members of the jury to believe in Ambergris?

X: It wasn't easy. It wasn't even easy to get my attorney to pursue the case in the rather insane way

I suggested. He went along with it because he believed the jury would find me crazy and remand me to the psychiatric care I'm sure he thought I needed. There seemed no question that I would be convicted—my own wife was a witness.

I: But you convinced some of the jurors.

X: Perhaps. Maybe they just didn't like the prosecuting attorney. It helped that nearly everyone had read the books or heard about them. And, yes, it proves my imagination is magnificent. The world was so complete, so fully-realized, that I'm sure it became as real to the jurors as that squalid, musty backroom they did all their deliberations in.

I: So you convinced them by the totality of your vision. And by your sincerity—that *you* believed Ambergris was real.

X: Don't *do* that. As I told you before we began, I don't believe in Ambergris anymore.

I: Can you describe the jurors at the first trial for me?

X: What?

I: I said, describe the jurors. What did they look like? Use your famous imagination if you need to.

X: They were jurors. A group of my peers. They looked like . . . People.

I: So you cannot remember their faces.

X: No, not really.

I: If you made them believe in Ambergris so strongly that they would not convict you, why can't you believe in it?

X: Because it doesn't exist! It doesn't exist, Alice! I made it up. Or, more properly, *it* made *me* up. It does not exist.

X was breathing heavily. He had brought his left fist down hard on the desk.

"Let us sum up, for there are two crucial points that have been uncovered by this interrogation. At least two. The first concerns the manta ray. The second concerns the jury. I am going to ask you again: *Did you never think that the manta ray might be a positive influence, a saving impulse?*"

"Never."

"I see it as a manifestation of your sanity—perhaps a manifestation of your subconscious, come to lead you into the light."

"It led me into the darkness. It led me into never never land."

"Second, there was no trial, except in your head as you ran from the scene of the crime. Your jurors who believed in Ambergris—they represented the part of you that still clung to the idea that Ambergris was real. No matter how you fought them, they—faceless, anonymous—continued to tell you Ambergris was real!"

"Now you are trying to trick me," X said. He was trembling. His right hand had closed around his left wrist in a vice-like grip.

"Do you remember how you got here?" I asked.

"No. Probably through the front door, don't you think?"

"Don't you find it odd that you don't remember?"

"In comparison to what?" He laughed bitterly.

I stared at him. I said nothing. I think it was my silence, in which I hoped for some last minute redemption, that forced him to the conclusion my decision would not be favorable.

"I don't believe in Ambergris. How many times do I have to say it?" He was sweating now. He was shaking.

When I did not reply, he said, "Are there any more questions?"

I shook my head. I put the transcripts back in my briefcase and locked it. I pushed the chair back and got up.

"Then I am free to go. My wife is probably waiting in—"

"No," I said, putting on my jacket. "You are not free to go."

He rose quickly, again pounded his fist against the desk. "But I've told you, I've told you—I don't believe in my fantasy! I'm rational! I'm logical! *I'm over it!*"

"But you see," I said, with as much kindness as I could muster as I opened the door, "that's precisely the problem. This *is* Ambergris. You are *in* Ambergris."

The expression on X's face was quite indescribable.

As he locked the door behind him and ascended the staircase, he realized that it was all a horrible shame. Clearly, the writer had lost contact with reality, no matter how desperately that reality had struggled to get his attention. And that poor woman, still unidentified, that X had pushed into the path of a motored vehicle (he hadn't quite had it in him to tell X just how faulty his memory was)—she was proof enough of his illness. In the end, the fantasy had been too strong. And what a fantasy it was! A place where people flew and "made movies." Disney, tee-vee, New York City, New Orleans, Chicago. It was all very convincing and, within limits, it made sense—to X. But as he well knew, writers were a shifty lot—not to be trusted—and there were far too many lunatics on the streets already. How would X have coped with freedom anyhow? With his twin fantasy of literary success and a happy marriage revealed as a lie? (And there were X's last words as the door had closed: "All writers write. All writers edit. All writers have a little darkness in them.")

They had found no record of him in the city upon his arrest, so he had probably come from abroad—from the Southern Isles, perhaps—carrying his pathetic book, no doubt self-published by "Spectra," a vanity operation by the sound of it. He knew those sounds himself from his modest dabbling in the written arts. In fact, he reflected, the only real benefit of the session, between the previous transcripts and the conversation itself, had been to his fiction; he now had some very interesting elements with which to compose a fantasy of his own. Why, he could already see that the report on this session would be a kind of fiction itself, as he had long since concluded that no delusion could ever truly be understood. He might even tell the story in first *and* third person, to both personalize and distance the events.

When he reached the place where he had plucked the rose, he took it from his buttonhole and stuck its stem back in the crack. He regretted having picked it. But even if he had not, it would have been doomed to a short, brutish life in the darkness.

Out on the street the rain had stopped, although the moist rain smell lingered, and the noontime calls to prayer from the Religious Quarter echoed through the narrow streets. He could almost taste the wonderful savoriness of the hot sausage sold by the sidewalk vendors. After lunch, he would take in some entertainment. The Manzikert Opera Theater had decided to do a Voss Bender revival this season, and with any luck he could still catch the matinee and be home to the wife before dinner. With this thought uppermost in his mind, he stepped out onto the street and was soon lost to view amongst the lunchtime crowds. ❧

Voss Bender Memorial Mental Institute
1314 Albumuth Boulevard
Ambergris I13-24

Doctor William Simpkin
Central Records Office
Psychiatric Studies Division
c/o Trillian Memorial Hospital
8181 Sallowskull Avenue
Ambergris M14-518

Dear Doctor Simpkin:

As requested, enclosed please find all personal
effects left behind by X, save for his pen, a
blank notebook, and that tattered paperback
copy of City of Saints & Madmen he insisted on
clasping to his bosom like a talisman. I have
kept these items for my personal collection.
(You may recall that I have an extensive
selection of souvenirs from my many years here.
If you should ever again visit our humble
outpost of insanity, I will be happy to give
you a guided tour as I have recently begun
to catalogue my collection in anticipation of
the day when we will receive funding for its
proper display. Each item comes complete with
an exhibit card explaining the history of
the item. If I may say so, the organization and
presentation are exquisite. I am lacking only a
display case and monies for maintenance.)

Most of X's possessions consisted of various
writings, which either originated with him or
which he acquired during that brief period
when he walked the streets of Ambergris a free
man. As you requested, I have carefully read

through all of these writings, despite the
time it has taken away from those other of my
patients who have had the courtesy to remain
in my care. I now present my findings to you:

(1) X's Notes. The notes typed up on the following
pages came from crumpled sheets of paper
found in the wastepaper basket. They consist
of a series of reminders, observations, word
sketches, drawings (X has had a lot of free time
to perfect his doodling), and a short account
of one of X's dreams that I like to call "The
Machine." The notes seem self-explanatory. "The
Machine," on the other hand, demonstrates an
extreme paranoia directed toward the gray
caps. One must learn not to read too much
into nightmares-- my own nightmares usually
concern having to close down vital services due
to lack of funds--but I would hazard the guess
that X suffers from anxiety about his studies.
This would be consistent with his case history.

(2) The Release of Belacqua. Although an
attached note attributed this manuscript to
Sirin, a secretary at his office assured us
via telephone (ours being broken, I walked
five blocks to a colleague's house to use his)
that Sirin did not write it. Therefore, we must
conclude that X wrote it himself. Nothing in the
story sheds light on X's whereabouts, however. If
anything, the protagonist is as puzzled about
X as we are. The cold little reference to Janice
Shriek puts the lie to X's protestations that
he felt remorse for his actions. Throughout the
story, X communicates to the reader "between the
lines" in a rather pathetic manner. Such self-
consciousness has clearly corrupted his writing.
(Consulting my abridged version of Bender's

Trillian, I find no mention of a "Belacqua,"
although this is a point of curiosity only.)

(3) King Squid by Frederick Madnok. At first,
I assumed that this slim pamphlet had been
privately printed by X under a pseudonym.
However, further inquiries revealed that
Madnok does indeed exist and that for a few
months he hawked this pamphlet, among other
self-published oddities, on the corner of
Albumuth Boulevard and Beak Drive. His present
whereabouts are unknown. Although our records
could be incorrect, it appears he was never a
patient here. (You may wish to use the impressive
resources at your disposal to verify this
fact, as many of our records have been damaged
by water seepage. In many cases, your copies
should now be considered the originals.) Given
that King Squid did not originate with X and
there are no margin notes from him, I cannot
extrapolate much about X from it. On a surface
level, however, one might assume that X envied
the transformative qualities of Madnok's prose.
Perhaps he saw Madnok as a kindred spirit.
Again, we lack the personnel to perform the
kind of analysis necessary to make such a third-
party document "speak" to us about X's condition.

(4) The Hoegbotton Family History. This document,
although fascinating to me personally, seems at
best something X may have read as background
for enjoyment of item (5), below. It was found
stuffed between his mattress and bed frame.
There is a possibility it belonged to the former
occupant of the cell, a Mr. M. Kodfan.

(5) The Cage. I also checked with Sirin's
secretary about this manuscript, given X's
scrawled note of attribution. (I wish I had

discovered said attribution before having
returned to the asylum; as it was, I had to
turn right back around to use my colleague's
telephone.) This time, she confirmed that Sirin
had indeed written the story. She found it
remarkable that X had galleys, given that the
story is due to be released next month as part
of Sirin's new collection. She was most anxious
that we return the manuscript to Sirin. I told
her this was impossible until I had secured
your approval. As for any connection between
Sirin and X, it hardly seems credible--more the
case of an "admirer and an admiral," as they say.
While X's possession of the story confirms his
obsession with the gray caps, I'm not sure that
The Cage is otherwise of much use to us. Sirin's
characterization of Hoegbotton struck me as
perverse. But, then, I am not a fan of Sirin's
fiction, although I did much admire his book of
verse, "The Metamorphosis of Butterflies."

(6) In the Hours After Death. X tore this story
by Nicholas Sporlender out of last month's
Burning Leaves, the creative journal enjoyed
by so many of our patrons. I can confirm that
the pages did indeed originate with our library
copy. Several other pages had been ripped from
the journal, but none of these pages remained
in X's room. I want to discuss the absent pages
first because they perplex me. In comparing a
complete copy of Burning Leaves with the torn
one, I found that X may have absconded with an
advertisement for women's underthings, an article
on the origins of water puppetry, a caricature
of the current Truffidian Antechamber, a short,
experimental (and completely incomprehensible)
fiction by Sarah Beeside entitled "Bedbugs and
Ballyhoo," and yet another advertisement for
women's underthings. (Sticking to the letter of

your instructions, I have not included these
items since you specifically asked for what X
left behind, not what-he-didn't-leave-behind-
but-had-torn-out-at-some-point-from-a-creative-
arts-journal. I must note that we often follow
the letter of instructions due to lack of
funding; anything that deviates, other than our
incarcerated deviants, costs money.) "In the Hours
After Death" itself sheds no enduring light on
X's condition. It points to a simple death wish,
by which wish we would expect to have found X's
corpse, not the absence of his corpse, in his cell
that very interesting morning when I decided, on
a whim, to talk with X before the appointed hour.

(7) Encrypted story. Several pages, folded and
stuck inside City of Saints & Madmen, consisted
of a long series of numbers. Rather than bore you
with them, I took an amateur's stab at deciphering
what appeared to be a code, even though we are
really not prepared here at V.B.M.M.I. to interpret
encrypted materials. (You will recall that we lost
our funding for even such a basic necessity as
a frenziologist last year; perhaps you could put
in a word with Flauntimer?). After much tortuous
experimentation, I discovered that each number
series referred to a page, paragraph, line, and
word in X's book. I then decoded the manuscript in
some haste, keeping in mind the urgency of your
request for the materials to be examined by your
investigator at Central Records. Some of the words
I have translated seem to make no sense--in my
haste I have made errors--but the last paragraph
has escaped my efforts completely. It seems to
draw on some other type of decryption. What seems
clear from what I have decrypted, however, is
that X seeks to make a parallel between the gray
caps and us, his "captors" at the Institute. Such a
crude comparison is spurred on by a childish need

for revenge. I am sure your expert will have his
own theories.

(8) The Exchange. This festival story by Nicholas
Sporlender has been in X's possession for some
time, but he did not arrive with it. Someone
handed it to him, I believe. He has scrawled
some notes on the envelope the booklet came in,
specifically, "Sporlender hated Verden by the
end. But I don't yet hate Eric. I wonder if that
'echo' will ever appear, or if it's simply not a
one-for-one resonance." X then carefully cut the
pages out, glued them to larger sheets, and added
his own typewritten notes. (I am also intrigued
by X's insinuation that he met Madnok while in
this institution. Again, I don't see how this
could be--no patient by that name ever stayed
with us.) Clearly, I should have given X more to
do in his spare time.

(9) Learning to Leave the Flesh. Although I took
this story from X at the beginning of his sojourn
in this delightful place, I include it as an item
of potential interest, having carefully cut it
from X's collection. I have read the story several
times in hopes of deciphering it. It, I feel, far
more than even the typed numbers, holds some
clue to X's whereabouts. The story is luminous--it
almost seems to glow as one reads it. I must admit
to sending it to you mostly to be rid of it.

(10) The Ambergris Glossary. This item, received
by X via mail the week before his disappearance,
is a strange alliance of the original entries
from Duncan Shriek's The Early History of
Ambergris and X's added entries, so intertwined
that it will require a detailed comparison to
determine the extent of X's changes. I will leave
this analysis in your capable hands since mine

are full of such interesting decisions as which sub-department to shut down due to crumbling facilities: farkology or incrementology.

The facts in this case remain the same, my good Simpkin: X gone with no trace of how he accomplished the feat and no sign of where he might have sought refuge. The most telling clue is that he left his beloved copy of City of Saints & Madmen behind. But we've certainly made no further progress in our investigations. (Some wags among the long-suffering kitchen staff--who last week resorted to poaching from the nearby zoo for supplies--have noted that X took all pens but one and conclude he must have "written his way out." It's as good a theory as any at this point.) It seems of little use to note that most of these written materials deal with some form of transformation, a common enough concern of those who wish to leave their insanity behind.

As soon as I can buy a new typewriter ribbon, I will of course submit a full report to the Board. For now, however, the Strange Case of X, as it might be termed, remains open.

Sincerely,

Dr V.

P.S. I said the notebook I kept is blank, and it is, but on the inside back cover, I found scrawled the following words: "Zamilon," "convergence," and "the green lights of the towers." Could they be a clue, I wonder? The words mean nothing to me in this context.

P.P.S. When possible, please return X's possessions--for my display.

NOTES

-A writer who is having difficulties with his
masterwork--too old or just unmotivated? Read H's
Portrait of the Artist as an Old Man, first.

-A writer in a prison. The prison is his own
story. How can he make himself free?

-Ask the attendant for a better night lamp,
not to mention another typewriter ribbon.

-Tonsure kept two journals, one that he
wanted to be found. Why, really, would it be
important for a fake account to be found?

-Always exercise when you first get up in the
morning!

-Could easily write a
biography of Voss Bender
while in here. Start
with childhood. Picture
him this way: in the
Truffidian Cathedral,
surrounded by people yet
utterly alone, sitting
in the place of honor at
the head of the altar,
his left leg crossed
over his right, an arm
and fist supporting his
head--a wild shock of
black hair that goes
to his shoulders, the olive skin, the darkness
under the eyes, accentuating the darkness
of the eyes themselves. These are eyes that
see a lot without seeming to. The thick lips,

the hint of a smile on those lips, while all around the congregation continues to chant. His foot is tapping. But the tapping foot is not a sign of boredom. Inside his head, he is already, at 12, composing an opera. Beside him-- shriveled, white-haired grandfather, vacant sad-eyed mother, a father to whom everything in the world is cause for indifference. As the ceremony progresses and each of the relatives comes up to say something, most stress that he should "use his skills for good." He looks up at them from beneath the wall of black hair as if they were all made from scraps of paper. Throughout it all, his foot is still tapping. And as he receives the benediction with his parents, their hands placed gently atop his head, he stands with his arms behind his back, his hands clasped together as if he has been shackled . . . and still the foot taps to the great swelling of symphonies in his head . . . He will always be this way--half in the real world, half in the next. (How, then, does he go from this idealism to despotism of old age?)

     -Don't forget that the director needs a letter to his superiors about funding.

     -In the future, the gray caps will probably have taken over the city no matter what I write--how might the city change as a result? What will be the dangers of writing in such a milieu? Simple incarceration or something much worse? Is it worth the risk? Is it a good staging ground anyway?

     -Ask for new books, even if theoretically you wrote them all.

-An encoded message from the future, itself
with a message embedded in it?

-Is there more to
the Martin Lake story?
Later years?

-Oxygenated squid
blood is blue, not red.

-"His dreams will
rise to the surface like
bubbles of air, and when
they pop open, he will
finally remember the
one thing he had hoped
to forget." Bad B-movie
material?

-Visions that I am not sure are mine. I'm not
quite sure what to make of them. They suggest
answers to some questions about the gray caps.
It is always underground. And it is dark. There
is a machine. The front of the machine has a
comforting translucent or reflective quality.
You will never be able to decide which quality
it possesses, although you stand there staring
at it for days, ensnared by your own foolish hope
for something to negate the horrible negation
of the machine's innards. Ghosts of images cloud
the surface of the machine and are wiped clean
as if by a careless, a meticulous, an impatient
painter. A great windswept desert, sluggish
with the weight of its own dunes. An ocean,
waveless, the tension of its surface broken only
by the shadow of clouds above, the water such a
perfect blue-green that it hurts your eyes. A
mountain range at sunset, distant, ruined towers
propped up by the foothills at its flanks. Images

of jungles and swamps inhabited by strange
birds, strange beasts. Always flickering into
perfection and back into oblivion. Places that
if they exist in this world you have never seen
them or heard mention of their existence. Ever ...
After several days, your eyes stray and unfocus
and blink slowly. You notice, at the very bottom
of the mirror, the glass, a door. The door is
as big as the machine. The door is as small as
your fingernail. The distance between you and
the door is infinite. The distance between you
and the door is so small that you could reach
out and touch it. The door is translucent--
the images that flow across the screen sweep
across the door as well, so that it is only by
the barely-perceived hairline fracture of its
outline that it can be distinguished beneath
the desert, ocean, mountains, that glide across
its surface. The door is a mirror too, you
realize, and after so long of not focusing on
anything, letting images run through you, you
find yourself concentrating on the door and the
door alone. In many ways, it is an ordinary door,
almost a non-existent door. And yet, staring
at it, a wave of fear passes over you. A fear so
blinding it paralyzes you. It holds you in place.
You can feel the pressure of all that meat, all
that flesh, all the metal inside the machine
amassed behind that door. It is an unbearable
weight at your throat. You are buried in it,
in a small box, under an eternity of rock and
earth. The worms are singing to you through the
rubble. You cannot think. You cannot breathe.
You dare not breathe. Your head is full of blood.
     There is something behind the door.
     There is something behind the door.
     There is something behind the door.
     The door begins to open inward, and something
fluid and slow, no longer dreaming, begins to

come out from inside, lurching around the edge
of the door. You run you run you run you run
from that place as fast as you possibly can,
screaming until your throat fills with the
blood in your head, your head now an empty
globe while you drown in blood. And still
it makes no difference, because you are back
in that place with the slugs and the skulls
and the pale dreamers and the machine that
doesn't work that doesn't work that doesn't work
thatdoesn'twork hatdoesnwor atdoeswor tdoeswor
doeswor doewor dowor door . . .

Patient 19-9-18-9-14
Voss Bender Memorial Mental Institute
1314 Albumuth Boulevard
Ambergris I13-24

THE RELEASE OF BELACQUA

The shade of the composer Voss Bender himself might have passed Belacqua in the back corridors of the opera house; the aging critic Janice Shriek might have half-noticed the stoic humor of his performance, just not thought it important enough to mention in her review.

Much about him cried out for attention. Above the black shoes: the long red socks, matched only by the outrageous pink-blue chessboard buttons of his jacket, mimicked in lazy rural fashion by the green eyes on his yellow shirt. His hair—in a twisted red braid (frayed at the end)—hung down in front like the fuse to the bomb of his head. His made-up face reflected a certain forethought mirrored in the shrewd miscalculation of his clothes. The eyebrows (more than one opera-goer may have thought, attention wandering momentarily from the major players) had been stolen from the flourishes on the body of a violin: they overpowered the small, terrified eyes, melted into the lines of the long, garrulous (fake) nose, which itself loomed over the parrotfish mouth (flanked by vertical lines like gills) and sometimes slid down in mock surrender to gravity by performance's end. This farce was pigmented with sow-pink skin, paler above the rarefied heights of the dueling eyebrows, as overdone in description as in life.

But we would know all of this if we had attended a performance, his costume blaring at us like a bawdy horn. *Belacqua, Belacqua,* the horns blared—*this is Belacqua. See him move across the stage. See him briefly speak, and turning burn his image across our eyes.* We could never know that he lives on the fifth floor of a hideous old hotel, in a cramped apartment with indifferent lime-green wallpaper. Neighbors who move around above and below like blunt objects with a dulled sense of direction. Children who cry in the dark like ragged ghosts. A flutter of wings at the windowpane, delicate as eyelashes, and then gone. The repeated banging of a bedpost like some erotic gunshot aimed at his heart. (Next door, for ease of transition and translation, a necropole awaits those who grow cold in the hotel's embrace.)

On weekend mornings, he sits on the balcony, an unlit cigar between his lips. Dressed in a plain white robe, renouncing all make up, he feels the wind move through him as if he does not exist. He watches the people who pass by on the street below and anoints them all with secret lives, breathes into them qualities to match the golden light that filters down between the rooftops.

Sometimes, his gaze blurs upon the filigreed balcony railing as he remembers his dreams. His dreams are all disturbing jokes with obscure punchlines. In one dream, he sees his father: a dark figure at the far end of an alley, briefly illuminated by the glare of a bulb that cuts through the murk. He hears the sound of running water or beer poured from a bottle. Shards of glass lacerate his feet as he runs across the cobblestones. But the joke is, no matter how fast he runs, he can never come close enough to read his father's eyes. Motionless, frictionless, his father glides ahead, continually twenty, thirty feet beyond his grasp.

The filigree of the balcony at first seems like protection from the dream, not protection from falling. He drops the cigar, stands up, goes back inside, dresses in subdued pants and shirt, descends the stairs, walks out onto the street, loses himself there, glad to be anonymous. He leaves his opera persona behind him like an abandoned skin: a husk that has as little to do with him as his clothes.

As he walks toward Albumuth Boulevard (possibly to buy a book at Borges Bookstore, possibly just to wander), a black flame burns inside of him—it lights up his eyes and lends his speech (a word to the fruit vendor, a brief exchange with a more talented but unemployed actor) a subdued yet incandescent fury. Each word arrives burnt around the edges, consumed. His mother used to talk that way, as she let her life be created by his father. The Great Actor. The Drowned Man. The Drunkard.

Even now, he cannot completely forget his role in Bender's most popular opera, the last written before his death and staged posthumously under a one-word title: *Trillian*. The opera recounts, in six raucous acts lasting four hours, the reign of Trillian the Great Banker, leaving out nothing, presenting every scene as a painting of the sort in which a thousand brightly-colored details battle for the viewer's attention. His role, as the Great Banker's gray cap advisor Belacqua, consisted of four lines and two hours of pratfalls.

The part was based on hearsay, heresy, and innuendo, for no history he had ever read mentioned Trillian's advisor. Bender had made it up, and he had played the falsehood for ten years now, the opera's undiminished popularity both blessing and curse. His father would never have taken such a role, but he had no choice. He had always recognized both the limitations of his acting style and that he lacked any spark of talent in other trades. Belacqua he was and Belacqua he would always be. Thus doomed to replay this other self night after night, while his father's ghost hooted and howled, besotted, from some upper balcony seat.

The role, though small, required work, if only because the directors could require work of him without complaint. They told him exactly where to stand, and he stood there. They told him when to make absurd little motions in time to the main players pouring out in perfect pitch and tone the words that now to his ears had no meaning, much as any repetition reduces function and content to a void. He also studied gray caps when he came upon them slumped in alleys or, from a distance, at dusk as they began to waken—observed their hunching gait, their distinctive clothing, their deep, unknowable eyes. He even took lessons on how to project *small* upon the audience, making his five-foot-six-inch height look like four-foot-four (this last a precaution against getting the boot).

In his pocket, he kept a crumpled piece of paper. On the paper he had scribbled stage directions and The Lines.

> BELACQUA approaches the front of the stage, holding the bloody knife. When he reaches TRILLIAN, he sternly sings:
>
> What you cannot know and will not trust
> Will find you here because it must—
> I fly away now, the night to bring
> Down upon Trillian's head, and then?
> No-thing.

Below this, he had written what he thought Belacqua felt in that moment: "Everything that had been building up for so long—dissipated in the pool of blood bubbling up from X's body."

He knew how Belacqua felt, but he didn't know what

the lines meant, even after ten years. For ten years, he had been saying these lines, show after show, and they were incomprehensible to him. He didn't even believe the lines were particularly relevant to the opera. They seemed to have arrived from some other opera, confused in Bender's mind, glittering darkly and spun into *Trillian* on a whim. Not that it should bother him as much as it did—he hadn't actually written the lines. Although he would have liked to be a writer, he had always been written.

Late one afternoon, he brought home a loaf of fresh bread, a squid pie, and a bottle of red wine imported from Morrow. As he entered the apartment, the telephone rang. He froze at the sound, did not at first recognize it. Phones did not often ring in such an old and sleeping city. Then, as if awakened from dream, he dropped the bag. He walked into the kitchen, picked up the receiver.

"Hello?" he said. "Hello?" No response, only a low splashing gurgle of water in the background, so he said, "Who is this?"

Like an imperfect echo, refracted by the corrosion of static, a voice replied, "Hello. Is this Henry? Henry, is that you?"

A vague disappointment settled into his stomach like a smooth, gray stone. "No. It's not. I'm sorry—you have a wrong number."

"But I have no other number. This is the only number." A distressed tone had entered her voice. Such an achingly beautiful voice even without the new element of loss, even through the background interference.

"I'm sorry," he forced himself to say. "I'm not Henry." I wish I was, Belacqua thought to himself, *but I'm not even sure I'm Belacqua.*

The static raged, faded, raged, as the woman said, "Can you connect me to Henry?"

"I don't know Henry," he said, a hint of desperation in his voice, "but if I did, I'd gladly connect you."

The woman began to weep. Such lovely weeping. He felt himself start to reach out through the phone line to comfort her. The whine of static stopped him. Now he listened to her and did not dare to interrupt.

"We've run out of time," she said. "There is no time. I can't call again. They're coming now. I have to give you the message and leave here. It's very important . . . They come up through the floor. If you've got metal floors, they come up even through the steel. They sneak around in your rooms at night. If they don't like you, you're dead, Henry."

"But—"

"Please. Don't say a word. I know what you want to say, but please don't say it. You shouldn't say it. Here is the message: I delivered the last package to X last week. I'm to explain the writing was fine and the lock has been picked. He can find me if he tries. Make him try."

"I'll make him try," he said, resigned to his role. "I have the message. But tell me one thing. What is your name? Please tell me your name. Maybe I can help you. Please . . . "

Any answer she might have given was drowned out by the maniacal grinding of unseen engines of the night. The lapping of water against a dock. The clacking of keys against paper.

For a long time afterwards, he sat in semi-darkness, puffing on a cigar. The bag with his dinner in it lay forgotten by the open apartment door, the broken wine bottle leaking red wetness into the hall. It was the longest telephone conversation he had had in months. With a complete stranger. He watched the spark from the tip of his cigar. His skin felt tight, uncomfortable. His head was a mortar balanced atop a pestle. His fingers around the cigar were thick and slow. And yet, his heart beat as delicately as that of a stunned thrush he had once found on his way to the theater.

He could make no sense of it, all through the night. What could he do? Why should he do anything? But in the morning he left a message for Henry and the woman on a note card at the central telephone exchange. So many lines got crossed that they had set up a special series of bulletin boards devoted to chronicling that very problem. He left the note card impaled on a thumbtack, a white moth lost amongst all the other white moths. When he looked back after having walked several paces, the message had disappeared into the blur of all the other distressed signals of miscommunication.

The very next day, he became Belacqua again and stalked the stage as if he owned a very small portion of it. He opened his mouth and out leapt The Lines, crisp and insignificant as ever. As he gazed through the sparkling glare, past the frantic insectile movements of the orchestra, he wondered if the woman sat in one of those seats, or had attended some past performance. He felt helpless, lost, alone.

The next weekend, he visited the message board. His message was still pinned there, writhing in the wind. No one had written a reply.

* * *

One day the city froze over, the snow falling in muffled flakes. The lizards turned white, developed protective skin over their eyes, and grew thick fur. Lit by holiday lamps even on sunny days, the hotel took on an odd glow, a blanched light usually found only in paintings. He and Belacqua both thought it sad. He imagined the surprised gasping of the fish as they drowned on snow, their scales tipped with frost. The screams of the swans on the river, their legs trapped in the ice. (His silent screams at the sight of the unchanged message board.) The seasons had become strange in Ambergris. The seasons did not know how to change, just as the telephones did not know how to connect.

In the midst of this, he came down with a fever that burrowed into his head like the most terrible word for torment. His limbs on fire, he trudged to the theater and donned his ridiculous costume. All through the performance, which he remembered only as a blur of sequins and song, his head ached and his eyes smoldered as if with smoke.

Afterwards, mumbling his lines under his breath, he put his street clothes back on and drifted out the theater's back entrance. The snow came down in clumps and clots. Not a single leaf had survived on the trees lining the avenue. The lamps had frosted over, trapping the light inside them. The sky resembled a writer's idea of the worst kind of gray: streaked with shadow, shot through with darker shades. He trembled in the cold, breathed the sting of it into his lungs. The fever had worked so far into him that he had succumbed to a fatigued restlessness. He could not return to his apartment. He could not stand still. The message board. He would check it again, although only a day had passed since the last time.

As he set off down the avenue, the fever lent everything he passed a terrible clarity. The polished brass of a lamp post shone so brightly it hurt his eyes. A boy dragged a wooden wagon past him and the dirty wheels revealed the inner mysteries of their polished grain to him. The pink faces of passersby ate into his mind with a cruel precision. He refused to grant them a secret life;

he could forgive none of them for what he had done to himself. Yet he allowed himself this lie: he decided as he walked that he would never give up his quest to find the woman. He would return to the message board again and again until the thrush that was his heart could no longer bear it.

His sense of despair so deep he would have drowned had he not already frozen, he approached the snow-flecked bulletin board. He found his message readily enough, faded around the edges, gray with ash, ink smeared but legible:

THIS MESSAGE IS FOR HENRY AND FOR THE WOMAN WHO CALLED ME. HENRY: THE LAST PACKAGE HAS BEEN SENT. THE WRITING IS FINE BUT THE LOCK HAS BEEN PICKED. TO THE WOMAN: I TALKED TO YOU ON THE TELEPHONE. I'D LIKE TO TALK TO YOU AGAIN. PLEASE GIVE ME SOME WAY TO CON-TACT YOU. YOU HAVE A VERY BEAUTI-FUL VOICE.

A chill slipped over him, extinguishing the fever. No one had written on it. No one would ever write on it. But then his roving gaze found another message on a card next to his own. It was new. It had no snow on it. The ink was still bright with the memory of forming words.

HE IS NOT A CHARACTER. THIS HAS NEVER BEEN A STORY. NOW THAT WE HAVE FILLED HIM UP, WE RELEASE HIM. LET HIM BECOME WHATEVER HE WILL BECOME. LET HIM NO LONGER BE WRITTEN. X.

He stood there, looking up at the message. Was it meant for him? It could have been pure coincidence, as peripheral to his existence as the telephone call. It could have meant nothing. But even knowing this, he felt something loosen within him, thawing, as he read the words. *He is not a character. This has never been a story.* "Belacqua" began to fade away, and with him the lines, the costume, the opera. His father's face. The woman's voice.

He blinked back tears as he read the message over and over again, memorizing it. His fingers curled around the crumpled piece of paper in his pocket. The edges cut against his palm. Somehow he knew that when he took the paper out of his pocket, the words written there would be utterly, irrevocably transformed.

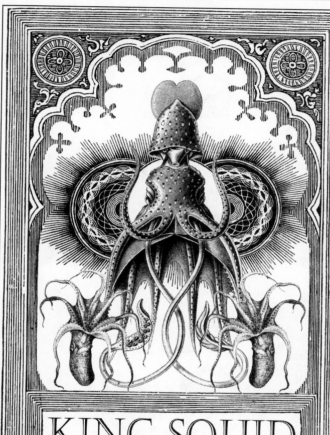

KING SQUID

Being a Brief Monograph By Frederick Madnok
(with some additional research by
librarian Candace Harpswallow)

KING SQUID:

→Being a Brief Monograph Explaining Both the Phenomena of the Giant Freshwater Squid and of Related Squid Folklore (Including the Festival of the Freshwater Squid), While Also Containing Much by Way of Personal Experience, in Four Parts— Part I Describing What the Squid Is Not, Part II What the Squid Is, Part III Expounding with Brevity on the Peculiarities of Squid Lore, and Part IV Divulging an Accurate Scientific Theory that Explains a Number of Otherwise Puzzling Things that Have Long Preyed Upon the Mind of this Writer (And a Vision)—and Concluding with a Bibliography (Intermittently Annotated)⋐

By Frederick Madnok (with some additional research by librarian Candace Harpswallow)

CONTENTS

About the Author: Born on the Madnok family estate 33 years ago, Frederick Madnok has, in his interests, long mimicked his illustrious ancestors. His father, James Madnok, was the author of several books on the study of mushrooms; his scientific bent fostered an early love of analysis in his son. His mother, Henrietta Madnok, served as the choir leader and Home Matron of the local branch of the Truffidian Church. Her devotion to spiritual matters instilled in him the discipline to pursue his interests in Squidology. The presence of squid mills on the family property no doubt fed his curiosity as well.

An excellent student at the Blythe Academy, Frederick graduated with high honors and a degree in general biology (no squidology degree being available at that time). Despite a brief flirtation with illustration and cartoons, he soon found himself in the field observing the King Squid in its natural habitat. Several of his more interesting observations have been published in chapbook, pamphlet, and broadsheet form (refer to the bibliography for more information). After the sale of his family's estate at the age of 27 and following a series of misfortunes, Frederick eventually regained the seclusion necessary to expand upon his studies and his writings. For the past four years, the generosity of his current benefactors has allowed him to make the important discoveries set out in this monograph.

I — WHAT THE SQUID IS NOT

⇉ INTRODUCTION ⇇

T IS A SAD BUT INCONTROVERTIBLE FACT THAT the world stands in profound ignorance of the King Squid—and the related festival. Although some might say that more has become known of this creature than evidenced by the mistakes contained in a few naturalist guides published abroad, I am not among their number. To my wandering eye, such errors of fact have multiplied, as have the inaccurate estimates of the number of the King Squid's tentacles. Firstly, squid have both tentacles and arms. Secondly, the arms do *not* number five, six, seven, nine, ten, or, most absurdly, fourteen—as suggested by the no doubt severely landlocked Dr. Alfred Kubin, a man who probably also thinks he himself has seven arms and no leg to stand on. The correct number of squid limbs is ten—eight arms and two tentacles— and it is from the foundation of this tenant of fact that all else in this institution shall build. The tentacles, of course, distinguish themselves from the arms by their ingenious hooks, with which they grip prey in a manner improbable for the arms.

From these examples, and such grievous ignorables as "squid is my favorite kind of fish," a statement I overheard Madame Tuff's farctated daughter proclaim from an adjacent table in the cafeteria just last Thursday, it should be clear that before we approach the mad misconceptions of the Festival's history and associated customs, we must first disperse current layperson fogginess about the squid itself.[1]

Firstly, the squid does *not* "lay its eggs on the banks of the muddy River Moth in the Spring, whence they hatch in late Autumn and pull themselves by means of proto-tentacles and their scrappy little beaks into the water" as has been suggested by the jarkman Leo Pulling in his crapulous treatise "An Account of the Squidlings' First Hours by the Banks of the Great River," published in that soggy sack of lies known as *The Ambergris Journal of Speculative Zoology.*

Secondly, although pustulated by a certifiable army of morons, including Blas Skinder, Volmar Gort, Maurice Rariety, Frank Blei, and Nora Kleyblack, the King Squid is *not* related to any of the lesser squid. It is not related to the Morrow Barking Squid, the Stockton Burrowing Squid, the Exploding Kalif Squid, the Detachable Mandible Squid, the Truffidian Monk's Head Squid, the Fallowpine Honking Squid, the Burning Leopard Squid, the Myopic Slorvorian Howling Squid, the Northern Batwinged Squid, the Eastern Red-faced Mongoose Squid, the Three-Eyed Leaf Squid, the Scintillating Button Squid, the grossly-named Daffed Dancing Sapphire Squid, or even the Nicean Scuttlefish.[2]

It is *none* of these things—nor related to any of them—I must repeat for those of you who may have lost the thread or are hard of reading.

MISS FLOXENCE'S PRETTY THEORIES

I realize at this point that some readers may think it important for me to say what the King Squid *is* rather than what it continually *is not.* However, I am not yet finished with my essential ablutions, which must be completed to purge the reader of the impure negative energy created by so many madcap theories.

For we have yet to encounter the pathologically inane and scientifically unsound utterances of one Edna Floxence, primarily remembered as the unbalanced astrologer of the Banker-Cappan Trillian, but whom, under Trillian's auspices, suborned the public's attentions in such a way that certain myths engendered there continue to feast upon the brains of Ambergrisian school children to this very day. *The Strange World of the Freshwater Squid* is only trumped in its bilious and breezy antidotes for the truth by *The Mysteries of the Freshwater Squid Revealed:* six hundred continuous pages of spurious text that no true squidologist can read today without bleeding profusely from the nose, ears, and mouth.[3]

The problem, for one, is that in amongst the straitjackets of commonsense in the closet of her looney-ness, Miss Floxence makes the amazing claim to have "swum with the squid on a daily basis for an entire summer" in order to learn their secrets. The dust jacket for *The Strange World* even sports an engraving of Miss Floxence in a fetching frock, a petticoat bathing suit made all of frills and dangling tangles.

Why should the foolish Miss Floxence's claim seem so bogus? For two reasons: (1) At the time of setting herself adrift like so much floppery amongst the no doubt perturbed (and forever traumatized) squid, the River Moth's silt content was higher than it had been in years, thus ensuring that any swimmer in those mad murky waters could hardly have seen their own mud-sloppy hand in front of their wet leaf-obscured face, let alone observed and documented over one hundred complex mating rituals, alarm strobes, feeding frenzies, and "quaint ancestral games" and (2) In her frilly petticoat bathing suit and with her pale skin and bulbous eyes, Miss Floxence bears an uncanny resemblance to the common fopgrinder, a fish in the *toxicana* family. This fish, with its frilly fins and dead white pallor, is the King Squid's favorite delicacy.[4] One can only imagine the eye-popping jubilant salivation of a hungry pack of teenage King Squid upon encountering a fopgrinder of such magnificent size and proportions.

No, I'm afraid that Miss Floxence never swam with the squid—this delusion is not supported by the evidence. Even supposing clear visibility and a bathing suit not as likely to trigger close-up observations of squid eating habits, the reader must keep in mind that a King Squid routinely reaches speeds of 14 knots. I doubt the flouncy Miss Floxence could reach one knot on a really ambitious day.

We must thus jettison and watch float out of sight, perhaps sparing a curt wave, all of Miss Floxence's pretty theories, from the idea of squid changing partners every three months (a popular practice among humans in Ambergris at the time), to the ridiculously complex courtship rituals that combined the worst attributes of a spasmodic seizure with the most daring escapades from a romance novel, topped off by a very optimistic use of tools. (Owning up to your crimes is, as they say, very important for redemption. Dear Miss Floxence has yet to achieve that state of grace and, undiscovered letters and notes notwithstanding, may never achieve it.)

BLITHERING ANECDOTAL EVIDENCE

Early eyewitness accounts range from the choicest pulpatoons to the worst trillibubs of information. Such inaccuracies should be put aside along with our alphabet blocks, mother's too-frequent goodnight kisses, and therapy sessions.

A single example should suffice to catalog a mountain of mariner anecdotes, this selection ripped from a book actually paid for by the Society of Morrowean Scientists Abroad, entitled *Squidologist Enoch Sighly's and Doctor Bernard Povel's Journey Up the River Moth by Way of Native Canoe and Indigenous Ingenuity, Culminating in a Boat Wreck, a Near Escape, Alcoholism, and Some Unfortunate Negotiations with the Aforementioned Natives:*

> A wondrous Fish or Beast or Other Creature that was lately Killed or Speared or Shot washed up by its own

Accord, Being Dead, on a nearby Sandbank on the 20th Day of our Expedition. We bade the curiously mirthful Natives Heave To! And when they did not, Asked Again, that we might Examine the Specimen. It had two Heads and ten Horns and on eight of the Horns, it had 800 Fleshy Bumpies; and in each of Them, a set of Teeth, the said Body bigger than three Cows of the Largest Size and with the Abnormal Horns being of almost 40 hoofs in length. The Greater Head carried only the Horns and two very large Eyes, much pecked by the birds that the natives call Birds. And the Little Head thereof carried, in addition to an Unwholesome Stench and an Odd Putrefaction, a Wondrous Strange Mouth and two Tongues within it, which had the Unnatural Power to draw itself out or into the Body as Necessity required. Other remarkable things observed in the Monster must be said to include its reddish Colored Wrapper sticking fast to the back thereof, and loose laps on both sides, white and red throughout. As well as Blubberous Skin that the Natives will not touch. It hath the most Monstrous Nose ever seen within or without the World.

From the fractured description of a "fish or beast or other creature" to the "bumpies," the "horns," the "little head" (clearly a funnel), the "tongues," and the "wrapper," not to mention the comically mis-diagnosed "laps," it becomes simultaneously clear that the "fish or beast or other creature" in question is a King Squid and that the Society of Morrowean Scientists Abroad was unwise to choose as observers the Fatally Unobservant.[5]

At least in such accounts, however, we come closer to the beast itself, the life's blood of Ambergris, the bounty of plenty, the squidologist's beakish wet dream, the freshwater monster known simply as "King Squid."

⇒ Notes ⇐

1   As my father used to say, "Layperson fogginess is the leading cause of hatred directed toward scientists." (See: Madnok, James, *A Theory of Mushrooms.*) The context of this statement? A discussion of the city's subterranean inhabitants, the semi-mysterious gray caps, and the mass disappearances they supposedly induced, known as "The Silence."

2   The King Squid eats all of these species, with great relish, on a weekly basis.

3   I first encountered Miss Floxence's text in the family library. My father and I had gone there to escape mother's wrath over some trivial offense and he pulled out the tome both because it was mother's favorite and because he thought I might enjoy a good laugh. He read me bits aloud to my cackling response. So I cannot pretend to be objective about Miss Floxence's books.

4   A fact lovingly recorded by D. S. Nalanger in his paper "The Fish Preferences of the Giant Freshwater Squid as Recorded During a Controlled Experiment Involving a Hook, Bait, a Boat, and a Strong Line of Inquiry," publication pending.

5   Indeed, although the Society never published the monogram from the second expedition, such a (slim) pamphlet could have been titled "Enoch and Bernard's Cut-Short Journey Wherein the Canoe Overturned and the Crocodiles Danced a Merry Jig Upon Our—"

II – WHAT THE KING SQUID IS

APPROACHING THE TRUE KING SQUID

Now WE SHALL TALK OF WHAT THE KING SQUID *is* INSTEAD OF what it is not. It is magnificent and vast. It is mythical and, to some of the misguided, Divine. It is, to more practical souls, a fine meal with a side of potatoes and a glass of brandy.

That it can be all things to all people may be explained by the fact that squidologists have identified over 600 species of squid. Large, small, medium-sized, oblong, squat, lithe, and long—all kinds exist in oceans, in rivers, in lakes. Beaks like parrots. Skin that flames and gutters with its own potency; depending on the time of day and temperature/ment, sometimes mute gray or festooned with self-made light like the Festival route at night. Some tough, some soft, some muscular, some gelatinous. Some can fling their bodies out of their watery domain and seem to fly! Others live in the deepest depths of the River Moth. Some commune together like swimming judges without scales to do them justice. Some, solitary, cannot stand even their own company. Yet others must, by their very nature, endure the company of an inferior species until they can metamorphose to a more exalted state.

UNCOMMON CHARACTERISTICS

While I shall attempt to recite shared characteristics in an orderly[6] fashion, as rote as any children's song, I must admit that the closer we approach to the squid itself, the more excited I become: my mantle turns cerulean with pleasure, my funnel juts more prominently, my suckers tremble. So to speak.

As every young squidologist—released to happily squat over tidal pools (if in the Southern Isles) or lurk around the dock pilings (if in Ambergris)—knows, almost every squid has eight arms and two tentacles, grappling hooks, etc. As I may have mentioned. (The bookish squidologist will find case files on the now extinct Morrowean Mud Squid, whose tentacles reabsorb into the body upon attaining adulthood, leaving only flaccid nubs. This embarrassing condition is not shared by the King Squid.)

Some defective species—the malodorous Stunted Beak Squid, the aptly-diagnosed Stockton Disabled Squid, and the repugnant Saphant Arse Squid—have arms of differing lengths. However, the King Squid is by contrast a paradigm of good health, its eight arms the exact same thickness and length, its two tentacles longer by only a few feet.

The tentacles, a marvel of biological engineering, serve a number of graceful functions, but primarily bring prey to the doom that is its mouth. Not a particularly swift doom, however. The King Squid does not swallow its food whole as does the Swollen Mantle Squid peculiar to the Alfar Lake Region. Nor does it batter its food against underwater rocks to tenderize it as does the Purple Bullheaded Squid popular along the coast of Scatha. Instead, the King Squid must chop up and grind down its food using its beak, teeth, and pistolaro (a tongue-like organ).

Why must the King Squid do this? Alas, as every aspiring young squidologist knows, the squid's cartilaginous head capsule has little elasticity. It already houses a miraculous clamor of inmates: luminous eyes, a large brain, the esophagus.

Is this a flaw or some forethought the squidologist has not yet deciphered?

A SHORT DIGRESSION ON SQUID EYES

And the eyes! If the eyes function as a window on the soul as so many doctors seem to believe,[7] then the King Squid is a being from the Truffidian's Heaven. Firstly, a squid's eyes are not binocular: each sees what is on that side of the head. As a result, a squid can see twice as well as a human being; four times as well as those of you with glasses. Secondly, these eyes come in all shapes and sizes, from eyes as big as wagon wheels to eyes as small as buttons. Oblong, circular, ovoid, slitty, triangulated, spherical, octagonal. In colors that range from the exact shade of the green-gold sunset over Ambergris through the bars (of distant music) to the red-silver shimmer of a rich woman's skirt at visiting time.

The King Squid's eyes number not one like the Cyclopedic Swelling Squid, nor two like Every Other Type of Squid, but three! Three eyes! The third and most exciting lies hidden on the underside of the mantle. The third eye performs two miraculous functions. Firstly, it detects bioluminescence only. Secondly, certain retina secretions suggest that this third eye *produces a beam of light to aid the squid in seeing through the murky silt of the Moth River.*

I can shed no further light on this subject as profound as the King Squid's own.

CONTINUING ON WITH LESSER-KNOWN UNCOMMON CHARACTERISTICS

But this, as I have said, any enterprising[8] young squidologist must already know—if not from first hand adventures than from any of the treacly but beloved kiddie squid cartoons that I believe still run amok in the various Ambergris broadsheets.

What the bemuddened, water-splashed, invertebrate-loving young rascal may be unaware of are certain aspects of the King Squid's physiology and behavior that separate it from its squidkin. This should come as no surprise, given the paucity of quality sources for squidfact.

Firstly, the King Squid may reach adult lengths of 150 feet and weights of more than 5,000 pounds (would that the Moth were wider, deeper, and therefore more hospitable to larger specimens). As a result, the King Squid has the largest beak of any known squid. Squid beaks run small in relation to the body, but this still means a brave man with arms outstretched could just touch a large King Squid's open upper and lower mandibles. Since this would require said man's head to be inside said squid's mouth, I cannot recommend it as a measurement technique except when approaching the deadest of squid.

But size alone cannot explain our lifelong fascination with the King Squid. Indeed, not even the most reputable amateur squidologist would recognize the creature in its juvenile phase, when it resembles the larva of some aquatic insect.[9] This has caused several unfortunate errors over the years.

TAKE THE CASE OF RICHARD SMYTHE, AMATEUR SQUIDOLOGIST

For example, even a published amateur squidologist such as Mr. Richard Smythe—a traveling salesman residing in the landlocked city of Leander—can make a mistake. Mr. Smythe scooped up a jar of Moth water on a trip to Nicea precisely because it was full of what he believed to be insect larvae. Once home, he added the water to his aquarium to feed his patient fish and promptly departed in pursuit of a rumor of umbrellas needed in an umbrella-less land. Upon his return three weeks later, an angry King Squid the size of a small dog greeted him from the fishless tank. The starving squid promptly set upon the unfortunate Mr. Smythe, arms and tentacles flailing. Only the unsold umbrellas from his trip saved this silly man from an otherwise grinding fate.[10] That he and the squid later became the best of friends does not alter the two basic lessons to be derived from this story: Always strain your water for juvenile squidlings and *never* trust water from the River Moth.

ENEMIES AND EATABLES

According to Clyde Aldrich, hailed by inaccurate blateroons as the "leading expert" on the King Squid, this beast among squid has no natural enemies. (This is not the case for its closest relative, the southern saltwater Saphant Squid, which must fend off the treacherous predations of the schizophrenic Saphant Whale—the whale that framed an empire, so to speak.)

As for the King Squid's consumables, we can say with some authority that it eats with more variety than those released at the appointed hour to graze the cafeterias or even kitchens. The King Squid is a rapturous meativore that hunts relentlessly for prey ranging from insects, crustaceans, fish, other squid, and cows (when available), to the contents of badly placed houses.[11] In short, the King Squid will eat anything it can wrap its limbs around, including the deadly but stupid freshwater shark. However, contrary to George Edgewick's *A Study of the Link Between Invertebrates & Garbage,* the King Squid, due to its highly developed sense of smell, does not follow garbage scows any more than it would care to order out from an Ambergrisian tavern.[12]

THE PLAYFUL SIDE OF THE KING SQUID

All talk of predators and prey aside, the King Squid express-es a playful side when released from the prison of rote in-stinct. This sense of play usually manifests itself through its propulsion system. To move about, the squid depends upon its funnel—a short, hose-like organ that projects from the mantle below the head.[13] Because the mantle swivels, the squid has remarkable funnel control. From which point derives one of the most remarkable of the King Squid's habits.

Namely, the King Squid has been known to shoot long streamers of water at unsuspecting travelers who walk on paths along the riverbank. These high-speed columns of water can travel as far as 80 feet inland and douse a soon-spluttering pedestrian with a pungent dose of silty water.[14]

Such preternatural aim requires excellent eyesight and remarkable intelligence. The displays are often accompanied by a "huffing" sound that I believe is laughter, despite what my neighbor John says about my theories. The so-called experts—who could be locked up forever in a cell for all I care—believe this is just an effect created by refilling the funnel with water to have another go.

Regardless, as an unfortunate result, those bloated ticks who congregate under the name "The Ambergrisian Safety League" drafted a resolution allocating monies to train squid as firefighters for those sections of Ambergris accessible by water. Less laughable although more absurd are the oft-fatal and crackpot "squid baptisms" performed by the Church of the Squid Children, a cult that attempts to provoke "the holy act of absolution" from the squid. As might be expected from a confirmed meativore, the King Squid rarely obliges with anything approaching civilized behavior.

FURTHER INKLINGS OF SQUID INTELLIGENCE—AND A BROD SIGHTING

Meanwhile, further inklings of King Squid intelligence continue to surface, the ripplings of a case for cognitive ability long established by physiological evidence.[15] Surely it cannot be coincidence that the squid's two mighty hearts pump blood not only into its stalwart gills, but into its large and complex brain as well? The average King Squid brain receives three gallons of blood more each day than the average resident—fed a lunch of dried-out fish strips, curdled yogurt, and a disappointed-looking green bean—receives in a week. The only animal with a larger brain, the Odecca Bichoral White Whale, is said to list to one side from the weight of its cranium.[16]

The King Squid—like some lesser squid but unlike the Spastic Alarming Squid—also maintains direct control over its coloration and patterns, which appears to provide further evidence of craftiness. Phosphorescent displays over the river at night bring to mind the strange lights seen over the ruined town of Alfar ten years ago and attributed to an unknown intelligence. (The careful reader will begin to catch a glimpse of the context for my unique theories, imparted to you in Part IV of this monograph.)

From a base of translucent silver, the King Squid can strobe to green, blue, red, yellow, orange, purple, black, or any combination thereof. They can camouflage themselves against any background, with lightning-fast color changes.[17] Although such changes may originally have "evolved"—to use the much-abused Xaver Daffed's over-analyzed word—to interrupt predator attack sequences or to assist in mating rituals, the skill now appears to form a sophisticated communication system, more effective than sound or the tentacle sign language Maxwell Brod once hallucinated he observed on a deep river dive.[18]

FURNESS AND LEEPIN'S REVELATORY DISCOVERY

If people were not by nature insane and resistant to self-improvement or therapy, the joint research of the under-appreciated Raymond Furness and Paulina Leepin would have long ago replaced the buffoonish efforts of ludicrines like Brod.

Furness and Leepin's first stroke of inspiration was to bypass the Silt Problem by setting up a blind much like those used for birding. Made of glass and located in the hollowed out bottom of a houseboat tethered to a sandbank in the middle of an otherwise deep part of the Moth, this device represented a classic advancement in the tools available to the squidologist.[19]

In time, various King Squid overcame their wariness and peered curiously into the glass while Furness and Leepin, motionless and somewhat terrified, stared back. It took several months of study, according to their journals, but they eventually recorded evidence of squid "flash communication" as they called it. Later, these two pioneers were able to glean meaning from the "flash communication"—and actually communicate back! Thus was the barrier between squidologist and squid broken, if only for a moment, altering forever the relationship between scientist and tidal pool, observer and observed.[20]

To start with, Furness and Leepin sketched out some basic communication patterns,[21] reproduced on page 20.[22]

As even a mythomaniac can see, such communication operates at a much higher level than that of a dog, a cat, or a pig, even considering recent experiments in that area.

But Furness and Leepin's research had not yet reached its full potential. With the help of a lamp and crepe paper, they projected letters into the water alongside their squid equivalents, first in random strings such as RIEKHITMLALFEYD and then as words and phrases such as I AM A SQUID. HOW ARE YOU TODAY?

At first, the squid did not reply. After a week of such stimuli, however, Furness and Leepin were astonished to find that the squid would display the letters on their glowing skin—and not only display the letters but send them in motion, circling their bodies, so that dual messages of I AM A SQUID and HOW ARE YOU TODAY might collide like ghostly alphabet trains.

Such findings should have led to further revelations, with fame and fortune awaiting Furness and Leepin once they had documented all of their observations. However, an odd incident then occurred to discredit them utterly in the eyes of other scientists. This incident hints at a higher level of squid intelligence than previously reported in even such optimistic publications as *Squid Thoughts*. The journal entry makes for riveting reading, but also distresses me. What might have been if only they had held their ground?[23]

Today Furness and I decided to abandon our research. It is too dangerous. The squid make it so. I never thought that the squid themselves could dissuade us from our love of squidology, but, alas, it has happened. To explain—

After an uneventful morning, a series of huge bubbles breached the water's surface near our houseboat around noon. A slow, ponderous wave, as of something enormous coming toward us below the surface, buffeted the boat. We immediately donned our emergency animal skin flotation devices, our globular fishbowl masks, and our seal fins and, thus safe (or so we thought), descended into the glass blind at the bottom of the houseboat. Flashing red and orange, the King Squid we had nicknamed Squid #8, Squid #5, Squid #12, Squid #16, and Squid #135 hovered in front of the blind for a moment, receded into the middle distance, and then sped away into the murk. At first, we thought our odd attire had startled them. Even so, their reaction unnerved us. Yet we stayed in the houseboat because of our devotion to the Cause[24] . . . only to scream in terror as a tentacle the size of our entire boat slid through the water beneath the glass. Across its vast greenish surface, as Truff is our witness, we read, in gold letters: LEAVE NOW OR I WILL DEVOUR YOU, SUCK OUT

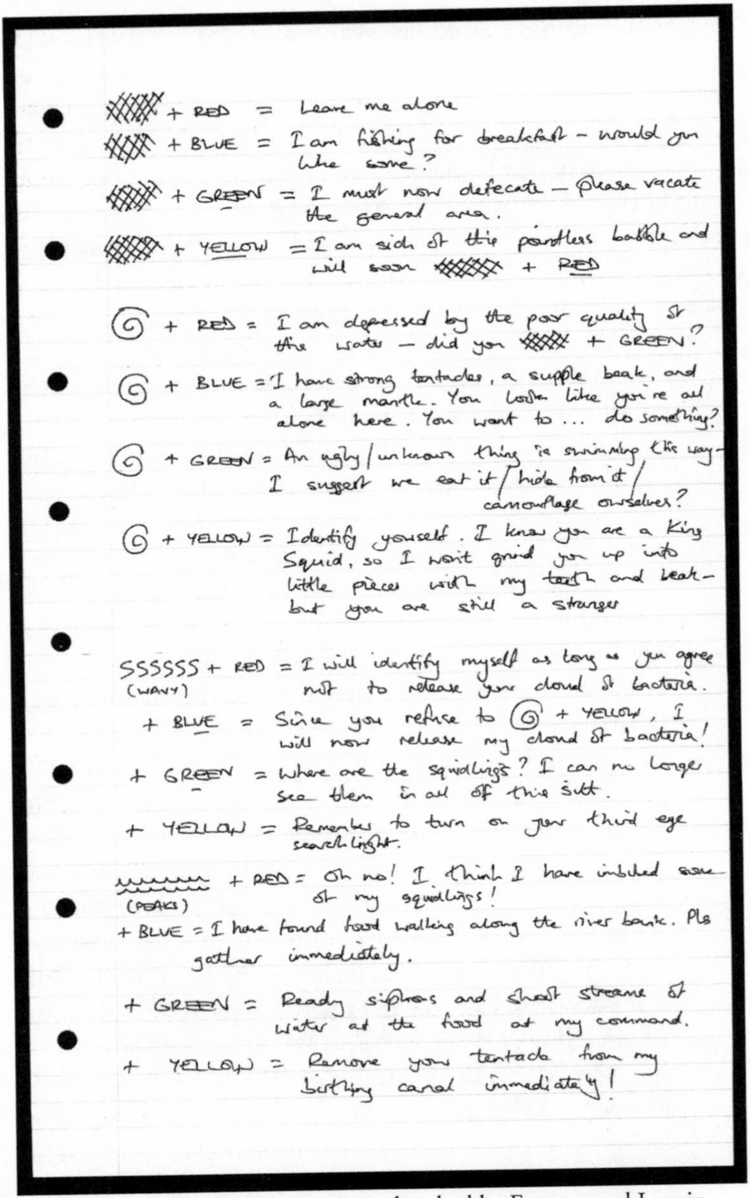

XXXX + RED = Leave me alone

XXXX + BLUE = I am fishing for breakfast — would you like some?

XXXX + GREEN = I must now defecate — please vacate the general area.

XXXX + YELLOW = I am sick of this pointless babble and will soon XXXX + RED

(spiral) + RED = I am depressed by the poor quality of the water — did you XXXX + GREEN?

(spiral) + BLUE = I have strong tentacles, a supple beak, and a large mantle. You look like you're all alone here. You want to ... do something?

(spiral) + GREEN = An ugly/unknown thing is swimming this way — I suggest we eat it / hide from it / camouflage ourselves?

(spiral) + YELLOW = Identify yourself. I know you are a King Squid, so I won't grind you up into little pieces with my teeth and beak — but you are still a stranger

SSSSSS + RED = I will identify myself as long as you agree
(WAVY)   not to release your cloud of bacteria.

+ BLUE = Since you refuse to (spiral) + YELLOW, I will now release my cloud of bacteria!

+ GREEN = Where are the squidlings? I can no longer see them in all of this silt.

+ YELLOW = Remember to turn on your third eye searchlight.

mmmm + RED = Oh no! I think I have imbibed some
(PEAKS)   of my squidlings!

+ BLUE = I have found food walking along the river bank. Pls gather immediately.

+ GREEN = Ready siphons and shoot streams of water at the food at my command.

+ YELLOW = Remove your tentacle from my birthing canal immediately!

Fig 1: Communication patterns as sketched by Furness and Leepin.

YOUR MARROWS, AND USE THE BONES TO MAKE A NEST FOR MY YOUNG. For a moment, we sat there in terror. We could not move. It was only a sharp slap of tentacle tip against the boat, a sudden stench of ammonia, and an added squidular message of HURRY UP! that unparalyzed us.

It is difficult to reconstruct what happened next, but we remember running onto the deck and jumping onto the sandbar, screaming all the while, and then, behind us, the houseboat crunching into bits from tentacle lashings. We threw ourselves into the waters opposite in a state of utter hysteria and scrambled for shore, bits of broken planks slicing through the air all around us, our masks obscured by silt, our seal fins impeding our progress and, most annoying of all, our animal skins filling with water because we had clutched them so tightly they had begun to leak from puncture marks. When at last we reached the safety of the shore, only a few floating timbers remained of the houseboat. A sudden lunging wave of water convinced us to seek more permanent shelter far, far inland—where we have remained to this day.

Alas, muddleheads with all-powerful spectacles pushed up on their brows, doltish jury lumps with puddings for brains—what constituted Established Squidology—swept Furness and Leepin's findings aside as easily as their houseboat and they were lucky to escape *that* catastrophe with even the integrity of their earlier studies intact. Confined to the bin of rejects, labeled as "lunatics," despite having made perhaps the single most important squidology discovery since Rebecca Yancy's revelations concerning the air-water gill ratio, Furness and Leepin descended into that nightmare half-lit world of pseudo-science and alcoholism that so many of our practitioners enter never to return.[25] (For more information on the circumstances surrounding this, our primary affliction, please refer to *Hops and the Amateur Squidologist* by Alan Ruch and *The Squid on Our Backs, The Tentacles in Our Brains: An Account of a Descent into Madness* by Macken Clark.)

SQUID CROSS-COUNTRY ADVENTURES

Reliable scientific study aside, at least two pieces of anecdotal evidence also point to squid intelligence *and* squid creativity.

The first evidence concerns reports of squid perambulations on solid ground! On six separate occasions, individuals reported seeing groups of giant squid come up out of the water and "walk around" using shimmering globes of water encased around their gills and eyes to protect them from the villainous air. In all cases, the globe of water, tension unbroken, was held in place by four arms wound above the head, while the remaining four arms and two tentacles sufficed for the King Squid to drag itself over the grass. As they *gafflocked* along (a term I myself coined while experimenting with the squidly means of transportation out in the yard), intense communication shimmered like heat lightning across their skin, strobing from silver to red to blue to green to purple to black and back again within a matter of seconds. Where these adventurous squid were headed, the eyewitnesses could not say,[26] being too shocked at the sight of these hardy invertebrate explorers of terror firma to do much more than bleat in panic and run away. One man even dropped his pipe and started a fire—quickly put out by a nonchalant water blast from the squid.

As further proof of squid wiles, every witness encountered the squidpeditions in sparsely habitated regions near dusk, while walking alone. In each case, the delusional local authorities explained it away as a result of "poor light and bad eyesight." In one case, the witness was asked if she hadn't in fact seen a "balloon of some kind." However, the more advanced and dedicated squidologist will note that the King Squid is, in its natural habitat, most active at dusk—and surely a cross-country jaunt of some length suggests a high level of activity! Alas, all of the accounts on this matter are protected under the quaint laws governing doctor-client privilege, as each witness has since been hospitalized for various and sundry psychological ailments, squidanthropy chief among them.

HELLATOSE & BAUBLE: FACT OR FICTION?

It has been more difficult for skeptics to scuttle the case of Baron Bubbabaunce & His Amazing Performing Squid. This act, associated with many a circus, from the Amazing Two-Headed Trilobite Brothers' Cavalcade of Miracles to High Priest David Thornton's Abyss of Sinfully Good Fun, consisted of George Bubbabaunce (known by his carny friends as "Bauble") and his King Squid Hellatose Jangles performing a water puppet show. While "Bauble" narrated from the side, Hellatose Jangles created complex psychodramas based on the work of the obscure playwright Hoffmenthol (an influence on the great Voss Bender). Flanked on three sides by bleacher seating, the "theater" consisted of a rectangular pool of murky water siphoned in from the River Moth. Hellatose's mantle and head provided an island or "stage" within the pool. Bauble would fit Hellatose's arms with tentacle puppets. This meant that up to 10 puppets could inhabit a single scene—leading to extremely sophisticated productions[27] that rivaled the pomp and circumstance of Machel and Sporlender. Two of Bauble's comrades at the Abyss of Sinfully Good Fun recall that he did not seem to be the one in control of the artistic relationship. As quoted in Sneller's *A History of Traveling Medicine Shows and Nefarious Circi,* the Four-Faced Lizard Boy, Samuel Pippin, indicated that "In their tent at night, they would have long arguments. Bauble would shout. Hella would respond with high-pitched squealings from his traveling pond. If the light was on in the tent, you could see Hella's arms writhing as he tried to make some point with body language. Bauble would just stand there with shoulders slumped, like a hen-pecked husband."

Three-Jawed Shark Fin Girl claims to have witnessed even more damning evidence of squid intelligence. She entered the Bauble-Hellatose tent only to find the squid dictating new scenes to Bauble, Bauble reacting with severe annoyance as he wrote down a line only for Hellatose to object and force him to erase it and start over. "It seemed," she said, "as if Bauble was just a scribe for Hella, the master playwright."

Certainly, the very public argument over set design that ended their relationship conveyed a succinct affirmation of squid intelligence, as Hellatose used his arms to make a rude gesture in Bauble's general direction. Following this altercation, recorded in Elaine Feaster's article for *The Amateur Squidologist* (see: Feaster, Elaine) neither man nor squid was ever heard from again.[28]

Much nonsense has been expelled into print over the years about Bauble and Hellatose. The worst of this revolves around rumors, silly to the extreme, that both Sporlender and Bender owed many of their best lines to "a mysterious Mr. H," to whom they would send dead scenes when their creativity had dried up . . . "only to receive back, by anonymous messenger, a fortnight later, wonderful revisions . . . in a delicate handwriting that used squid ink."[29]

I need not point out the ridiculousness of this assertion—a squid would rather write with its own vomit than use its ink. The very thought is repugnant.

⇒ NOTES ⇐

6   A classic case study of the day-to-day reality of a noun transformed into mad adverb.

7   My father's eyes were a steely gray that locked in on the subject of his stare with a scientist's ardor. Once seen, you could not be unseen by his gaze, even were he to turn away. My mother had pale blue eyes that never stared for long. They did not follow the fastidious detail of the stern words that issued from her mouth, but fluttered here and there. I recommend to every young squidologist that they study first their parents' eyes before looking into the eyes of a King Squid. For you will then be surprised by how similar, despite the differences, the two species, in such different families, can be . . .

8   Truant or troublemaking squidologists may actually know more but find themselves confined to restrictive settings in which it is difficult to obtain the proper books and tools to advance themselves in their chosen profession. See: Footnote #3. (In those early years, some sort of transformation may seem necessary, even desirable. Usually, this is just a condition of youth. However, in rare cases, it may develop into something miraculous. Refer to Roberts, M.A., for more information.)

9   I would compare the problem to my father's reliance on "fruiting bodies" when discussing mushrooms with the general populace. My father was a firm believer in the Invisible World simply because so much of his research depended upon the microscope. This formed a marked contrast to my mother, who used the widest celestial and psychic telescopes in hopes of catching a glimpse of God. Somewhere between

the two extremes lie the young of the King Squid, which, although observable by microscope, must often feel like tiny gods adrift in some limitless expanse of darkness.

10   See: *An Amateur Squidologist's Journey Toward Self-Realization: The Squid and I,* by Richard Smythe.

11   See Frederick Roper's fascinating study, *Incidences of Squid Incursions Among the Communities of the Lower Moth: Anecdotal Evidence Supporting the Need for Squid-Proof Habitats.*

12   Which leaves Edgewick with one valid conclusion, only implied by his book: "George Edgewick follows garbage scows." My father used to call this sort of thing the "bookless theory."

13   It would be easier to just show you the infernal and uncomfortable thing than have to describe it, frankly.

14   Eyewitness accounts convey a sense of embarrassed terror. John Kuddle, a financial officer and former banker-warrior under Trillian, related that "I was walking down a quiet path by the river, on my way to the town of Derth, a big bag of money over my shoulder, when suddenly something hit me and knocked me off my feet. The coins in my bag went flying. It was only when I got up and surveyed my situation and found I was all wet and covered in bits of algae that I realized I had been doused—and there the big brute of a bastard was, lazing in the water with his mantle up, that tin plate eye staring at me as if to say 'What are you going to do about it?'" (Local washerwomen also tell of being taunted by squid for sport.)

15   As for evidence of souls, I can offer no evidence more circumstantial than the words of my mother upon our fre-

quent returns from the Truffidian Church: "Nothing without bones to rattle can truly be said to have a soul." (She was herself merely parroting the priest to whom she had expressed concerns about my interest in squidology. Needless to say, such fears were unfounded.)

16   Zoologists have never caught a good glimpse of this whale, let alone been able to perform a taxonomy.

17   Some squid have even been known to camouflage themselves perfectly as human beings. (See: Kranch, George, who claimed that he "often came upon squid masquerading as human beings." How to tell the difference? "You must look at the purported human being from the corner of your eye. If you experience a shimmering ripple effect around the edges of its form, then it is actually a squid." The ridiculous Kranch then writes, "Of course, sometimes I just see sunspots. And it can be embarrassing to net a squid camouflaged as a human and then have to let them go.")

18   Brod is clearly a congenial idiot hailing from a long line of idiots of the first order who would be better off counting the fins of the dull fish with which his name rhymes. Brod's dive took place within the confines of a metal suit connected to an airhose. Assuming Brod was even receiving enough oxygen through his fragile lifeline to avoid brain damage, he had less than a slit of visibility through the poor quality glass of his face plate. Such visibility is, as I have previously pointed out while disposing of the mal-efficient Floxence, rendered moot by the silt content of the Moth anyway. I therefore have great difficulty believing his description of an "intricate device of communication that held me in thrall, the lithe sweep of tentacles forming signs and arcane letters that I could not decipher but nonetheless held me in awe of their magical meaning." To which I reply: it's the silt, man! The silt!

Remember the silt before you fabricate outrageous lies. (This is good advice for any aspiring squidologist, I believe.)

19   A replica of the blind has apparently been put on display in the Morhaim Museum for Scientific Advancement in the Biological Sciences just this past Thursday, according to a letter I have received.

20   It would be of benefit to the general populace if this inversion of the usual professional relationship were applied to other fields.

21   By an odd coincidence, the color scheme matches that of the Ambergrisian flag.

22   That the notebooks of these two pioneers in squidology remain unpublished and must be crudely mimeographed by attendants and passed around to their colleagues at squid conferences is a travesty of science, the blame for which falls squarely upon the anti-invertebrate shoulders of the so-called "academic" journals.

23   My father suffered from a similar affliction in his relationship with my mother. Although he did not allow it to ruin his studies, it did "mute" them to a degree. I would like to say that my mother misunderstood my father's work, but I am afraid she understood it all too well. I loved her very much, despite the circumstances, but I do wonder what might have been for my father if she had left him to his own devices for more than ten minutes at a time.

24   Of Science, one assumes. Not, as one twisted ambivert with mesomorphic tendencies shared with me recently, some anti-squid terrorist organization. Most of the theories one hears are not worth repeating.

25 I sneer at those who claim Furness and Leepin were drunk long before they recorded the fateful events that ruined their reputation. As for a plot to collect insurance on the houseboat—such a rumor will not even receive a reply from me.

26 Certainly not to rescue me, apparently, despite my efforts these many years on their behalf.

27 Eyewitnesses believed Bauble used ventriloquism to create the voices of the characters. However, what if, instead, Hellatose was throwing his voice?

28 Except for the odd children's comic strip "The Adventures of Hellatose & Bauble" that ran for several years in local broadsheets. A sample of the text:

> Bauble & Hellatose are sitting in their circus tent, Bauble on a chair, Hellatose in his wading pool. Bauble is reading a broadsheet on the current state of Ambergrisian politics. Hellatose is imbibing, through a very long straw, a slightly alcoholic beverage with a tiny umbrella in it. It's been a long day performing complex psycho-dramas for uncaring snot-nosed children . . .

> *Hellatose:* Bauble?
> *Bauble:* Yes, Hellatose?
> *Hellatose:* Bauble, why aren't I better known?
> *Bauble:* Better known as what, Hellatose?
> *Hellatose:* As a playwright, Bauble. A playwright. I should be as well known as Voss Bender.
> *Bauble (absorbed in his broadsheet):* Really?
> *Hellatose:* Yes. I should be. I definitely shouldn't be *here.* (Waves tentacles around to indicate the confines of the tent.)

Bauble: You're a squid, Hellatose.
Hellatose: All the more reason. I should be splashing around in my very own place of honor in a private pud-dlebox at the theater.
Bauble: There's no such thing as a puddlebox, Hellatose.
Hellatose (sighing): There should be, Bauble. There should be.

29   My family used squid ink to write with for a time, while we had the squid mills. The squiders would bring it up in a glass container whenever we needed a refill. If I had known what indignities squid endure during ink collection, I would have used more conventional substances. My father, however, continued to use the ink and so it was never entirely exorcised from our house.

III – EXPOUNDING WITH BREVITY ON THE PECULIARITIES OF SQUID LORE

A WARY INTRODUCTION TO THE FESTIVAL[30]

THOSE WITH MAGGOTS FOR BRAINS, WHO NUMBER MANY AND cure so few, often refer to the "misunderstood" Festival, as if it were some sort of sorely maligned creature, unfairly subjected to electric shock therapy and short rations due to a vice that, if viewed in a more sympathetic light, might be revealed as virtue. The boobish Bellamy Palethorpe, in his weekly tirade for the *Ambergris Daily Broadsheet,* "Bellamy Retorts," would take precious column inches away from spraying the arterial blood of his enemies across the printed page to reminisce about youthful festival indulgences, referring to them as "innocent," "fun-loving," and "harmless antics." Even the great lackbrain Voss Bender would at times shrug his shoulders and look to the heavens, as if the Festival existed independent of its participants. It is this kind of cloddish thinking that my mother, for all of her faults, railed against on a weekly basis. For if this theory of non-responsibility were universally applied, many an insensate, myopic fool, tripping through life in undeserved freedom, could hope for "redemption through reinterpretation"—a ham-fisted piece of Truffidian theology and a favorite dream of prison/asylum inmates.

The "truth"—and every squidologist is always painfully aware that today's truth may be tomorrow's chum—is that the Festival, as Martin Lake once put it, "exists whole and darkly glittering in the mind of each citizen of Ambergris." I would travel farther than Lake and state that each separate version/vision creates a splinter Festival—and another, and another, until, turning upon that distant stage, no stars above for comfort, one finds oneself trapped in a hall of fractured mirrors comprised of so many reflected Festivals that it becomes impossible to choose the real Festival, even should freedom depend upon it.[31] The various accumulations of rituals and odd customs, gathered together and twisted into a beggar's pack before being offered up by smug experts as the "festival experience," have no intrinsic worth.[32]

The true "festival experience" cannot be fully explained even by the most learned squidologist. At the height of the Festival, one almost feels at home as, surrounded by squid floats and revelers in squid masks and squid balloons and the musky odor of fresh fish and seaweed, one can almost pretend that the trail of the light-festooned street is the Moth itself, and the revelers freshwater squid, gathered for social intercourse. The giddy energy, the sense of swimming upstream caused by the heavy thickness of the people you must brush up against to walk along the sidewalk, the sloshing of drinks in their glasses and cups, the wild surge of conversations, like the trickling of water over rocks downstream . . . There is such longing in these memories.

I experienced my first Festival more than 15 years ago.[33] Freed finally from the ancestral home, from the magnifying-glass attentions of my mother and the febrile energy of my father, I was taking classes with the esteemed squidologist Chamblee Gort and breathing in such liberty as I have not known since. The Festival came as a revelation to me. It wakened in me all of those long-repressed feelings that I had accumulated in my youth among the books, reading tome after tome in that library as large as many people's houses. Like many others, I ran naked[34] through the revelers, clad only in my squid mask and lost myself in the crowds. It was only later, when I remembered the attendant violence,[35] that I realized the Festival was a poor substitute.[36]

AN ATTEMPT TO ATTEMPT THE SUBJECT REGARDLESS

However, despite my introduction, why not attempt (and tempt) the impossible.[37] Therefore:

The Festival did not originate as so many feckless historians (from Mr. Shriek on down) have suggested—namely, with an order by Cappan Manzikert I, first ruler of Ambergris, a year after founding the city. No, the Festival echoes a much earlier Festival put on by the indigenous tribe called the Dogghe.[38]

The Dogghe worshipped what we now call the "Mothean Scuttlefish," a dour type of squid, primitive by invertebrate standards, that likes nothing better than to wallow in the silt at the river's bottom and siphon gross sustenance from the rotting refuse to be found there.

The Dogghe believed—for reasons forever lost to us along with most of the Dogghe—that the flesh of the scuttlefish held regenerative powers and heightened the amorous abilities of those who ate of it. Their annual celebration, held at roughly the same time as the modern day Festival, culminated with the choosing of one man to hunt the scuttlefish. Given that the average Mothean Scuttlefish, flattened against the riverbed, forms a circle roughly six feet across and that their primary defense consists of stuffing as much of their invertebrate bodies as possible down their attacker's mouth and other available orifices, being selected cannot have been considered much of an honor by the selectee. (Imagine being suffocated underwater rather than drowned.)

No doubt the Manzikert clan, opportunists as always, usurped the Dogghe's festival for the practical reason that it marked the start of the best ("best" is a relative term in this context) time to hunt the King Squid but also to replace the Dogghe's rituals with stronger "magic."

From dubious sources such as Dradin Kashmir's third-person autobiography, *Dradin, In Love,*[39] we can extract a few additional "facts":

> The Festival is a celebration of the spawning season, when the males battle mightily for females of the species and the fisher folk of the docks set out for a month's trawling of the lusting ground, hoping to bring enough meat back to last until winter.

Beyond the obvious errors in this silly passage, I would point out the pathetic phallacy of battle. No such contests occur, except within the syllables of overheated ultra-decadent purple prose. The depiction of a "spawning season/lusting ground" conjures up a depraved scene of tentacular orgies with great strobing bodies entangled and writhing as they thrash about in the silt. Alas, King Squid mate for life and do not congregate to breed.[40] Only "widowed" or "unwed" squid maneuver for mates, and then only in solitary, scattered rituals that occur at another time of year entirely.

No, in fact, the squid gatherings at Festival time appear to consist of an orderly convocation of conferences—a convention of squid, at which a good deal of intense strobing occurs, but very little sexual activity.

I cannot overstate the dangers involved in disrupting such meetings for the purpose of hunting squid. One year, Ambergris lost 20 ships and over 600 sailors. On average, the squid-hunting season results in at least 30 casualties and the loss of more than a dozen ships.[41] Even the casual researcher begins to wonder, scrutinizing the statistics, whether the King Squid congregate merely to hunt humans.

What benefits does Ambergris gain from this yearly sacrifice of men and materials? The answer is "an abundance of riches," from the skin used as airtight containers and the meat sold to the Kalif's empire, to the experimental new motored vehicle fuels developed by Hoegbotton & Sons Industrial Branch from squid oil and ink. Every part of the squid is used for some product, even the beak, which, ground down, comprises a key ingredient in the perfume exports that have, in recent years, brought money pouring into the Ambergris economy (little of which has gone into invertebrate research).

THE SQUID MILLS OF MY YOUTH

As an offshoot of the hunt—and perhaps to offset its unpredictable nature, Ambergris and many other Southern river cities experimented with squid mills for a time. Such attempts to breed the squid in semi-captivity were doomed to failure: the mills required too much space, blocking river traffic, and the squid were, at best, uncooperative.

In a depressingly familiar scenario, replicated throughout my life with regard to the objects of my desire, I remember the squid mills precisely because I was not, at first, allowed near enough to them to satisfy my curiosity (and when I finally was allowed, I could not enjoy the experience).

Framed by the third-story window of the locked library, the River Moth wound its way through the vast expanse of grounds to the west. With the naked eye, all I could make out of the squid mills was a glint of sun off metal and a suggestion of movement. With the aid of a spyglass, smuggled up from my rooms, I could just discern the unsubmerged portions of the squid mills: the tops of the huge metal cages, the great white pontoons that separated and supported them. Around these cages, from which I often fancied I saw a tip of tentacle creep out, strode the squiders in their red boots, overalls, thick gloves, and wide-brimmed hats. The single-minded attention they paid to their tasks only underscored the dangers of farming the squid.

Those men assigned to the deeper parts of the river, which contained completely submerged squid cages, used "squilts"—long, thick stilts that required great strength to maneuver through the turgid water. The top half of the squilts could be detached for use as a weapon against either the captive squid or the wild squid that often attempted to free their brethren.

From my vantage, through the selective eye of the spyglass, those squiders in the deepest parts of the river seemed miraculous—"walking" on the water, the squilts completely submerged as they trudged along, gaze intent upon the swirling silt below them. The job of the squider took a tremendous sensitivity, for they "felt" the water with the squilts, searching for the vibrations of wild squid, sometimes sweeping special hand-held hooks through the water, hoping to encounter rubbery flesh.[42] When the caged squid were used as bait for juvenile wild King Squid, the squiders would herd the wild squid into nets using nothing but the hooks and squilts. On one occasion, I observed a sudden frantic splashing of water, the suggestion of a large, dark body shooting up from the river bed, followed by a squider suddenly disappearing, his squilts still upright and vibrating . . .

Little wonder that to be "put through the squid mill" still means accomplishments gained through tedious yet danger-ous labor. As we were driven through the local village on our way to the Truffidian Cathedral,[43] I would often hear the children of the squiders singing:

Oh, stop the squid mill, stop it, I pray
For I have been tending squid a good deal today
My head is quite sore from the thrashing I've received.
And my squilty bosses ache so much that sorely I am grieved.
Oh, stop the squid mill, stop it today, and I'll be relieved.

For a long time, stuck in that library for so many months, forbidden by my mother to go outside, I wanted to be a squider. Alas, eventually the village children got their wish and the squid mills died out. I turned to squidology and the library became associated not with squid mills but with a series of other banal events.

RELATED SQUIDLORE

Many of the folk remedies attributed to lesser squid do not apply to the King Squid, which seems oddly resistant to being of use. For example, the old remedy in which one "lays a squid on the feet of the afflicted" to cure toothache or headache would take on a nightmarish context should a two-ton squid be winched into position and dropped on the patient! Nor does the ground beak of the King Squid, mixed with wine, stimulate sexual prowess or draw the poison from the bite of a venomous snake.

This also applies to the "squid cap"—a popular folk remedy to cure headaches and insomnia, immortalized in these lines from a play by Machel:

Bring in the squid cap. You must be shaved, sir
And then how suddenly we'll make you sleep.

Traditionally, the "squid cap" placed on countless hapless heads consisted of a mixture of raw squid tentacles, milk, honey, rice, and wine, contained within a poultice. Relatedly, to have a "head squid" means to have a head cold—an apt metaphor since a cold could often feel to the patient as if a squid had reached its arms down into his or her skull. Alas, the squid cap has never been touted as a cure for the common head squid. Alas, too, some folks have a more serious, permanent case of squid head. (Not to mention "squidlick," a badly curled haircut.)

Actual squid recipes have been around for many hundreds of years, as exemplified by this children's rhyme taken from the *Blythe Academy Squid Primer:*

> Here's water in your eye
> From a half-baked squid pie
> With the tentacles still a'twitching
> And the gummy arms still itching
> To catch you up to the beak
> The beak beak beak beak beak

The Ambergris Gourmand Society has recorded 1,752 squid recipes originating from Ambergris alone.

Many squid-related words have entered the Ambergrisian vocabulary. While "ambiloquent" still means to be dexterous in doubletalk, to be "squidiloquent" is a much higher compliment. A "squid wife" sells squid. A "squidler," as opposed to a "squider," is one who handles squid for entertainment. Bauble would have been a good example of a squidler. A "chamber squid" is a common Mud Squid placed in a hotel room during the Festival for luck. A "squidpiece," no longer much used now that Cappans do not rule Ambergris, used to refer to what can only be termed a kind of ornamental protective gear worn outside of the clothing, covering the genitals. An "obsquidium" would refer to an act of compliance in squid cult orations.

Of course, squidanthropy is the most famous aspect of squidlore.

SQUIDANTHROPY

Squidanthropy is not, as some have misidentified it, the domain of squid philanthropists but, rather, a form of supposed insanity in which a man imagines himself to be a squid. This may result in the subject taking to the waters in an attempt to rejoin his squidkin, with often fatal consequences if one wants to be honest about it, or simply a confused physiology: the subject may believe he or she is drowning while on dry land or feel the absence of gills or a mantle, or lose the ability to walk and find oneself swimming around in public fountains.

The most committed of amateur squidologists will always empathize with the underlying urge toward squidanthropy. It is no empty promise, no empty threat of a cure. It is simply one way in which to fulfill the dream known since childhood: to understand the squid in all of its manifestations. What squidologist has not thought of what it would be like to have a mantle? What squidologist, while spraying water on his boyhood friends, many or few, has not thought how much more fun to have a funnel? It is inevitable that in the quest to get under the King Squid's skin, the squidologist learns to think like the squid. Like the detective who, in investigating a murder, loses himself in the identity of the murderer, the squidologist may, at times, lose himself in the identity of the squid (which, admittedly, has committed no crime). That some few do not come back out the other side to "sanity" is to be expected—and, perhaps, applauded. Those who follow a singular obsession their entire lives should not be castigated for achieving the object of that obsession. Would we punish an artist for, through one last burst of genius flecked with insanity, creating the masterwork for which the world had been waiting since the beginning of the artist's career? For make no mistake—in squidanthropy, the amateur squidologist longs to make the final, synergistic leap that separates observer from observed, patient from doctor. The doctor studies the thing the patient has become, whereas the patient longs to study and understand himself. The correlation and the corollary are clear . . . [44]

{

⇒ Notes ⇐

30 Ironically, my mother loved the Festival for its colors and its spectacle. She truly believed the Truffidian Church's proclamation that the Festival had been "reclaimed for God." My father, on the other hand, found it frivolous and dangerous—he forbade me from going at first, although he would never tell me why.

31 Sometimes, one's freedom, as any squidologist knows, depends on the patterns a squid's ink makes as it lingers in the water.

32 The situation is not without humor, for it closely resembles the situation that exists within a mental institution: in tight quarters, in similar garb, dissimilar minds attempt to build a consensus reality that, with a monumental effort of empathy, cannot—can never!—take concrete form. (If you do not like this new tone I have adopted, O Reader, remember that tone can change depending on the mood of the day and the amount of medication.)

33 Better that I be deprived of the "Festival" as practiced *here*—it resembles the real Festival only in the way a soggy cupcake resembles a wedding cake.

34 Alas, young squidologists, you are unlikely to see a woman in the places you'll be traipsing through in your waterproof boots. Only a female squidologist will truly understand you—and they are few and far between; not every Furness finds his Leepin. You may find some comfort in documenting the sensual activities of the female King Squid, but danger lies therein as well.

35   Issues of Festival violence and the involvement of Ambergris' subterranean inhabitants, the gray caps, lie outside of this section's purview and therefore I have chosen to ignore such unpleasantries for the moment.

36   See: Cane, Albert.

37   At least at the level of drought-like fact, one may make statements about the history of the Festival that, while boring, could be sworn to before a board of inquiry.

38   As do, to be brutally honest, half of Ambergris' current stuporstitions, including raw, chopped-up rabbit as a cure for eating poison mushrooms and the enchanting thought that lying in a pool of blood extracted from deer livers will bring back the dead. Believe me, if I thought it worked, I would have tried it first. (See: Stindle, Bernard.) At least the modern welt that is psychotherapy cannot be laid at the Dogghe's door.

39   Written by a madman, if you can believe that, and yet still read today.

40   Unlike many human beings. Some, like my mother, could not stop preying off the local help.

41   Squid baiting has never been a popular sport.

42   These silent, solitary men must be of the sternest and calmest disposition while pursuing their work. Many, in fact, left the employ of the squid mills to become solo squid hunters, or "squidquellers," and were often found in remote parts of the River Moth, waiting patiently on their squilts for the slightest ripple of squid.

43 My mother was a devout Truffidian. My father and I would spend an hour at night with her, praying. Although I did not, as a rule, get to go out—as now as then—mother did insist we go to church: that stale and perfunctory place where all the cattle sit like people in the pews.

44 I feel a great (s)urge, suddenly, to wax autobiographical, but shall contain the impulse until once again among my ancestral books. (Is this the "breakthrough" in my personal development long promised by the resident gods? Strange. It feels more like a death knell. I sense a great abyss opening up beneath me, a vein of deep water not previously negotiated by fish or squid.)

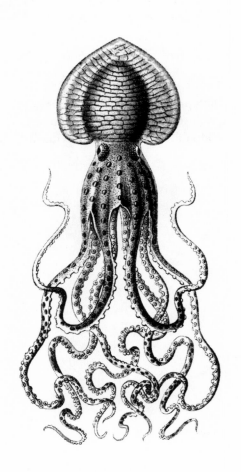

PART IV – DIVULGING AN ACCURATE SCIENTIFIC THEORY THAT EXPLAINS A NUMBER OF OTHERWISE PUZZLING THINGS THAT HAVE LONG PREYED UPON THE MIND OF THIS WRITER (AND A VISION)

THE THEORY

NOW, AS WE COME TO THE CRUCIAL POINT, I SHALL BEGIN TO shed my horrible verbosity as if it were just my human skin. My words, I promise, shall become sure and fleet, as if my feet were different than those a poet knows (this squidologist's fleeting fancy).[45] I realize that I have, for the most part, documented the ridiculous theories of others in hopes of dissuading the reader from holding credence in them. However, I beg for the reader's indulgence and endurance as I expound upon my own, scientifically-based theory about the King Squid, derived from my ceaseless and exhaustive study of this fascinating creature,[46] both in its natural state and flatly two-dimensional within the pages of various books. (I have tried to hold back and speak only of these matters at the end, when you might be most receptive to what could, in the light of day that is the beginning of an essay rather than the dusk at the end, appear absurd. But now I am duty-bound to discuss it.)

Preamble is overrated: In short, I believe that the King Squid serves as host for the so-called King Fungus cultivated by the gray caps—the purple wedge of evil that so proliferated across the city's streets and dwellings prior to the murder we call The Silence. I do not suggest, as some have, that the gray caps' spores alone cause the violence and disorientation that is the Festival. No, the truth is more insidious and invasive, dear reader. The unique *symbiosis* between fungi and squid is the reason why we remain in subconscious thrall to the gray caps.[47] We should not eat the flesh of the squid, for it has been contaminated by the fungus. (I say this having momentarily set aside my mantle as squid advocate.) Or, more specifically, the fungus incubating within the flesh of the squid. The fungus in the squid.

The concept may be difficult for the layperson to understand, or to accept, but I base it on very sound invertebrate intuition. Squidologists, for example, have long wondered how the King Squid attains the raw intensities of red and green that make it burn with light under the stress of hunger or courtship—intensities impossible in any other squid, and strangely akin to the lights seen over landbound Alfar directly prior to the mass murder of The Silence. Not to mention the evidence of intelligence, landward jaunts, and messages sent to squidologists writ in pulsing skin.

As all of these developments have occurred over the past 100 years, I believe it is only recently that the gray caps have fed a special fungus to the squid, using their submerged metal boats. These feedings have increased the squid's color intensity and its ingenuity, while simultaneously contaminating the meat in such a way as to make Ambergrisians more susceptible to the gray caps' spores during the (ironically-named) Festival of the Freshwater Squid. From squid steaks to squid stews, we poison ourselves more and more each year. Thus does the Festival violence spread and intensify.[48]

If this monograph serves any useful purpose beyond the mundane, it is to caution against the eating of squid flesh.

A Vision

A vision may have no place in a serious monograph, but having come this far, I am reluctant to stop. This vision comes to me on days when I am fed squid meat. Alas, I cannot, even now, knowing what I know, being what I am, stop eating squid meat, such is the compulsion of the fungus within the squid.

The vision that has reached me in my sleep of recent months is worthy of the likes of Hellatose: I travel across a great chasm of Time that passes as quickly as clouds in a storm and as that time trickles past I see the squid taking more and more to the land, their bewitching eyes hidden by the globes of water, their skin a translucent silver, while, fed on spores and the meat of an animal more intelligent than they know, Ambergris' true inhabitants grow watery and ill, their flesh moist, sallow, and ever more boneless, until eventually the squid take their place and the current Ambergrisians recede into the waters as if they had never been anything but a fiction, remnants, revenants, in this great city, globules of infected fat and skin—too dazed and decadent to fight back when the gray caps flood the city and we, long-prepped for invasion, scuttle into Ambergris, our arms and tentacles wrapped around buildings and vehicles, the very stones marked by the claw and the sucker, while the humans, pale underclass, pale underbelly, are but servants for our will.

The advance guard and scouting parties have already begun—what are the water-globed squid if not this? I would not be at all surprised if the King Squid were already among us, their spies having perfected the art of camouflage so as to replicate setting and human alike.

There are those idiots here who would escape their fate more literally, and with haste, their means as simple as they are and yet myriad—sneaking into the pill cabinet, sharpening a spoon for their wrists, tearing their clothes up for a noose. You see it here all the time. None of them in death will better understand the mysteries of their lives and I do not envy them this state, even when my own transformation seems so far away.

⇒ Notes ⇐

45   Perhaps too tentative a pentameter.

46   What else is there to do here? The other patrons of this fine establishment share neither my interests nor my temperaments. Were I to awaken a vague interest in squidology amongst the general populace, I might take solace in lectures or even idle conversations during the blank hours, but, alas, this is not to be . . .

47   I believe my morelean father was, at the time of his demise, working on just such a theory. Perhaps this explains his own morbid interest in the abandoned squidmills. Unfortunately, he did not have the background in squidology necessary to develop his theory.

48   During the rule of the Cappans, the gray caps had not yet perfected this system and the city had not become as dependent on squid flesh. Why, it may be that the gray caps have worked to make squid meat more succulent to us and therefore more addictive.

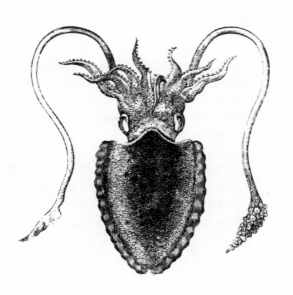

❧ BIBLIOGRAPHY ❧

(INTERMITTENTLY ANNOTATED)

This bibliography allows the reader to follow up on the subject matter set out in my monograph. Many of these books I conjure whole from memory, the originals having haunted the shelves of my long-abandoned childhood library. (Thus this bibliography serves as a kind of memorial to the one saving grace of my youth.) As for the question of publication dates, even those books found in the pathetic library I currently have access to are likely to be hopelessly antiquated editions. Most of these tomes are either so common or so rare as to make the question of time moot, even if I could set out the dates with anything approaching consistency. Where necessary, I have placed my own comments about a particular book in parentheses following the bibliographical information, in the hopes that my added insight will be of some small value.

Absence, Thrasher T., *Squid Camouflage: What Are They Trying to Hide?*, Squid Mill Library Press.

Aldrich, Clyde, *Squid?*, Distant Bells Press.

Allans, John, *The Hoegbotton Guide to Nymphomania,* Hoegbotton & Sons Press.

Alsop, Seymour, *Ammonia Among Old Beaks: Essays and Idylls of a Squid Lover,* Dyfold Press.
    (Precise in its data yet utterly false in its conclusions.)

Anon, *The Hoegbotton Book of Absurd Synonyms,* Hoegbotton & Sons.

Anon, *The Hoegbotton Book of Obscure Insults,* Hoegbotton & Sons.

Anon, *The Hoegbotton Guide to Psychological Terminology,* Hoegbotton & Sons Press.

Babbit, Cynthia, *A Child's Coloring Book of Squid, Featuring Three Imaginary Ones,* Libyrinth Press.

Bamardot, Allison, *The Squidularch and His Watery World,* Nicea Publishers.
    (An interesting argument for a crude form of squid government.)

Batton, Sarah, ed., *Squid Sightings Magazine,* Vols. 1–23, Renegade Mollusk Press.

Bender, Voss, "A Refutation of the Claim that Certain of My Operas Have Been Aided by Squid-Written Arias," *Ambergris Drama Digest,* Vol. 234, No. 12, Front Row Publications.
    (Would that they had been.)

Bender, Voss, *Bender for Riverside Reading,* Frankwrithe & Lewden.

Bender, Voss, *Libretto with Squid,* Frankwrithe & Lewden.

Bentinck, Bargin, *The Library of Robert Quill: An Instance of Squidophilia,* Borges Bookstore Publishing.
(Bentinck's library far exceeded that of my parents, especially in the area of squid-related books. It is one of the great tragedies of my life that I have been unable to visit it. If I ever do, it will blissfully eclipse memories of my own red-spined volumes.)

Blade, Jeremy, *The Hoegbotton Guide to Oikomania,* Hoegbotton & Sons Press.

Blei, Frank, "Invasive Foreign Squid: The Visitors That Never Leave," *The Morrow Wildlife Quarterly,* Vol. 400, No. 4, Mandible & Crossclaw.

Bordman, Ann K., *Squidopolis,* Buzz Press.
(A novel, this book is, in fictional form, the twin to my nonfiction and, lacking my purpling prose, my better half.)

Brecht, Richard, Jr., *Jackaclock Squidulous:* The Life of a Squid Boxer, Savor Press.

Breitenbach, Joseph A., ed., *The Hoegbotton Guide to Common Cephalopod Mannerisms* (chapbook), Hoegbotton & Sons.

Breitenbach, Joseph A., "Caudal Fin Exercises You Can Do at Home," published in *The Amateur Squidologist,* Vol. 19, Issue 7, Ambergris Squidology Society.
(Quite useful—these exercises do indeed strengthen the arms.)

Breitenbach, Joseph A., ed., *Hoegbotton & Sons Parts Catalog for Squid-Grade Freshwater Filters,* Hoegbotton & Sons.

Breitenbach, Joseph A., *Mating Rituals of the Freshwater Squid* (Illustrated Edition), Hoegbotton & Sons.

(As debauched a book as one is likely to own. Salacious and steamy—complete with hard-to-follow diagrams.)

Breitenbach, Joseph A., *The Book of Squid Sense,* Alfar Publishing Consortium.

Breitenbach, Joseph A., *The Hoegbotton Pricing Guide to Collectible Ceramic Squid* (chapbook), Hoegbotton & Sons.

Brek, George, *The Squid and the Shade-Head: Philosophical Loci of the New Art,* Tarzia Publishers.

(I much prefer the views on the New Art set out in Rogers' *Torture Squid* books.)

Brisk, Susan, *A Compendium of Squid Sounds and Squid-Related Sounds,* Southern Cities Press.

(What, you might ask, is a "squid-related" sound? The unexpected gush of a water funnel. The wet slap of a tentacle against a railing. Suckers clamping down on skin.)

Brisk, Susan, *The Illustrated Book of Squid,* Hoegbotton & Sons.

Brod, Maxwell, *Classic Fallacies in the Work of Jonathan Madnok,* Debunked Press.

(I include this misshapen and monstrous text only to provide a balanced bibliography. Not a word of this book, except for some conjunctions and prepositions, contains any truth.)

Burden, Rosetta, *The Cephalopod's Colophon,* House & Garden.

Burke, K. Craddock, *The Short Lives of Squid Cults: Annals of a Long Legacy,* Hoegbotton & Sons.
  (Squid cults have afflicted us since before the rise of the Dogghe Tribes. This fascinating book traces their development and frequent demise. The most interesting chapter explains the intricacies of the Squid Head Cult that arose during the civil unrest caused by the Reds and the Greens.)

Burlveener, William Barnett, *Encyclopedia Cephalopodia,* Frankwrithe & Lewden.

Burlveener, William Barnett, *The Compleat Squider,* Outdoor Adventure Publishing.

Burlveener, William Barnett, *The Inkmaker's Reference Guide,* Borges Bookstore Publishing.
  (Most relevant for the whimsical aside on Hellatose the performing squid.)

Butterhead, R.G., *The Double Cephalopod Folio: The Story of Daffed's "Squids of Ambergris,"* Hoegbotton & Sons.

Butterhead, R.G., *The Squidqueller's Handbook,* Fisherman's Hook Publications.

Cane, Albert, *Squidanthropy: Causes and Appropriate Reactions,* Modern Psychiatrics Press.
  (One of the few doctors to grasp the true nature of this tragically misunderstood phenomenon.)

Chisler, John, *The Hoegbotton Guide to Anthomania,* Hoegbotton & Sons Press.

Chisler, John, *The Hoegbotton Guide to Paramania,* Hoegbotton & Sons Press.

Clark, Machen, *The Squid on Our Backs, the Tentacles in Our Brains: An Account of a Descent into Madness,* Grievance Press.

Cram, Louis, *A List and Description of Ambergris Squid Clubs,* Blackmarket Publications.
    (Squid clubs, for the uninitiated, constitute one of Ambergris' dirty little secrets. Squid clubs vary in degeneracy, from those that feature betting on squid fights to those that boil live squid right in front of you. And in some of the city's most dangerous establishments, you can partake of debaucheries best left to the shadows of wordlessness.)

Cram, Louis, *Squidphilobiblon,* Squid-Lover's Press.

Cram, Louis, *The Cephalopod Codex,* Squid-Lover's Press.

Cross, Templeton, "An Analysis of the Mating Call of the Crimson Bull Squid," *Bulletin of the History of Mollusk Studies,* Vol. 676, No. 6, Libyrinth Press.

Cross, Templeton, "Maestros of the Deep: A Proposal Towards Revising Our Notions on the Intelligence of the Crimson Bull Squid," *Bulletin of the History of Mollusk Studies,* Vol. 678, No. 4, Libyrinth Press.

Cross, Templeton, "A Note on Rook's Misappropriation of Crimson Bull Squid Mating Calls in his Proposed 'Opera,'" *Bulletin of the History of Mollusk Studies,* Vol. 679, No. 12, Libyrinth Press.

Ditchfield, Marc, *Squid Fatal to Their Owners,* Frankwrithe & Lewden.
    (It astonished me to read just how many squid have been fatal to their owners throughout Ambergris' history.)

Dormand, Samuel T., *The Hoegbotton Guide to Bruxomania,* Hoegbotton & Sons Press.

Dormand, Samuel T., *The Hoegbotton Guide to Pathomania,* Hoegbotton & Sons Press.

Drabble, Smocke, *A Compleat Dictionary of Squid Types with Small But Comprehensible Drawings of Tentacles and Beaks,* Diverse Kinds Press.

(The dictionary is compleat, all right. Alas, the drawings are *not* comprehensible, consisting as they do of a series of spasmodic scribbles.)

Dribble, Larken, *Squid Inks: A Catalog of Cephalopod Political and Personal Satire Preserved by the Ambergris Department of Broadsheet Licensing,* Ambergris Department of Broadsheet Licensing Publications.

Dundas, Elayne, *"And I Heard of a Mollusk in Your Ear": Folk-Humor Among the Squid Fishermen of the Moth River Delta,* Tarzia Publishing.

(So this is what the squiders said to each other as they tended the squid mills! It was a revelation to discover this book one sticky sweet summer day stuck—bliss and torment—in the library. It gave voice to those far-off men otherwise only visible to me through my spyglass.)

Enamel, George, *The Hoegbotton Guide to Cheromania,* Hoegbotton & Sons Press.

Enamel, George, *The Hoegbotton Guide to Phaneromania,* Hoegbotton & Sons Press.

Evens, Langerland, "Squid Mating Activity on the Southern Coastal Plain During the Late Pre-Trillian Period," Vol. 29,

No. 11, *Squidologist Digest*, Morrow Squidologist Association.

Everlane, Brian, *Gentleman Squid*, Frankwrithe & Lewden.
(A risky and risque novel that charts the downward course of a promising young architect as he tries unsuccessfully to deal with his squid obsession. The evocation of the infamous Oleander Squid Club—closed down twenty years ago—has true poignancy.)

Everlane, Brian, *Squidy Jenkins: The Great Prize Fighters of Yesteryear, Volume 9*, Southern Cities Press.
(Gerald Jenkins received his "Squidy" nickname for the rapidity of his punches, which at times made his arms appear multiplied to a more cephalopodic number.)

Fain, Corbett, "An Analysis of Squid Feces Obtained at Various and Divers Locations Around the City," published in *The Amateur Squidologist*, Vol. 10, Issue 5, Ambergris Squidology Society.
(The less said, the better.)

Fain, Corbett, *Nicean Cuttlefish Rarities Discovered in a Second Portfolio of Louis Verden's Squid Plates*, Southern Cities Press.

Fangmountain, Eliza, *Squid in Myth, Magic, and Medicine*, Frankwrithe & Lewden.
(The myth, the magic, if not the medicine, are all, as far as I'm concerned, to do with the author's dangerously precipitous surname.)

Farmore, Arthur, "Rising Bubbles: The Case for Squid Indiscretions," published in *The Amateur Squidologist*, Vol. 19, Issue 7, Ambergris Squidology Society.

(Farmore would have enjoyed talking to Fain, no doubt—both covered their subject from the same end.)

Feaster, Elaine, "B&H: The Circumstantial Evidence," *The Amateur Squidologist,* Vol. 44, Issue 4, Ambergris Squidology Society.

Feeney, Dora, *The Hoegbotton Guide to Poriomania,* Hoegbotton & Sons Press.

Fisher, Marian T., "Wrede's Aporia: A Refutation of Gendered Hydrotherapy," *Current Cephalopodic Remedies,* Vol. 21, No. 7, Libyrinth Press.

Fisher, Marian T., "Spilled Ink: A Deconstructionist Critique of Wredian Methodology," *Current Cephalopodic Remedies,* Vol. 21, No. 11, Libyrinth Press.

Flack, Harry, *Squid Stalking at Home and Abroad,* Action-Danger Press.

Flack, Harry, *The Further Deadly But True Adventures of the Squid Hunter,* Hoegbotton & Sons.

Flack, Harry, *The Latest Horrifying and Yet Oddly Magnificent Adventures of the Courageous Squid Hunter,* Frankwrithe & Lewden.
(Probably the best of this tough-man series. Ironic, really, that I read him as a child and fill him out as an adult.)

Flack, Harry, *The Return of the Squid Hunter and His Horribly Dangerous Profession,* Hoegbotton & Sons.

Flack, Harry, *The Squid Hunter's Ferocious Adventures in the Wilds,* Hoegbotton & Sons.

Flack, Harry, *Voss Bender Memorial Mental Institute Clinic Check-In Form.*

Flack, Harry, *Voss Bender Memorial Mental Institute Handbook of Regulations.*

Flack, Harry, *Voss Bender Memorial Mental Institute Patient Evaluation Form.*

Flack, Harry, *Voss Bender Memorial Mental Institute Patient Sign-in Sheet.*

Flaunt, Contense T., *How to Order Your Bibliography for Maximum Reader Impact,* The Writing Life Consortium.

Flex, Drednaught, *Squid Squinting: The Elmor Brax Story,* Mathew Press.

Floxence, Edna, *The Mysteries of the Freshwater Squid Revealed,* Credence, Ltd.
    (Acarpous!)

Floxence, Edna, *The Strange World of the Freshwater Squid,* Credence, Ltd.
    (Feeble-brained theorists should not tackle squidology!)

Forrest, Hayden A., *An Outspoken Condemnation of Squid Wrestling,* Six Doors Press.

Forrest, Hayden A., *Beaks to Beakers: The History of Squid Science,* Mollusk Medicine Press.
    (A harrowing volume in which electric squid experiments and nerve ending research make me cringe in sympathy even now.)

Forrest, Hayden A., *Cephalopodectomy in Theory and Practice,* Mollusk Medicine Press.

Forrest, Hayden A., *Famous Tentaclopheliacs,* Snark & Daughters.
(Even Trillian, apparently, was one—and most of his Banker Warriors.)

Forrest, Hayden A., *Kraken Dawn: An Investigation of the Post-Celebration Sleep Patterns of Festival Attendees,* Wry Investigations, Inc.

Forrest, Hayden A., *Squid Wrestling for Fun and Profit,* Engelbrecht Club Publishing.

Fragnall, Dibdin, *Puddling by the Docks: An Ecstacy of Collecting,* Frankwrithe & Lewden.
(Truly a career-affirming experience for any aspiring squidologist. Dibdin understands the squidology subculture better than any living author.)

Fragnall, Dibdin, *The Coffee Table Book of Squid Forgeries,* Frankwrithe & Lewden.

Furness, Raymond and Leepin, Paulina, *Anatomy of a Betrayal: Why We Left the Water After 20 Years of Squid Studies,* Bypass Press.

Furness, Raymond and Leepin, Paulina, *Discredited: Why We Have Been the Target of Unfair Ridicule and Persecution by Other Squidologists* (chapbook), privately published.

Furness, Raymond and Leepin, Paulina, *King Squid Nocturnal Prey Stalking Tactics,* Buzzard Publishing.

Furness, Raymond and Leepin, Paulina, *Some Interesting Metaphors Conveyed to Us By the King Squid* (chapbook), Ambergris Squidology Society.

Furness, Raymond and Leepin, Paulina, *Squid Communication in Murky Conditions* (chapbook), Leoprand Collective Publishing.

Furness, Raymond and Leepin, Paulina, *Sucker Strength in King Squid Juveniles,* Nicea Publications for the Betterment of Science.

Furness, Raymond and Leepin, Paulina, *That Which Cannot Be Said: The Real Case for Squid Intelligence,* Cephalopod Press.
    (Although not specifically cited within my monograph, this book most influenced my arguments for squid intelligence.)

Furness, Raymond and Leepin, Paulina, *The Darkness of Squid Ink: Our Personal Journey into Obscurity* (chapbook), privately printed.

Furness, Raymond and Leepin, Paulina, *The Loss of Dignity in the Face of Persecution: Scientists Forced to Beg for Food* (broadsheet), privately published.

Furness, Raymond and Leepin, Paulina, *The Sociological Significance of Beak Size in King Squid Communities,* Southern Cities Press.

Furness, Raymond and Leepin, Paulina, *The Terrifying King Squid Speaks,* privately published.

Furness, Raymond and Leepin, Paulina, *Vital Similarities Between the King Squid and the Skamoo Icicle Squid of the Extreme North,* Absence Publications.

Gambol, Nils, *Flashions: The Influence of Squid Tentacles on Ambergrisian Hair Salons,* Nail Biter Productions.
   (One might consider the recent squid fads in hair styles and other primpings to be a kind of passive squidanthropy—although to one truly afflicted with the disease, it no doubt feels like cruel mockery.)

Gevers, Nicholas, *Last and First Squid,* Johannes Publishing.

Giflank, Henry, *The Hoegbotton Guide to Cresomania,* Hoegbotton & Sons Press.

Giflank, Henry, *The Hoegbotton Guide to Pseudomania,* Hoegbotton & Sons Press.

Gort, Joan, *Investigations, According to Licensed Dock Number and Maritime Phratry, of Squid-Haul Tallymen on Public Aid: Volume Seven of the Statistical Survey of Mothian Municipalities, With Figures Representing the Flux of Civil Posts During the Partition of the Ruling Government,* Tarzia Public Document Archives.

Gort, Marmy, "A Select Listing of Squid Catalogued at the Fish Markets of the Ambergris Docks," published in *The Amateur Squidologist,* Vol. 12, Issue 6, Ambergris Squidology Society.

Gort, Marmy, "Remarks Addressed to an Ignorant Squid Fancier," published in *The Amateur Squidologist,* Vol. 11, Issue 5, Ambergris Squidology Society.
   (This speech is perhaps the funniest rebuttal of ignorance

ever published. It consists of a conversation between two squid as they perform an autopsy on a drowned human. The squids' absurd mislabeling of parts and purpose—the heart is determined to be a tumor, the liver a misplaced tongue—still makes me chuckle.)

Gort, Marmy, "Seven 'Profane' Properties of King Squid Ink," published in *The Amateur Squidologist,* Vol. 15, Issue 3, Ambergris Squidology Society.

Gort, Marmy, *A Detailed Diary of Mold,* Great Moments in Science Press.
    (This boring tome chronicles the spread of fungus to the river's bank over 300 long pages; however, there is some pay-off for the amateur squidologist at the end of the account, as a tentacle flicks briefly from the water and then disappears.)

Gort, Marmy, ed., *Homage to a Squidman: Essays on Cephalopods Written for Clyde Aldrich on the Occasion of His 75th Birthday,* Ambergris Squidology Society Press.
    (I had the great pleasure of meeting Clyde Aldrich at this event. Whatever one may think of Aldrich's ridiculous theories, his passion for squidology has done more to legitimize this noble science than a hundred more logical theorists.)

Gort, Volman, *The History of Tenticular Creatures,* Southern Cities Press.
    (Perhaps a bit fanciful—for example, I do not personally consider frogs to be tenticular creatures unless born deformed.)

Griffin, Magni, *The Vanished Squid: An Exploration of the Extinguished White Ghost Squid,* Walfer-Barrett Publishers.

Halme, J. P., *An Annotated Bibliography of References Pertaining to the Biology, Fisheries, and Management of Squids,* The Squid Lover's Press.

Halme, J. P., *Squid Strandings,* Southern Cities Press.

Halme, J.P., *"There Are Giants in the River": Monsters and Mysteries of the River Moth,* Frankwrithe & Lewden.

Hatepool, J. D., *The Dictionary of Obscure Insults,* Up Yer Arse Publications.

Hewn, Reese, *Decadence with Decapods,* The Real Cephalopod Press.

Hewn, Reese, *Nine Arms Are Not Enough,* Cephalopod Publications.
     (My good friend Reese is wrong—nine arms are *more* than enough. *Seven* arms are not enough.)

Hoegbotton, Henry, ed., *Henry Hoegbotton's Squid Primer,* Hoegbotton & Sons.

Hortent, Nigel, *The Hoegbotton Guide to Dipsomania,* Hoegbotton & Sons Press.

Hortent, Nigel, *The Hoegbotton Guide to Pyromania,* Hoegbotton & Sons Press.

Istlewick, James, *The Hoegbotton Guide to Doramania,* Hoegbotton & Sons Press.

Istlewick, James, *The Hoegbotton Guide to Siderodromomania,* Hoegbotton & Sons Press.

Jakes, Laura, *My Life As a Squid,* The Squid Lover's Press.

Jitterness, Jonathan, *The Hoegbotton Guide to Sitomania,* Hoegbotton & Sons Press.

John, Samuel, *Confessions of an Asylum Inmate* (chapbook), Sensational True Life Story Serials Press.

Keater, Mathew, *A Report from the Cappan's Ministers on an Odd Occurrence Involving Certain Types of Intractable Squid,* Bits and Scraps Publications.

(To Keater, the president of the Ambergris Gourmand Society, any squid that resists being harpooned and eaten is an "intractable" squid. Although I am sure that any squid sampled by his rubbery lips must at least feel somewhat at home.)

Keensticker, Harrod, *The Malicious Monster: An Experienced Seaman's Heated Oral Ejaculations on the Coming Battle Between Squid and Man,* Tales of the Sea Press.

Kickleback, John, *The Hoegbotton Guide to Drapetomania,* Hoegbotton & Sons Press.

Kickleback, John, *The Hoegbotton Guide to Squidomania,* Hoegbotton & Sons Press.

Kleyblack, Nora, *Squid of the Southern Isles, Being an Abridged Description of the Cephalopods and Other Mollusks of Saphant, Nicea, Briand, and Wrayly, Arranged According to the Natural System,* Pulsefire Products.

Kron, Michael, "Sensory-Motor Skills of the Injured Squid," *Squidology Journal,* Vol. 1, No. 1, Southern Cities Press.

Kron, Michael, *Squid Death Danses & Habitual Mourning,* Southern Cities Press.

Laglob, E.A., *The Story of My Boyhood Amongst the Squid Folk and What Became of Me Because of It,* privately printed.
(Laglob's story, although poorly written, is a poignant, sometimes heartbreaking, tale of acceptance and ultimate betrayal. Too intense for me to finish.)

Larsen, David, *Ambush Courtship in the Moth River Delta,* Source Press.

Larsen, David, *Beak Soup: A Season Tracking Bull Squid, With a Note About Night and a Caution Regarding Riverbank Assignations,* Source Press.

Lawler, L. Marie, *Combating Compression,* Cephalopod Publications.
(Compression is usually more of a problem for squidologists writing essays than for the squid.)

Lawler, L. Marie, *Critical Inking,* Frankwrithe & Lewden.

Lawler, L. Marie, *Invisible Ink: Tentacles from the Dark Side,* Cephalopod Publications.

Lawler, L. Marie, *Squibble: An Indepth Look at Squid Personality Disorders,* Cephalopod & Cuttlefish.

Lawler, L. Marie, *The Colors of Fear: Squid Self Defense,* The Real Cephalopod Press.

Lawler, L. Marie, *The Curious Case of Changed Careers: The Tragedy of Freelance Writer Harry Flack, Ex-Squid Hunter,* Hoegbotton & Sons.

Lorstain, Michael, *The Hoegbotton Guide to Eleuthromania,* Hoegbotton & Sons Press.

Lorstain, Michael, *The Hoegbotton Guide to Timbromania,* Hoegbotton & Sons Press.

Madnok, Frederick, "Squidanthropy: The Silent Disease," published in *The Thackery T. Lambshead Pocket Guide to Eccentric & Discredited Diseases,* M. A. Roberts, ed., Chimeric Press.
     (In retrospect, I chose a bad title. The disease is not so much "silent" as "inappropriate.")

Madnok, Frederick, *Certain Subtle Aspects of Squidanthropy* (chapbook), Madnok Press.
     (What many do not realize is how disconcerting sudden non-binocular vision can be to sufferers—not to mention the loss of muscular control as one's hindquarters "melt" into a funnel and mantle and one's legs "dissolve" into eight arms.)

Madnok, Frederick, *Tentative Tentacles: A Failure of Nerve Among Amateur Squidologists* (chapbook), privately printed.
     (The publication that resulted in the Ambergris Squidology Society banning me from any future meetings. Even so, I stand by every statement I made.)

Madnok, James, *The Meaning of Mushrooms,* Murmur Press.
     (Even then the house was crumbling. Many of my father's finest experiments revolved around fruiting bodies situated in some dark corner of the basement or wine cellar. My mother, dedicated to the eradication of all rot, hated this situation—especially since my father sometimes went out of his way to encourage rot ["but not rubbish," as he was fond of saying]. When my father was at his most mischievous, my mother might open the tea cupboard and find tendriled gray-

and-crimson fungi peeking out from the side of each perfect saucer.)

Madnok, James, *Experiments into the Transformative Element of Fruiting Body Absorptions,* Southern Cities Press.
(The most amazing transformation my father ever made involved the alchemy of merging metal and mushroom. The result was uncanny. For days, my father slowly weaned the red-dappled gort cap from its normal diet of compost and dead beetles, replacing its sustenance with iron shavings. After months of careful regulation, the mushroom became shiny, gray, and hard. After a year, it became almost entirely metallic, with but a few flecks of red-and-beige to hint at its formerly edible nature. It had become a decorative ornament. [My own experiments have been of an opposite nature: turning the decorative into the sinuous and fleshy . . .] He gave it to my mother for her birthday; she gave it to me soon thereafter and I still have it somewhere in storage.)

Madnok, James, *The Invisible World,* Frankwrithe & Lewden.
(My father's masterwork: A beautifully-designed 400-page book that was unfairly ignored by reviewers and readers at the time of publication but which is now widely recognized in certain circles as the definitive statement on Southern fungi. I still have a copy of this book. The sarcastic jabs at Truffidian "theories" on the gray caps drove a wedge between my parents.)

Madnok, James, *A Unified Theory of Spore Migration,* Frankwrithe & Lewden.
(I would like to believe that my father was on the right track in this, his final book, posthumously published—alas, he was forced to abuccinate; the book never saw print in the Southern Cities—and that he felt no pain.)

Mannikan, A., *The Great Cephalogod* (fiction), Hoegbotton & Sons.

Marmont, E.D., *A Raucous Yet Commercial People: Living on the Banks of the Moth, A Study,* Not Worthy Publishers.

Midan, Pejora "The Architectural Marvel That Is the Cephalopod", published in *Architecture of the Southern Cities,* Vol. 95, Issue 12, Barqology Press.

Midan, Pejora, *Squid Iconography as Expressed in Ambergrisian Architecture,* Blueprint Publications.
    (Midan's infatuation with squid did not last. His planned Mollusk Palace and Tentacle House never came to fruition; all we have now are the plans for such wonders.)

Midan, Pejora, *The Underwater Gardens of the Mollusk: God's Design,* Blueprint Publications.

Mipkin, Siffle, *The Hoegbotton Guide to Entomomania,* Hoegbotton & Sons Press.

Morge, Ralph, *Squid Theories Involving the Sabotage of Haragck Flotation Devices* (chapbook), Ambergris Squidologist Society.
    (Morge's postulation that squid sabotaged the Haragck during their famous attack by puncturing their flotation devices seems circumstantial at best.)

Nanger, D.T., "The Fish Preferences of a Freshwater Squid in a Controlled Experiment Involving a Hook, Bait, a Really Big Boat, and a Strong Line of Inquiry," *Hablong Research Institute Quarterly Report,* Hablong Publications.

Nick, Robert, *The Edge of Madness,* Frankwrithe & Lewden.

Nick, Robert, *The Role of Madness and Creativity,* Frankwrithe & Lewden.

(That squidanthropy should be cited so inappropriately in this context discredits the book before the reader has even finished a quick skim of the index.)

Norman, Hugh. *Beware of Random Letters: The History of Non-Human Communication,* Frankwrithe & Lewden.

Nymblan, Kever, *The Hoegbotton Guide to Erotographomania,* Hoegbotton & Sons Press.

Parsons, Kevin, *A Field Guide to Freshwater Squid,* Southern Cities Press.

Pickleridge, Timothy, *A Serious Call to a Devout and Holy Life, Adapted to the State and Condition of All Orders of the Religious, Being a Call to Worship Our Father the King Squid* (chapbook), privately printed.

Plate, S. N., *Eight Arms to Choke By: The Suicide of a Squidler* (poems), Tarzia Publications.

Pond, Samuel, *The Hoegbotton Guide to Florimania,* Hoegbotton & Sons Press.

Povel, Bernard and Sighly, Enoch, *Vice Squidologist Enoch Sighly's and Doctor Bernard Povel's Journey Up the River Moth by Way of Native Canoe and Indigenous Ingenuity, Culminating in a Boat Wreck, a Near Escape, and Some Unfortunate Negotiations with the Aforementioned Natives,* Society of Scientists Abroad in Morrow Press.

Pulling, Leonard, "An Account of the Squidlings' First Hours by the Banks of the River Moth," *Ambergris Journal of Speculative Zoology,* Fungoid Press.

Quiddity, Teresa, *Sucker Punches,* Feeble Bleatings Press.

Quiddity, Teresa, *The Case to be Made for Hellatose Authorship of Various and Sundry Theatrical Performances,* Front Row Publications.
  (Leave it to Quiddity to spend nearly 300 pages digging around in the archives of various Ambergris theaters only to conclude that "the evidence for Hellatose authorship of any dramatic production, other than those sponsored by the carnivals and circuses he was associated with, is circumstantial at best.")

Quork, Corvid, *The Hoegbotton Guide to Ornithomania,* Hoegbotton & Sons Press.

Rariety, Maurice, *The Ambergris of James Kinkel Lightner: His Species and Types, Collecting Localities, Bibliography, and Selected Reprinted Works by Guyerdram,* Historic Archive Publications.
  (The first of an accursed breed, the "gentleman squidologist," Lightner hired others to observe the squid in its natural habitat—while he frequented bankers' clubs and other dens of equity. In smoke-filled back rooms, Lightner would then recount, as if he had experienced them first-hand, exploits and dangers related to him by his underlings. Guyerdram, Lightner's chief expert, snapped one night and murdered Lightner in mid-sentence, using nothing more complicated than a Nicean Mud Squid wound around the old man's neck. Unfortunately, the perception that Lightner was a great scientist has not died as easily as the man himself.)

Redfern, Kathryn, *The Odd Account of Malfour Blissbane and His Squid of Fear,* Frankwrithe & Lewden.
  (Sensationalist stories for young adults and impressionable adults.)

Redfern, Kathryn, *The Strange Tale of Ronald Battlebuss and His Seven Squid of Doom,* Frankwrithe & Lewden.

Redfern, Kathryn, *The Stranger Tale of Bartley Gangrene and His Three Squid of Destiny,* Frankwrithe & Lewden.

Riddle, William, *The Hoegbotton Guide to Hamartomania,* Hoegbotton & Sons Press.

Riddle, William, *The Clash of Science and Religion: Personal Explorations,* Squid Mill Library Press.
   (One day, my father entered his workshop to find that my mother had cut off the fruiting bodies of the King Fungus central to his research. It had taken 17 years of trial-and-error to grow them in the artificial environs of his laboratory. Mother had methodically snipped them with a small scythe, placed them in his wastepaper basket, and put them to the match. All that remained was a little ash and a stringent smell. I would imagine he stared into that circle of smolder and smoke until his eyes watered. Then he got up and went into the library.)

Roberts, M.A., *The Big Book of Squid,* Chimeric Press.
   (Marred in its otherwise splendid authenticity by illustrations showing the mature Morrowean Mud Squid with two tentacles.)

Roberts, M.A., *The Captain's Advanced Freshwater Squid Telemetry,* Tales of the Sea Press.

Roberts, M.A., *The Odd Case of Hellatose & Bauble* (chapbook), Chimeric Press.

Rogers, Vivian Price, *Laying Low with the Torture Squid,* Small Books/Big Dreams Incorporated.

(The Torture Squid will always remain my favorite fictional creations. The books take as their premise that five jackanapes, steeped in the ways of petty thuggery, are transformed by the gray caps, through the medium of squidanthropy, into King Squid. As squid, the five of them—renamed Squidy Johnson, Squidy Macken, Squidy Slakes, Squidy Taintmoor, and Squidy Barck (the leader)—have lost none of their criminal ways. They take up their old prowling grounds in the decrepit Bureaucratic Quarter and wreak havoc on its citizenry. In this installment, Squidy Taintmoor suggests that the Torture Squid lay low for awhile, since the Cappan's men are after them. By the end of this blackly humorous story, "laying low" has resulted in burglary, arson, armed robbery, and many other offenses against the law.)

Rogers, Vivian Price, *The Return of the Torture Squid,* Small Books/Big Dreams Incorporated.

(Squidy Barck and his mates decide to visit their mums, with disastrous results. Stepfathers take a beating, as does most of the criminal code.)

Rogers, Vivian Price, *The Torture Squid and the Magnetic Rowboat,* Small Books/Big Dreams Incorporated.

(Squidy Macken finds a magnetic rowboat, possibly left behind by the gray caps, and the Torture Squid have fun propping it up near major thoroughfares and cackling as motored vehicles driving past suddenly find themselves stuck to it—windshield glass flying in all directions—and soon on the receiving end of demands from the knife-wielding Squidy Barck, Squidy Johnson, and Squid Slakes. At the end, they hijack one motored vehicle and smash it into a tree, laughing through their bruises.)

Rogers, Vivian Price, *The Torture Squid Beat Up Some Priests,* Small Books/Big Dreams Incorporated.

(Squidy Slakes remembers how the priests who brought him up in the orphanage used to do mean and nasty things to him. Squidy Johnson suggests getting some revenge and Squidy Barck seconds the motion. The Torture Squid cruise the Religious District, punching out mendicants and stealing donations from collection boxes. In the stunning conclusion, they smash the stained glass of the Truffidian Cathedral and beat a confession of sodomy out of the Antechamber himself before Squidy Slakes breaks down and begins to cry—but, no: he's not crying, he's snickering. Squidy Slakes has been having everyone on—he wasn't an orphan and a priest never raised him. The Torture Squid all share a good laugh.)

Rogers, Vivian Price, *The Torture Squid Get Drunk in Trillian Square,* Small Books/Big Dreams Incorporated.

(One day, Squidy Barck wakes up in the Torture Squid's west Albumuth Boulevard hovel and finds that Squidy Johnson is missing! Have the Cappan's men found him and arrested him? Squidy Barck and the rest of the remaining Torture Squid spread out and cover the adjoining streets. No Squidy Johnson. Where could he be? As the Torture Squid search ever more desperately for their companion, they inevitably become thirsty. Many a pub receives their gruff demands for alcohol, until finally, after a number of adventures—one involving a squid club—the Torture Squid converge on Trillian Square, as pre-arranged. Who should they find there but Squidy Johnson, curled up on a bench, nursing a massive hangover from having snuck out for a "quick pint" the night before. The Torture Squid assuage their irritation by kicking Squidy Johnson into unconsciousness.)

Rogers, Vivian Price, *The Torture Squid Pillage the Towers of the Kalif,* Small Books/Big Dreams Incorporated.

(In this slightly less successful book, Rogers takes the Torture Squid out of the familiar environs of Ambergris and sets them on a quest to plunder the Kalif's treasure. By the time they reach the gates of the Kalif's capital city, they are so drunk on cheap wine that they are mistaken for merry-making pilgrims and allowed into the city. Once there, they proceed to pinch the bottoms of women, steal fruit from grocery stands, rob wealthy merchants, and generally make a nuisance of themselves. Eventually, the Kalif's soldiers arrest them, sober them up by torturing them in the dungeons, and then release them, naked, into the wastelands beyond the city's walls. Less clothed, but a bit wiser, the Torture Squid sadly wander home. As Squidy Johnson remarks, "Foreign conquest is not as exciting as I thought it would be.")

Rogers, Vivian Price, *The Torture Squid Take on the New Art,* Small Books/Big Dreams Incorporated.

(Squidy Macken points out, one fine morning as the Torture Squid sit imbibing refreshments at the Cafe of the Ruby-Throated Calf, that, as a group, they are under-educated. True, Squidy Barck once spent a semester at the Blythe Academy as a janitor, thus qualifying him to lead the Torture Squid, but in general they lack refinement. After Squidy Slakes punches Squidy Macken several times, Squidy Barck decides Squidy Macken is right. But how to become better educated? After some thought, Squidy Barck suggests that they attend a retrospective of the New Art down at the Gallery of Hidden Fascinations. So the Torture Squid don their best clothes, sharpen their knives, slick back their hair, and head off for the gallery exhibit. Once there, however, they are sorely disappointed. Most of the canvases seem unfinished—one is just a blotch of blue with some white blobs on it. Squidy Barck, embarrassed, decides maybe he should try to finish a few of the paintings—show the other Torture Squid some true culture. Alas, the museum guards try to stop them and the room erupts into a prolonged tussle, accompanied by the sound of knives tearing canvas. When the museum guards are finally disposed of, the

Torture Squid turn their back on the gallery—and all "refinements"—although they read in the Ambergris Broadsheet the next day that spectators found their resulting performance art piece "oddly appealing.")

Rogers, Vivian Price, *The Torture Squid Torch an Underground Passage,* Small Books/Big Dreams Incorporated.
(One of Rogers' simplest books, this title delivers exactly what it promises—the Torture Squid torch an underground passage. They spend 50 pages planning the torching. They spend 50 pages torching the passage. They spend 50 pages escaping from the Cappan's men as a result. Many critics believe this book was ghost-written for Rogers.)

Rogers, Vivian Price, *The Torture Squid Trash a Restaurant,* Small Books/Big Dreams Incorporated.
(For once, the Torture Squid do not instigate the nastiness. Squidy Barck and Squidy Johnson sit in the River Moth Restaurant minding their own business when they are recognized by members of a rival gang, the Moth Heads, who happen to be walking by. A fight ensues, during which Squidy Barck holds off the Moth Heads by throwing chairs and dishes at them while Squidy Johnson goes around the corner for reinforcements. When Squidy Slakes, Squidy Johnson and Squidy Taintmoor join the fracas, the Moth Heads soon find themselves on the receiving end of too many blows to count and wind up being chased down the street by the Torture Squid. Not content with the evening's activities, the Torture Squid then proceed to blow up a bakery and set a motored vehicle on fire. As Squidy Johnson says, "Them Moth Heads provocatated us.")

Rogers, Vivian Price, *The Torture Squid's Stint in Prison: Memories of Beastly Childhoods,* Small Books/Big Dreams Incorporated.

(Perhaps Rogers' masterpiece, this book relates, in six chapters, the childhood experiences of Squidy Johnson, Squidy Macken, Squidy Slakes, Squidy Taintmoor, and Squidy Barck—while, in the story's present-day, all five occupy the same prison cell. Surprise, surprise: only Squidy Barck had a genuinely bad childhood, his mother a prostitute, his father unknown, and out on the street by the age of 10. The rest were the sons of privileged members of society who simply preferred thuggery to honest work. In chapter six, the Torture Squid break out of prison after beating the guards half to death and the previously nostalgic feel of the book gives way to the usual merry mayhem.)

Rogers, Vivian Price, *The Torture Squid's Last Stand,* Small Books/Big Dreams Incorporated.

(Enraged by the Torture Squid's criminal activities, the Cappan raises a small army dedicated to their eradication. In the climactic final scene, the Torture Squid, cornered in a barn outside of the city, escape by setting themselves on fire and running through the shocked encircling troops to the freedom of the River Moth. Finally released into their natural element, they never return to the city, "although even today mothers tell the story of Torture Squid's exploits to their aspiring young thugs.")

Rook, Alan B., *Passion in Crimson; Pelagian Love; Rosy Tentacles; Dido and the Squid: Four Libretti and Scores for Unrealized Operas,* Quail Note Publishers.

Rook, Alan B., *Chamber Mass for the Nautilus & Requiem for the White Ghost Squid: Two Liturgical Scores After the Noran and Stangian Modes,* Quail Note Publishers.

(There is no bliss in all the world as complete as listening to the Requiem for the White Ghost Squid [based on Spacklenest's classic novel]. It is especially sublime if listened to on phonograph while relaxing in a small wading pool.)

Roper, Frederick, *Incidences of Squid Incursions Amid the Communities of the Lower Moth: Anecdotal Evidence Supporting the Need for Squid-Proof Residences,* Not Easily Read Publications.

Roper, Frederick, *The Significance of Bookshelves in Domestic Squabbles,* Squid Mill Library Press.
 (In the library, through a trick of light in some cases, the books sat in their rows, steeped in red. Red were the bindings. Red was the floor.)

Roundtree, Jessica, *Husbands Who Kill Their Wives,* Squid Mill Library Press.

Rowan, Iain, "Tentaculon: An Approach to Human-Squid Communication," *Journal of Squid Studies,* Vol. 52, No. 3.

Rowan, Iain, "The Squid As Other: Transgressive Approaches to Hegemonic Dualities," *Journal of Aquatic Hermeneutics,* Vol. 34, No. 1.

Ruch, Alan, *Hops and the Amateur Squidologist,* Tornelain Publications.

Savant, Charles, *An Invitation to Squid Sightings: Its Pleasures and Practices: With Kindred Discussions of Maps, Depth Charts, and Physiology Tables* (chapbook), Ambergris Squidology Society.

Savant, Charles, *Historical Notes on the Relationship Between Fires in Quiet Port Towns and the King Squid,* Ambergris Squidologist Society.

Savant, Charles, *Sunset Over the Squid Mills,* Squid Mill Library Press.

(He must have known I would find her there. Every summer, returning from Blythe Academy or from my expeditions, I would go there first, although they had been long abandoned—wooden husks where once the squiders swished to and fro on their squilts. Her head rocked gently against the rotted pontoons, gold-gray hair fanning out. Her gaze seemed peaceful although I could read nothing in her eyes. The echo of her words now as gentle as her caress. She had been in the water for more than a week. I almost did not recognize her.)

Shannon, Harold, *Sorrowful Wake for Mother Squid: The Attachments of Juvenile King Squid,* Mournful Press.

Shannon, Harold, *Adaptations of Cephalopod Organisms to Non-Saltwater Environments,* Woode-Holly Productions.

Shannon, Harold, *Cephalopod Mating Behavior (Freshwater Seduction Rituals),* Woode-Holly Productions.

Shriek, Duncan, *The Hoegbotton Guide to the Early History of Ambergris,* Hoegbotton & Sons.

Shriek, Janice, *The Blythe Academy Squid Primer,* Blythe Academic Press.

Sidlewhile, Henry, *The Life and Times of Thackery Woodstocking, Amateur Squidologist,* Ashbrain Press.

Simpkin, A.L., *Gladesmen, Squidlers, Moonshine, and Sniffers,* Candon Press.

(A rollicking adventure that properly immortalizes the tough, solitary life of the squidlers and the gladesmen who insure them.)

Sirin, Vlodya, *Verse by Tentacle: An Anthology of Poetry Featuring Squid Down Through the Ages—Saphant Empire to William Buckwheat,* Running Water Publications.

Skinder, Blas, *Extraordinary Popular Delusions and the Madness of Festival Crowds,* Southern Cities Press.

Slab, Thomas, *The Redeeming Noose: The Reception of Doctor R. Tint Tankle's Ideas on Social Discipline, Mental Asylums, Hospitals, and the Medical Profession as They Relate to Squid-Induced Suicide Attempts,* Reed Publications.

Slab, Thomas, *The Anatomy of Madness,* Reed Publications.

Slay, Jack, *Cephalopods: A Handbook of Decapodian Grammar,* Frankwrithe & Lewden.

Sleeter, M. J., *The Hoegbotton Guide to Hippomania,* Hoegbotton & Sons Press.

Sleeter, M. J., *A Guide to the Mushrooms of Late Summer: The Poisonous and the Benign,* Squid Mill Library Press.
(He was picking mushrooms in the forest behind the house and humming softly to himself. I paused a moment to marvel at his calm, even though the late afternoon sun, mottled through the deep silence of the fir trees, cast my shadow far in advance of his gaze. He must have known I would find him there.)

Smutney, Jones, *The Squid That Killed His Own Father: A Novel of Cephalopodic Revenge,* True Tales Press.

Smutney, Jones, *Wealth, Virtue, and Seafood: The Shaping of a Political Economy in Ambergris,* Archival Squid Press.

Smythe, Alan, *The Physiology and Psychology of the King Squid* (illustrations by Louis Verden), Frankwrithe & Lewden.

Sneller, Anne, *A History of Traveling Medicine Shows and Nefarious Circi,* Spectacular Press.

Sourby, Pipkick, *A Carousel for Squidophiles: A Treasury of Tales, Narratives, Songs, Epigrams, and Sundry Curious Studies Relating to a Noble Theme,* Borges Bookstore Publishing.

Sourby, Pipkick, *Mollusk Wise, Squid Foolish,* Borges Bookstore Publishing.

Spacklenest, Edgar, *Lord Hood and the Unseen Squid,* Frankwrithe & Lewden.
   (This tale of a Nicean nobleman haunted by the ghost of the squid he jigged has a simple poignancy to it. In the book, Lord Hood lives alone in his ancestral home, his parents murdered in a terrible double tragedy some years before. Once a year, Lord Hood leaves his property to attend a fishing expedition with his fellow lords. On one such expedition, he spears the mantle of a young female King Squid. The squid dies and is eaten that night by the aristocratic fishermen. The very next day, as Lord Hood sits reading in his extensive library, the apparition of the squid appears before him, beseeching him with mournful eyes. At first, Lord Hood flees in terror, but over time, as the visitations become more frequent, he becomes used to the company of the squid ghost. As the reader learns more about Lord Hood's tortured past and his parents' fate, it is clear that he is as much a ghost haunting his own house as the squid. Eventually, he comes to feel affection for the squid who haunts him and he begins a kind of squidanthropic transformation on an emotional level. He finds himself drawn to the nearby River Moth—and as the squid

ghost manifests itself more often the closer the proximity of water, Lord Hood begins to spend most of his time in the river. Lord Hood finds himself less and less attached to the land. In the heart-breaking final scene, he—not truly blessed with squidanthropy—sinks beneath the waters and drowns . . . only to liberate his ghost, which finds union with the ghost of the squid.)

Stang, Napole, *Edict the Fifth: On the Question of Whether Squid Shall Have Souls, as Written by the 12th Antechamber of Ambergris, Napole Stang,* Truffidian Religious Books, Inc.

Stark, Rokham, *Further Adventures in Squidology,* Tannaker Publications.

Starling, Lee D., *Squid Dish: An Esoteric Seafood Lovers' Cookbook,* Bait & Hook Press.

Starling, Lee D., *The Squid Scrolls,* Frankwrithe & Lewden.

Stiffy, Madeline, *An Argument on Behalf of the New Science Known as Squidology* (chapbook), Ambergris Squidologist Society.

Stiffy, Madeline, *The Curious Case of Manzikert VII and the Squid What Burped,* Arcanea Publishing Collective & Outdoor Market.
    (An undignified, mocking, and completely worthless amalgamation of rumor, hearsay, and libel.)

Stim, Zyth, *Sarah Volume (I) and the Great Squid Migration,* Small Books/Big Dreams Incorporated.

Stim, Zyth, *Sarah Volume (II) and the Mysterious Squid of Zort,* Small Books/Big Dreams Incorporated.

Stim, Zyth, *Sarah Volume (III) and the Treasure of the Squid,* Small Books/Big Dreams Incorporated.

Stim, Zyth, *Sarah Volume (IV) and the Squid With No Name,* Small Books/Big Dreams Incorporated.

Stim, Zyth, *Sarah Volume (V) and the Underwater Valley of the Squid,* Small Books/Big Dreams Incorporated.

Stim, Zyth, *Sarah Volume (VI) Goes Squidless,* Small Books/ Big Dreams Incorporated.

Stim, Zyth, *Sarah Volume's Eight-Armed Volume of Squid Stories for Bedtime,* Small Books/Big Dreams Incorporated.

Stindel, Bernard, *A Refutation of the Theories of Jessica Roundtree,* Squid Mill Library Press.

Stine, Allison, ed., *Squid Lover, The: A Magazine of Squid Lore, Being a Miscellany of Curiously Interesting and Generally Unknown Facts About Squid-dom and Squid-Related People; Now Newly Arranged, with Incidental Divertissement and All Very Delightful to Read,* The Squid-Lover's Press.

Sumner, Geoffrey T., *Behind a Cloud of Ink: A Biography of the Enigmatic A. J. Kretchen, Squid Hunter,* Southern Cities Publishing Company.

Sumner, Geoffrey T., *Cuttlefishing,* Ecropol Press.

Sumner, Geoffrey T., *How to Make Jewelry from Polished Squid Beak,* Arts & Crafts Publishers (Squidcraft imprint).

Sumner, Geoffrey T., *The Squid as Aquatic Angel in Religious Visitations,* Truffidian Cathedral Publishing.

Tanthe, Meredith, *Taste & Technique in Squid Harvesting* (chapbook), Ambergris Gastronomic Society.

Tribbley, Jane, *The Hoegbotton Guide to Hypomania,* Hoegbotton & Sons Press.

Umthatch, Wiggins, *The Hoegbotton Guide to Mentulomania,* Hoegbotton & Sons Press.

Ungdom, George, *Squid Anatomy for the Layperson* (illustrated by Louis Verden), Frankwrithe & Lewden.

Vielle, C. M., *Naughty Lisp and the Squid: A Polyp Diptych,* Frankwrithe & Lewden.

Viper, Arnold, *The Hoegbotton Guide to Mesmeromania,* Hoegbotton & Sons Press.

Vosper, Robert, *The Pauseback Collection of Rare Squid Children's Books,* Small Books/Big Dreams Incorporated.

Willis, Sarah, *The Book of Average Squid,* Savor Press.

Willis, Sarah, *The Book of Greater Squid,* Savor Press.

Willis, Sarah, *The Book of Lesser Squid,* Savor Press.

Wortbell, Randall, *The Hoegbotton Guide to Mythomania,* Hoegbotton & Sons Press.

Wrede, Christopher, "'I Think You're Both Quacks': The Controversy Between Doctor Blentheen Skrill and Squidologist Croakley Lettsom," *Bulletin of the History of Mollusk Studies,* Vol. 689, No. 7, Recluse Press.

Wrede, Christopher, "Gender, Ideology and the Water-Cure Movement," *Current Cephalopodic Remedies,* Vol. 21, No. 5, Recluse Press.

Wrede, Christopher, "Hysteria, Squid Hypnosis, and the Lure of the Invisible: The Rise of Cephalo-mesmerism in Post-Trillian Ambergris," *Bulletin of the History of Mollusk Studies,* Vol. 699, No. 3, Recluse Press.

Wrede, Christopher, "Squidology and Spiritualism in the Pre-Trillian Era," *Bulletin of the History of Mollusk Studies,* Vol. 700, No. 9, Recluse Press.

Wrede, Christopher, "The Chronic Squidanthropist, the Doctor, and the Play of Medical Power," *Journal of Squid-Related Psychological Diseases,* Vol. 377, No. 2, Recluse Press.

Wrede, Christopher, *Institutions of Confinement, Hospitals, Asylums, and Prisons in the Southern Cities,* Recluse Press.

Wrede, Christopher, *Squidologist Quackery Unmasked,* Recluse Press.

Xyskander, Melanie, *The Hoegbotton Guide to Nosomania,* Hoegbotton & Sons Press.

Yit, Florence, *The Hoegbotton Guide to Nudomania,* Hoegbotton & Sons Press.

Yowler, John, *The Beaten Child: The Essential Iniquity of Physical Abuse,* Mother's Milk Publishing.
      (The noted writer Sirin once said, "Every unhappy family is the same. Every happy family is unique." The beatings could be bad, but not as bad as the ones here.)

Yowler, John, *The Present-Absent Father,* Mushroom Studies Press.

(The old grandfather clock dolling out my doom. The nightly "calls to prayer" that he could not protect me from.)

Zeel, George H., *The Book of Squidanthropy,* Frankwrithe & Lewden.

(It is coming sooner than I thought—the transformation they wish to deny me. One night, although it is forbidden, I shall sneak past the guards and slide out into the yard, sidle up to the fence, and flow through and over it as suits my new self . . .)

Zenith, C. N., *Effective Techniques for Building Suspense,* Frankwrithe & Lewden.

Zither, Marianne, *The Triumph of Madness Over Guilt,* Frankwrithe & Lewden.

(. . . under the light of the moon, with sweet, sweet longing, I make for the River Moth. Through the tangle of branches and moon-bright leaves, I surge toward the river. I can smell it, mad with silt, and hear its gurgling roar. Finally, the mud of the riverbank is under my tentacles, firm yet soft, and the grass can no longer lacerate my arms. For a moment, I remain on the river bank, looking out across the black waters reflecting the clouds above, and just watch the slow current, the way the water wavers and flows . . . I remember my mother, my father, the squid mills of my youth, the vast, silent library . . .)

Zonn, Crathputt, *How to Hold Your Audience in Thrall to the Very End,* Frankwrithe & Lewden.

Zzy, Veriand, *Satisfying Conclusions: Epiphanies in Squid Transformations,* Frankwrithe & Lewden.

(. . . then, with the strobing lights of my fellow squid to guide me, I baptize myself in the water, let it take me down into the silt, the sodden leaves, my lungs filling with the essence of life, my mantle full, my third eye already raking through the darkness, filling it with luminescence. The water smells of a thousand wonderful things. I am feather-light in its embrace. I want to cry for the joy of it. Slowly, slowly, I head for my brothers and sisters, disappearing from the sight of the doctors and the attendants, impervious to their recriminations, once more what I was always meant to be . . .)

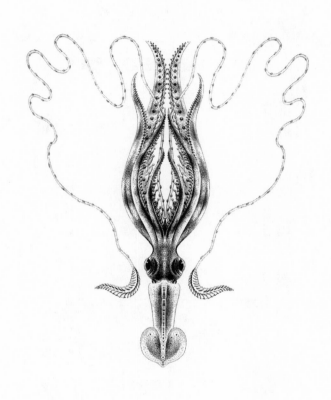

PRAISE FOR PREVIOUS WORK BY MR. MADNOK

"Thanks for sending us your new booklet."
Raymond Furness, co-author of
King Squid Nocturnal Prey Stalking Tactics

"The illustrations are very interesting indeed!"
Vivian Price Rogers,
author of the *Torture Squid* series

"This booklet has left me speechless."
J. P., author of
Monsters and Mysteries of the River Moth

"Thank you for your latest tome, which confirms many of
my own theories."
Christopher Wrede, author of
Squidologist Quackery Unmasked

THE HOEGBOTTON FAMILY HISTORY
by Orem Hoegbotton

Nine souls we were in the old city. Now, there remain of us only two: myself and my brother Myon. Our father and mother knew what it meant to have a homeland, but lived to see it taken from them by the Kalif. Once, we were a united people living in Yakuda—a long, wide valley through which ran the Dalquin River. It was hilly territory and my ancestors liked nothing better than to ride through the thick forests on our sturdy horses. Before we settled in the valley, we had come from a place farther to the west where, for a time, we had been members of a mighty empire, much greater than that of the Kalif. Some even breathed the word "Saphant." We were also known for our rug weaving and the elaborate ceremonies, lasting for weeks, by which we said farewell to our dead. But by the time I was born, the Kalif's armies had driven us from our homes and we had become refugees. We lost our valley first. Then we lost our horses to the ice and cold as we circled far to the north to avoid death at the hands of the Kalif. As we entered the eastern lands, we lost our very name, "Hyggboutten" become "Hoegbotton" because this sounded less like the names of our distant cousins, the warlike Haragck.

I have tried in this account to tell what our daily lives were like and how we came to survive and to prosper.

The Early Days

My brothers and sisters and I were all brought up in Urlskinder, south of the lands of the Skamoo, but far north
of Morrow. Urlskinder lay upon the southeast bank of the
Gebernia River, in that territory claimed by the Kalif's
Empire but rarely taxed or visited by his men. The city had
been built on unending plains, with no escape from the
cold winds that blew in from the river.

Our house stood on a street that stretched from the
Gebernia itself up to the market square and eventually
to the larger city of Orsha, some seventeen miles to the
north. My father would add rooms onto the house whenever we had the money. Behind the house, we made a very
large garden, and in the front of the house a small garden
with two cherry trees.

I do not know the number of people who lived in Urlskinder, but I do know that we had one high church surrounded
by five lesser buildings, all devoted to the northern-most
outposts of the Truffidian faith. We had ten shops for
supplies, 250 houses, and three schools. Everywhere, even
with the muffling snow that caused such hardship, we
could hear the students reciting from their texts through
the late afternoon.

The greatest majority of our people at that time were
workers; very few merchants, although we would grow
strong in that line. Most of them wove prayer shawls,
shirts, and curtains. Some made the religious icons that
the Truffidians used in their church and often exported to

greater areas of worship in the south. Yet others learned to write the sacred words that were inserted into the icons.

The best weavers were the artists who could weave as many as 60, 70, or even 80 threads into each inch of material. These weaver-artists were sought out by the wealthy buyers, and they were always busy. Everything they produced was bought. At the market, there would often be traders from far away, their ships anchored in the middle of the Gebernia and their longboats a common sight on the riverbank.

We had five or six weaver stools in our house. Every adult wove, and even some girls were hired to work with us, but we were not of those who had steady work. There was a fixed price for the raw material, and every store would buy it in exchange for merchandise, but when we put our hard work into them and made the prayer shawls, few would buy them. They looked like the other shawls to us, but the people knew that we were not Truffidians.

As I grew older, I could see that our father was a sick man. He could not work. In the summer, he would sit in our front garden trying to catch his breath. In the winter, he stayed in the house. His ambition was that at least one child of his should leave behind the old ways and become learned in the ways of the Truffidian priests, so as to advance the family. The old ways, tied more to the earth and the sky than to the idea of a God, marked us as different from the others. But, as insult added to injury, my father had to pay a fee for such teachings. I know this pained him since food was always scarce. An aura of poverty existed in our house. Sometimes I was sent away to the nearby town, to a hostel for the poor, and there I ate "days." (This meant I was supposed to be given a meal in a different wealthy family's house each day of the week. This was a customary way of seeing to it that students—who were generally poor—would get a good meal every day.) Often, there were "days" missing and I had to go hungry. I was ashamed to let anyone know of this, and I often starved. A few times, hoping for some frozen fish to thaw, I would go begging from the lone Skamoo who haunted the edges of the town like ghosts, but they were wary and would vanish into the snow before I could approach them.

I remember that my father was learned in the old ways and read from the faded prayer books every afternoon, although he had to be careful to put such books away when the Truffidians made their rounds. Often, he would wake up in the middle of the night and study and groan. When I asked him why he groaned, he would say that it was his burden, which meant that ever since we had lost our home to Kalif and we were scattered throughout the world, his soul could find no rest.

Our father was a wise man. People would come to him and ask him to settle their disputes. He would always give the verdict for the good of all, although in times of need our mother became mad at him because he refused payment for those services. He could also speak the language of the Skamoo and so he would help trappers discuss rights of land use. For this last service, he did accept payment.

When I look back, I recall that we children lived in harmony together before we dispersed to our separate fates. There was even among us a certain discipline because we were careful not to mention our sick father. We felt a great respect for our parents and a special empathy for our mother, who constantly cared for us. She cooked and baked and was always busy, without rest.

I can remember the serene atmosphere of the forbidden holy days when we would throw the windows open and those neighbors who dared came in to sing with us heartily and with pleasure. (We would always have a boy hidden on a rooftop to warn us of approaching priests.) After dinner, our father would go to his room to rest and my mother would read to a few women the battered prayer books. Already, our native language was beginning to be lost, because so few of the youth could read it, or wished to read it. Everything the Truffidians brought, they embraced, in rebellion.

Sometimes, too, at night, by the fireplace, our mother would tell us stories of the old country, especially of daring raids on horseback against our enemies. I knew the stories of our resistance to the Kalif could not all be true or we would not have been driven from Yakuda, but I liked to hear them. Before we became displaced, my mother had been a great breaker and trainer of horses. There was no call for such a gift in our adopted home.

Our father died at 48 years of age, in the year 7590 of our calendar. At the time, my oldest brother was in Kretchken, a village outside of Zamilon, with his wife and child. This left me as the oldest one at home, for my brother Myon was younger. I became the leader of the household. (I gave up my studies in the Truffidian faith, although I did not miss them.)

It was recorded in the books of the local government that my brothers Myon and Bestrill were twins. According to the law, as the youngest brothers one of them had to go into the Kalif's army, and this lot fell to Myon. But Bestrill felt that Myon could better help our household so he volunteered to go into the army. Bestrill died in battle against Stretcher John's army, at a place called Thraan. We were told in a letter from one of his fellow soldiers that Bestrill had ridden to his death, his regiment attacking into the mouths of cannon. I am glad my father was dead before he could hear of this. When Bestrill died, they called up Myon to take his place. Our mother was heart-broken.

Our Life Changes

A short time after our father died and I became the head of the family, an organization of benefactors from Orsha tried to help the workers in Urlskinder in their poverty by constructing a big building for communal weaving. A man came from Morrow to manage the workers. His name was Frederick Alsomb, an agent of the respected Frankwrithe & Lewden. He raised wages and paid us with coins instead of the paper that was redeemable for food in the stores. It took from two to four sels per week for a family to exist in poverty and he paid six to seven sels.

They needed a finisher (one who prepares the pattern) and they hired me because I knew how from preparing the pattern for weaving the prayer shawls. I do not remember my father ever weaving, but he prepared the threads and this I learned from him. (He was a big man and although he became gaunt in later years, his hands were always lithe and nimble.)

I soon figured out quicker ways to make the patterns and Alsomb increased my wages. He also hired other relatives to work for him. We threw away our weaver stools and my mother had only to prepare meals for us. They spoke of us in the town: that we were buying bread in a bakery and that we ate meat every day and not just on holidays. Most important to me was the respect between Alsomb and myself. When he walked out of the office to inspect the weaving area every morning, he always talked to me for a few minutes. However, when he found out I was not a Truffidian, he began to ignore me.

At that time all of the people in the town, especially the youth, were listening to revolutionaries and offshoots of religions. There were those who wished to raise an army and fight against the Kalif. There were those who called for a holy war against Morrow. There were those who wanted the mayor to make Truffidianism the official faith of the region. Everyone was against the Kalif, but most of it was talk only. We all knew that sooner or later the Kalif's spies would make those who talked loudest disappear. And so it would happen—men and women taken from their homes, never seen again. It was rumored that in the prisons of the Kalif, the sound of our people chanting became ever louder.

We had a bitter winter that year and because of this and the unrest, we received lower payment for our work. Some of us were let go, including me. As things became worse, many people wanted to settle in Morrow. It was a long journey to Morrow. It took a lot of money. I had already saved up enough money so that when Myon ran away from the army, I gave him money to go to Morrow, where I would go to meet him later. It took longer than I had thought, but eventually I made it to Morrow.

Life in Morrow

Morrow was usually not as cold as Urlskinder and its dark green forests reminded me of the stories our mother told of the old lands. We had already heard in Urlskinder that for one of us, displaced from our lands, to become employed as a weaver would be most difficult. Therefore, I began to learn how to make cloaks. My brother Myon was more worldly than I and more important he was sturdier; the army had strengthened him. Myon worked as a clerk for Frankwrithe & Lewden and we hoped to save enough to bring our whole family over. But the situation in Morrow became bad after we had been there for several months. Sometimes the agents of Frankwrithe & Lewden saw my people as competition and attacked us openly in the streets. There was no more work for Myon and he joined me in making cloaks and taking courier jobs. Still, we continued to send our money home.

At that time, an office was opened in Morrow's main square. It was supported by certain of our countrymen, to help the displaced spread even further south so they would not all have to live in Morrow. Myon went to the office and was advised to go to Nicea. There he would find work or he would be able to peddle in the "country." We decided that he would go to Nicea and that I might follow later.

In Nicea, my brother Myon used to ride on a cart and get off many miles from the city. There he would peddle at the farms where he sold various necessities that he had bought in Nicea on credit and sought to sell them for money. But as there was still a crisis, the farmers who purchased the merchandise paid with butter, eggs, and chickens.

That second winter was long and bitter. Myon could not return to help and my peddling small articles from house to house made hardly enough money for one meal a day. My shoes were ruined and I could not afford to replace them. I gave up my living space in a loft to buy second-hand shoes and for two months I hid in the back of the Truffidians' cathedral, sometimes stealing bread when I could not bear the hunger. If I was lucky, I could afford to buy a hard-boiled egg for lunch.

When the winter had passed, I returned to peddling. For the first few days of the week, I would peddle in various parts of the city. Later in the week, I would stay around Dekkle Street, there to sell my merchandise to passersby in front of the furniture and antique stores. After a few months, one store owner took me aside and said, "I can see from the way you talk and your bearing that you are a fine young man and willing to work. I want to sell my store. I will teach you and you can buy my store. You have peddled enough. You will pay me weekly or monthly." That was Wolf Shalzan, a kind man to whom I owe everything.

Myon came home a few weeks later, broke and tired, and we talked it over. We decided to accept Shalzan's offer. We had no choice. Through the office run by our countrymen, we were able to receive a loan with payments spread out over several years. After I bought the store, Myon also bought a store and we were partners until his marriage.

Many more displaced peoples had arrived in Urlskinder by this time, some of them blood kin and others northern neighbors also forced to flee by the Kalif's armies. The news spread that we had made more of our lot than most and there arrived in the city dozens of men and women who wished to work for us. Our credit was good, and through small banks we could borrow up to 500 sels to pay back in a year. As most of the newcomers were young unmarried men, we bought stores for them. We also lent them cash money from time to time and so each one lived sparingly and paid back the borrowed money. The result was that we assured all newcomers from Urlskinder that they could eat and sleep with us until they could become established for themselves. That was the beginning and the cause of so many new immigrants to Morrow becoming store owners.

Gradually, our own family made the trip from Urlskinder to Morrow. When our mother arrived with Praidal, our sister, and "Itchi", our young cousin, our whole life changed for the good. At the place where newcomers were inspected, the officials and doctors would talk to each person in his own language. Praidal and Itchi were immediately passed through, but mother was held back. It took awhile to examine her eyes. They were fearful of disease brought in by foreigners. We knew this and understood, and were satisfied, and then forgot it. Once, though, much later, when our mother and a few women were talking in Praidal's house, she told them that at the examination the doctor spoke to her and asked why she had come to the city. When she told them that she had come to meet the Hoegbottons, her children, they then immediately let her through. This was not true, but it shows the pride she took in us.

We had already prepared a house so that Praidal and my mother could live in a certain style. I, not being married, shared the house with them. We were all very happy. Then Praidal got married and my mother went to live with her. I would visit them during the week. Our mother visited us very often in our stores and would take money from us to send to her poor sister, who had moved to Nysimia (a far western province of the Kalif's Empire) with her husband. Even when we had lived in Urlskinder she felt it was her duty to help her sister, who was poorer than us. My mother, when she went to the market in Urlskinder, would stop on the way home at her sister's, who had not yet left for Nysimia and had a house full of children, and there my mother would leave some food and then come home. We all knew of this, except for my father, but none of us children ever said a word about it.

Our mother felt quite content for a time. She sent money and letters to her sister and received letters in return, until the beginning of several wars conducted by the Kalif against his own people. The mail from the empire was discontinued abruptly. No more letters arrived from Nysimia and mother became uneasy. We all assured her that the wars could only last a few months. That is what everyone thought at the time. But as each month went by, she became more concerned and worried, and she changed completely.

She would sit for hours at a time in her room, often in silence. One evening when we were all sitting in the dining room talking pleasantly, our mother came out of her room upset and tearfully asked us how it could be that they wouldn't let a letter through from a sister. She asked us to go in force to the Kalif and ask him how he could allow for sisters to be out of touch for such a long time. How could he allow such a thing! Such agony was in her question that we were gripped by more pain than we could bear.

A few days later, we experienced the first death in the family since our arrival in Morrow. Somehow, I will always connect my mother's distress and this death. Praidal became ill from wheat infected with fungus. Others recovered, but in Praidal the illness became more profound. It made her unable to keep down food and it changed the pallor of her skin so that it became almost clear. After four days, she died. This was a shock to us. We wept for days. We had survived so much and come so far that I suppose we had thought we could endure anything. Washing her body for burial and knowing the hardship she had suffered in Urlskinder, I could not forget her. It was then, in the cemetery, as I held my mother close to me, that I first grieved for the homeland.

What Came After

At the present time, all of us original Hoegbottons have multiplied and become intertwined with other families. Because the agents of Frankwrithe & Lewden have been hostile to us, we have had to spread out—to Nicea, to Stockton, even, as I write this, to Ambergris. From the nine of our generation, most have gone to their eternity, including my mother, just two years ago. The children and the children's children do not know who they are and how they came to Morrow. They are here and that is enough for them. They are different than us—sharper and less kind (although they will laugh if they read this).

Some of our people still lived in Yakuda, under the Kalif's rule, for many years. We did not hear from them, but we used to send money to Yakuda after the wars had ended, each to his own people. One time, we undertook to send a large sum of money through the Kalif's ministers to Yakuda. We told them it was for everyone in Yakuda, even those who had been resettled there from distant lands and had helped to drive us out. We did this so as to not create any ill-feeling.

I don't remember the amount of money, but it was a very large sum and they never received it. After a time, one of the leaders in Yakuda—a pale man whose family must have originated far to the West—came to Morrow and we called a meeting. He was a good speaker. He spoke for a long, long time. He said that the Kalif knows better who is in need and that if the Kalif's ministers did not give the money to the people in Yakuda, then it is certain that it was needed more elsewhere. We were naïve. We still had not heard the reports of the atrocities performed in the name of the Kalif, or could know that many of those remaining in Yakuda would be uprooted or killed in the coming months.

After the repressions had subsided, many years later, we tried to find out something about Yakuda and as a last resort sent out letters to the regional administrator for the area. We did not get an answer. Later, we heard a story that the Kalif had dammed the river, flooding the valley. It was strange to hold in our minds the thought of our homeland lost to the river—our homes, our cities, underwater. For years, I told people that this story was not true. But lately, I have come to realize it does not matter. There are no Hyggboutten left there.

Many evenings now, I have a dream. It is probably not a dream so much as a wish. I should like to tell it to my children, but I do not know that it will mean anything to them. I am frightened that it will mean nothing.

In the dream, my brothers and I are riding through the valley we have never seen, up the hills that border the river. Our parents gallop ahead of us and we try to catch up to them. The sun fills the leaves of the trees with shadow. We laugh as we ride, the underbrush lashing against our leather-clad legs. The river is a line of silver light below us. The horses are very fast. And we are happy because we are home.

THE CAGE

1

The hall contained the following items, some of which were later catalogued on faded yellow sheets constrained by blue lines and anointed with a hint of mildew:

- 24 moving boxes, stacked three high. Atop one box stood
- 1 stuffed black swan with banded blood-red legs, its marble eyes plucked, the empty sockets a shock of outrushing cotton (or was it fungus?), the bird merely a scout for the
- 5,325 specimens from far-off lands placed on shelves that ran along the four walls and into the adjoining corridors—lit with what he could only describe as a black light: it illuminated but did not lift the gloom. Iridescent thrush corpses, the exhausted remains of tattered jellyfish float-ing in amber bottles, tiny mammals with bright

eyes that hinted at the memory of catastrophe,
their bodies frozen in brittle poses. The stink of
chemicals, a whiff of blood, and

- 1 Manzikert-brand phonograph, in perfect condition, wedged beside the jagged black teeth of
11 broken records and
- 8 framed daguerreotypes of the family that
had lived in the mansion. On vacation in the
Southern Isles. Posed in front of a hedge. Blissful
on the front porch. His favorite picture showed a
boy of seven or eight sticking his tongue out, face
animated by some wild delight. The frame was
cracked, a smudge of blood in the lower left corner. Phonograph, records, and daguerreotypes
stood atop
- 1 long oak table covered by a dark green cloth
that could not conceal the upward thrust that
had splintered the surface of the wood. Around
the table stood
- 8 oak chairs, silver lion paws sheathing their legs.
The chairs dated to before the reign of Trillian the
Great Banker. He could not help but wince noting the abuse to which the chairs had been subjected, or fail to notice
- 1 grandfather clock, its blood-spattered glass face
cracked, the hands frozen at a point just before
midnight, a faint repressed ticking coming from
somewhere within its gears, as if the hands sought
to move once again—and beneath the clock
- 1 embroidered rug, clearly woven in the north,
near Morrow, perhaps even by one of his own

ancestors. It depicted the arrival of Morrow cavalry in Ambergris at the time of the Silence, the horses and riders bathed in a halo of blood that might, in another light, be seen as part of the tapestry. Although no light could conceal

- 1 bookcase, lacquered, stacks with books wounded, ravaged, as if something had torn through the spines, leaving blood in wide furrows. Next to the bookcase

- 1 solicitor, dressed all in black. The solicitor wore a cloth mask over his nose and mouth. It was a popular fashion, for those who believed in the "Invisible World" newly mapped by the Kalif's scientists. Nervous and fatigued, the solicitor, eyes blinking rapidly over the top of the mask, stood next to

- 1 pale, slender woman in a white dress. Her hooded eyes never blinked, the ethereal quality of her gaze weaving cobwebs into the distance. Her hands had recently been hacked off, the end of the bloody bandage that hid her left nub held by

- 1 pale gaunt boy with eyes as wide and twitchy as twinned pocket watches. At the end of his other arm dangled a small blue-green suitcase, his grasp as fragile as his mother's gaze. His legs trembled in his ash-gray trousers. He stared at

- 1 metal cage, three feet tall and in shape similar to the squat mortar shells that the Kalif's troops had lately rained down upon the city during the ill-fated Occupation. An emerald green cover hid its bars from view. The boy's gaze, which

required him to twist neck and shoulder to the
right while also raising his head to look up and
behind, drew the attention of

- 1 exporter-importer, Robert Hoegbotton, 35 years
  old: neither thin nor fat, neither handsome nor
  ugly. He wore a drab gray suit he hoped displayed
  neither imagination nor lack of it. He too wore a
  cloth mask over his (small) nose and (wide, sar-
  donic) mouth, although not for the same reasons
  as the solicitor. Hoegbotton considered the mask
  a weakness, an inconvenience, a superstition. His
  gaze followed that of the boy up to the high perch,
  an alcove set half-way up the wall where

the cage sat on a window ledge. The dark, narrow
window reflected needlings of rain through its tu-
bular green glass. It was the season of downpours
in Ambergris. The rain would not let up for days on
end, the skies blue-green-gray with moisture. Fruiting
bodies would rise, fat and fecund, in all the hidden
corners of the city. Nothing in the bruised sky would
reveal whether it was morning, noon, or dusk.

The solicitor was talking and had been for what
seemed to Hoegbotton like a rather long time.

"That black swan, for example, is in bad condition," Hoegbotton said, to slow the solicitor's relentless chatter.

The solicitor wiped his beaded forehead with a
handkerchief tinged a pale green.

"The bird itself. The bird," the solicitor said, "is in
superb condition. Missing eyes, yes. Yes, this is true.

But," he gestured at the walls, "surely you see the richness of Daffed's collection."

Thomas Daffed. The last in a long line of famous zoologists. Daffed's wife and son stood beside the solicitor, last remnants of a family of six.

Hoegbotton frowned. "But I don't really need the collection. It's a fine collection, very fine" —and he meant it; he admired a man who could so single-mindedly, perhaps obsessively, acquire such a diverse yet unified assortment of *things* —"but my average customer needs a pot or an umbrella or a stove. I stock the odd curio from time to time, but a collection of this size?" Hoegbotton shrugged his famous shrug, perfected over several years of haggling.

The solicitor stared at Hoegbotton as if he did not believe him. "Well, then, what *is* your offer? What *will* you take?"

"I'm still calculating that figure."

The solicitor loosened his collar with one sharp tug. "It's been more than an hour. My clients are not well!" He was sweating profusely. A greenish pallor had begun to infiltrate his skin. Despite the sweat, the solicitor seemed parched. His mask puffed in and out from the violence of his speech.

"I'm sorry for your loss—all of your losses," Hoegbotton said, turning to the mother and child who stood in mute acceptance of their fate. "I won't keep you much longer." The speech never sounded sincere, no matter how sincerely he meant it.

The solicitor made a noise between a groan and a choke that Hoegbotton did not bother to catalog.

His thoughts had returned to the merchandise—rug, clock, bookcase, phonograph, table, chairs. What price might they accept?

Hoegbotton would not have included the cage in his calculations if the boy's stare had not kept flickering wildly toward it and back down again, gliding like Hoegbotton's own over the remnants of a success that had become utter failure. For all the outlandish things in the room—the boy's own mother to be counted among them—the boy most feared the cage, an object that could no more hurt him than the green suitcase that hung from his arm.

A reflexive sadness for the boy ran through Hoegbotton, even as he noted the delicacy of the silver engravings on the chair legs; definitely pre-Trillian.

He stared at the boy until the boy stared back. "Don't you know you're safe now?" Hoegbotton said a little too loudly, the words muffled by the cloth over his mouth. An echo traveled up to the high ceiling, encountered the skylight, and descended at a higher pitch.

The boy said nothing. As was his right. Outside, the bodies of his father, brother, and two sisters were being burned as a precaution, the bodies too mutilated to have withstood a Viewing anyway. The boy's fate, too, was uncertain. Sometimes survivors did not survive.

Nothing could make one safe. There had been a great spasm of buying houses without basements or with stone floors, but no one had yet proven that such a measure, or any measure, helped. The random nature of the events, combined with their infrequency, had instilled a certain fatalism in Ambergris' inhabitants.

The solicitor had run out of patience. He stood uncomfortably close to Hoegbotton, his breath sour and thick. "Are you ready yet? You've had more than enough time. Should I call Slattery or Ungdom instead?" His voice seemed more distorted than the mask could explain, as if he were in the grip of a new, perhaps deadly, emotion.

Hoegbotton took a step back from the ferocity of the solicitor's gaze. The names of his chief rivals made a little vein in Hoegbotton's left eyelid pulse in and out. Especially Ungdom—towering John Ungdom, he of the wide belly, steeped in alcohol and pork lard.

"Call for them, then," he said, looking away.

The solicitor's gaze bored into his cheek and then the foul presence was gone. The solicitor had slumped into one of the chairs, a great smudge of a man.

"Anyway, I'm almost ready," Hoegbotton said. The vein in his eyelid would not stop pulsing. It was true: neither Slattery nor Ungdom would come. Because they were afraid. Because their devotion to their job was incomplete, insufficient, inadequate. Hoegbotton imagined them both taken up into the rain and torn to pieces by the wind.

"Tell me about the cage," Hoegbotton said suddenly, surprising himself. "The cage up there"—he pointed—"is it for sale, too?"

The boy stiffened, stared at the floor.

To Hoegbotton's surprise, the woman turned to look at him. Her eyes were black as an abyss; they did not blink and reflected nothing. He felt for a moment as if he stood balanced precariously between the son's alarm and the mother's regard.

"The cage was always open," the woman said, her voice gravelly, something stuck in her throat. "We had a bird. We always let it fly around. It was a pretty bird. It flew high through the rooms. It— No one could find the bird. After." The terrible pressure of the word *after* appeared to be too much for her and she fell back into her silence.

"We've never had a cage," the boy said, the dark green suitcase swaying. "We've never had a bird. They left it here. *They* left it."

A chill ran through Hoegbotton that was not caused by a draft. The sleepy gaze of a pig embryo floating in a jar caught his eye. Opportunity or disaster? The value of an artifact *they* had left behind might be considerable. The risks, however, might also be considerable. This was the third time in the last nine months that he had been called to a house visited by the gray caps. Each of the previous times, he had escaped unharmed. In fact, he had come to believe that late arrivals like himself were impervious to any side effects. Yet even he had experienced moments of discomfort, as when, at the last house, he had walked down a white hallway to the room where the merchandise awaited him and found a series of dark smudges and trails and tracks of blood. Halfway down the hallway, he had spied a dark object, shaped like a piece of dried fruit, glistening from the floor. Curious, he had leaned down to examine it, only to recoil and stand up when he realized it was a human ear.

This time, the solicitor had experienced the most unease. According to the talkative messenger who had summoned Hoegbotton, the solicitor had arrived in the early afternoon to find the bodies and survivors. Arms and legs had been stuck into the walls between specimen jars, arranged in intricate poses that displayed a perverse sense of humor.

The light glinted softly off the windows. The silence became more absolute. All around, dead things watched one another, from wall to wall—a cacophony of gazes that saw everything but remembered nothing. Outside, the rain fell relentlessly.

A tingling sensation crept into Hoegbotton's fingertips. A price had materialized in his mind, manifested itself in glittering detail.

"Two thousand sels—for everything."

The solicitor sighed, almost crumpled in on himself. The woman blinked rapidly, as if puzzled, and then stared at Hoegbotton with a hatred more real for being so distant. All the former protests of the solicitor, even the boy's fear, were nothing next to that look. The red at the end of her arms had become paler, as if the white bandages had begun to heal her.

He heard himself say, "Three thousand sels. If you include the cage." And it was true, he realized—he wanted the cage.

The solicitor, trying to mask some small personal distress now, giggled and said, "Done. But you must retrieve it yourself. I'm not feeling well." The cloth of the man's mask moved in and out almost imperceptibly as he breathed. A sour smell had entered the room.

On the ladder, Hoegbotton had a moment of vertigo. The world spun, then righted itself as he continued to the top. When he peered onto the windowsill, two eyes stared up at him from beside the cage.

"Manzikert!" he hissed. He recoiled, almost lost his balance as he flailed at empty air, managed to fall back against the ladder . . . and realized that they were just the missing marble eyes of the swan, placed there by some prankster, although it did not pay to think of who such a prankster might be. He caught his breath, tried to swallow the unease that pressed down on his shoulders, his tongue, his eyelids.

The cage stood to the right of the ladder and he was acutely conscious of having to lock his legs onto the ladder's sides as he slowly leaned toward the cage.

Below, the solicitor and the boy were speaking, but their voices seemed dulled and distant. He hesitated. What might be in the cage? What horrible thing far worse than a severed human ear? The odd idea struck him that he would pull the cord to reveal Thomas Daffed's severed head. He could see the bars beneath the cloth, though, he told himself. Whatever lived inside the cage would remain inside the cage. Now that it was his property, his acquisition, he refused to suffer the same failure of nerve as Slattery and Ungdom.

The cover of the cage, which in the dim light appeared to be sprinkled with a luminous green dust, had a drawstring and opened like a curtain. With a sharp yank on the drawstring, Hoegbotton drew aside the cover—and flinched, again nearly fell, a sensation of displaced air flowing across his face, as of *some-*

thing moving. He cried out. Then realized the cage was empty. He stood there for an instant, breathing heavily, staring into the cage. Nothing. It contained nothing. Relief came burrowing out of his bones, followed by disappointment. Empty. Except for some straw lining the bottom of the cage and, dangling near the back, almost as an afterthought, a perch, swaying back and forth, the movement no doubt caused by the speed with which he had drawn back the cover. A latched door extended the full three feet from the base to the top of the cage and could be slid back on special grooves. Stained green, the metal bars featured detail work as fine as he had ever seen—intricate flowers and vines with little figures peering out of a background rich with mushrooms. He could sell it for 4,000 sels, with the right sales pitch.

Hoegbotton looked down through a murk diluted only by a few lamps.

"It's empty," he shouted down. "The cage is empty. But I'll take it."

An unintelligible answer floated up. As his sight adjusted to the scene below, the distant solicitor in his chair, the other two still standing, he thought for a horrible second that they were melting. The boy seemed melded to his suitcase, the green of it inseparable from the white of the attached arm. The woman's nubs were impossibly white, as if she had grown new bones. The solicitor was just a splash of green.

When he stood on solid ground again, he could not control his shaking.

"I'll have the papers to you tomorrow, after I've catalogued all of the items," he said.

All around, on the arms of the chairs, on the table, atop the bookcase, white mushrooms had risen on slender stalks, their gills tinged red.

The solicitor sat in his chair and giggled uncontrollably.

"It was nice to meet you," Hoegbotton said as he walked to the door that led to the room that led to the next room and the room after that and then, hopefully, the outside, by which time he would be running. The woman's stubs had sprouted white tendrils of fungus that lazily wound their way around the dried blood and obscured it. Her eyes were slowly filling with white.

Hoegbotton backed into the damaged table and almost fell. "As I say, a pleasure doing business with you."

"Yes, yes, yes, yes," the solicitor said, and giggled again, his skin as green and wrinkly as a lizard's.

"Then I will see you again, soon," Hoegbotton said, edging toward the door, groping behind him for the knob, "and under . . . under better . . . " But he could not finish his sentence.

The boy's arms were dark green, fuzzy and indistinct, as if he were a still life made of points of paint on a canvas. His suitcase, once blue, had turned a blackish green, for the fungi had engulfed it much as ivy had engulfed the eastern wall of the mansion. All the terrible knowledge of his condition shone through the boy's eyes and yet still he held his mother's arm as the white tendrils wound round both their limbs in an ever more permanent embrace.

Hoegbotton later believed he would have stood at the door forever, hand on the knob, the solicitor's giggle a low whine in the background, if not for what happened next.

The broken clock groaned and struck midnight. The shuddering stroke reverberated through the room, through the thousands of jars of preserved animals. The solicitor looked up in sudden terror and, with a soft popping sound, exploded into a lightly falling rain of emerald spores that drifted to the floor with as slow and tranquil a grace as the seeds of a dandelion. As if the sound had torn him apart.

* * *

Outside, Hoegbotton tore off his mask, knelt, and threw up beside the fountain that guarded the path to Albumuth Boulevard. Behind him, across a square of dark green grass, the bodies of Daffed, his daughters, his other son, smoldered gray and black. The charred smell mixed with mildew and the rain that stippled his back. His arms and legs trembled with an enervating weakness. His mouth felt hot and dry. For a long time, he sat in the same position, watching pinpricks break his reflection in the fountain. He shivered as the water shivered.

He had never come this close before. Either they had died long before he arrived or long after he left. The solicitor's liquid giggle trickled through his ears, along with the soft pop of the spores. He shuddered, relaxed, shuddered again.

When his assistant Alan Bristlewing questioned, as he often did, the wisdom of taking on such hazardous work, Hoegbotton would smile and change the subject. He could not choose between two conflicting impulses: the upswelling of excitement and the desire to flee Ambergris and return to Morrow, the city of his birth. As each new episode receded into memory, his nerve returned, somehow stronger.

The boy's arm, fused to his suitcase.

Holding on to the lichen-flecked stone lip of the pool, Hoegbotton plunged his head into the smooth water. The chill shocked him. It prickled his skin, cut through the numbness to burn the inside of his nose. A sob escaped him, and another, and then a third that bent him over the water again. The back of his neck was suddenly cool. When he pulled away, he looked down at his reflection—and the mask he had made to hide his emotions was gone. He was himself again.

Hoegbotton stood up. Across the courtyard, the Cappan's men had abandoned the bodies to begin the task of nailing boards across the doors and windows of the mansion. No one pulled the shades open to protest being trapped inside. No one banged on the door, begging to be let out. They had already begun their journey.

One look at his face as he staggered to safety had told the Cappan's men everything. No doubt they would have boarded him in too, if not for the bribes and his previous record of survival.

Hoegbotton wiped his mouth with his handkerchief. The merchandise he had bought would molder in the mansion, unused and unrecorded except in his ledger of "Potential Acquisitions: Lost." Depending on which hysteria-induced procedure the Cappan had adopted this fortnight, the mansion grounds might be cordoned off or the mansion itself might be put to the torch.

The clock struck midnight.

The cage stood beside him, slick with rain. Hoegbotton had gripped its handle so hard during his escape—from every corner, Daffed's infernal collection of dead things staring innocently at him—that he had been branded where the skin had not been rubbed off his palm. He bore the mark of the handle: a delicate filigree of unfamiliar symbols from behind which strange eyes peered out. In the fading light, with the rain falling harder, the fungi appeared to have been washed off the cover of the cage. Perversely, this fact disappointed him. With each new encounter, he had come to expect further revelations.

Blinking away the rain, Hoegbotton let out a deep breath, stuffed his mask in a pocket, wrapped the cloth around his injured hand, and picked up the cage. It was heavier than he remembered it, and oddly balanced. It made him list to the side as he started walking up the path to the main road. He would have to hurry if he was to make the curfew imposed by the Cappan.

Ambergris at dusk, occluded and darkened by the rain that splattered on sidewalks, rattled against rooftops, struck windows, hinted at a level of debauchery almost as unnerving to Hoegbotton as the way, whenever he stopped to switch the cage from his left to his right hand and back again, the weight never seemed the same.

The city that flourished from wholesome activity by day became its opposite by night. Orgies had been reported in abandoned churches. Grotesque and lewd water puppet shows were staged down by the docks. Weekly, the merchant quarter held midnight auctions of paintings that could only be termed obscene. The fey illustrated books of Collart and Slothian enjoyed a popularity that placed the authors but a single step below the Cappan in status. In the Religious Quarter, the hard-pressed Truffidian priests tried to wrest back authority from the conflicting prophets Peterson and Stratton, whose dueling theologies infected ever-more violent followers.

At the root of this immorality: the renewed presence of the gray caps, who in recent years came and went like the ebb and flow of a tide—now underground, now above ground, as if in a perpetual migration between light and dark, night and day. Always, the city reacted to their presence in unpredictable ways. What choice did the city's inhabitants have but to go about their business, hoping they would not be next, blind to all but their own misfortunes? It was now one hundred years since the Silence, when thousands had vanished without a trace, and people could be forgiven their loss of memory. Most people no longer thought of the Silence on a daily basis. It did not figure into the ordinary sorrows of Ambergris' inhabitants so much as into the weekly sermons of the Truffidians or into the worries of the Cappan and his men.

As Hoegbotton walked home, street lamps appeared out of the murk, illuminating fleeting figures: a priest holding his robe up as he ran so he wouldn't trip on the hem; two Dogghe tribesmen hunched against the closed doors of a bank, their distinctive green spiraled hats pulled down low over their weathered faces. Of the recent Occupation, no sign remained except for painted graffiti urging the invaders to go home. But Hoegbotton still came upon the faintly glowing, six-foot-wide purplish circles that showed where, before the Silence, huge mushrooms had been chopped down by worried authorities.

Hoegbotton's wife was already asleep when he walked up the seven flights of stairs and entered their apartment. She had turned off the lamps because it gave her the advantage in case of an intruder. The faint scent of lilacs and honeysuckle told him the flower vendor from the floor above them had been by to see Rebecca.

A dim half-light shone from the living room to his left as he set down the cage, took off his shoes and socks, and hung his raincoat on the coat rack. Directly ahead lay the dining room, with its mold-encrusted window, the purple sheen burning darkly as the rain fed it. He had checked the fungi guard just a week ago and found no leakage, but he made a mental note to check it again in the morning.

Hoegbotton found a towel in the hall closet and used it to dry his face, his hair, and then the outside of the cage. Again picking up the uncomfortable weight of the cage, he tiptoed into the living room, the rug beneath his feet thick but cold. A medley of dark shapes greeted him, most of them items from his store: Lamps and side tables, a couch, a long low coffee table, a book case, a grandfather clock. Beyond them lay the balcony, long lost to fungi and locked up as a result.

The fey light almost transformed the living room's contents into the priceless artifacts he had told her they were. He had chosen them not for their value but for their texture, their smell, and for the sounds they made when moved or sat upon or opened. Little of it appealed visually, but she delighted in what he had chosen and it meant he could store the most important merchandise at the shop, where it was more secure.

Hoegbotton set the cage down on the living room table. The palms of his hands were hot and raw from carrying it. He took off the rest of his clothes and laid them on the arm of the couch.

The light came from the bedroom, which lay to the right of the living room. He walked into the bedroom and turned to the left, the closed window above the bed reflecting back the iridescent light that came from her and her alone. Rebecca lay on her back, the sheets draped across her body, exposing the long, black, vaguely tear-shaped scar on her left thigh. He ran his gaze over it lustfully. It glistened like obsidian.

Hoegbotton walked around to the right side and eased himself into the bed. He moved up beside her and pressed himself against the darkness of the scar. An image of the woman from the mansion flashed through his mind.

Rebecca turned in her sleep and put an arm across his chest as he moved onto his back. Her hand, warm and soft, was as delicate as the starfish that glided through the shallows down by the docks. It looked so small against his chest.

The light came from her open eyes, although he could tell she was asleep. It was a silvery glow awash with faint phosphorescent sparks of blue, green, and red: shivers and hiccups of splintered light, as if a half-dozen tiny lightning storms had welled up in her gaze. What rich worlds did she dream of? And, for the thousandth time: What did the light mean? He had met her on a business trip to Stockton, after the fungal infection that had resulted in the blindness, the odd light, the scar. He had never known her whole.

Who was this stranger, so pale and silent and beautiful? A joyful sorrow rose within him as he watched the light emanating from her. They had argued about having children just the day before. Every word he had thrown at her in anger had hurt him so deeply that finally he had been wordless, and all he could do was stare at her. Looking at her now, her face unguarded, her body next to his, he could not help loving her for the scar, the eyes, even if it meant he wished her to be this way.

2

The next morning, Hoegbotton woke to the fading image of the woman's bloody bandages and the sounds of Rebecca making breakfast. She knew the apartment better than he did—knew its surfaces, its edges, the exact number of steps from table to chair to doorway—and she liked to make meals in a kitchen that had become more familiar to her than it could ever be to him. Yet she also asked him to bring back more furniture for the living room and bedroom or rearrange existing furniture. She became bored otherwise. "I want an unexplored country. I want a hint of the unknown," she said once and Hoegbotton agreed with her.

To an extent. There were things Hoegbotton wished would stay unknown. On the mantel opposite the bed, for example, lay those of his grandmother's possessions that his relatives in Morrow had sent to him: a pin, a series of portraits of family members, a set of spoons, a poorly copied family history. A letter had accompanied the heirlooms, describing his grandmother's last days. The package had been waiting for him on the doorstep of the apartment one evening a month ago. His grandmother had died six weeks before that. He had not gone to the funeral. He had not even brought himself to tell Rebecca about the death. All she knew of it was the crinkling of the envelope as he smoothed out the letter to read it. She might even have picked up the pin or the spoons and wondered why he had brought them home. Telling her would mean explaining why he hadn't gone to the funeral and then he would have to talk about the bad blood between him and his brother Richard.

The smell of bacon and eggs spurred him to throw back the covers, get up, put on a bathrobe, and stumble bleary-eyed through the living room to the kitchen. A dead sort of almost-sunlight—pale and green and lukewarm—suffused the kitchen window through the purple mold and thin veins of green. A watermark of the city appeared through the glass: gray spires, forlorn flags, the indistinct shapes of other anonymous apartment buildings.

Rebecca stood in the kitchen, spatula in hand, framed by the dour light. Her black hair was brightly dark. Her dress, a green-and-blue sweep of fabric, fit her loosely. She was intent on the skillet in front of her, gaze unblinking, mouth pursed.

As he came up behind Rebecca and wrapped his arms around her, a sense of guilt made him frown. He had come so close last night, almost as close as the boy, the woman. Was that as close as he could get without . . . ? The question had haunted him throughout his quest. A sudden deep swell of emotion overcame him and he found that his eyes were wet. What if, what if?

Rebecca snuggled into his embrace and turned toward him. Her eyes looked almost normal during the day. Flecks of phosphorescence shot lazily across the pupils.

"Did you sleep well?" she asked. "You came home so late."

"I slept. I'm sorry I was late. It was a difficult job this time."

"Profitable?" Her elbow nudged him as she turned the eggs over with the spatula.

"Not very."

"Really? Why not?"

He stiffened. Would Rebecca have realized the mansion had become a deathtrap? Would she have smelled the blood, tasted the fear? He served as her eyes, her contact with the world of images, but would he truly deprive her by not describing its horrors to her in every detail?

"Well . . . " he began. He shut his eyes. The sick gaze of the solicitor flickering over the scene of his own death washed over him. Even as he held Rebecca, he could feel a distance opening up between them.

"You don't need to shut your eyes to see," she said, pulling out of his embrace.

"How did you know?" he said, although he knew.

"I heard you close them." She smiled with grim satisfaction.

"It was just sad," he said, sitting down at the kitchen table. "Nothing horrible. Just sad. The wife had lost her husband and had to sell the estate. She had a boy with her who kept holding on to a little suitcase."

The remnants of the solicitor floating to the ground, curling up like confetti. The boy's gaze fluttering between him and the cage.

"I felt sorry for them. They had some nice heir-looms, but most of it was already promised to Slattery. I didn't get much. They had a nice rug from Morrow, from before the Silence. Nice detail of Morrow cavalry coming to our rescue. I would have liked to have bought it."

She carefully slid the eggs and bacon onto a plate and brought it to the table.

"Thank you," he said. She had burned the bacon. The eggs were too dry. He never complained. She needed these little sleights of hand, these illusions of illumination. It was edible.

"Mrs. Bloodgood took me down to the Morhaim Museum yesterday," she said. "Many of their artifacts are on open display. The textures were amazing. And the flower vendor visited, as you may have guessed."

Rebecca's father, Paul, was the curator for a small museum in Stockton. Paul liked to joke that Hoegbotton was just the temporary caretaker for items that would eventually find their way to him. Hoegbotton had always thought museums just hoarded that which should be available on the open market. Rebecca had been her father's assistant until the disease stole her sight. Now Hoegbotton sometimes took her down to the store to help him sort and catalog new acquisitions.

"I noticed the flowers," he said. "I'm glad the museum was nice."

For some reason, his hand shook as he ate his eggs. He put his fork down.

"Isn't it good?" she asked.

"It's very good," he said. "I just need water."

He got up and walked to the sink. The faucet had been put in five weeks ago, after a two-year wait. Before, they had gotten jugs of water from a well down in the valley. He watched with satisfaction as the faucet spluttered and his glass gradually filled up.

"It's a nice bird or whatever," she said from behind him.

"Bird." A vague fear shot through him. "Bird?" The glass clinked against the edge of the sink as he momentarily lost his grip on it.

"Or lizard. Or whatever it is. What is it?"

He turned, leaned against the sink. "What are you talking about?"

"That cage you brought home with you."

The vague fear crept up his spine. "There's nothing in the cage. It's empty." Was she joking?

Rebecca laughed: a pleasant, liquid sound. "That's funny, because your empty cage was rattling earlier. At first, it scared me. Something was rustling around in there. I couldn't tell if it was a bird or a lizard or I would have reached through the bars and touched it."

"But you didn't."

"No."

"There's nothing in the cage."

Her face underwent a subtle change and he knew she thought he doubted her on something at which she was expert: the interpretation of sound. On a calm day, she had told him, she could hear a boy skipping stones down by the docks.

For a moment, he said nothing. He couldn't stay quiet for long. She couldn't read his face without touching it, but he suspected she knew the difference between types of silence.

He laughed. "I'm joking. It's a lizard—but it bites. So you were wise not to touch it."

Suspicion tightened her features. Then she relaxed and smiled at him. She reached out, felt for his plate with her left hand, and stole a piece of his bacon. "I knew it was a lizard!"

He longed to go into the living room where the cage stood atop the table. But he couldn't, not just yet.

"It's quiet in here," he said softly, already expecting the reply.

"No it's not. It's not quiet at all. It's loud."

The left corner of his mouth curled up as he replied by rote: "What do you hear, my love?"

Her smile widened. "Well, first, there's your voice, my love—a nice, deep baritone. Then there's Hobson downstairs, playing a phonograph as low as he can to avoid disturbing the Potaks, who are at this moment in an argument about something so petty I will not give you the details, while to the side, just below them"—her eyes narrowed—"I believe the Smythes are also making bacon. Above us, old man Clox is pacing and pacing with his cane, muttering about money. On his balcony, there's a sparrow chirping, which makes me realize now that the animal in your cage must be a lizard, because it sounds like something clicking and clucking, not chirping—unless you've got a chicken in there?"

"No, no—it's a lizard."

"What kind of lizard?"

"It's a Saphant Click-Spitting Fire Lizard from the Southern Isles," he said. "It only ever grows in cages, which it makes itself by chewing up dirt, changing it into metal, and regurgitating it. It can only eat animals that can't see it."

She laughed in appreciation and got up and hugged him. Her scent made him forget his fear. "It's a good story, but I don't believe you. I do know this, though—you are going to be late to work."

Once on the ground floor, where he did not think it would make a difference if Rebecca heard, Hoegbotton set down the cage. The awkwardness of carrying it, uneven and swaying, down the spiral staircase had unnerved him. He was sweating under his rain coat. His breath came hard and fast. The musty quality of the lobby, the traces of tiny rust mushrooms that had spread along the floor like mouse tracks, the mottled green-orange mold on the windows in the front door, did not put him at ease.

Someone had left a worn umbrella leaning against the front door. He grabbed it and turned back to stare at the cage. Was this the moment that Ungdom and Slattery's ill wishes caught up with him? He drove the umbrella tip between the bars. The cover gave a little, creasing, and then regained its former shape as he withdrew the umbrella. Nothing came leaping out at him. He tried again. No response.

"Is something in there?" he asked the cage. The cage did not reply.

Umbrella held like a sword in front of him, Hoegbotton pulled the cover aside—and leapt back.

The cage was still empty. The perch swung back and forth madly from the violence with which he had pulled aside the cover. The woman had said, "The cage was always open." The boy had said, "We never had a cage." The solicitor had never offered an opinion. The swinging perch, the emptiness of the cage, depressed him. He could not say why. He drew the cover back across the cage.

Footsteps sounded on the stairs behind him and he whirled around, then relaxed. It was just Sarah Willis, their landlady, walking down from her second floor apartment.

"Good morning, Mrs. Willis," he said, leaning on the umbrella.

Mrs. Willis did not bother to respond until she was standing in front of him, staring up at him through her thick glasses. A flower pattern hat covered her balding head. A matching flower dress, faded, covered her ancient body, even her presumably shoed feet.

"No pets allowed," she said.

"Pets?" Hoegbotton was momentarily bewildered. "What pets?"

Mrs. Willis nodded at the cage. "What's in there?"

"Oh, that. It's not a pet."

"No animals allowed, pets or meat." Mrs. Willis cackled and coughed at her own joke.

"It's not . . . " He realized it was useless. "I'm taking it out now. It was just there for the morning."

Mrs. Willis grunted and pushed past him.

At the door, just as she walked out into the renewed patter of rain, apparently counting on her hat to protect her, she offered Hoegbotton the following advice: "Miss Constance? On the third floor? She'll have your head if you don't put back her umbrella."

* * *

Located on Albumuth Boulevard, half-way between the docks and the residential sections that descended into a valley ever in danger of flooding, Hoegbotton's store—"Robert Hoegbotton & Sons: Quality Importers of Fine New & Used Items From Home & Abroad"—took up the first floor of a solid two-story wooden building owned by a monk in the Religious Quarter. The sign exhibited optimism; there were no sons. Not yet. The time was not right, the situation too uncertain, no matter what Rebecca might say. Someday his shop might serve as the headquarters for a merchant empire, but that wouldn't happen for several years. Always in the back of his mind, spurring him on: his brother Richard's threat to swoop down with the rest of the Hoegbotton clan to save the family name should he fail.

The display window, protected from the rain by an awning, held a battered mauve couch, an opulent, gold-leaf-covered chair (nicked by Hoegbotton, along with several other treasures, during the panicked withdrawal of the Kalif's troops), a phonograph, a large red vase, an undistinguished-looking saddle, and Alan Bristlewing, his assistant.

Bristlewing knelt inside the display, carefully placing records in the stand beside the phonograph. He had already wiped the window clean of fungi that had accumulated the night before. The detritus of the cleaning lay on the sidewalk in curled up piles of red, green, and blue. A sour smell emanated from these remnants, but the rain would wash it all away in an hour or two.

When Bristlewing saw Hoegbotton, he waved and inched his wiry frame out of the window. A moment later, shielding his head from the rain with a newspaper, he was opening the huge lock in the iron grille of the door, his mouth set in the familiar laconic grin that itself displayed some antiques, courtesy of a sidewalk dentist. A few button-shaped mushrooms, a fiery red, tumbled out of the lock as the key withdrew, rolling to a stop on the wet sidewalk.

Bristlewing was a scruffy, short, animated man who smelled of cigar smoke and often disappeared for days on end. Stories of debaucheries with prostitutes and week-long fishing trips down the River Moth buzzed around Bristlewing without settling on him. Hoegbotton could not afford to hire more dependable help.

"Morning," Bristlewing said.

"Good morning," Hoegbotton replied. "Any customers last night?"

"None with any money . . . " Bristlewing's grin vanished as he saw the cage. "Oh. I see you went to another one."

Hoegbotton set the cage down in front of Bristlewing

and took the ring of keys from him at the same time. "Just put it in the office. Are the inventory books up-to-date?" Hoegbotton's hand still stung from where the imprint of the handle had branded itself on his skin.

"Course they're current," Bristlewing said, turning stiffly away as he picked up his new burden.

By design, the way to Hoegbotton's office at the back of the store was blocked by a maze of items, from which rose a collective must-metal-rotted-dusty smell that to him formed the most delicate of perfumes. This smell of antiquity validated his selections as surely as any papers of authenticity. That customers tripped and frequently lost their bearings as they navigated the arbitrary footpaths mattered little to Hoegbotton. The received family wisdom said that thus hemmed in the customer had no choice but to buy something from the stacks of chairs, umbrellas, watches, pens, fishing rods, clothes, enameled boxes, deer racks, plaster casts of lizards, elegant mirrors of glass and copper, reading glasses, Truffidian religious icons, boards for playing dice made of oliphaunt ivory, porcelain water jugs, globes of the world, model ships, old medals, sword canes, musical clocks, and other ephemera from past lives or distant places. Hoegbotton loved knowing that a customer might, in seeking out a perfectly ordinary set of dinner plates, come face-to-face with the flared nostrils and questing tongue of a Skamoo erotic mask. An overwhelming sense of the secret history of these objects could sometimes send him into a trance-like state. Thankfully, Rebecca understood this feeling, having been exposed to it from an early age.

Emerging from this morass of riches, Hoegbotton's office lay open to the rest of the store like an oasis of sparseness. Five steps led down to its sunken carpeting—crimson with gold threads, bought from the old Threnody Larkspur Theater before it burned to the ground—and a simple rosewood desk whose only flourishes were legs carved into the shape of writhing squid. A matching chair, two work tables against the far wall, and a couch for visitors rounded out the furniture. To the left of the office space stood two doors. The first led to a private bathroom, recently installed, much to Bristlewing's delight.

The desk lay beneath an organized clutter of books of inventory, a blotter, a selection of fountain pens, stationery with the H&S logo emblazoned upon it, folders full of invoices, a metal message capsule with a curled up piece of paper inside, a slice of orange mushroom in a small paper bag, a shell he had found while on vacation in the Southern Isles when he was six, and the new Frankwrithe & Lewden edition of *The Mystery of Cinsorium* by Blake Clockmoor. Daguerreotypes of Rebecca, his brother Stephen (lost to the family now, having signed up for the Kalif's cavalry on a monstrous but historically common whim) and his mother Gertrude standing on the lawn of someone else's mansion in Morrow added a personal touch.

Bristlewing had already made himself scarce—Hoegbotton could hear him pulling some artifact out from behind a row of old bookcases stacked high with cracked flowerpots—and the cage stood on the sideboard of his desk as if it had always been there.

Hoegbotton hung his raincoat on one of the six coat racks lined up like soldiers in the farthest corner of the office. Then he took the past day's book of inventory and purchases and walked to the door that led to the room next to the bathroom. The door was very old, wormholed, and studded with odd metal symbols that Hoegbotton had taken from an abandoned Manziist shrine.

Hoegbotton unlocked the door and went inside. The door shut silently behind him and he was alone. The light that cast its yellowing glare upon the room came from an old-fashioned squid oil lamp nailed into the room's far wall.

Nothing, at first glance, distinguished the room from any other room. It contained a tired-looking dining table around which stood four worn chairs. To one side, plates, cups, bowls, and utensils sat atop a cabinet with a mirror that served as a backboard. The mirror was veined with a purplish fungus that had managed to infiltrate minute fractures in the glass. He had worried that the Cappan's men might confiscate the mirror on one of their weekly inspections of his store, but they had ignored it, perhaps recognizing the age of the mirror and the way mold had itself begun to grow on the fungus.

The table held three place settings, the faded napkins unfolded and haphazard. Across the middle of the table lay a parchment of faded words, so old that it looked as if it might disintegrate into dust at the slightest touch. A bottle of port, half-full, stood on the table next to a bare space in front of the fourth chair.

By tradition, recently-established, Hoegbotton sat there for his daily readings from the books of inventory. Bound in red leather, the books were imported from Morrow. The off-white pages were thin as tissue paper to accommodate as many sheets as possible. The two books Hoegbotton had taken with him represented the inventory for the past three months. Sixteen others, as massive and unwieldy, had been wrapped in a blanket and carefully hidden beneath the floorboards in his office. (Two separate notebooks to record unfortunate but necessary dealings with Ungdom and Slattery, suitably yellow and brown, had been tossed into an unlocked drawer of his desk.)

Yesterday had been slow—only five items sold, two of them phonograph records. He frowned when he read Bristlewing's description of the buyers as "Short lady with walking stick. Did not give a name." and "Man looked sick. Took forever to make up his mind. Bought one record after all that time." Bristlewing did not respect the system. By contrast, a typical Hoegbotton-penned buyer entry read like an investigative report: "Miss Glissandra Beckle, 4232 East Munrale Mews, late 40s. Gray-silver hair. Startling blue eyes. Wore an expensive green dress but cheap black shoes, scuffed. She insisted on calling me 'Mr. Hoegbotton.' She examined a very expensive

Occidental vase and commented favorably on a bone
hairpin, a pearl snuffbox, and a watch once worn by
a prominent Truffidian priest. However, she only
bought the hairpin."

If Bristlewing disliked the detail required by
Hoegbotton for the ledgers, he disliked the room itself
even more. After carefully cataloguing its contents
upon their arrival three years before, Hoegbotton had
asked Bristlewing a question.

"Do you know what this is?"

"Old musty room. No air."

"No. It's not an old musty room with no air."

"Fooled me," Bristlewing had said and, scowling,
left him there.

3

But Bristlewing was wrong. Bristlewing did not understand the first thing about the room. How could
he? And how could Hoegbotton explain that the room
was perhaps the most important room in the world,
that he often found himself inside it even while walking around the city, at home reading to his wife, or
buying fruit and eggs from the farmers' market?

The history of the room went back to the Silence itself. His great-great-grandfather, Samuel Hoegbotton,
had been the first Hoegbotton to move to Ambergris,
much against the wishes of the rest of his extended
family, including his twenty-year-old son, John, who
stayed in Morrow.

For a man who had uprooted his wife and daughter from all that was familiar to take up residence in an unknown, sometimes cruel, city, Samuel Hoegbotton became remarkably successful, establishing three stores down by the docks. It seemed only a matter of time before more of the Hoegbotton clan moved down to Ambergris.

However, this was not to be. One day, Samuel Hoegbotton, his wife, and his daughter disappeared, just three of the thousands of souls who vanished from Ambergris during the episode known as the Silence— leaving behind empty buildings, empty courtyards, empty houses, and the assumption among those who grieved that the gray caps had caused the tragedy. Hoegbotton remembered one line in particular from John's diary: "I cannot believe my father has really disappeared. It is possible he could have come to harm, but to simply disappear? Along with my mother and sister? I keep thinking that they will return one day and explain what happened to me. It is too difficult to live with, otherwise."

Sitting in his mother's bedroom with the diary open before him, the young Robert Hoegbotton had felt a chill across the back of his neck. What had happened to Samuel Hoegbotton? He spent many summer afternoons in the attic, surrounded by antiquities, speculating on the subject. He combed through old letters Samuel had sent home before his disappearance. He visited the family archive. He wrote to relatives in other cities. His mother disapproved of such inquiries; his grandmother just smiled and said sadly, "I've often wondered myself." He could not talk to his father about it; that cold and distant figure was rarely home.

His sister also found the mystery intriguing. They would act out scenarios with the house as the backdrop. They would ask the maids questions to fill gaps in their knowledge and thus uncover the meaning of words like "gray cap" and "Cappan." His grandmother had even given them an old sketch that showed the apartment's living room—Samuel Hoegbotton surrounded by smiling relatives on a visit. But for his sister it was just relief of a temporary boredom and he was soon so busy learning the family business that the mystery faded from his thoughts.

When he reached the age of majority, he decided to leave Morrow and travel to Ambergris. No Hoegbotton had set foot in Ambergris for 90 years and it was precisely for this reason that he chose the city, or so he told himself. In Morrow, under the predatory eye of Richard, he had felt as if none of his plans would ever be successful. In Ambergris, he had started out poor but independent, operating a sidewalk stall that sold fruit and broadsheets. At odd times—at an auction, looking at jewelry that reminded him of something his mother might wear; sneaking around Ungdom's store examining all that merchandise, so much richer than what he could acquire at the time—thoughts of the Silence wormed their way into his head.

The day after he signed the lease on his own store, Hoegbotton visited Samuel's apartment. He had the address from some of the man's letters. The building lay in a warren of derelict structures that rose from the side of the valley to the east of the Merchant Quarter. It took Hoegbotton an hour to find it, the carriage ride followed by progress on foot. He knew he was close when he had to climb over a wooden fence with a sign on it that read "Off Limits By Order of the Cappan." The sky was overcast, the sunlight weak yet bright, and he walked through the tenements feeling ethereal, dislocated. Here and there, he found walls where bones had been mixed with the mortar and he knew by these signs that such places had been turned into graveyards.

When he finally stood in front of the apartment—on the ground level of a three-story building—he wondered if he should turn around and go home. The exterior was boarded up, fire-scorched and splotched with brown-yellow fungi. Weeds had drowned the grass and other signs of a lawn. A smell like dull vinegar permeated the air. The facing rows of buildings formed a corridor of light, at the end of which a stray dog sniffed at the ground, picking up a scent. He could see its ribs even from so far away. Somewhere, a child began to cry, the sound thin, attenuated, automatic. The sound was so unexpected, almost horrifying, that he thought it must not be a baby at all, but *something* mimicking a baby, hoping to lure him closer.

After a few more moments, he reached a decision and took a crowbar from his pack. Half an hour later, he had unpried the boards and the door stood revealed, a pale "X" running across the dark wood.

He realized he was breathing in shallow gasps, anticipation laced with fear. No one could help him if he opened the door and needed help, but he still wanted whatever was inside the apartment. It could be anything, even the end of his life, and yet the adrenalin rushed through him.

Hoegbotton pulled the door open and stepped inside, crowbar held like a weapon.

It took a moment for his eyes to adjust to the darkness. The air was stale. Windows to the right and left of the hallway, although boarded up, let in enough light to make patches of dust on the floor shine like colonies of tiny, subdued fireflies. The hallway was oddly ordinary, nothing out of place. In the even more dimly-lit living room, Hoegbotton could make out that some vagrant had long ago set up digs and abandoned them. A sofa had been overturned and a blanket used as a roof for a makeshift tent, broadsheets strewn across the floor for a bed. Dog droppings were more recent, as were the bones of small animals piled in a corner. A rabbit carcass, withered but caked with dried blood, might have been as fresh as the week before. The wallpaper had collapsed into a mumbling senility of fragments and strips. Paintings that had hung on the wall lay in tumbled flight against the floor, their hooks having long since given out. A faint, bitter smell rose from the room—a sourness that revealed hidden negotiations between wood and fungi, the natural results of decay. Hoegbotton relaxed. The gray caps had not been in the apartment for a long time. He let the crowbar dangle in his hand.

Hoegbotton entered the dining room. Brittle fragments of newsprint lay scattered across the dining room table, held in place by a bottle of port with glass beside it. Colonized by cobwebs, by dust, by mottled fragments of wood that had drifted down from the ceiling, the table also held three plates and place settings. The stale air had preserved the contents of the plates in a mummified state. Three plates. Three pieces of ossified chicken, accompanied by a green smear of some vegetable long since dried out. Samuel Hoegbotton. His wife Sarah. His daughter Jane. All three chairs, worm-eaten and rickety, were pulled out slightly from the table. A fourth chair lay off to the side, smashed into fragments by time or violence.

Hoegbotton stared at the chairs for a long time. Had they been moved at all in the last hundred years? Had freak winds blowing through the gaps in the boarded up windows caused them to move? How could anyone know? And yet, their current positioning teased his imagination. It did not look as if Samuel Hoegbotton's family had gotten up in alarm—unfolded napkins lay on the seats of two of the chairs. The third—that of the person who would have been reading the newspaper—had not been used, nor had the silverware for that setting. The silverware of the other two was positioned peculiarly. On the right side, the fork lay at an angle near the plate, as if thrown there. Something dark and withered had been skewered by the fork's tines. Did it match an irregularity in the dry flesh of the chicken upon the matching plate? The knife was missing entirely. On the left side of the table, the fork was still stuck into its piece of chicken, the knife sawing into the flesh beside it.

It appeared to Hoegbotton as if the family had been eating and simply . . . disappeared . . . in mid-meal. A prickly, cold sensation spread across Hoegbotton's skin. The fork. The knife. The chairs. The broadsheet. The meals uneaten, half-eaten. The bottle of port. The mystery gnawed at him even as it became ever more impenetrable. Nothing in the scenarios his sister and he had drawn up in their youth could account for it.

Hoegbotton took out his pocketknife and leaned over the table. He carefully pulled aside one leaf of the broadsheet to reveal the date: the very day of the Silence. The date transfixed him. He pulled out the chair where surely Samuel Hoegbotton must have sat, reading his papers, and slowly slid into it. Looked down the table to where his daughter and wife would have been sitting. Continued to read the paper with its articles on the turmoil at the docks, preparing for the windfall of squid meat due with the return of the fishing fleet; a brief message on blasphemy from the Truffidian Antechamber; the crossword puzzle. A sudden shift, a dislocation, a puzzled look from his wife, and he had stared up from his paper in that last moment to see . . . what? To see the gray caps or a vision much worse? Had Samuel Hoegbotton known surprise? Terror? Wonder? Or was he taken away so swiftly that he, his daughter, and his wife, had no time for any reaction at all.

Hoegbotton stared across the table again, focused on the bottle of port. The glass was half-full. He leaned forward, examined the glass. The liquid inside had dried into sludge over time. A faint imprint of tiny lips could be seen on the edge of the glass. The cork was tightly wedged into the mouth of the bottle. A further mystery. Had the port been poured long after the Silence?

Beyond the bottle, the fork with the skewered meat came into focus. It did not, from this angle, look as if it came from the piece of chicken on the plate.

He pulled back, as much from a thought that had suddenly occurred to him as from the fork itself. A dim glint from the floor beside the chair caught his eye. Samuel Hoegbotton's glasses. Twisted into a shape that resembled a circle attached to a line and two "u" shapes on either end. As he stared at the glasses, Hoegbotton felt the questions multiply, until he was not just sitting in Samuel Hoegbotton's chair, but in the chairs of thousands of souls, looking out into darkness, trying to see what they had seen, to know what they came to know.

The baby was still screaming as Hoegbotton stumbled outside, gasping. He ran over bits of brick and rubble. He ran through the long weeds. He ran past the buildings with mortar made from bones. He scrambled over the fence that said he should not have been there. He did not stop running until he had reached the familiar cobblestones of Albumuth Boulevard's farthest extreme. When he did stop, gasping for breath, the pressure in his temples remained, the stray thought

lodged in his head like a disease. What had Samuel
Hoegbotton seen? And was it necessary to disappear
to have seen it?

That was how it had started—following a cold, one
hundred-year-old trail. At first, he convinced himself
that he was just pursuing a good business opportunity: buying up the contents of boarded up homes,
fixing what was in disrepair, and reselling it from
his store. He had begun with Samuel Hoegbotton's
apartment, hiring workmen to take the contents of
the dining room and transplant it to the room next to
his office. They had arranged it exactly as it had been
when he first entered it. He would sit in the room for
hours, scrutinizing each element—the bottle of port,
the plates, the silverware, the napkins haphazard on
the chairs—but no further insight came to him. After
a few months, he dusted it all and repaired the table,
the chairs, restoring everything but the broadsheet to
the way it must have been the day of the Silence. In
his darker moments, he felt as if he might be ushering
in a new Silence with his actions, but still he came no
closer to an answer.

Soon even the abandoned rooms of the Silence lost
their hold on Hoegbotton. He would go in with the
workmen and find old, dimly-lit spaces from which
whatever had briefly imbued them with a ghastly intensity had long since departed. He stopped acquiring
such properties, although in a sense, it was too late.
Ungdom, Slattery, and their ilk had already begun to
slander him, spreading rumors about his intent and

his sanity. They made life difficult for him, but by ignoring their barbs, he had survived it.

Hoegbotton did not give up. Whenever he could, he bought items that had some connection to the gray caps, hoping to find the answers necessary to quell his curiosity. He read books. He spoke to those who remembered, vaguely, the tales their elders had told them about the Silence. And then, finally, the breakthrough: a series of atrocities at one mansion after the other, bringing him closer than ever before.

Hoegbotton finished reading the ledger, took a last sip of the port he had poured for himself, and walked out of the room in time to hear the bell that announced the arrival of a customer. He put the books back in their place and was about to lock the door to Samuel Hoegbotton's dining room when it occurred to him that the cage might be more secure inside the room. He picked it up—the handle seemed hot to the touch—walked back into the room, and placed the cage on the far end of the table. Then he locked the door, put the key in his desk, and went to attend to the needs of his customer.

4

That night, he made love to Rebecca. Her scar gleamed by the light from her eyes, which, at the height of her rapture, blazed so brightly that the bedroom seemed transported from night to day. As he came inside of her, he felt a part of her scar enter him. It registered as an ecstatic shudder that penetrated his muscles, his bones, his heart. She called out his name and ran her hands down his back, across his face, her eyes sparking with pleasure. At such moments, when the strangeness of her seeped through into him, he would suffer a sudden panic, as if he was losing himself, as if he no longer knew his own name. He would sit up, as now, all the muscles in his back rigid.

She knew him well enough not to ask what was wrong, but, sleep besotted, the light from her eyes dimming to a satisfied glow, said, simply, "I love you."

"I love you, too," he said. "Your eyes are full of fireflies."

She laughed, but he meant it: entire cities, entire worlds, pulsed inside those eyes, hinting at an existence beyond the mundane.

Something in her gaze reminded him suddenly of the woman with the missing hands and he looked away, toward the window that, though closed, let in the persistent sound of rain. Beside the window, his grandmother's possessions still lay in shadows on the mantel.

The next day, as he sat in Samuel Hoegbotton's room writing out invoices for the past week's exports—Saphant carnival masks, rare eelwood furniture from Nicea, necklaces made by yet another indigenous tribe discovered at the heart of the great southern rainforests, all destined for Morrow—he noticed something odd. He drew his breath in sharply. He pushed his chair back and stood up.

There, growing at a right angle from the green cloth that covered the cage, was a fragile, milk-white fruiting body on a long stem, the gills tinged red. It was identical to the mushrooms that had appeared in Daffed's mansion. He cast about for a weapon, his gaze fixed on the cage. There was nothing but the bottle of port. Beyond the cage, the fungus that had infiltrated the cracks of the mirror appeared to have darkened and thickened. Irrationally, he decided he had to remove the cage from the room. The room had caused the fruiting body. Picking up a napkin, he wound it around the handle of the cage and carried it out of the room, to his desk.

He stared across the store, trying to locate Bristlewing. His assistant stood in a far corner helping an elderly gentleman decide on a chair. Hoegbotton could just see the back of Bristlewing's head, nodding at something the potential customer had said, both of them obscured by a column of school desks.

Slowly, as if the mushroom was watching him, Hoegbotton slid his hand over to the top drawer of his desk, pulled it open and took out a silver letter opener. Holding it in front of him, he approached the cage. Images of the woman and her son flickered in his mind. He couldn't keep his hand still. He hesitated, wavered. A vision of the mushroom multiplying into two, three, four came to him. Hoegbotton leaned over his desk, chopped the mushroom off the side of the cage. It fell onto his desk, leaving behind only a small, circular white spot on the green cover, as innocent as a bird dropping.

Hoegbotton pulled his handkerchief out of his breast pocket and squashed the mushroom in its folds, careful not to touch any part of it. Then he stuffed the handkerchief into the wastebasket at his side. A moment's hesitation. He fished it out. Decided against it and placed the handkerchief back into the wastebasket. Fished it out again.

Hoegbotton realized that both Bristlewing and his customer were now standing a few feet away, staring at him. He froze, then smiled.

"My dear Bristlewing," he said. "What can I help you with?"

Bristlewing gave him a disgusted look. "Mr. Sporlender here was interested in a writing desk, for his son. We've a good, solid chair but nothing appropriate in a desk. Anything in storage?"

Hoegbotton smiled, extremely aware of the dead mushroom in his hand. The irritation caused by the handle of the cage flared up, pulsing across his palm. "Yes, actually, Mr. Sporlender, if you would come back tomorrow, I believe we might have something to show you . . . " Or not. Just so long as he left the shop—now.

Hoegbotton nudged Bristlewing out of the way and guided the man toward the door, through the crowded stacks of artifacts—babbling about the rain, about the importance of a writing desk, about anything at all, while Bristlewing's disgusted stare burned into the back of his skull. Hoegbotton had never been more impatient to reach the rain-scoured street. When it came, it was like a wave—of light, of fresh air. It hit him with such force that he gasped, drawing a sharp look from Mr. Sporlender.

As they stood there, on the cusp of the street, the iron door at Hoegbotton's back, the man stared at him through narrowed eyes. "Really, Mr. Hoegbotton—should I come back tomorrow? Would you truly advise that?"

Hoegbotton stared down at his hand, which was about to rebel and throw the handkerchief and mushroom as far away as possible. Some of the early afternoon passersby already stared curiously at the two of them.

"I suppose you shouldn't, actually. We don't have a desk in storage or anywhere else . . . I have a condition of sudden claustrophobia. It comes and goes. I cannot control it."

The man sneered. "I saw what you put in the handkerchief. I know what it is. Will I tell? Why bother—you'll be dead soon enough." The man stalked off.

Hoegbotton immediately began to fast-walk in the opposite direction, past sidewalk vendors, a thin stream of pedestrians, and an even thinner stream of carts and carriages, which the rain rendered in smudges and humid smells. Only after three or four blocks, soaked to the skin, did he feel comfortable tossing the handkerchief and its contents into a public trashcan. He already had an image in his head of the Cappan's men searching his store for traces of fungi.

A man was throwing up into the gutter. A woman was yelling at her husband. The sky was a uniform gray. The rain was unending, as common as the very air. He couldn't even feel it anymore. Everywhere, in the cracks of the sidewalk, in the minute spaces between bricks in shop fronts, new fungi was growing. He wondered if anything he did mattered.

Back at the store, Bristlewing was grumpily moving some boxes around. He spared Hoegbotton only a quick glance—watchful, wary. Hoegbotton brushed by him and headed for the bathroom, where he scrubbed his hands red before coming out again to examine the cage. It looked just as he had left it. The green cover was unblemished but for the white spot. There had been no proliferation of mushrooms in his absence. This was good. This meant he had done the right thing. (Why, then, was it so hard to draw breath? Why so difficult to stop shaking?)

He sat down behind the desk, staring at the cage. The inside of his mouth felt dry and thick. Nothing happened without a reason. The mushroom had not appeared by coincidence. This he could not believe. How could he?

Almost against his will, he reached over to the cage and pulled the cover aside, the green giving way to the finely-etched metal bars, the shadows of the bars letting the light slide around them so that he saw the perch, gently swinging, and, below it, a pale white hand. Slender and delicate. The end a mass of dried blood. A vision overtook him: that he was Samuel

Hoegbotton, staring across the dining room table at the cage, which was the last thing he ever saw . . . The hand, he had no doubt, was from Daffed's wife. What would it take to make it go away?

But then his mind registered a much more important detail, one that made him bite down hard on his lower lip to stop from screaming. The cage door was open, slid to the side as neatly as the cover. He sat there, motionless, staring, for several seconds. Throughout the store, he could hear the hands of myriad clocks clicking forward. No mask could help him now. The hand. The open cage. The fey brightness of the bars. A *rippling* at the edges of his vision.

Somewhere, Hoegbotton found the nerve. He reached out and slid the door back into position with both hands, worked the latch shut—just as he felt a sudden weight on the other side, rushing up to meet him. It brushed against his fingers and chilled them. He drew back with a gasp. The door rattled once, twice, fell still. The perch began to swing violently back and forth as if something had pushed up against it. Then it too fell still. Suddenly.

He could not breathe. He could not call out for help. His heart was beating so fast, he thought it might burst. This was not how he had imagined it. This was not how he had imagined it.

Something invisible picked up the hand and forced it through the bars. The hand fell onto his blotter, rocked once, twice, and was still.

It took five or six tries, his fingers nimble as blocks

of wood, but he managed to find the cord to the cover and slide it back into position.

Then he sat there for a long time, staring at the green cover of the cage. Nothing happened. Nothing bad. The sense of weight on the other side of the bars had vanished with the drawing of the veil. The hand that lay on his blotter did not seem real. It looked like alabaster. It looked like wax. It was a candle without a wick. It was a piece of a statue.

An hour could have passed, or a minute, before he found a paper bag, nudged the hand into it using the letter opener, and folded the bag shut.

Bristlewing appeared in his field of vision some time later.

"Bristlewing," Hoegbotton said. "I'm glad. You're here."

"Eh?"

"You see this cage?"

"Yes."

"I need you to take it to Ungdom."

"Ungdom?" Bristlewing's face brightened. He clearly thought this was a joke.

"Yes. To Ungdom. Tell him that I send it with my compliments. That I offer it as a token of renewed friendship." Somewhere inside, he was laughing at Ungdom's future discomfort. Somewhere inside, he was screaming for help.

Bristlewing snorted. "Is it wise?"

Hoegbotton stared up at him, as if through a haze of smoke. "No. It isn't wise. But I would like you to do it anyway."

Bristlewing waited for a moment, as if there might be something more, but there was nothing more. He walked forward, picked up the cage. As Bristlewing bent over the cage, Hoegbotton thought he saw a patch of green at the base of his assistant's neck, under his left ear. Was Bristlewing already infected? Was Bristlewing the threat?

"Another thing. Take the rest of the week off. Once you've delivered the cage to Ungdom." If his assistant was going to dissolve into spores, let him do it elsewhere. Hoegbotton suppressed a giggle of hysteria.

Suspicious, Bristlewing frowned. "And if I want to work?"

"It's a vacation. A vacation. I've never given you one. I'll pay you for the time."

"All right," Bristlewing said. Now the look he gave Hoegbotton was, to Hoegbotton's eye, very close to a look of pity. "I'll give the cage to Ungdom and take the week off."

"That's what I said."

"Right. Bye then."

"Goodbye."

As Bristlewing negotiated the tiny flotsam-lined pathway, Hoegbotton could not help but notice that his assistant seemed to list to one side, as if the cage had grown unaccountably heavy.

Five minutes after Bristlewing had left, Hoegbotton closed up the shop for the day. It only took seven tries for him to lock the door behind him.

5

When he arrived at the apartment, Hoegbotton told
Rebecca he was home early because he had learned
of his grandmother's death. She seemed to interpret
his shakes and shudders, the trembling of his voice,
the way he needed to touch her, as consistent with
his grief. They ate dinner in silence, her hand in his
hand.

"Tell me about it," she said after dinner and he
catalogued all the symptoms of fear as if they were the
symptoms of loss, of grief. Everywhere he turned, the
woman from the mansion confronted him, her gaze
now angry, now mournful. Her wounds bled copi-
ously down her dress but she did nothing to staunch
the flow.

They went to bed early and Rebecca held him until
he found a path toward sleep. But sleep held a kaleidoscope of images to torment him. In his dreams, he
walked through Samuel Hoegbotton's apartment until
he reached a long, white hallway he had never seen
before. At the opposite end of the hallway, he could see
the woman and the boy from the mansion, surrounded
by great wealth, antiques fit for a god winking at him
in their burnished multitudes. He was walking across
a carpet of small, severed hands to reach them. This
fact revolted him, but he could not stop walking: the
promise of what lay ahead was too great. Even when
he began to see his head, his arms, his own legs, crudely soldered to the walls using his own blood, he could

not stop his progress toward the end of the hallway.
The hands were cold and soft and pleading.

Despite the dreams, Hoegbotton woke the next morning feeling energetic and calm. The cage was gone.
He had another chance. He did not feel the need to
follow in Samuel Hoegbotton's footsteps. Even the
imprint on his hand throbbed less painfully. The rain
clattering down made him happy for obscure, childhood reasons—memories of sneaking out into thun-
derstorms to play under the dark clouds, of taking to
the water on a rare fishing trip with his father while
drops sprinkled the dark, languid surface of the River
Moth.

At breakfast, he even told Rebecca that perhaps
he had been wrong and they should start a family. Rebecca laughed, hugged him, and told him
they should wait to talk about it until after he had
recovered from his grandmother's death. When she
did not ask him about the funeral arrangements, he
wondered if she knew he had lied to her. On his way
out the door, he held her close and kissed her. Her
lips tasted of honeysuckle and rose. Her eyes were, as
ever, a mystery, but he did not mind.

Once at work, Bristlewing blissfully absent, Hoegbotton searched the store for any sign of mushrooms.
Donning long gloves and a fresh mask, he spent most
of his time in the old dining room, scuffing his knees
to examine the underside of the table, cleaning every
surface. The fungus embedded in the mirror had lost
its appearance of renewed vigor. Nevertheless, he

took an old toothbrush and knife and spent half an hour gleefully scraping it away.

Then, divesting himself of mask and gloves, he went through the same routines with his ledgers as in the past, this time reading the entries aloud since Bristlewing was not there to frown at him for doing so. Fragments of disturbing images fluttered in his mind like caged birds, but he ignored them, bending himself to his routine that he might allow himself no other thoughts.

By noon, the rain had turned to light hail, discouraging many erstwhile customers. Those who did enter the store alighted like crows escaping bad weather, shaking their raincoat wings and unlikely to buy anything.

By one o'clock, he had only made 100 sels. It didn't matter. It was almost liberating. He was beginning to think he had escaped great danger, even caught himself wondering if another rich family might experience a gray cap visitation.

At two o'clock, his spirits still high, Hoegbotton received a shock when a grim-faced member of the Cappan's security forces entered the store. The man was in full protective gear, clothed from head to foot, a gray mask covering his entire face except for his eyes. What could they know? It wasn't time for an inspection. Had the man looking for a desk talked to them? Hoegbotton scratched at his wounded palm.

"How can I help you?" he asked.

The man stared at him for a moment, then said, "I'm looking for a purse for my mother's birthday."

Hoegbotton burst out laughing and had to convince the man it was not directed at him before selling him a purse.

No customers entered the store for half an hour after the Cappan's man left. Hoegbotton had worked himself into a fever pitch of calm by the time the messenger arrived around three o'clock: a boy on a bicycle, pinched and drawn, wearing dirty clothes, who knocked at the door and waited for Hoegbotton to arrive before letting an envelope flutter to the welcome mat outside the door. The boy pulled his bicycle back to the sidewalk and pedaled away, ringing his bell.

Hoegbotton, softly singing to himself, leaned down to pick up the envelope. He opened it. The letter inside read, in a spidery scrawl:

> *Thank you, Robert, for your very fine*
> *gift, but your bird has flown away home.*
> *I couldn't keep such a treasure. My*
> *regards to your wife. – John Ungdom.*

Hoegbotton stared at the note, chuckling at the sarcasm. Read it again, a frown closing his lips. Flown away home. Read it a third time, his stomach filling with stones. My regards to your wife.

He dropped the note, flung on his raincoat, and, not bothering to lock the store behind him, ran out onto the street—into the blinding rain. He headed up Albumuth Boulevard, through the Bureaucratic Quarter, toward home. He felt as if he were running in place. Every pedestrian hindered him. Every horse and cart blocked his path. As the rain came down harder, it beat a rhythmic message into Hoegbotton's shoulders. The raindrops sounded like tapping fingers. Through the haze, the dull shapes of buildings became landmarks to anchor his staggering progress. Passersby stared at him as if he were crazy.

By the time he reached the apartment building lobby, his sides ached and he was drenched in sweat. He had fallen repeatedly on the slick pavement and bloodied his hands. He took the stairs three at a time, ran down the hallway to the apartment shouting "Rebecca!"

The apartment door was ajar. He tried to catch his breath, bending over as he slowly pushed the door open. A line of white mushrooms ran through the hallway, low to the ground, their gills stained red. Where his hand held the door, fungus touched his fingers. He recoiled, straightened up.

"Rebecca?" he said, staring into the kitchen. No one. The inside of the kitchen window was covered in purple fungi. A cane lay next to the coat rack, a gift from his father. He took it and walked into the apartment, picking his way between the white mushrooms as he pulled the edge of his raincoat up over his mouth. The doorway to the living room was directly to his left. He could hear nothing, as if his head were stuffed with cloth. Slowly, he peered around the doorway.

The living room was aglow with fungi, white and purple, green and yellow. Shelves of fungi jutted from the walls. Bottle-shaped mushrooms, a deep burgundy, wavering like balloons, were anchored to the floor.

Hoegbotton's palm burned fiercely. Now he was in the dream, not before.

Looking like the exoskeleton shed by some tropical beetle, the cage stood on the coffee table, the cover drawn aside, the door open. Beside the cage lay another alabaster hand. This did not surprise him. It did not even register. For, beyond the table, the doors to the balcony had been thrown wide open. Rebecca stood on the balcony, in the rain, her hair slick and bright, her eyes dim. Strewn around her, as if in tribute, the strange growths that had long ago claimed the balcony: orange strands whipping in the winds, transparent bulbs that stood rigid, mosaic patterns of gold-green mold imprinted on the balcony's corroded railing. Beyond: the dark gray shadows of the city, dotted with smudges of light.

Rebecca was looking down at . . . nothing . . . her hands held out before her as if in supplication.

"Rebecca!" he shouted. Or thought he shouted. His mouth was tight and dry. He began to walk across the living room, the mushrooms pulling against his shoes, his pants, the air alive with spores. He blinked, sneezed, stopped just short of the balcony. Rebecca had still not looked up. Rain splattered against his boots.

"Rebecca," he said, afraid that she would not hear him, that the distance between them was somehow too great. "Come away from there. It isn't safe." She was shivering. He could see her shivering.

Rebecca turned to look at him and smiled. "Isn't safe? You did this yourself, didn't you? Opened the balcony for me before you left this morning?" She frowned. "But then I was puzzled. You had the cage sent back even though Mrs. Willis said we couldn't keep pets."

"I didn't open the balcony. I didn't send back the cage." His boots were tinged green. His shoulders ached.

"Well, someone brought it here—and I opened it. I was bored. The flower vendor was supposed to come and take me to the market, but he didn't."

"Rebecca—it isn't safe. Come away from the balcony." His words were dull, unconvincing. A lethargy had begun to envelop his body.

"I wish I knew what it was," she said. "Can you see it? It's right here—in front of me."

He started to say no, he couldn't see it, but then he realized he could see it. He was gasping from the sight of it. He was choking from the sight of it. Blood trickled down his chin where he had bitten into his lip. All the courage he had built up for Rebecca's sake melted away.

"Come here, Rebecca," he managed to say.

"Yes. Okay," she said in a small, broken voice.

Tripping over fungi, she walked into the apartment. He met her at the coffee table, drew her against him, whispered into her ear, "You need to get out of here, Rebecca. I need you to go downstairs. Find Mrs. Willis. Have her send for the Cappan's men." Her hair was wet against his face. He stroked it gently.

"I'm scared," she whispered back, arms thrown around him. "Come with me."

"I will, Rebecca. Rebecca, I will. In just a minute. But now, I need you to leave." He was trembling from mixed horror at the thought that he might never say her name again and relief, because now he knew why he loved her.

Then her weight was gone as she moved past him to the door and, perversely, his burden returned to him.

The thing had not moved from the balcony. It was not truly invisible but camouflaged itself by perfectly matching its background. The bars of a cage. The spaces between the bars. A perch. He could only glimpse it now because it could not mimic the rain that fell upon it fast enough.

Hoegbotton walked out onto the balcony. The rain felt good on his face. His legs were numb so he lowered himself into an old rotting chair they had never bothered to take off the balcony. While the thing watched, he sat there, staring between the bars of the balcony railing, out into the city. The rain trickled through his hair. He tried not to look at his hands, which were tinged green. He tried to laugh, but it came out as a rasping gurgle. The thought came to him that he must still be back in the mansion with the woman and the boy—that he had never really left—because, honestly, how could you escape such horror? How could anyone escape something like that?

The thing padded up to him on its quiet feet and sang to him. Because it no longer mattered, Hoegbotton turned to look at it. He choked back a sob. He had not expected this. It was beautiful. Its single eye, so like Rebecca's eyes, shone with an unearthly light, phosphorescent flashes darting across it. Its mirror skin shimmered with the rain. Its mouth, full of knives, smiled in a way that did not mean the same thing as a human smile. This was as close as he could get, he knew now, staring into that single, beautiful eye. This was as close. Maybe there was something else, something beyond. Maybe there was a knowledge still more secret than this knowledge, but he would never experience that.

The thing held out its clawed hand and, after a time, Hoegbotton took it in his own.

☙❧

In the Hours After Death

By Nicholas Sporlender

☙❧

Nicholas Sporlender has contributed more than a dozen fictions to *Burning Leaves* over the years, including such memorable works as "The Exchange" (since published as a stand-alone chapbook by Hoegbotton & Sons), "The Smoldering Eye," "A Nail, Driven Deep" and "The Game of Lost and Found." Recently, Mr. Sporlender severed his long professional relationship with the artist (and art director of this publication) Louis Verden. The editorial board of *Burning Leaves* would like to take this opportunity to express its wish that the worthy gentleman will reconsider and provide Ambergris with many more years of macabre delights.

I

In the first hour after death, the room is so still that every sound holds a terrible clarity, like the tap of a knife against glass. The soft pad of shoes as someone walks away and closes the door is profoundly solid—each short footstep weighted, distinct. The body lies against the floor, the sightless eyes staring down into the wood as if some answer has been buried in the grain. The back of the head is mottled by the shadows of the trees that sway outside the open window. The trickle of red from the scalp that winds its way down the cheek, to puddle next to the clenched hand, is as harmless now, leached of threat, as if it were colored water. The man's features have become slack, his mouth parted slightly, his expression surprised. The wrinkles on his forehead form ridges of superfluous worry. His trumpet lies a few feet away . . . From outside the window, the coolness of the day brings the green-gold scent of lilacs and crawling vines. The rustle of leaves. The deepening of light. A hint of blue through the trees. After a time, a mouse, fur ragged and one eye milky white, sidles across the floor, sits on its haunches in front of the body, and sniffs the air. The mouse circles the man. It explores the hidden pockets of the man's gray suit, trembles atop the shoes, nibbles at the laces, sticks its nose into a pant cuff. A metallic sound, faint and chaotic, rises through the window. The mouse stands unsteadily on its hind legs and sniffs the air again, then scurries back to its hole underneath the table. The sound intensifies, as of many instruments lurching together in drunken surprise. Perhaps the noise startled the mouse, or perhaps the mouse was frightened by some changed aspect of the man himself. The man's chin has begun to sprout tendrils of dark green fungi that mimic the texture of hair, curling and twisting across the man's face while the music comes ever closer. The tendrils move in concert. The clash of sounds has more unity than raw cacophony, yet no coherence. It seems as if several people tuning their instruments have begun to play their own separate, unsynchronized melodies. Somewhere in the welter of pompous horns and trumpets, a violin whines dimly. The tendrils of fungi wander in lazy attempts to colonize the blood. The music rollicks along, by turns melancholy and defiant. The man hears nothing, of course; the blood has begun to crust across his forehead. The smell of the room has become fetid, damp. The shadows have grown darker. The table in the corner—upon which lies a half-eaten sandwich—casts an ominous shade of purple. Eventually, the music reaches a crescendo beneath the window. It has a questioning nature, as if the people playing the instruments are looking at one another, asking each other what to do next. The man's face moves a little from the vibration. His fungi beard is smiling. In a different light, he might almost look alive, intently staring at the floorboards, into the apartments below. Bells toll dimly from the Religious Quarter, announcing dinner prayers. The afternoon is almost gone. The room feels colder as the light begins to leave it. The music becomes less hesitant. Within minutes, the music is clanking up the stairs, toward the apartment. The music sounds as if it is running. It *is* running. The tendrils, in a race with the music, have spread farther, faster, covering all of the man's face with a dark green mask. As if misinterpreting their success, they do not spread out over the rest of his body but instead build on the mask, until it juts hideously from the face. The door begins to buckle before a blaring of horns, a torrid stitching of violins. Someone puts a key into the lock and turns the doorknob. The door opens. The music enters in all its chaotic glory. The man lies perfectly still on the floor beside the almost dry puddle of blood. A forest of legs and shoes surround him. The music becomes a dirge, haunted by the ghost of some strange fluted instrument. The musicians circle the body, their distress flowing through their music, their long straight shadows playing across the man's body. But for a tinge of green, the man's face has regained its form. The fungus has disappeared. Who could have known this would happen? Only the dead man, who had been looking into the grain as if some mystery lay there. The dead man lurches to his feet and picks up his trumpet. Smiles. Takes his hat from the table and places it on his head, over the blood. Wets his lips. He puts the trumpet to his mouth as all the other instruments become silent. He begins to blow, the tone clear yet discordant, his own music but not in tune. The faces of his friends come into focus, surround him, buzzing with words. His friends laugh. They hug him, tell him how glad they are it was all a joke; they had heard the most terrible things; please, do not scare them that way again. They did not know whether to play for a funeral or a rumorless resurrection. Unable to decide, they had played for both at once. He laughs, pats the nearest on the back. Play, he says. But he is not part of them. Play, he implores. But he is not one of them. And they play—marching out the door with him, they play. He is no longer one of them. When the door closes, the room is as empty as before, although the stairs echo with music. Over time, the sound fades. It fades until it is not even the memory of a sound, and then not even that. Nothing moves in the room. The man has been returned to himself. This is the first hour of death in the city of Ambergris. You may not rest for long. You may, in a sense, become yourself again. Worst of all, you may remember every detail but be unable to do anything about it.

II

In the second hour after death, the man finds himself with his musician friends playing a concert in a public park. A crowd has gathered, some standing, others kneeling or sitting on benches. The trumpet is hot and golden in the man's hands. With each breath he blows into his trumpet, he feels the surge of an unidentifiable emotion and a detail from his past appears in his mind. The man feels as if he were filling up with Life, each breath enhancing him rather than maintaining him. He remembers his name— the round, generous vowels of it—but resists the urge to shout it out. A name is a good foundation on which to build. The members of the audience are cheerful smudges compared to the clear, sharp lines of his friends as they move in time-honored synchronicity with their instruments. Their names, too, pop into his head—each a tiny explosion of pleasure. Soon, he swims in a sea of names: mother, father, brother, daughter, postman, baker, bartender, butcher, shopkeeper . . . He smiles the radiant smile of a man who has recalled his life and found it good. This is the pinnacle of the second hour, although not all are so lucky. To some, the knowledge of identity seems to be escaping through their pores, each exhaled thought just another casualty of the emptying. The man, however, is not so truthful with himself. He smells the honeysuckle, tastes the pipe smoke from a passerby, hears the tiny bells of an anklet tinkling through a pause in the music and does not wonder why these sensations are dull, muffled. His friends' faces are so near and sharp. Why should he worry about the rest? The blur of the world shouldn't be his concern. The instruments that seem so cruel, all honed edges, the metal reflecting at odd angles to create horrible disfigurements of his face? Why, it is just a trick of the shadows. The quickness of his breath? Why, it is just the aftermath of musical epiphany. The fluttering of his eyelids. The sudden pallor. The smudge of green that he wipes with irritation from his cheek . . . When the concert ends and the crowds disperse under threat of night, the man is quick to nod and laugh and join in one last ragged musical salute. An invitation down narrow streets to a café for a drink elicits a desperate gratitude—he slaps the backs of his friends, nods furiously, already beginning to lose the names again: pennies fallen through a hole in a shirt pocket. On the way to the café, he notices how strangely the city now speaks to him, in the voices of innuendo and suggestion, all surfaces unknown, all buildings crooked or deformed or worse. The sidewalk vendors are ciphers. The passersby count for less than shadows; he cannot look at them directly, his gaze a repulsing magnet. He clutches his trumpet, knuckles white. He would like to play it, bring the jovial wide vowels of his name once more into focus, but he cannot. The names of his friends fast receding, his laughter becomes by turns forced, nervous, sad, and then brittle. When they reach the café, the man looks around the beer-strewn table at his friends and wonders how he fell in with such amiable strangers. They call him by a name he barely remembers. The sky fills with a darkness that consists of the weight of all the thoughts that have left him. The man wraps his jacket tight. The street lamps are cold yellow eyes peering in through the window. The conversations at the table tighten around the man in layers, each sentence less and less to do with him. Now he cannot look at them. Now they run away to the edge of his vision like a trickle of blood from a wound. The man's last image of his dead wife leaves him, his daughter's memory lost in the same moment. Even the dead do not want to die. Stricken, face animated by fear, he stands and announces that he must leave, he must depart, he must go home, although thoughts of the grainy apartment floor leave a dread like ice in his bowels . . . This, then, is the last defiant act of the second hour: to state a determination to take action, even though you will never take that action. The world has become a mere construct—a hollow reed created that you might breathe. You may hear echoes of a strange and sibilant music, coursing like an undercurrent through inanimate objects. This music may bring tears to your eyes. It may not. Regardless, you are now entering the third hour of death.

III

In the third hour after death, all other memories having been emptied and extinguished, the repressed memory of lifelessness returns, although the man denies the truth of it. Denies the sting of splinters against his face, the taste of sawdust, the comfort of the cool floorboards. He thinks it is a bad dream and mutters to himself that he will just walk a little longer to clear up the headaches pulsing through his head. The man still holds his trumpet. Every few steps, he stops to look at it. He is trying to remember what he once used it for. The third hour can last for a very long time. After awhile, staring at his trumpet, an unquenchable sadness rises over him until he is engulfed in a sorrow so deep it must be borne because nothing better lies beyond it. It is the sorrow of lost details; the darkness of it hints at the echoes of memories now gone. Indirectly, the man can sense what grieves him, but the very glittering reflection of its passage is enough to blind him. To him, it feels as if the natural world has made him sad, for he has wandered into a park and the sky far above through the branches seethes with the light of a restless moon. If the man could only see his way to the center of a single memory and hold it in his mind, he might understand what has happened to him. Instead, from the edge of his attention, the absence of mother, father, wife, daughter, leaves only outlines. It is too much to bear. It must be borne . . . In some cases, recognition may take the form of violent acts—one last convulsion against the inevitable. But not in the man's case. In him, the sorrow only deepens, for he has begun to suspect the truth. The man wanders through gardens and courtyards, through tree-lined neighborhoods and along city-tamed streams, all touched equally by the blank expanse of night. He is without thought except to avoid thought, without purpose except to avoid purpose. He does not tire—nothing without will can ever tire—and as he walks, he begins to touch what he passes. He runs his hands through the scruffy tops of bushes. He rubs his face against the trunk of a tree. He follows the line of a sidewalk crack with his finger. As the night progresses, a tightness enters his face, a self-aware phosphorescence. When he leans down to float his hand through a fountain pool, his face wavers in the water like a green-tinged second moon. Passersby run away or cross the street at his approach. He has no opinion on this; it does not upset or amuse him. He is rapidly becoming Other: Otherwhere, Otherflesh. His trumpet? Long ago fallen from a distracted grasp . . . Eventually, the trailing hand will find something of more than usual interest. For the man, this occurs when he sits down on a wooden bench and the touch of the grain on his palm brings a familiarity welling up through his fingertips. He runs his arms across the wood. He strokes the wood, trying to form a memory from before the sorrow. He lies down on the bench and presses his face against the grain . . . until he sees his apartment room and the blood pooling in the foreground of his vision and knows that he is dead. Then the man sits up, his receding sorrow replaced by nothing. Tendrils of fungi rise from their hiding places inside his body. The man waits as they curl across his face, his torso, his arms, his legs. And he sees the night for possibly the first time ever.

And he sees *them* coming out from the holes in the night. But he does not flinch. He does not run. He no longer even tries to breathe. He no longer tries to be anything other than what he is. For this is the last phase of the third hour of death. After the third hour, you will never be unhappy again. You will never know pain. You will never have to endure the sting of an unkind word. Every muscle, every sinew, every bone, every blood vessel in your body will relax to let in the darkness. When they come for you, as they surely will, you will finally understand, under the cool weavings of the tendrils, what a good thing this can be. You will finally understand that there is no fourth hour after death. And you will marvel that the world could be so still, so silent, so *clear.*

Dr. Simpkin:

You will find my (almost complete) decryption
of X's numbers below. I did not enjoy tackling
this assignment. What began as a lark became
an unnerving experience. At first, I fixated on
two irritating thoughts: (1) that X had double-
spaced his story just to waste paper; (2) that
he had written it just to waste typewriter
ribbon. As I decrypted the first few sentences,
I could not help but feel that X, from some
distant place, was peering over my shoulder
and laughing at me. (Such laughter was
depressingly common during his stay with us.)

My mood of irritation changed as I began to
realize the discipline X had brought to his
endeavors. The sheer persistence required to
translate so many words into numbers impressed
me. If the story was this difficult to decode--
I began, for example, to experience blinding
headaches--then how much more difficult had
it been to encrypt in the first place? Had his
escape involved the daily removal of a single
fragment of brick from the wall of his cell, I
don't believe X could have demonstrated greater
patience.

As I continued to work, fatigue transformed my
banal task into grim revelation. The shadows
grew long; the light left the window of my
cramped office. X's phantom laughter faded
and the only sound was the dry scritch of
my pen against paper. A belief at odds with
the rationality of my profession colonized
me: that I was creating the events uncovered
with each excavated word. This sensation, so
unexpected, made me shiver and suck in my

breath. It brought my efforts to a shuddering
halt. I literally felt that I was bringing into
existence an entire future for Ambergris--a
future so horrible I would not conjure it up for
all the typewriter ribbons in the world. I threw
down my pen; then picked it up and bent it until
it broke, as if to guard against any possibility
of continuing. That said, I could not bring
myself to try to decrypt the final paragraph.
I felt the ramifications would be too earth-
shattering.

When I summoned the nerve to review my
decryption effort (which I call "The Man Who
Had No Eyes"), I discovered I had "mistranslated"
at least seven words. I got up to retrieve
X's book from the filing cabinet where I
had quarantined it, intending to correct my
errors, but immediately sat down again, terror
paralyzing me. I could not move or speak for
several minutes, frozen from the belief that the
book itself had changed and was now writing
me. During this negative epiphany, the shadows
seemed to undulate like wings. The air was close
and thick. When I emerged from my trance state, I
knew that the results of correcting those seven
words would be unthinkable. (Such an episode,
had it originated with one of my patients, would
have been the stuff of five or six therapy
sessions.)

As I type this note, I realize it is nonsense
to believe words on a page can affect reality.
It is just a story. It is just X's final goodbye.
However, I cannot bring myself to send the book
to you along with the other items. Yes, I do
need it for my collection, but there are more
important reasons to keep it here.

You should visit us. You could stay a few days, assist us in those areas where we lack personnel, maybe bring us some supplies. I do not think the text that next you read will much resemble what you may remember, but this place is the same, if in worse disrepair.

I wonder if there is already a name for my affliction.

Dr. V

P.S. Some of the words I have translated seem to make no sense--in my haste I have made errors--but the last paragraph has escaped my efforts completely, for reasons I will touch on later.

The Man Who Had No Eyes

There came a day when the gray caps changed the course of the River Moth and flooded the city of Ambergris. Abandoning their PLOTTED lair, they came out into the light, put the rulers of the city to flight, and took over the islands that were now Cinsorium once again.

At first, people found that life did not change much under the new rulers. It certainly did not change for the most famous writer in Ambergris. Born in the city, he used the city as his palette, bending every word in the world to his will. He could create paragraphs so essential that to be without their smooth, wise forms was to be without a soul. If his mood was grim, he would create suicide paragraphs: words from the almost dead to the definitely dead. He could, I tell you, describe an object in such a way that forever after his description replaced the original.

Perhaps if he had been less talented, he would
have been less APED. For praise rose all about
him as naturally as the fog that came off the
River Moth and he came to think of himself
as unbound by any laws other than those of
fiction.

Thus, he felt a growing need to break the
labyrinthine rules of the gray caps. He laughed
at daybreak in front of the watery ruins of
Truffidian Cathedral. After dusk, he distributed
his stories on public streets for free. He read
his work from a boat above the flooded and
now ANONYMITY statue of Voss Bender. He wrote
paragraphs in honor of the Lady in Blue (who,
from the underground passages of the gray caps,
confronted them with the evidence of their own
cruelty).

After the fifth such offense, the gray caps
cut out his tongue and threw it into the now
BONFIRES River Moth, for the fish had grown
fond of such flesh. They plucked out his eyes
and used them on their barges. They cut off
his hands and used them as candles at their
administrative offices. They mutilated his
torso with their symbol, in fungus green.
Then they sent him to the one-room stilt
house of his birth, by the water, so that
he could, in GORGEOUS, contemplate his fate
where once he had watched swallows fly,
snatching insects.

For a long time, no one visited the writer out
of fear. His own wife left him because she was
not BLINDING enough. Every week, a Truffidian
priest would come close enough to leave food and
water on his doorstep.

The writer sat in a chair facing the wall as
the stories built up inside of him until he was
so full that he thought he would die from the
SNARL of them in his lungs. But he had no tongue
with which to speak. He had no eyes with which
to see the world. He had no hands with which
to write down his stories. He lived inside a box
inside a box. What now could he do?

For many weeks, he thought about killing
himself and might have done so except that one
day he bumped against the table on which he set
the supplies and a pen rolled off the edge. It
fell against his left foot. The touch was cold
and sharp. The sensation spread up his leg and
up into his torso until, inside the boxes inside
his head, something awoke.

The writer spent the next three weeks feeling
his way across every inch of his room much as
you, dear reader, are feeling your way through
this story. He picked up anything that lay
against the walls until the table, the chair,
the bed, and a few books all stood in the middle
of the room. Then, holding the pen between his
toes, he began to write on the wall.

It took many months to learn how to write with
his feet. It was weeks before the visiting priest
could read a single letter and much longer
before anything more complex appeared on the
walls. Words formed without form: "crashing am
worry depends on the continuing earth exists
can Zamilon." Each letter became an act of will--
a playing out in his mind of what it should look
like and then making his toes, his foot, his leg,
apply the correct pressure to the wall so that
the pen did not break and the shape took form
correctly.

Over time, the writer covered the walls of
his room with the visions that blossomed in
the dark gardens of his mind. Words formed
sentences, sentences paragraphs, paragraphs
stories. With each word, a great burden lifted
itself from the writer and he began to feel
like himself again. Later, with sheets of paper
and more pens begged from the priest, more
words spilled out in a jumble, his pages a flood
greater than that brought by the gray caps.

I saw one of the stories the writer wrote on the
wall--in red ink, surrounded by thousands of
other, disconnected words. It read:

There once was a cage in an empty room. A
soft, soft sound like weeping came from the
cage. After a time, a man entered the room.
He was gray and sad. He held a small animal
by the ears. It was battling to escape. The
cage grew silent. The man approached the
cage. He pulled the cage door open, threw in
the animal, and slammed the door shut. As
the man watched, the animal screamed, its
paws sliding off the bars. A wound appeared
in its left leg. A wound appeared in its left
shoulder. Slowly, the animal was eaten alive
until it was just a pile of bone and blood. The
weeping became relentless. Everything the man
placed within the cage died. Every time, the
man felt a corresponding thrill of delight.
But eventually the thrill died too. It became
ordinary, something he had to do. Would it
ever stop? He could not decide. One day, he grew
so bored that he opened the cage to let the
nothing out. He expected it would kill him,
but it did not. It let him live. It followed him
everywhere. Over time, it killed everything he

held dear, weeping the entire time. When nothing
was left to care about, it abandoned the man.
The man sat in his room with the empty cage and
made the weeping sound the cage had once made.

Before the gray caps had mutilated him, the
writer had published dreams and long, absurd
stories. He had published fake histories and
travel guides. I cannot say I care much for what
he writes now, although he became famous for
it. Within a short time, readers began to come
from far away to buy a page from him. The writer
would be able to continue to do what he had
always done. He just had no tongue. He just had
no eyes. He just had no hands. Was that really so
bad?

At least, this is the story the man wrote for me
when, as a traveler to Ambergris--fresh from
an encounter with the giant squid that had
scuttled my boat--I visited him in his room.
Later, others told me that he had been born in
his current state and that all of his ideas came
from old books by obscure authors, read to him
by a friend.

When I first saw him, he sat by a window, his
head thrown back as if to receive the light. (I
now know he was listening. Intently.) The writer
was a wiry man whose face, with its wrinkles
and mouth of perpetual grimace, hinted at
tortures beyond imagining. His arms did indeed
end in nothing. His legs, curled beneath him,
were tight with muscle and ended in muscular
feet. His toes seemed as supple as my fingers.
When I came in, he smiled at me. He uncurled his
feet, stood, and held his leg up in a ridiculous
position. I thought he wanted to "shake hands,"
but no: he held a piece of paper between his toes.

He nudged it toward me. I took it. What did it
say? I could not read it. It was just a series of
numbers. What do numbers mean to a man like me?
Nothing.

1:1   15:4   1:3   15:8   2:56   5:35   4:66   14:34   4:33.
4:56   14:34   2:25   1:3   5:74   5:75   13:191   7:43   5:96
5:97   5:98   5:99.   1:6   5:96   7:79   10:91   13:208
3:18   1:6   4:35   10:59   10:60   16:59   4:78.   1:6
5:96   7:79   10:91   13:208   13:209   1:6   12:22   1:45
2:90,   9:20   9:21,   14:33   7:63.   5:31   7:79   10:91
16:23   1:45   1:23   13:116   1:39   10:43   12:10   2:90
10:46   1:38   7:63   9:26   9:27   14:12   2:100   13:77
16:53.   5:31   7:79   10:91   16:23   9:26.   2:67   2:90
13:152   1:26   2:46   14:48   10:40   1:38   2:92   10:47
1:45   7:58   10:27   10:48.   (12:1   10:41   4:40   14:33.)
10:57   2:90   14:64?   (16:143   10:91   10:42.)   10:49
2:90?   (12:1   3:10   2:4   10:50.)   9:24   13:22   10:5
13:156   15:4   4:5   14:43.

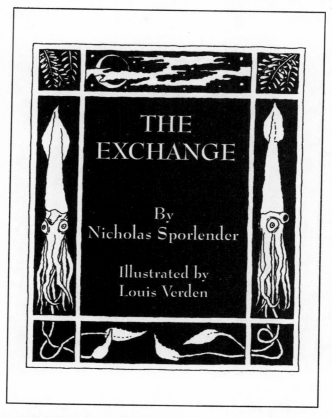

THE
EXCHANGE

By
Nicholas Sporlender

Illustrated by
Louis Verden

Frederick Madnok told me once that the idea
first occurred to Louis Verden during his
collaboration with Nicholas Sporlender on The
Exchange. Whether Verden's idea was sparked by
violent disagreement or by the nature of the
story, Madnok could not tell me . . .

. . . Sporlender followed the teachings of
Richard Peterson, the Fighting Philosopher.
Verden had always been a rabid Strattonist--
and strategist, as it turned out. At least,
according to Madnok, who seems a reliable sort.

Madnok confirms that copyright pages always
brought out the worst in Verden. At one
party, a drunken Verden (never a pleasant
sight) cursed the day he had been brought
into the world "a Verden, rather than, say,
an Aardvark." He was forever fated to have
his name come second to Sporlender's, and for
admirers of their collaborations to flock to
Sporlender.

The Exchange

THE NIGHT came down crookedly on Ambergris, and the slanted darkness, in sheets, reflected back on itself. It came down like a flood. It smelled of the river. It smelled of mud and reeds. It smelled like the forethought of smoke. Through the winking

This especially rankled because Verden would make corrections to the text--additions and enhancements--while Sporlender often felt that his responsibility ended after he had turned in the final typed manuscript and illustration instructions. As for the idea behind The Exchange, Sporlender never commented, except to say in one interview, "It's all there, for those who read it correctly."

of the blinkered buildings, the night smothered others and itself. But the blinkered buildings kept winking out. The wind that rose up was like an animal. It used the trees as its claws; it suborned the stars for eyes. It needed only eyes and claws to lay Albumuth Boulevard bare. No one walked in that night except the insane and the gray caps with their blood-red flags.

At the very end of Albumuth Boulevard, in a small apartment on the ground floor of a tired-looking building, an old couple ate dinner across from each other at an antique table. They could have been 70 or 700 from the implacable calm, the senseless peace, that occluded their faces. The food on their plates squirmed and wrestled with itself in the dim gas light. Even a gray cap would not have known what manner of meal had been prepared in the small, grubby kitchen. Their plates held a microcosm of the city: filled with a sustenance unrestrained, its

---

In Ambergris, despite all of the city's quirks, food does not squirm and wrestle with itself on the plate. In Ambergris, most things are possible, but not that. I do wonder about the nature of "food" in The Exchange. In all the literature I have read about the city, there is scarcely a recipe to be found, not even in the Hoegbotton guides. Yet here, we have a very explicit mention of a meal, in a pamphlet that serves as a Festival grace note. Odd.

This panel shows Verden's devotion to
Strattonism--apparent in the leaf patterns, the
clouded moon, the squid tentacles. In the upper
right panel, the number of leaves equals the
number of Strattonism's Commandments. In the
upper left panel, the number of leaves matches
the list of proscribed activities set out in
the <u>Book of the Stratton</u>. The moon? A moon as a
lidded eye is a secret symbol of Strattonism. As
for the tentacles, observe how two Strattonists
greet each other when they meet.

movements swift and unpredictable. Her fork skewered a piece of tentacle, still twitching as it entered her mouth. But the creature lurching through her salad greens refused to die. Frightened eyes in clumps and bunches stared up at her from her plate.

The woman wore a plain yellow dress that had acquired the antique tint of parchment paper. She had gray-white hair modestly curled, and her slate-gray eyes slid from her husband to her food to the gas light above their heads, but she never stared out the window. Her arms and wrists had a faded delicacy, a clockwork intricacy, to them, but her hands were wide and wing-like, especially when she used them to gesture. She moved her lips and words flickered briefly in the space between them before entering her husband's ears. From her husband's mouth came more words, infiltrating her ears with a careless familiarity.

Her husband also refused to stare out the

Some have thought that Sporlender, intentionally or not, used Verden as his model for the wife. This would certainly have rankled Verden, as it comes close to revealing one of his many secrets. From Ambergris' outlawed squid clubs, Madnok has told me, comes the rumor of a woman resembling Verden who used to frequent the most diabolical of establishments. After paying for a night's entertainment, this woman would take out a sketch pad and begin drawing the debaucheries.

window through which I watched them both. He wore a white shirt with a conservative black tie and plain black dress pants. Bald headed, he had bushy gray eyebrows that gave him a falsely-fierce demeanor, reinforced by the abrupt way he stabbed at the food moving on his plate. His hands moved speedily with knife and fork to halt the escape of his food and then pin it down before guiding it to his mouth. Even from the window, I could tell dirt had gathered in the whorls of his fingers. The knuckles of his hands had sprouted unsubtle gray hairs as if in defiance of his smooth scalp.

On the table between them stood a single lit candle. By the side of their sharply serrated silverware, each had placed a sealed, wrapped present. I suppose it could have been the celebration of an anniversary, if it did not signify some acknowledgment of the Festival.

They did not smile as they ate, and who could blame them: dinner was a grim business

Certainly, with some embellishment the description of the old man fits Sporlender quite well. It is for this reason that many experts less eccentric than Madnok believe that The Exchange was meant as a complex allegory--describing the creative process Sporlender and Verden went through on each project.

and several times the limbs they guided to their mouths smacked against their lips and tried to grab hold. It was, in fact, a war rather than a ritual, and if they did not relax the vigilance of their stony gazes when the final morsel of flesh had squealed its last, I guess it was because they knew that the darkness could not long contain the Festival of the Freshwater Squid. The festival would soon extinguish the city's darkness in the most violent of lights. (I myself would soon have to be going, but for awhile I lingered at the window for no good reason. Did I need one?)

The wife cleared the slaughter fields from the table and placed them in the sink. She brought two glasses and a bottle of wine back to the table.

After a brief battle with the cork screw—it seemed reluctant to perform its function, or perhaps the ghosts of their meal haunted them—the husband managed to open the

It is, perhaps, key that Verden takes credit for suggesting the hidden "I" narrator who suddenly manifests within the narrative.

Madnok believes that this illustration
predicts a terrible act committed in Ambergris,
an act known to only a few. His further
observation that the squid "seem less irritable
than sensually disposed" toward one another
reflects, I believe, his only failing as a
reliable observer.

bottle. He poured the amber-colored liquid, frothy as the Moth River Delta, into the two glasses, and only then did their gazes meet and a secret smile pass between them. They said so much with the smile that I could not catch every word, every nuance of the exchange. And I wanted to unravel that smile. I wanted to dissect it in all of its meanings, for all it said about this old couple on the eve of Festival. The regret, the wry humor, the knowledge of all they had shared together—this I could discern, and still see reflected in their eyes as they sat back down, wine glasses raised in a toast.

She drank her wine smoothly, effortlessly, with such an elegant series of gestures that I deduced she had attended many a social gathering. He, on the other hand, managed to spill the wine onto his chin, where it dribbled onto his white shirt and formed a stain of red.

He ignored it, and so did she. He because

Sporlender often made it a point of pride that he had few social graces, but Verden's editing from the original manuscript has softened the mockery of the old woman in this section.

he had only the minimum social graces, she because she had acquired too glittering an array of social graces. In that small non-gesture, I discovered the secret, if any, to their compatibility.

Still they refused to look at the window, whether to negate my presence or the presence of the night, I do not know. But now I sensed a lightness about them, a sudden levity unlocked by the wine. Their hands became less heavy, rose in the air about them like pale birds, and their head movements accelerated, accompanied by more rapid eye blinks. He said something that made her blush. She said something that made him laugh.

As one, as if remembering for the first time, they pushed their presents across the table at each other. The husband had a childish, greedy expression on his face; clearly, the present meant a great deal to him. Her expression, a thin smile, hid a certain wariness, and I

Madnok suggests that Sporlender here provides a glimpse into secret Fighting Philosopher rites. I have no way of verifying this information given the restrictions put on my movements.

wondered how many times before he had disappointed her. She looked up at him and back down at the present. He held out his hand in an unmistakable gesture of "Go ahead— open it."

The size of a small child, his present to her had been wrapped in gold paper with green ribbon. He had taken great care to curl the ribbon. The present vibrated as it lay on the table.

With one wrinkled, age-spotted hand, she pulled the ribbon loose. Then she pried off the tape and meticulously unwrapped the paper, revealing a brown box with a dozen small holes puncturing the sides. She refolded the paper and, still hesitant, looked up at her husband. Go ahead, he gestured, all smiles. Open it. I think he was impatient to open his own present.

When she opened the lid, she started, moved back abruptly.

"I found this in the marshes, in the

I surmise that the "exchange" is clearly an exchange of ideas. That the ideas ultimately prove incompatible may be unimportant--if the friction created during conflict is recorded as art, so to speak.

Is this how Verden felt about his creative
relationship to Sporlender? Bound to
Sporlender, trapped by him? Did Sporlender
feel just as much of a need to break free as
Verden? The moon is almost completely covered
by clouds. The squid are ready for just about
anything. The squid look oddly identical to me.
Could it be that Verden and Sporlender were too
much alike?

sourweeds near the old boat house, not far from the docks. It tried to disguise itself in the mud, but I found it."

By this time, I had put my ear up to the dusty, cold window. If they turned toward the window, they would see the imprint of my ghastly pale ear, but at the moment the box held their attention.

Out of the box crawled a blackish-green creature with huge yellow eyes, four legs or hands, and a lurching gait due to the curled claws at the ends of its webbed toes. It revealed its wet red tongue and made a gurgling sound as it took a few hesitant steps across the table.

The husband looked at the creature with utter surprise, as if he had never seen it before, despite having placed it in a box and then wrapped it for his wife.

"Do you...like it?" he said, as if asking the question of himself.

"Oh yes," she said. "Open yours. I found

Here, Sporlender teases Verden, by making the creature frog-like. Verden hated frogs. He grew up in an old rotted mansion by the River Moth. The basement and ground floor of that place had been flooded for months at a time. From the safety of his bedroom on the third floor, he had for years heard the incessant bleat and croak of the frogs--"as if they mocked my family's old money poverty."

yours in a ditch under a drain in the oldest part of the city, where if you wait long enough you will hear a rustling that isn't the leaves in the breeze..." Her husband's present to her flopped wetly across the table, narrowly missing the wine bottle and her husband's lap.

Her present to her husband was hastily wrapped in purple paper with ragged silver ribbon. It also was the size of a small child. Her husband tore it open, to reveal a box very similar to the one he had presented to his wife. It too had breathing holes. His eyebrows shot up.

Nonetheless, his hand crept over to the box, and he opened the lid.

A delicate miracle of silver metal and red muscle emerged from the box. The beating crimson of its central fleshiness was offset by spindly metal legs, dainty as a dragonfly, the sad cyclopean headlight of its face, and the slender hypodermic needles that were its arms.

Sporlender had an obsession with the idea of flesh and metal interwoven, as a way of staving off death. A coward in many ways, Sporlender came closest to acting on his desires by adorning himself with metal bracelets, earrings, and rings. At one point, he commissioned the great inventor Porfal to construct a metal "skin suit" for him, but the execution of the plan proved too much even for the likes of Porfal.

Lighter than any of the needlessly heavy things in the apartment, it glided across the table as the wife looked expectantly at her husband.

Slowly, he nodded, the expression on his face one of relief. "I've always wanted one," he joked. "I love it."

I took my ear from the windowpane, to see better. The two creatures circled each other while the husband and wife, presents forgotten, stared at each other, once again using an inscrutable smile to shut out the night, the city, and me from their most private thoughts.

The green flopping creature let out a soundless howl as it glared at the metal-flesh creature. With a moist scuttle, it closed the distance between itself and its adversary. With a single cruel blow of its webbed hand, it pulled off the metal creature's right leg. The metal creature gave out a cry of anguish and fell to the table while the couple watched, immobilized by surprise.

Combat joined! The Dogghe versus Manzikert I! The Kalif versus Stretcher John! The gray caps versus Ambergris! The Festival versus itself! Mimicry of Ambergris' great history of conflict. The night before Sporlender left for Morrow, abandoning Ambergris forever, a mob armed with flaming torches gathered outside the gates of his house. A band of Strattonists, out late carousing, irritable and high-strung because of the recent spate of uncommonly mild Festivals. Soon set upon by a group of passing adherents of the Fighting Philosopher.

According to his alibi, Verden was on the other side of town when the melee broke out. It was a cloudy night. Cast in darkness, the city became unfamiliar even to the most hardened nighttime traveler. What had at first been an organized battle between religious fanatics became a miserable chaos of wounds and shrieks.

The green creature leapt upon its wounded counterpart, tearing away the other leg. It fastened its fang-engorged mouth on the central thick red meat. The metal creature spasmed, waved one needle arm weakly, made a sound like a snapping branch. The green creature's eyes were greedy with its victory. Alas, just as it crushed its enemy's heart in its mouth, the metal creature managed to pierce the webbed flesh of the green creature's left foot, discharging the purple contents of its needle. The metal creature shuddered and lay still. The green creature spasmed, shook violently, and fell over on its side, jaws still closed around its opponent.

Inside the window, husband and wife sat on either end of the table, wine glasses beside them, between them an empty wine bottle, a guttering candle, and the carcasses of their gifts to each other. The carcasses bore an uncanny resemblance to their earlier meal.

In the great slaughter, very few from either side survived. But where was Sporlender during all of this? Those few who bothered to look up from their work saw two shadowy figures in the window of Sporlender's living room. They appeared to be arguing with one another. Most are certain that one was Sporlender and the other was not his wife. The second figure appeared to be sitting down. No one could tell who it might be.

She looked at him with unrelenting sadness. "I didn't mean it," she said, pleading. "I love you. I didn't mean it."

For a moment, he was silent. Then he sighed, leaned forward, and placed his hands over hers. "I know," he said. "I didn't mean it either."

But such sentiments were too late, of course, for the green and metal creatures. And in saying what they had said, they had cracked open the sealed container of their secret smile in such a way that it would never mean exactly the same thing again.

Yet the woman accepted the man's hands with such infinitely graceful body language, effortlessly placing one of her hands over his, tenting her knuckles softly, that she might also be a comfort to him. I almost regretted that behind me I could hear the Festival of the Freshwater Squid destroying the night with its customary eruption of flames and chaotic

A light came from the window, so bright that it blinded the combatants. Sporlender's house, the figures inside, became momentarily illumined, yet none could see them.

uncommon sense. Nonetheless, it was time to abandon the window for the pleasures of the Festival.

One.

My plank of wood shattered the window.

Two.

I stared in at them, revealed, and smiled their secret smile back at them, although it did not comfort them much. I was as alone as the wind with its branches for claws and its pitiless stars for eyes.

Three.

The light disappeared. The figures remained. Then there was the sound of glass breaking and the window exploded into shards. Something small and round and heavy rolled to a stop at the feet of the Strattonists and the followers of the Fighting Philosopher . . .

A moment later it disintegrated and
disappeared into the air. Each Strattonist who
saw it thought of it as something different.
To some it was a seed pod. To others, a small
mushroom. To yet others, a child's ball. But
to a man, the followers of the Fighting
Philosopher saw a curled up flower inside
of a dodecahedron. Meanwhile, both figures
had disappeared from the window. When the
Strattonists stormed the house a few minutes
later, it was empty. Sporlender was never seen
in Ambergris again, nor was his wife.

Nicholas Sporlender has authored over 100 books and instructional religious pamphlets, including *Sarah and the Land of Sighs*, *Truffidian Votives for the Layperson*, and *A List of Daily Sacrifices for Members of the Church of the Seven-Edged Star*. Many of Sporlender's books incorporate the ideas of the "fighting philosopher" Richard Peterson. A five-time recipient of the Southern Cities' most prestigious literary award, The Trillian, Sporlender lives in Morrow with his wife of 25 years and three dogs.

Louis Verden first established his reputation with gargoyle-inspired jewelry (the highlight of many a Festival parade). From jewelry, Verden progressed to book illustration, illuminating such popular texts as *The Physiology and Psychology of the Giant Squid* and *Squid Anatomy for the Layperson*. He is currently contributing art director for *Burning Leaves*. A fervent acolyte of Strattonism, Verden has for many years headed up the Ambergris chapter of the Free Thinkers Guild.

As Madnok was fond of saying about this page, "Here they rest side-by-side even though in life, they are as distant as can be possible." Does Sporlender actually reside in the city of Morrow with his wife, as many claim? Every once in a long while, a letter will come, or a new story, stamped "Morrow," but no one has actually seen Sporlender since that night.

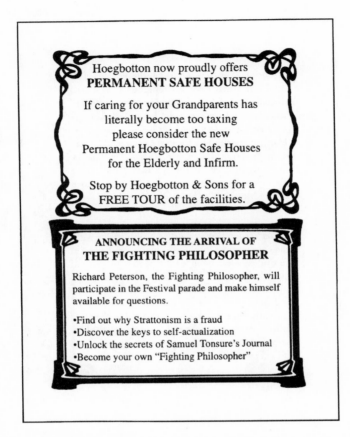
The editors of <u>Burning Leaves</u> launched an
investigation into the odd occurrences that
night. They charged both Hoegbotton & Sons
and the Fighting Philosopher's acolytes with
collusion in Sporlender's disappearance. When
a letter arrived from Sporlender indicating
he had simply moved to Morrow to "get away
from Verden," <u>Burning Leaves</u> dropped its
investigation and published the story
Sporlender had attached to the letter, "In
the Hours After Death," with the appropriate
editor's note.

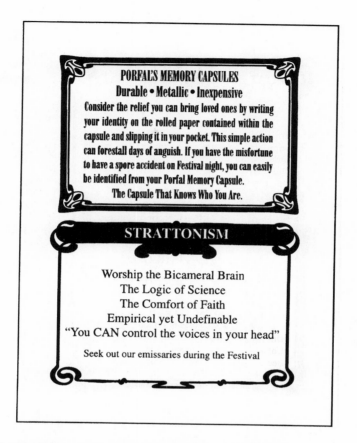

PORFAL'S MEMORY CAPSULES
Durable • Metallic • Inexpensive
Consider the relief you can bring loved ones by writing
your identity on the rolled paper contained within the
capsule and slipping it in your pocket. This simple action
can forestall days of anguish. If you have the misfortune
to have a spore accident on Festival night, you can easily
be identified from your Porfal Memory Capsule.
The Capsule That Knows Who You Are.

STRATTONISM

Worship the Bicameral Brain
The Logic of Science
The Comfort of Faith
Empirical yet Undefinable
"You CAN control the voices in your head"

Seek out our emissaries during the Festival

As Madnok reminded me, Verden has also
retreated from the public eye since that night,
although perhaps not in such a dramatic
fashion. He is rarely seen without a robe
with a cowl, due to, as he puts it, "a disease
of the skin that has reduced my handsomeness
to whatever comes out of my pen and pencil."
He has also done far fewer illustrations in
recent years.

The houseboat theatre production "Remarkable Water Puppet show" is excellent. The two main puppets are modeled after Sporlender and Verden. This puppet show postulates that Sporlender and Verden were visited by the gray caps that fateful night. It chronicles Sporlender's slow disintegration into fungi in Morrow. It also shows how Verden is permanently disfigured by spores. In the dramatic finale, Verden and Sporlender meet one last time when Verden visits Morrow in search of his former friend. They dissolve in one another's arms. Not recommended for children.

Hoegbotton Publishers provides the Southern Cities with a fine selection of pamphlets that range from historical discussion to travel guides for the casual tourist.

The Hoegbotton Ambergris Pamphlet Series

The Hoegbotton Guide to Ambergris Artists
The Hoegbotton Guide to Literary Walking Tours in Ambergris
The Hoegbotton Guide to Ambergris Indigenous Janitors
The Hoegbotton Guide to Ambergris Bars, Pubs, Taverns, Inns, Restaurants, Brothels, and Safe Houses
The Hoegbotton Guide to the Early History of Ambergris
The Hoegbotton Guide to the Religious Quarter
The Hoegbotton Guide to the Architectural Highlights of Albumuth Boulevard

I have almost all of these pamphlets. <u>The Guide to Literary Walking Tours</u> includes a section on Sporlender. The Sporlender Walking Tour includes a stop at Sporlender's former house, as well as stops at the various publishing houses that presented his work to the public. For a rather steep fee, a Hoegbotten guide will accompany you. According to Madnok, the weekend narrators are the best, and will provide you with the most entertainment value.

The Guide to Bars, Pubs, Taverns, Inns,
Restaurants, Brothels, and Safe Houses contains
several mentions of Verden. It appears he had
quite a reputation.

The Hoegbotton Safe Houses still give out The
Exchange and the deluxe Exchange box during
the Festival. Due to an error in the contract,
neither Sporlender nor Verden receives any
monies from sales of the booklet. However, the
widespread popularity of the booklet still
gains them many new admirers each year.

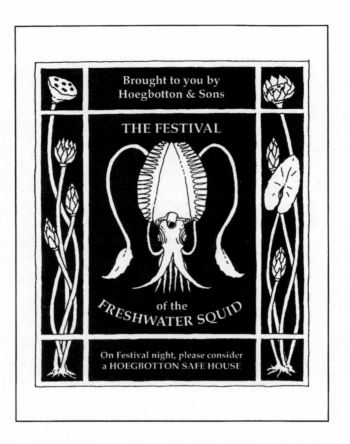

Brought to you by
Hoegbotton & Sons

THE FESTIVAL

of the
FRESHWATER SQUID

On Festival night, please consider
a HOEGBOTTON SAFE HOUSE

Once we get out of here, Madnok has promised to
show me some of his favorite Festival haunts.
As far as I'm concerned, it can't be too soon.

LEARNING TO LEAVE THE FLESH

I

Browsing through the Borges Bookstore, on a mission for my girlfriend Emily, I am suddenly confronted by a dwarf woman. The light from the front window strikes me sideways with the heat of late afternoon and, when she upturns her palm, the light illuminates all the infinite worlds enclosed in the wrinkles: pale road lines, rivers that pass through valleys, hillocks of skin and flesh. A matrix of destinies and destinations.

Before I can react, the dwarf woman takes my hand in hers and stabs me with a thorn, sending it deep into my palm. I grunt in pain, as if a physician had just taken a blood sample. I look down into her large, dark eyes and I see such calm there that the pain winks out, only returning when she shuffles off, hunchback and all, out of the bookstore.

The walls rush away from me, the shelves so distant that I cannot even brace myself against them. I bring my hand up into the light. The thorn has worked itself beneath the surface and might even burrow deeper, if I let it. I examine the blood-blistery entrance hole. It throbs, and already a pinkish-red color spreads across my palm like a dry fire. The hole itself could be a city on a map, a citadel torn apart by the angry pulse of warfare that will soon spread into the countryside. A war within my flesh.

I leave the bookstore and walk back to my apartment. The boulevard, Albumuth, has a degree of security, but only two blocks down, on graffiti-choked overpasses, young teenage futureperfects carouse and cruise through the night-to-come, courting pleasures of the flesh, courting corruption of the soul. Albumuth is my lifeline, the artery to the downtown section where I work, buy groceries, and acquire books. Without it, the city would be dangerous. Without it, I might be unanchored, cast adrift.

As it is, I drag my shoes on the sidewalk, taking every opportunity to run my fingers along white picket fences, hunch down to pet cocker spaniels, converse with smiling apple grannies, and stare into the deep eyes of children.

Even now, so soon after, the wound has begun to change. I manage to pry out the thorn. The hole looks less and less like a city in flames and more like part of my own hand. Rarely has a portion of my anatomy so intrigued me. No doubt Emily has traced the lines between my freckles, explored the gaps between my toes, run her hands through the sprawl of hair on my chest, but I have never examined my own body in such detail. My body has never seemed relevant to who I am, except that I must keep it fit so it will not betray my mind.

But I examine my palm quite critically now. The wrinkles do not share consistency of length or width and calluses gather like barnacles or melted-down toothpaste caps. Abrasions, pinknesses, and a few tiny scars mar my palm. I conclude that my palm is ugly beyond hope of cosmetic surgery.

I reach my apartment as the sun fades into the blocky shadows of the city's rooftops and scattered chimneys. My apartment occupies the first floor of a two-story brownstone. The bricks are wrinkled with age and soft as wet clay in places. The anemic front lawn has been seeded with sand to keep the grass from growing.

Inside my apartment, the kitchen and living room open up onto the bedroom and bath to left and right respectively. In my bedroom there is a window seat from which, through the triangular, plated-glass window, I can see nothing but gray asphalt and a deserted shopping mall.

In the kitchen and living room, my carefully cultivated plants behave like irrational but brilliant sentences; they crawl up walls, shoot away from trellises despite my best efforts. I have wisteria, blossoms clustered like pelican limpets, sea grapes with soft round leaves, passion fruit flowers, trumpet vines, and night-blooming jasmine, whose petals open up and smell like cotton candy melted into the brine-rich scent of the sea. Together, they perform despotic Victorian couplings beyond the imagination of the most creative ménage à trois.

Emily hates my plants. When we make love, we go to her apartment. We make such perfect love there, in her perfectly immaculate bedroom—a mechanized grind of limbs pumping like pistons—that we come together, shower together afterwards, and rarely leave a ring of hair in the bathtub.

II

I suppose I did not think much about the thorn at the time because now, as I lie in bed listening to the dullard yowls and taunts of the futureperfects riding their cars halfway across the city, the wound's pulsating, pounding rhythm leads me back to my first real memory of the world.

Orphaned very young, my parents lost at sea in a shipwreck, yet not quite a baby to be left on a doorstep, I remember only this fragment: the sea at low tide with night sliding down on the world like a black door. Water licked my feet and I felt the coolness of sand between my toes, the bite of the wind against my face. And: the *plop-plop* of tiny silver fish caught in tidal pools; the spackle of starfish trapped in seaweed and glistening troughs of sand; ghost crabs scuttling sideways on creaking joints, pieces of flesh clutched daintily in their pincers.

I do not know how old I was or how I came to be on that beach. I know only that I sat on the sand, the stars faded lights against the cerulean sweep of sky. As dusk became nightfall, hands grasped me by the shoulders and dragged me up the dunes into the stickery grass and the sea grape, the passionflower and the cactus, until I could see the ferris wheel of a seaside circus and hear the hum-and-thrum hollow acoustic sob of people laughing and shouting.

Whether this is a real place or an image from my imagination, I do not know. But it returns to center me in this world when I have no center; it gives me something beyond this city, my job, my apartment. Somewhere, magical, once upon a time, I lay under the stars at nightfall and I dreamed the fantastic.

I have few friends. Foster children who move from family to family, town to town, rarely maintain friendships. Foster parents seem now like dust shadows spread out against a windowpane. I can remember faces and names, but I feel so remote from them compared to the memory of the wheeling, open arch of horizon before and above me.

Now I have a wound in my palm. A wound that leads me back to the beach at dusk, of my grief at my parents' death, that I had not drowned with them. Living but not moving. Observing but not doing. At the center of myself I am suggestibility, not action. Never action.

My parents took actions. They *did* things. And they died.

III

Despite my wound—not a good excuse—I drive to work down Albumuth Boulevard, turning into the parking lot where tufts of grass thrust up between cracks in the red brick. The shop where I work occupies a slice of the town square. It has antique glass windows, dark green curtains to deflect the gaze of the idly or suspiciously curious, and stairs leading both up and down, to the loft and the basement.

My job is to create perfect sentences for a varied clientele. No mere journalism this, for journalism requires the clarity of glass, not a mirror, nor even a reflection. I spend hours at my cubicle in the loft, looking out over the hundreds of rooftops, surrounded by the fresh sawdust smell of words and the loamy *must* of reference text piled atop reference text.

True, I am only one among many working here. Some are not artists but technicians who gargle with pebbles to improve the imperfect diction of their perfect sentences, or casually fish for them, tugging on their lines once every long while in the hope that the sentences will surface whole, finished, and fat with meaning. Still others smoke or drink or use illicit drugs to coax the words onto the page. Many of them are quite funny in their circuitous routines. I even know their names: Wendy, Carl, Daniel, Christine, Pamela, Andrea. But we are so fixated on creating our sentences that we might well pass each other as strangers on the street.

We must remain fixated, for the Director—a vast and stealthy intelligence, a leviathan moving ponderous many miles beneath the surface—demands it. We receive several paid solicitations each day that ask for a description of a beloved husband, a dying dog, or a housewife who wishes to tell her husband how he neglects her all unknowing:

> *He hugs her and mumbles like a sailor in love with the sea, drowning without protest as the water takes him deeper; until her lungs are awash and he has caught her in his endless dream of drowning.*

Ten years ago, we would have been writing perfect stories, but people's attention spans have become more limited in these, the last days of literacy.

Of course, we do not create *objectively* perfect sentences— sometimes our sentences are not even very good. If we could create truly perfect sentences, we would destroy the world: it would fold in on itself like a pricked hot air balloon and cease to be: poof!, undone, unmade, unlived, in the harsh glacial light of a reality more real than itself.

But I am such a perfectionist that, in the backwater stagnation of other workers' coffee breaks, in the *tapa-tap-tap* of rain trying to keep me from my work, I continue to string verbs onto pronouns, railroading those same verbs onto indirect objects, attaching modifiers like strategically placed tinsel on a Christmas tree.

By my side I keep a three-ringed, digest-sized notebook of memories to help me live the lives of our clients, to get under their skins and know them as I know myself. Only twelve pages have been filled, most of them recounting events after I reached my fifteenth birthday. Many notes are only names, like Bobby Zender, a friend and fellow orphan at the reform school. He had a gimp foot and for a year I matched my strides to his, never once broke ahead of him or ran out onto the playground to play kickball. He died of tuberculosis. Or Sarah Galindrace, with the darkest eyes and the shortest dresses and skin like silk, like porcelain, like heaven. She moved away and became an echo in my heart.

These memories often help me with the sentences, but today the wound on my hand bothers me, distracts me from the pristine longleaf sheets of paper on the drafting boards. The pen, a black quill that crisply scratches against the paper, menaces me. My fellow workers stare; their bushy black eyebrows and manes of blond hair and mad stallion eyes make me nervous. I sweat. I teeter uneasily on my high stool and try not to stare out the window at the geometrically pleasing telephone lines that slice the sky into a matrix of points of interest: church spires, flagpoles, neon billboards.

A woman who has finally found true romance needs a sentence to tell her boyfriend how much she loves him. My palm flares when I take up the pen; the pen could as well be a knife or a chisel or some object with which I am equally unfamiliar. My skin feels itchy, as if I have picked at the edges of a scab. But I write the sentence anyway:

When I see you, my heart rises like bread in an oven.

The sentence is awful. The Director leans over and concurs with a nod, a hand on my shoulder, and the gravelly murmur, "You are trying too hard. Relax. Relax."

Yes. Relax. I think of Emily and the book I was going to get for her at the Borges Bookstore: *The Refraction of Light in a Prison*. Perhaps if I can project from my relationship with Emily I can force the sentence to work. I think of her sharp cadences, the way she bites the ends off words as if snapping celery stalks in two. Or the time she tickled me senseless in the middle of her sister's wedding and I had to pretend I was drunk just to weather the embarrassment. Or this: the smooth, spoon-tight feel of her stomach against my lips, the miraculous tangle of her blond hair.

So. I try again.

When I see you, my heart rises like a flitting hummingbird to a rose.

Now I am truly hopeless. The repetition of "rises" and "rose" knifes through all alternatives and I am convinced I should have been a plumber, a dentist, a shoeshine boy. Words that should layer themselves into patterns—strike passion in the heart—become ugly and cold. The dead weight of cliché has given me a headache.

At dusk, I ask the Director for a day off. He gives it to me, orders me to do nothing but walk around the city, perhaps take in a ball game in the old historical section, perhaps a Voss Bender exhibit at the Teel Memorial Art Museum.

IV

I spend my day off contemplating my palm with my girlfriend Emily Brosewiser, she of the aforementioned blond hair, the succulent lips, the tactile smile, the moist charm. (My comparisons become so fecund I think I would rather love a fruit or vegetable.)

We sit on a lichen-encrusted bench at the San Matador Park, my arm around her shoulders, and watch the mallards siphoning through the pond scum for food. The gasoline-green grass scent and the heat of the summer sun make me sleepy. The park seems cluttered with dwarfs: litter picker-uppers armed with their steely harpoons; lobotomy patients from the nearby hospital, their stares as direct as a lover's; burly hunchbacked fellows going over the lawn with gleaming red lawnmowers. They distract me—errant punctuation scattered across a pristine page.

Emily sees them only as clowns and myself as sick. "Sick, sick, sick." How can I disagree? She smells so clean and her hair shines like spun gold.

"They were always there before, Nicholas, and you never noticed them. Why should they matter now? Don't pick at that." She slaps my hand and my palm thrums with pain. "Why must you obsess over it so? Here we are with a day off and you cannot leave it alone."

Emily works for an ad agency. She designs sentences that sell perfection to the consumer public. Before I ever met Emily, I saw her work on billboards at the outskirts of town: "Buy Skuttles: We Expect No Rebuttals" and "Someday You Are Gonna Die: In the Meantime, Buy and Buy—at the Coriander Mall." At the bottom, in small print, the billboards read: "Ads by Emily." At the time, I was girlfriendless so I called up the billboard makers, tracked down the ad agency, and asked her out. She liked my collection of erotic sentences and my manual dexterity. I liked the gossamer line of hair that runs down her forearms, the curves of her breasts with their tiny pink nipples.

But her sentences have become passé to me, too crude and manipulative. How can I expect more from her, given the nature of the business?

So I say, "Yes, dear," and sigh and examine my palm. She is always reasonable. Always right. But I am not sure she understands me. I wonder what she would think about my memory of the arc of sky above with night coming down and the sea rustling on the shore. She did not argue when I insisted on separate apartments.

The circle on my palm has gone from pink to white and the way the wrinkle lines careen into one another, the scars like tiny fractures, fascinates me.

Emily giggles. "Nicholas, you are so perfectly silly sitting there with that bemused look on your face. Anyone would think you'd just had a miscarriage."

I wonder if there is something wrong with our relationship; it seems as blank as my life as an orphan. Besides, "miscarriage" is not the appropriate logic leap to describe the look on my face. Granted, I cannot myself think of the appropriate hoop for this dog of syntax to leap through, but still . . .

We return to our separate apartments. All I can think about are dwarfs, hunchbacks, cripples. I sleep and dream of dwarfs, deformed and malicious, with sinister slits for smiles. But when I wake, I have the most curious of thoughts. I remember the weight of the dwarf woman's body against my side as she stuck the sliver into my palm. I remember the smell of her: sweet and sharp, like honeysuckle; the feel of her hand, the fingers lithe and slender; her body beneath the clothes, the way parts do not match and could never match, and yet have unity.

V

A most peculiar assignment lies on my desk the next morning, so peculiar that I forget my damaged palm. I am to write a sentence about a dwarf. The Director has left a note that I am to complete this sentence ASAP. He has also left me photographs, a series of newspaper articles, and photocopies from a diary. The lead paragraph of the top newspaper article, a sensational bit of work, reads:

> David "Midge" Jones, 27, a 4-foot-5 dwarf, lived for attention, whether he ate fire at a carnival, walked barefoot on glass for spectators, or allowed himself to be hurled across a room for a dwarf-throwing contest. Jones yearned for the spotlight. Sunday, he died in the dark. He drank himself to death. Tests showed his blood alcohol level at .43, or four times the level at which a motorist would be charged with driving under the influence of alcohol.

I pick up the glossy color print atop the pile of documentation. It shows Jones at the carnival, the film overexposed, his eyes forming red dots against the curling half-smile of his mouth. At either side stand flashy showgirls with tinsel-adorned bikini tops crammed against his face. Jones stares into the camera lens, but the showgirls stare at Jones as though he were some carnival god. The light on the photograph breaks around his curly brown hair, but not his body, as if a spotlight had been trained on him. He stands on a wooden box, his arms around the showgirls.

The film's speed is not nearly fast enough to catch the ferris wheel seats spinning crazily behind him, so that light spills into the dazzle of showgirl tinsel, showgirl cleavage.

Behind the ferris wheel, blurry sand dunes roll, and beyond that, in the valley between dunes, the sea, like a squinting eye.

The photograph has a sordid quality to it. When I look closer, I see the sheen of sweat on Jones's face, his flushed complexion. Sand clings to his gnarled arms and his forehead. The lines of his eyes, nose, and mouth seem charcoal pencil rough: a first, hurried sketch.

I turn the photograph over. In the upper right hand corner someone has written: *David Jones, September 19——. The Amazing Mango Brothers Seaside Circus and Carnival Extravaganza. He cleaned out animal cages and gave 50 cent blow jobs behind the Big Top.*

Jones is a brutish man. I want nothing to do with him. Yet I must write a sentence about him for a client I will never meet. I must capture David Jones in a single sentence.

I read the rest of the article, piecemeal.

> In his most controversial job, Jones ignored criticism, strapped on a modified dog harness, and allowed burly men to hurl him across a room in a highly publicized dwarf-throwing contest at the King's Head Pub.

> "I'm a welder, which can be dangerous. But welders are frequently laid off, so I also work in a circus. I eat fire, I walk on broken glass with bare feet. I climb a ladder made of swords, I lie on a bed of nails and have tall people stand on me. This job is easy compared to what I usually do."

I spend many hours trying to form a sentence, while sweat drips down my neck despite the slow swish of fans. I work through lunch, distracted only by a dwarf juggler (plying his trade with six knives and a baby) who has wrested the traffic circle away from a group of guildless mimes and town players.

I begin simply.

The dwarf's life was tragic.

No.

David Jones' life was tragic.

No.

David's life was unnecessarily tragic.

Unnecessarily tragic? Tragedy does not waste time with the extraneous. A man's life cannot be reduced to a Latin-esque, one-line, eleven-syllable haiku. How do I identify with David? Did he ever spend time in an orphanage? Did he ever find himself on a beach, his parents dead and never coming back? How hard can it have been to be an anomaly, a misfit, a mistake?

Then my imagination unlocks a phrase from some compartment of my brain:

David left the flesh in tragic fashion.

Again, my palm distracts me, but not as much. I see all the imperfections there and yet they do not seem as ugly as before. David may be ugly, but I am not ugly.

As I drive home in the sour, exhaust-choked light of dusk, I admire the oaks that line the boulevard, whorled and wind-scored and yet stronger and more soothing to the eye than the toothpick pines, the straight spruce.

VI

By now the plants have conquered my apartment in the name of CO_2, compost, and photosynthesis. I let them wander like rejects from '50s B-grade vegetable movies, ensuring that Emily will never stay for long. The purple and green passionflowers, stinking of sex, love the couch with gentle tendrils. The splash-red bougainvillea cat-cradles the kitchen table, then creeps toward the refrigerator and pulls on the door, thorns making a scratchy sound. Along with this invasion come the scavengers, the albino geckos that resemble swirls of mercury or white chocolate. I have no energy to evict them.

No, I sit in a chair, in underwear weathered pink by the whimsical permutations of the wash cycle, and read by the blue glow of the mute TV screen.

David grew up in Dalsohme, a bustling but inconsequential port town on the Gulf side of the Moth River Delta. His parents, Jemina and Simon Pultin, made their living by guiding tourists through the bayous in flatbottom boats. Simon talked about installing a glass bottom to improve business, but Jemina argued that no one would want to see the murky waters of a swamp under a microscope, so to speak. Instead, they supplemented their income by netting catfish and prawns. David was good at catching catfish, but Jemina and Simon preferred to have him work the pole on the boat because the tourists often gawked at him as much as at the scenery. It was Jemina's way of improving business without giving in to Simon's glass-bottom boat idea. Some of the documents the Director gave me suggested that Simon had adopted David precisely for the purpose of manning the boat. There is no record of what David thought of all of this, but at age fifteen he "ran away from home and joined a circus." He did whatever he had to on the carnival circuit in order to survive, including male prostitution, but apparently never saved enough money to quit, though his schemes became grander and more complex.

> "Most little people think the world owes them something because they're little. Most little people got this idea they should be treated special. Well, the world doesn't owe us anything. God gave us a rough way to go, that's all."

Soon the words blur on the page. Under the flat, aqua glow, the wound in my palm seems smaller but denser, etched like a biological Rosetta Stone. The itch, though, grows daily. It grows like the plants grow. It spreads into the marrow of my bones and I can feel it infiltrating whatever part of me functions as a soul.

That night I dream that we are all "pure energy," like on those old future-imperfect cardboard-and-glue space journey episodes where the budget demanded pure energy as a substitute for makeup and genuine costumes. Just golden spheres of light communing together, mind to mind, soul to soul. A world without prejudice because we have, none of us, a body that can lie to the world about our identity.

VII

The day my parents left me for the sea, the winter sky gleamed bone-white against the gray-blue water. The cold chaffed my fingers and dried them out. My father took off one of his calfskin gloves so my hand could touch his, still sweaty from the glove. His weight, solid and warm, anchored me against the wind as we walked down to the pier and the ship. Above the ship's masts, frigate birds with throbbing red throats let the wind buffet them until they no longer seemed to fly, but to sit, stationary, in the air.

My mother walked beside me as well, holding her hat tightly to her head. The hem of her sheepskin coat swished against my jacket. A curiously fresh, clean smell, like mint or vanilla, followed her and when I breathed it in, the cold retreated for a little while.

"It won't be for long," my father said, his voice descending to me through layers of cold and wind.

I shivered, but squeezed his hand. "I know."

"Good. Be brave."

"I will."

Then my mother said, "We love you. We love you and wish you could come with us. But it's a long journey and a hard one and no place for a little boy."

My mother leaned down and kissed me, a flare of cold against my cheek. My father knelt, held both my hands, and looked me up and down with his flinty gray eyes. He hugged me against him so I was lost in his windbreaker and his chest. I could feel him trembling just as I was trembling.

"I'm scared," I said.

"Don't be. We'll be back soon. We'll come back for you. I promise."

They never did. I watched them board the ship, a smile frozen to my face. It seems as though I waited so long on the pier, watching the huge sails catch the wind as the ship slid off into the wavery horizon, that snowflakes gathered on my eyes and my clothes, the cold air biting into my shoulder blades.

I do not remember who took me from that place, nor how long I really stood there, nor even if this represents a true memory, but I hold onto it with all my strength.

Later, when I found out my parents had died at sea, when I understood what that meant, I sought out the farthest place from the sea and I settled here.

VIII

At the office, I have so much work to do that I am able to forget my palm. I stare for long minutes at the sentence I have written on my notepad:

> *David was leaving the flesh.*

What does it mean?

I throw away the sentence, but it lingers in my mind and distracts me from my other work. Finally, I break through with a sentence describing a woman's grief that her boyfriend has left her and she is growing old:

> *She sobs like the endless rain of late winter, without passion or the hope of relief, just a slow drone of tears.*

As I write it, I begin to cry: wrenching sobs that make my throat ache and my eyes sting. My fellow workers glance at me, shrug, and continue at their work. But I am not crying because the sentence is too perfect. I am crying because I have encapsulated something that should not be encapsulated in a sentence. How can my client want me to write this?

IX

Emily visits me at lunchtime. She visits me often during the day, but our nights have been crisscrossed, sometimes on purpose, I feel.

We go to the same park and now we feel out of place, in the minority. Everywhere I look dwarfs walk to lunch, drive cars, mend benches. All of them like individual palm prints, each one so unique that next to them Emily appears plain.

"Something has happened to you." She looks into my eyes as she says this and I read a certain vulnerability into her words.

"Something has happened to me. I have a wound in my palm."

"It's not the wound. It's the plants out of control. It's the sex. It's everything. You know it as well as me."

Emily is always right, on the mark, in the money. I am beginning to tire of such perfection. I feel a part of me break inside.

"You don't understand," I say.

"I understand that you cannot handle responsibility. I understand that you are having problems with this relationship."

"I'll talk to you later," I say and I leave her, speechless, on the bench.

X

After lunch, I think I know where my center lies: it lies in the sentence I must create for David Jones. It is in the sentence and in me. But I don't want to write anything perfect. I don't want to. I want to work without a net. I want to write rough, with emotion that stings, the words themselves dangling off into an abyss. I want to find my way back to the sea with the darkness coming down and the briny scent in my nostrils, before I knew my parents were dead. Before I was born.

David Jones found his way. If a person drinks too much alcohol, the body forces the stomach to vomit the alcohol before it can reach a lethal level. Jones never vomited. As he slept, the alcohol seeped into his bloodstream and killed him.

My shaking fingers want to perform ridiculous pratfalls, rolling over in complex loop-the-loops and cul-de-sacs of language. Or suicide sentences, mouthing sentiments from the almost dead to the definitely dead. Instead, I write:

From birth, David was learning ways to leave the flesh.

It is nothing close to layered prose. It has no subtlety to it. But now I can smell the slapping waves of the sea and the alluring stench of passionflower fruit.

Before I leave for my apartment, Emily calls me. I do not take the call. I am too busy wondering *when* my parents knew they might die, and if they thought of me as the wind and the water conspired to take them. I wish I had been with them, had gone down with them, in their arms, with the water in our mouths like ambrosia.

XI

When I open my apartment door, I hear the scuttling of a hundred sticky toes. The refrigerator's surface writhes with milk-white movement against the dark green of leaves. In another second I see that the white paint is instead the sinuous shimmer-dance of the geckos, their camouflage perfect as they scramble for cover. I open the refrigerator and take out a wine cooler; my feet crunch down on a hundred molting gecko skins, the sound like dead leaves, or brittle cicada chrysalises.

I sit in my underwear and contemplate my wound by the TV's redemptive light. It has healed itself so completely that I can barely find it. The itching, however, has intensified, until I feel it all over, inside me. Nothing holds my interest on my palm except the exquisite imperfections: the gradations of colors, the rough pliable feel of it, the scratches from Emily's cat.

I walk into the bedroom and ease myself beneath the covers of my bed. I imagine I smell the sea, a salt breeze wafting through the window. The stars seem like pieces of jagged glass ready to fall onto me. I toss in my bed and cannot sleep. I lie on my stomach. I lie on my side. The covers are too hot, but when I strip them away, my body becomes too cold. The water I drank an hour ago has settled in my stomach like a smooth, aching stone.

Finally, the cold keeps me half-awake and I prop myself sleepily against the pillow. I hear voices outside and see flashes of light from the window, like a ferris wheel rising and falling. But I do not get up.

Then he stands at the foot of my bed, staring at me. A cold blue tint dyes his flesh, as if the TV's glow has sunburned him. The marble cast of his face is as perfect as the most perfect sentence I have ever written in my life. His eyes are so sad that I cannot meet his gaze; his face holds so many years of pain, of wanting to leave the flesh. He speaks to me and although I cannot hear him, I know what he is saying. I am crying again, but softly, softly. The voices on the street are louder and the tinkling of bells so very light.

And so I discard my big-body skin and my huge hands and my ungainly height and I walk out of my apartment with David Jones, to join the carnival under the moon, by the seashore, where none of us can hurt or be hurt anymore.

[Article excerpts taken from newspaper accounts in 1988 and 1989 by Michael Koretzky in *The Independent Florida Alligator* and by Ronald DuPont Jr. in *The Gainesville Sun*.]

THE AMBERGRIS GLOSSARY

– A –

AANDALAY, ISLE OF. The mythic homeland of the piratical Aan Tribes. According to the tales of the Aan, the Southern Hemisphere once consisted of a single landmass, the Isle of Aandalay, populated solely by the happy, peaceful Children of Aan. Only after a great cataclysm—the nature of which varies more from tale to tale than the weather in that part of the world—shattered the Isle into a thousand pieces did the Aan become warlike, each faction certain they possessed the mandate for restoration of a united Isle of Aandalay. Thus did piracy become rationalized as a quest for a homeland. Some Aan even attacked the mainland, claiming it was merely a huge splinter exiled from their beloved Isle. See also: *Calabrian Calendar.*

ABRASIS, MICHAEL. The first head librarian of the Manzikert Memorial Library. Abrasis is best known for his collection of erotic literature and lithographs. When he died, in his sleep, his body could not at first be removed from his apartment because the piles of pornography had blocked the only route from bed to door. Oddly enough, by the time Abrasis' relatives came to collect his things, the apartment had been picked clean. Abrasis bred prize-winning cababari in his spare time. See also: *Cababari; Manzikert Memorial Library.*

ALBUMUTH BOULEVARD. A rather famous thoroughfare cutting through the heart of Ambergris. The site of both the Borges Bookstore and the headquarters of Hoegbotton & Sons, Albumuth Boulevard has long been privy to the inner workings of the Festival of the Freshwater Squid. During the civil disturbances of the Reds and the Greens, Albumuth Boulevard served as the main battlefield. Certainly the recent armed struggle between Hoegbotton's publishing arm and the inscrutable Frankwrithe & Lewden could not have occurred without the events that first unfolded on the boulevard. No one can agree on the origin of the name "Albumuth," or on the limits of the boulevard. As Sirin once said, "Like the Moth, Albumuth Boulevard has a thousand tributaries and streams, so that, ultimately, who can determine its boundaries or the limits of its influence?" See also: *Borges Bookstore; Cappers; Frankwrithe & Lewden; Greens; Reds; Sirin.*

ALFAR. The ruins of Alfar form, with Zamilon, the only recorded instances of a particular architectural style reminiscent of gray cap buildings. Most structures at both Alfar and Zamilon have been constructed as circles within circles. Alfar, like Zamilon, is of unknown origin, but an additional peculiar tale is told by shepherds in both places: that, on certain nights, Alfar and Zamilon glow iridescent green and red, a sheen that spreads and intensifies so slowly that observers cannot at first recognize the change, but finally cannot doubt the evidence of their eyes. No one has as yet confirmed this claim independently, nor has anyone thought to time these "eruptions" of color, one to the other. What would it mean if Alfar and Zamilon became luminous on the same nights? See also: *Busker, Alan; Nysman, Michael; Zamilon.*

AMBERGRIS. In folklore, a marbled substance often found on the seashore and thought to be a "sea mushroom." Actually produced in the intestine of whales, ambergris can only be created when partially-digested squid beaks are present in the whale's system. Whalers long sought ambergris for use as an aphrodisiac, in perfumes, and as a folk medicine. Since the founding of the city of Ambergris, however, the popularity of the substance has decreased dramatically. The Truffidian Antechambers discontinued the habit of anointing their ears, eyebrows, and armpits with a tincture of ambergris before holiday sermons. The Kalif no longer eats raw ambergris to stimulate virility, substituting live snails. Male rats, however, still enter a sexual frenzy when they smell ambergris. See also: *Kalif, The; Moonrat; Rats.*

AMBERGRISIAN GASTRONOMIC ASSOCIATION. Founded during the days of Trillian the Great Banker, the AGA has published a number of books, including *One Thousand Squid Recipes* and *Experiments with Different Types of Grease.* The association achieved a degree of notoriety by uncovering the lost ingredients for Oliphaunt's Delight: 1 pound of cherries, 17 pounds of freshwater squid, 20 gallons of goat's milk, 5 pounds of fish paste (preferably flounder) and 1 ounce of asparagus. See also: *Oliphaunt, The.*

AMBERGRISIAN HISTORICAL SOCIETY. Completely unlike the Ambergrisians for the Original Inhabitants Society. The most adventure this group has seen is undercooked flounder at the annual Ambergrisian Historical Society Ball and the occasional paper cut (sweet red relief from boredom!) opening mail sent by similar dullards located in Morrow and Stockton. See also: *Ambergrisians for the Original Inhabitants Society.*

AMBERGRISIANS FOR THE ORIGINAL INHABITANTS SOCIETY. Completely unlike the Ambergrisian Historical Society. Never has membership in a historical society been so fraught with peril. Every two or three years, another few members succumb to the temptation to pry open a manhole cover and go spelunking amongst the sewer drains. Inevitably, someone gets stuck in a culvert and the others go for help, or the gray caps, presumably, catch them and they disappear forever. One imagines the hapless AFTOIS members waving their official membership cards at the approaching, unimpressed gray caps. When not conspiring to commit assisted suicide, the AFTOIS publishes *The Real History Newsletter.* See also: *Cappers; Martigan, Red; Real History Newsletter, The.*

– B –

BANFOURS, ARCH DUKE OF. Best known for being the first to bombard Ambergris with cannon fire. He ruled Ambergris for exactly 21 days. While sitting at a sidewalk cafe, surrounded by his bodyguards, a waiter casually walked up behind him and slit his throat. There appears to have been no particular motivation for the assassination except for the usual engrained Ambergrisian dislike of foreigner interlopers. See also: *Occupation, The.*

BANKER WARRIORS. This sect, comprising the most feared of Trillian's followers, grew out of the predations of highway robbery. Due to the rise of the merchant classes, large quantities of money had to be physically moved from one city to another. Generally, a banker's representative accompanied this transfer. Early transfers met with disaster. After years of robberies and payoffs to avoid robberies, the position of banker's representative evolved from paper-pusher to hardened veteran of weapons' training. By the time Trillian rose to power through the Ambergrisian banking system, the banker representatives had become a powerful, feared security force. Trillian himself named them the Banker Warriors and used them to consolidate his hold over Ambergris. Also influential in repelling attacks by the Kalif. Eventually assimilated into the Ambergris Defense Force, at which time women were excluded from participation. Several of these women (including the noted strategist Rebecca Gort, munitions expert Kathleen Lynch, and fencing master Susan Dickerson) founded their own chain of banks, bought several other businesses, and moved to Morrow, where they became the core of the most feared security force on the continent. The Ambergris Defense Force, on the other hand, perished to the last man during the Kalif's invasion. See also: *Frankwrithe & Lewden; Gort, Marmey; Kalif, The; Occupation, The; Trillian, The Great Banker.*

BEDLAM ROVERS. A southern ethnic group, known for living on house boats and incorporated at an early date into the Saphant Empire. These mystics thrived after the collapse of the empire, adopting their nomadic aquatic life to the River Moth and turning their seasonal perambulations into a lucrative business. Cloaking their mysterious religious tendencies in a veneer of the rational and scientific, the Rovers have developed a reputation as experts on madness and cast themselves in the role of "psychiatrists," much to the dismay of the mental health establishment in Ambergris. The Rovers' riverboats, topped with a multitude of light blue flags and crowded with mentally unstable customers, usually arrive in Ambergris for a fresh batch of patients the week after the Festival of the Freshwater Squid. See also: *Festival of the Freshwater Squid, The; Saphant Empire, The.*

BENDER, VOSS. A composer of operas, requiems, and minor rhymes, who, for a period of time, transcended his status as a cultural icon to become a politician and the unofficial ruler of Ambergris. His suspicious death spawned a civil war between the Greens, his most fanatical followers, and the Reds, his most fervent enemies. Famous for his defiant speech to the merchant barons during which he exclaimed, "Art always transforms money!" His many operas include *The Tragedy of John & Sophia, The King Underground, Hymns for the Dead, Wilted As the Flower Lay*, and his masterpiece, *Trillian*. Bender wrote an autobiography, *Memoirs of a Composer*, which contains more information on his early life. See also: *Greens; Midnight for Munfroe; Nunk, Autarch of; Reds.*

BIBBLE, MAXWELL. The owner of a restaurant supply business who changed careers at age 35 to become an art critic. Bibble's specialty was deep psychological profiles of artists based solely on their artwork. Best known for his misguided and fatuous attempts to identify Martin Lake as a member of a squid cult. For a time, Bibble was one of the most influential of the critics associated with the New Art movement, although he was unpopular with most New Artists. However, he died in poverty, using copies of his reviews to feed a fire during one of Ambergris' freak cold spells. The sculptor William Blaze took a plaster cast of Bibble's body, pasted his reviews on the outside of the cast, and exhibited the piece as "The Exhaustion of Criticism"—thereby reviving interest in Bibble's writings. See also: *New Art, The*.

BLGKKYDKS, HECKIRA. A Haragck military officer today best known for his oil paintings of remote landscapes. He often painted during campaigns and thus the paintings also have historical significance. The night before the Haragck amphibious assault on Ambergris, he completed preliminary sketches for a piece he intended to call "The Sack of Ambergris." During the ensuing rout, these sketches came into the possession of the Ambergris navy. For 20 years they were displayed at the Morhaim Museum, but the trader Michael Hoegbotton found them so compelling that, after the Haragck had largely faded as a political/cultural force, he paid Blgkkydks to live in Ambergris for a year to complete the actual painting. Poverty-stricken, the old general reluctantly agreed, but fell so in love with Ambergris that he lived out his remaining years there. He eventually became a fixture of Albumuth Boulevard, his craggy visage and rickety easel noted on tourist maps of the period. See also: *Grnnck, Haragck Khan; Morhaim Museum.*

BORGES BOOKSTORE. The oldest purveyor of printed words in Ambergris, thrice during its long history burned to the ground. Founded by and named after the Nicean brothers Bormund and Gestrand Kubtek, the Borges Bookstore has served many political and social functions over the years. During the conflict between the Reds and the Greens, Bender sympathizers hid in its basement. Before Festivals, patrons can book "reading slots" along its shelves, for it is well known that the gray caps will not pass the threshold. The westerner Kamal Bakar witnessed the third fire, set by looters during the 300th Festival of the Freshwater Squid, one of the worst in memory: "The sky was darkened by the smoke from the books; burned pages floated up into the air and fluttered back down again like a black snowfall all over the city. Those who caught a sheet could feel the heat and fleetingly read what had the strange appearance of a black-and-white dagguereotype. Once the heat had dissipated, the pages crumbled away between our fingers." See also: *Albumuth Boulevard; Bender, Voss; Burning Leaves; Festival of the Freshwater Squid; Greens; Reds.*

BRUEGHEL, MICHAEL. John Manzikert's nemesis eventually united the islands of the Aan despite several times coming close to total defeat. During his 50 years of rule, Brueghel not only annihilated the Kalif's troops in three historic naval battles, forever relegating the Kalif's ambitions to the continent, but also established an oligarchic form of government that served the Aan well for the next three generations. Perhaps his greatest achievement was to collect the remnants of the Saphant Empire under his aegis, preserving scientific and cultural advances that would otherwise have been lost. In later years, descendents of Brueghel, calling themselves Brueghelites, would seize large portions of the River Moth to the south of Ambergris and threaten Ambergrisian autonomy. See also: *Calabrian Calendar; Kalif, The; Saltwater Buzzard; Saphant Empire, The.*

BUBBABAUNCE, BARON. The real name of the circus performer "Bauble." See also: *Hellatose & Bauble; Kodfan, M.; Madnok, Frederick.*

BURNING LEAVES. A controversial arts journal, known for publishing macabre, disturbing fictions and illustrations. Published by the Borges Bookstore until the editors printed their infamous Black Tract, which included a perverse "map" of Voss Bender's naked body, diagramming the various worth of different parts and with short-short stories written about each part (most infamous: Sporlender's "Tree with Nuts"). Since then, the journal has been funded entirely by advertising and newsstand sales. *Burning Leaves* published the first works by such future luminaries as Louis Verden, Nicholas Sporlender, Martin Lake, and Janice Shriek, as well as the obscene mechanical diagrams of the eccentric inventor known simply as Porfal. The premiere issue featured Corvid Quork's short story "The Madness of Bird Masks." See also: *Bender, Voss; Borges Bookstore; Sporlender, Nicholas.*

EXHIBIT 1: THE ORIGINAL COVER OF *BURNING LEAVES*, VOLUME 1, ISSUE 1; ON DISPLAY IN THE MORHAIM MUSEUM'S "HISTORY OF SOUTHERN PERIODICALS" WING.

BUSKER, ALAN. Busker, long known as a fanatical (and often quite critical) traveler in both the north and south, may also have been a spy for the Kingdom of Morrow. Certainly, there was a time when Busker's travels among the northern cities resulted in disaster—Stockton, Belezar, Dovetown, and Tratnor all fell to Morrow shortly after Busker's visits to them. Most famous for attempting to enter the Kalif's Holy City by impersonating the Kalif himself. Some historians believe Busker spent a number of months in Alfar and Zamilon, his other journeys undertaken to provide cover for his true activities—research into the link between the gray caps and the monks of Zamilon. See also: *Alfar; Kalif, The; Stockton; Zamilon.*

– C –

CABABARI. Long-snouted, foul-smelling, fungus-eating, dirt-seeking pigs instrumental in the ouster of Trillian the Great Banker as ruler of Ambergris. See also: *Fungus; Trillian the Great Banker.*

CALABRIAN CALENDAR. A wonder of inefficiency that used an estimated count of the various islands the Isle of Aandalay had fragmented into as the number of days in its year. Months were named after the nearly unpronounceable monikers of old Aan leaders, but the names of months changed as new leaders rose and fell, with the result that many Aan towns employed month-tellers whose sole function was to untangle the knots of names. Making the situation more confusing, each group of Aan on each island began to name their months differently. The charts created by the month-finders began to dwarf those used by mathematicians and mapmakers. Several wars were fought over the allocation of days and months, including the famous War of the Three-Day Weekend, which left over 10,000 people forever unable to enjoy even a one-day weekend. Eventually, under the rule of Michael Brueghel, a reunited Aan people scrapped the Calabrian Calendar altogether in favor of the Kalif's calendar, itself based on the old Saphant Empire's calendar. Thousands of month-finders had to seek out other careers. Their color-coded charts still reside in many wealthy art collectors' mansions, although the largest collection can be found in the Morhaim Museum. See also: *Aandalay, Isle of; Brueghel, Michael; Morhaim Museum.*

CAPPERS. Individuals hired to clean the sewers. The profession requires nerve and cunning, due to the likelihood of encountering gray caps. The most dangerous duty involves rolling a huge metal-and-wood ball down the main stretch of Ambergris sewer, which runs roughly the length of Albumuth Boulevard. The purpose of rolling the ball (nicknamed "The Monster")—an invention of Porfal's—is to remove all impediments from the sewer. Sometimes, those rolling the ball will be surprised by a semi-crushed but still deadly piece of fungus or gray cap. The leaders of capper teams are called "martigans." See also: *Albumuth Boulevard; Martigan, Red; Monster, The; Porfal.*

CAROLINE OF THE CHURCH OF THE SEVEN-POINTED STAR. A heretic from Nicea who left the Cult of the Seven-Edged Star to found her own religion. Unlike the Cult of the Seven-Edged Star, the Church of the Seven-Pointed Star believed that God had seven points rather than seven edges. Therefore, rather than worshipping the journey toward self-realization symbolized by the edges, they worshipped the goals of self-realization as symbolized by the points. The specific points Caroline adhered to were: celibacy (during certain times of the year, if absolutely necessary), truth, beauty, self-realization, self-worth, love of others, and good hygiene (in some translations from the sacred text, literally, "negation of body odor through soapy immersions"). Adherents to the Church of the Seven-Pointed Star used swords with sharp points but no edge, while the Cult of the Seven-Edged Star used swords with sharp edges but no point. Alas, edges proved superior to points in most battles fought in the streets of Nicea. Caroline's followers were forced to either commit sacrilege and switch to edges, or become meals for the ever-present saltwater buzzard. Proving, one could say, the point of the edges. See also: *Mikal, Dray; Saltwater Buzzard.*

CHURCH OF THE FISHERMAN. Fish worshippers who abstain from eating "our watery brethren" but attain religious ecstasy by catching them and setting them free. Although the Odecca Bichoral White Whale is a mammal not a fish, the biology-challenged adherents of this religion have made it the centerpiece of their spiritual life. The high priest, or Fish Head, delivers his sermons from a lopsided marble altar chiseled to resemble the whale's head. Of late, Church of the Fisherman worshippers have been implicated in a series of crimes, from stealing dead fish on display at the markets and releasing them back into the River Moth, to freeing Odecca whales from the Daffed Zoo. See also: *Citizen Fish Campaign; Daffed Zoo; Odecca Bichoral White Whale.*

CITIZEN FISH CAMPAIGN. A practical joke, staged by the writer Sirin, seeking to replace the current Truffidian Antechamber with a stinking, five-day-old freshwater bass during the Holy Elections (held every decade). Sirin and his New Art friends created campaign posters featuring the dead bass, delivered stirring speeches in its name, and paraded the candidate around Ambergris on a cart. When the dead fish placed second as a write-in candidate in a field of eight, Sirin and his cohorts had to flee the city for a short period due to threats of physical violence. Groups offended included the Truffidian priesthood and the Church of the Fisherman (which felt Sirin's real aim was to ridicule the fish they held sacred). See also: *Church of the Fisherman; New Art, The; Sirin.*

COOKS OF KALAY. A clan of professional cooks who lived in the far western reaches of the Kalif's Empire, near the mountain fortress of Kalay. During frequent famines, these cooks learned to prepare meals from such unlikely items of sustenance as shoe leather, belts, grass, flowers, shirts, dirt, earthworms, and insects. Such was their prowess, according to legend, that when the famines passed, people still came to Kalay just to eat dirt. They became so famous that the Kalif forcibly transplanted the entire family to his palace at Vonaril, where they still languish, forced for generation after generation to cater to the Kalif's every craving for a midnight dinner or afternoon snack. See also: *Kalif, The.*

– D –

DAFFED, XAVER. An excellent observer of animal behavior whose reputation in recent years has been sullied by accusations he became too intimately involved with his subject matter. Daffed published numerous books on animals of the southern climes, including *Diary of an Aardvark, My Life Among the Sand Turtles of the Moth River Delta, A History of Animals, Vols. I—X,* and *The Hoegbotton Guide to Small, Indigenous Mammals.* He was found dead, of an apparent heart attack, in the tropical mountains near Nicea, wearing only a wooly monkey suit, several perplexed wooly monkeys watching from the nearby bushes. See also: *Cababari; Daffed Zoo; Hoegbotton Guide to Small, Indigenous Mammals, The.*

DAFFED ZOO. Founded by Xaver Daffed shortly before his death, his work completed by daughter Sarah Daffed, the Daffed Zoo has, over the years, hosted a wide assortment of the strangest animals ever seen, including the common banded snakblooter, the pigmy sanfangle, the red-and-white slout, and the metigulamated ratpig. Specializing in exotics, the zoo has at times fallen into disrepair and been closed for the public's safety. The zoo has also suffered from such outlandish claims as those promulgated by Xaver's great-grandson, Thomas Daffed, who, shortly before his death, hosted a rather redundant fungi exhibit that was to include a "fungal creature" he claimed to have caught near the ruined monastery-fortress of Zamilon, but which never made an appearance. More recently, the zoo's Odecca Bichoral White Whale exhibit was ruined when, in a daring raid, members of the Church of the Fisherman stole the centerpiece of the exhibit: the world's only captive Odecca Bichoral White Whale. See also: *Church of the Fisherman; Daffed, Xaver; Odecca Bichoral White Whale; Zamilon.*

DEFECATION, ORDER OF. The most reviled of the orders, although perhaps not the most disgusting. See also: *Living Saints.*

DISPOSSESSED. Some of the Ambergrisians "dispossessed" of their families because of The Silence became strange and fey to their friends. They would dig up animal bones, eat strange fungus, and visit graveyards, claiming to hear their brothers, sisters, sons, daughters, fathers, mothers, calling to them from the ground. In later years, these individuals became the official Dispossessed, wandering from place to place and burying the bones of their dead in the walls of buildings that others had boarded up after The Silence. For more than 70 years, these urban nomads roamed like lost souls, living by ever more desperate means, their numbers dwindling until they finally disappeared from the city. See also: *Fungus.*

DREADFUL TALES. A magazine of horror adventure tales published and edited by exploiter extraordinaire Mathew Palwine. Palwine's stable of authors included such hacks as Rachel Thorland, Gerrold Picklin, and Saltzbert Flounder. *Dreadful Tales* became popular chiefly due to the proliferation of typographical errors among its pages, which made it the darling of the "found object" adherents of the New Art movement. Nicholas Sporlender, among others, found cruel sport in writing letters to the editor on such subjects as "Why the Untoward Removal (Twice!) of a Very Important Vowel From the Word 'Countless' in Saltzbert Flounder's Story 'Tortured Love in the Middle Distance' Renders the Author's Vision Bleak Rather than Maudlin." See also: *Midnight for Munfroe; New Art, The; Sporlender, Nicholas.*

– E –

EJACULATIONS, ORDER OF. The most pleasurable yet socially-unacceptable of the Orders. See also: *Living Saints.*

– F –

FESTIVAL OF THE FRESHWATER SQUID, THE. A celebration specific to Ambergris that has, on occasion, led to untoward incidents.

EXHIBIT 2: "VIEW OF FESTIVAL FIREWORKS FROM SOPHIA ISLAND" BY LOUIS VERDEN, PUBLISHED IN *BURNING LEAVES*; ON DISPLAY IN THE MORHAIM MUSEUM'S "FAMOUS VIEWS OF THE CITY OF AMBERGRIS" GALLERY.

FIGHTING PHILOSOPHER, THE. See: *Peterson, Richard.*

FISH HEAD. Holy. Or rotting. Incidental to the Citizen Fish campaign. See also: *Church of the Fisherman.*

FLATULENCE, ORDER OF. The most deadly of the Orders. See also: *Living Saints.*

FRANKWRITHE & LEWDEN. A devious and conniving publishing company run by L. Gaudy and his family. Known for their insidious marketing strategies and accused by some of collaborating with the gray caps. Frankwrithe & Lewden was founded during the waning days of the Saphant Empire and claims to be the oldest publisher still extant on the Southern Continent. Books published by F&L have been banned by the Truffidian Antechamber of Ambergris 43 times. Most recently, as F&L has expanded into areas other than bookselling, it has been engaged in what amounts to a war with H&S over ownership of Sophia Island. See also: *Albumuth Boulevard; Banker Warriors; Manzikert Memorial Library; Midnight for Munfroe; Saphant Empire, The; Sophia Island.*

FUNGUS. A type of spore-reproducing "plant" that is usually quite harmless. One of Samuel Tonsure's favorite words—the most frequently-appearing word in his journal after the words "the," "a," "and," "that," "blood," and "fear." James Lacond, backed by evidence discovered in Marmey Gort's copious notes, has postulated that the gray caps have grown a giant fungus below the southern half of Ambergris.

According to Lacond, this fungus started as a single spore but, using black shoestring filaments to expand, now covers 2,000 acres and has a width of three feet. By mapping fungal concentrations of the golden mushrooms that pop up after rainfall—the physical manifestation of the "Monster" as Lacond calls it—he drew a controversial outline of its expanse that is strikingly similar to a mushroom in shape (now on display at the Morhaim Museum). Many trees in the city may actually be hollow husks, according to Lacond, their insides infiltrated by fungal spies. Lacond has not offered any theories as to the purpose behind this huge fungus, whether evil or benign. See also: *Cababari; Dispossessed, The; Gort, Marmey; Lacond, James; Monster, The; Morhaim Museum.*

FUNGUS SHIP, THE. See: *Thrush, The.*

– G –

GALLERY OF HIDDEN FASCINATIONS. A gallery often considered the flagship of the ideals of the New Art, founded by Janice Shriek. When it closed, the New Art movement lost its momentum and eventually fragmented into a number of splinter groups, including the Found Art movement, the Body Art movement (enthusiastically endorsed by the Living Saints), and the controversial Shadow Art movement. See also: *Living Saints; New Art, The; Shadow Art Movement, The.*

GLARING, MAXWELL. The author of *Midnight for Munfroe, The Problem With Krotch, Munfroe's Return, Krotch*

Strikes Back, Munfroe Reborn, Krotch Reborn, Krotch's Triumph, Munfroe's Legacy, Krotch's World, Son of Munfroe, Krotch's Last Stand, A Krotchless World, Krotch's Legacy, Son of Munfroe II, Krotch and Munfroe: The Lost Memoirs, and, post-humously, *The End of the Legacy of Krotch and Munfroe*. See also*: Bender, Voss; Krotch; Munfroe; Midnight for Munfroe.*

GORT, MARMEY. Marmey Gort kept minutely detailed records of city inhabitants' sanitary habits, including their storage of refuse. A typical entry reads: "Subject Z—outhouse use increase: av. 7x/day (5 min. av. ea.); note: garbage output up 3x for week: connex?" Gort even managed to track gray cap garbage pickup habits and concluded that if the gray caps were using the vast amounts of garbage as food or as mulch to grow food, the gray cap population under the city could exceed 300,000. No one listened to him. No one likes bad news. But Gort didn't care that no one listened to him—he went right on with his research, leaving behind 6,000 pages of observations when he died at the age of 70. Later, the Kalif would use the journals to successfully invade the city. See also: *Banker Warriors; Fungus; Occupation, The.*

GRAY TRIBES. Successors to the Aan in the Southern Islands. Implacable, cultured and barbaric at the same time. Thrilled to the opening of a book as much as to the opening of an enemy's throat. Denied a foothold on the continent by the Arch Duke of Malid, who thrilled only to the opening of throats and therefore put more enthusiasm into the endeavor. See also: *Aandalay, Isle of; Malid, Arch Duke of; Saltwater Buzzard.*

GREENS. A political movement and amateur military force intended to defend the interests and person of the composer nee politician Voss Bender. The remnants of the Greens ended their days as part of a music guild that provided piano lessons to youngsters. See also: *Bender, Voss; Borges Bookstore; Manzikert Memorial Library; Reds.*

GRNNCK, HARAGCK KHAN. Responsible for the failed amphibious attack on Ambergris during The Silence. Grnnck had complicated tastes. Utterly ruthless and without peer in the arts of deception, he was also enamored of frogs and all things connected to frogs. He may have possessed the largest collection of frog art in the world, from paintings to sculptures and wood carvings. Torn from his youth in the Southern swamps to join the Haragck who invaded his remote homeland, Grnnck quickly rose through the ranks until, by a stroke of luck, he managed to best the old Khan in single combat and replace him. No doubt love of frogs, a vestige of his youth he did not wish to relinquish, proved his downfall. Who can doubt this love made the idea of an amphibious invasion of Ambergris so attractive? See also: *Blgkkydks, Heckira.*

– H –

HELLATOSE & BAUBLE. Although real enough, this squid-and-man circus act reached its zenith of popularity as a cartoon strip inked and written by the reclusive M. Kodfan. See also: *Kodfan, M.; Madnok, Frederick.*

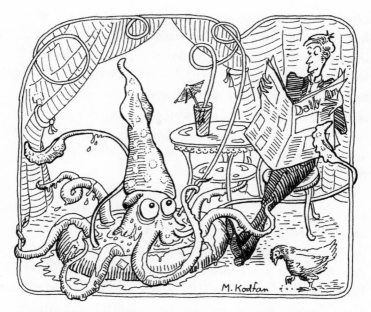

EXHIBIT 3: AN ORIGINAL PANEL FROM M. KODFAN'S FAMOUS CARTOON STRIP, RUN IN THE *AMBERGRIS DAILY BROADSHEET*; ON DISPLAY IN THE MORHAIM MUSEUM'S "ILLUSTRATION" GALLERY.

HOEGBOTTON, HENRY. A good friend and accomplice.

HOEGBOTTON, RICHARD. After several false starts, the Hoegbottons finally established a foothold in Ambergris due to this member of the clan. Over a period of 20 years, Richard Hoegbotton crushed Slattery and Ungdom, his main competitors, and established the beginnings of a mercantile network that today spans from the Southern Isles to the lands of the Skamoo. See also: *Hyggboutten.*

HOEGBOTTON GUIDE TO SMALL, INDIGENOUS MAMMALS, THE. The definitive guide to the fascinating variety of small, indigenous mammals found in the southern climes, including the tarsier, the wrinkled-lip bat, and the moonrat. The lengthy and rather dramatic chapter on the mating dance of the wooly monkey has long been considered an eccentric classic. See also: *Borges Bookstore, The; Cababari; Daffed, Xaver; Moonrat; Trillian the Great Banker.*

HOLY LITTLE RED FLOWER, THE. One of two central ideas behind the unnamed faith created by the fighting philosopher Richard Peterson, the other being the destruction of the "Strattonist bicameral brain followers." Peterson told the story of "The Holy Little Red Flower that Grows by the Side of the Road" at most of his gatherings, formal and informal. Taken from the third volume of his *Dodecahedron* (Book of Petals, Chapters 3–411, inclusive), published privately by the Holy Brotherhood of the Red Stamen, the tale is generally incomprehensible without the proper religious training. See also: *Peterson, Richard; Strattonism.*

HYGGBOUTTEN. A clan of nomadic horsemen originating in the far west, near Nysimia. A ruthless people driven east by the even more ferocious Haragck. The Hyggboutten forced the peaceful Yakuda peoples out of their valley and assimilated such Yakuda skills as weaving into their own culture. After driving the Haragck out of the Kalif's empire, the Kalif's armies turned their attentions to Yakuda, destroying the Hyggboutten and their bondsmen as a political and cultural force. The remnants of the Hyggboutten fled to the frozen north and eventually became assimilated into eastern cultures in such places as Urlskinder, Morrow, and Nicea. Some clan members changed their name to the more eastern-sounding "Hoegbotton" and, over time, descendents such as Richard Hoegbotton founded the Hoegbotton & Sons trading empire. The Hyggboutten were renowned for their skills with horses and their elaborate burial rites. After death, Hyggboutten leaders were flayed from head to foot, their organs scooped out and mummified. Priests purified the remaining skeleton and flesh by laying it out on a litter to dry. The priests also treated the skin with a preservative and a clan artist tattooed it with scenes from the leader's exploits while alive. The mummified organs were then placed back within the dried skeleton and the skin stretched over the bones and grinning skull. The next phase of burial included the ritualistic slaughter of the leader's horses, his servants, and his wife. The horses were transformed into spirit beasts by attaching antlers to their heads and scrawling sacred symbols across their skin. The Hyggboutten then dug a huge pit, built a small house in the pit, planted shrubs and trees around the house, and placed the leader, horses, servants, and wife inside the various rooms of the house. A period of ten days of mourning followed, after which the pit was filled in, burying the house and the dead alike. The Hyggboutten would wait for two weeks before building an identical house above ground on the same location as the buried house. This house would be filled with small pebbles carried by fast riders from any nearby sea or river and delicately placed within the house by virgins no older than 18. Once the house had been filled with pebbles, a Hyggboutten priest consecrated the ground and a tent stitched together by a dozen Hyggboutten women was placed over the house. The leader's eldest son or daughter would then set fire to the tent cloth, the flames also devouring the wooden beams of the house and leaving a pile of scorched pebbles. Each member of the clan would then take a pebble, while still hot—to remind them of the pain of their loss—to keep with them for the next six weeks, after which they would be required to bury the pebble wherever they had camped for the night. Then each member of the clan would carve a stick with the likeness of the fallen leader's "animal of power" and drive it into the ground to mark the location of the pebble. If the clan returned to that site in a year's time and all the pebbles were found, the leader's soul had passed on to the afterworld successfully. However, if even one pebble could not be found, the Hyggboutten were duty-bound to return to the place of burial and build another house full of pebbles atop the site, stitch together another tent, and repeat the entire process. Over time, and as they were dispersed by the Kalif, the Hyggboutten abandoned this ritual simply because they did not have time to observe it. See also: *Hoegbotton, Richard.*

– I –

IBONOF, IBONOF. A heretic once named simply Ibonof. A former member of the Truffidian Church. Excommunicated after having a vision in which he appeared to himself and proclaimed himself "divine." Spent the rest of his life talking to himself and seeing double.

INSTITUTE OF RELIGIOUSITY. See: *Morrow Religious Institute.*

<h1 style="text-align:center">– J –</h1>

JERSAK, SIMON. An unusually socially-mobile individual who eventually became known for his funny and insightful pamphlets about tax collecting and tax collectors. Although usually attributed to Sirin, the quote "those days when taxation has become a thing of beauty" was first written by Jersak. His advice to ordinary citizens is studded with laconic satire: "When a traveler came to some narrow defile, he would be startled by the sudden appearance of a tax-gatherer, sitting aloft like a thing uncanny." See also: *Sirin.*

JONES, STRETCHER. A poet and blacksmith born in Thajad, a southern province of the Kalif's Empire, who rose to become a leader of men. Driven to fight by the predations of Truffidian priests and the Kalif's troops upon the poor, Jones raised an army of his impoverished peers and, for a time, captured the southern expanse of the Kalif's Empire. A brilliant tactician and yet a gentle soul, his is a tragic story, too long to summarize here. If Stretcher Jones had been victorious, he would have led us all to a better place. There are still those in this world who hold fast to his ideals. His most famous speech was his shortest, to the satrap of Thajad demanding justice:

I feel that a man may be happy in this world. And I know that this world is a world of imagination and vision. I see everything in this world, but I know everyone does not see alike. To the eyes of your tax collectors, a sel is more beautiful than the sun and a bag worn with the use of money has more beautiful proportions than a vine filled with grapes. To the eyes of your soldiers, the shedding of blood brings tears of joy that might in others be brought forth only by the sight of a tree heavy with fruit. Some see in man's nature only ridicule and deformity, and by these I shall not regulate my proportions; and some scarce remark on man's nature at all. But to the eyes of the true, this is not so. As a man is, so he sees. As the eye is formed, such are its powers. You certainly mistake when you say that such visions are fancy and not to be found in this world. To me, this world should be all one continued vision of goodness.

See also: *Masouf; Nadal, Thomas; Oliphaunt; Saltwater Buzzard.*

– K –

KALIF, THE. Any one of 80 anonymous, sequential rulers of the great western empire. Known for taking great risks incognito. Often killed in freak accidents of a macabre but humorous nature. One of the more absurd theories put forth is that Samuel Tonsure was an incognito Kalif. Over time, the Kalif's scientists have invented such modern conveniences as the microscope, the gun, the telephone, and the cheese grater. See also: *Ambergris; Banker Warriors; Brueghel, Michael; Busker, Alan; Cooks of Kalay; Royal Genealogist; Saltwater Buzzard.*

KODFAN, M. The creator of the popular Hellatose & Bauble cartoon strip. Kodfan was never seen by the editors of the broadsheets in which his inked antics were eagerly consumed by children and adults alike. As one editor remembers, "Every third day of the week, a messenger would arrive at my office, usually on a unicycle for some reason. It was always a different messenger, perhaps because the unicycle is hard to master. I never saw Kodfan. One time I asked the messenger what he looked like. He told me Kodfan looked 'hooded.' I asked what on earth that meant. The lad said 'Kodfan had a hood on.' I never found out anything about him except that he was fond of squid. Then, one day, the messenger stopped coming. I never heard from Kodfan again. We had to hire that Verden character to ink the strip. It was never the same—Verden wanted Hellatose to pontificate about Strattonism. Eventually, I had to put a stop to it and we discontinued the cartoon altogether. That was when I began to have the fuzzy ribbon dreams, but that is an unrelated issue." See also: *Hellatose & Bauble; Frederick Madnok; Strattonism; Verden, Louis.*

KRETCHEN, THE GRAY CAP HUNTER. Around the time of The Silence, rumors began to spread of a man,

EXHIBIT 4: THE ORIGINAL PENCIL SKETCH FOR A PANEL OF THE HELLATOSE & BAUBLE CARTOON STRIP; ON DISPLAY IN THE MORHAIM MUSEUM'S "ILLUSTRATION" GALLERY.

cloaked in shadow, mystery, and something fashionably black with a silver lining, who went underground to kill gray caps. Some said he was the cousin of Red Martigan, seeking revenge. Others, that he was half gray cap himself and sought only to find his mother. Regardless, Kretchen never bothered to leave the shadows long enough to take a bow and so historians have placed him in that purgatory known as "possible but not probable." The cappers, on the other hand, have adopted him as their patron saint, putting out "scarecaps" dressed in long black cloaks. See also: *Cappers; Martigan, Red; Disappeared, The.*

KRISTINA OF MALFOUR, LEPRESS SAINT. With each little bit of her that fell off, she came a little bit closer to Sainthood. Other than her ability to shed body parts with apparent nonchalance, no historian has ever found any reason why she should have been sainted by the Truffidians. She appears to have sat around a lot and eaten hundreds of servings of rice pudding while watching her family work in the fields of the communal farm outside Ambergris. See also: *Living Saints.*

KROTCH. The villain of Maxwell Glaring's Krotch and Munfroe action/detective series. Krotch is described in the first book, *Midnight for Munfroe*, as "a tall man, so slender that sideways he might melt into the shadows that had already taken his soul. His gaze, when he brought it to bear upon a man, would show that man the dissolution of his own morals, so dead were they and carious. His mane of black hair cowled him in his evil." Yet by *Krotch's Last Stand*, Krotch is described variously as "stout," "portly," "emaciated," both a "black, scuttling beetle, low to the ground" and a "wisp torn from the wind in his ethereal height," with "dirty blonde hair" and later "reddish-tinged locks that hung like snakes to his waist." Perhaps signaling that Glaring had grown tired of the series. See also: *Glaring, Maxwell; Krotch; Midnight for Munfroe; Munfroe.*

KUBIN, ALFRED. A psychologist who specialized in the study of the underlying causes of squidanthropy. Over time, he came to comprehend these causes all too well, becoming a frequent patron of the most nefarious squid clubs.

When a Truffidian priest refused to marry him to a female squid he met in a club's wading pond, Kubin became violent and set fires all across the city during one delirious night of arson. Several historic institutions, including the oldest of the Hoegbotton safehouses, sustained severe fire damage. When finally captured, Kubin was incarcerated in the Voss Bender Memorial Mental Institute alongside his former patients, many of whom reportedly laughed uproariously before administering a severe beating. See also: *Madnok, Frederick.*

– L –

LACOND, JAMES. An eccentric historian whose theories of the gray caps have largely been dismissed (unfairly) by the reading public, other historians, and even by the unemployed carpenter who for years haunted the sidewalk outside Lacond's apartment overlooking Voss Bender Memorial Square. His pamphlets have been exclusively distributed by the Ambergrisians for the Original Inhabitants Society. Among his writings is the essay "An Argument for the Gray Caps and Against the Evidence of Tonsure's Eyes." Known for his frequent visits to Zamilon. See also: *Ambergrisians for the Original Inhabitants Society; Rats; Zamilon.*

LEOPRAN, GEORGE. A Scathadian writer and diplomat best known for his seven-page account of his journey to and from Ambergris. Also the author of the 3,000-page novel *A Sliver of Time*, which covers one day in the life of a lonely goat herder. In minute detail. The novel includes a 200-page diatribe castigating Manzikert III as an example of the abuse of power. See also: *Scatha*.

LIVING SAINTS. The long history of the Living Saints predates the Truffidian religion, which embraced the saints for their own purposes. Based on the premise that bodily functions are the most sacred signs of God in human beings, Living Saints endure solitary lives of poverty. There are four orders: the Order of Flatulence, the Order of Ejaculations, the Order of Defecations, and the Order of Urination. The saints spend years perfecting their particular specialty and thus honoring "the God that made us mortal" as the scriptures read. Many other religions hire these saints as guards because they are so disgusting they scare away criminals. Manzikert III was once mistaken for a Living Saint in the Order of Flatulence. See also: *Kristina of Malfour*.

– M –

MADNOK, FREDERICK. A flamboyant amateur squidologist of some renown who belonged to the spornspurn religion. (The numbers of this particular cult dwindled significantly upon the formal declaration of their views, due to a number of unexplained disappearances.) Suffered a nervous breakdown when, due to a printer's error, octopi images were placed in one of his squid monographs. See also: *Hellatose & Bauble; Kodfan, M.*

MALID, ARCH DUKE OF. Once upon a time, the Arch Duke of Malid was a little boy who tortured insects and small animals. He kept journals of these activities that have survived down to the present day (and which are of great interest to insect collectors and taxidermists for the intense detail of their descriptions). At first, the Duke's father applauded the Duke's industriousness in keeping a journal. No doubt he felt differently when he discovered himself, a little too late, on page 203: "Note to self: Above a battlement, on a wall, on a spike, the bloody head of my father." See also: *Gray Tribes, The; Saltwater Buzzard.*

MANDIBLE, RICHARD. One of Ambergris' foremost early economists and social scientists. Unfortunately, Richard's respectable reputation has been eclipsed by his brother Roger's artwork, which was at the center of the New Art's Great Earwax Scandal, as some wags have called it. Roger, it turned out, procured earwax from the lithesome ears of his sleeping lovers and mixed it into his paint; thus the marvelous amber tint to the sunsets on display at the Gallery of Hidden Fascinations. When the source of the amber tint was discovered, Roger suffered little career damage, but staid Richard, scandalized, never fully recovered from the incident. See also: *Gallery of Hidden Fascinations; New Art, The.*

MANZIISM. The rat-worshipping heretic religion inadvertently founded by Manzikert I near the end of his life. This cult has had little or no influence on history while inexplicably continuing to thrive, at least in Ambergris. Nothing sticks in the throats of Truffidian priests in the

Religious Quarter more than the sight of rat bishops, rat clerics, and just plain old rat-bastards paraded down the street during the Festival of the Freshwater Squid, a-glitter in their specially-made robes and silver crowns. See also: *Manzikert VI; Manzikert VII; Manzikert VIII; Moonrat; Rats.*

MANZIKERT VI. Death by bliss. In all fairness to the sixth Manzikert's moral fiber, he never really wanted to be Cappan of Ambergris. He was only too happy to retire to a monastery, especially a Manziist monastery. In those days, the only difference between a Manziist monastery and a brothel was that the latter attracted more priests. See also: *Manziism; Manzikert VII; Manzikert VIII.*

MANZIKERT VII. Death by an extreme miscalculation while flossing. Of his actual reign, the less said the better. See also: *Manziism; Manzikert VI; Manzikert VIII.*

MANZIKERT VIII. Death by tire tread. An expert at staging extravaganzas, Manzikert VIII had no notable political or military victories during his reign. He has the dubious distinction of being the first historical personage to be killed by a very early form of steam-powered motored vehicle (during the Festival). An entire line of motored vehicles was later named The Manzikert. See also: *Manziism; Manzikert VI; Manzikert VII.*

MANZIKERT MEMORIAL LIBRARY. Oddly enough, the ineffectual Manzikert III established the Manzikert Memorial Library. He established the library to house his ever-expanding collection of recipes and cookbooks. Since that time, the library has grown to include a healthy selection of fiction, secret documents, and erotica. The position of chief librarian has often been a political as well as administrative position, as when, during the conflict of the Reds and the Greens, the library became a repository for Voss Bender sheet music. Built in the same location as the gray caps' original "library," the Manzikert Memorial Library has experienced some of the strangest fungal outbreaks in Ambergris' history. See also: *Abrasis, Michael; Frankwrithe & Lewden; Fungus; Greens; Reds.*

MAP, BRANDON. An unfortunate splotch.

MARTIGAN, RED. Leader of a doomed underground expedition against the gray caps. This victim of his own curiosity would otherwise have passed out of history altogether. Instead, due to his overwhelming stupidity, Ambergris remembers him as being somehow larger-than-life. He is frequently an inhabitant of horror and ghost stories—in a sense, more substantial in memory than in the flesh. See also: *Ambergrisians for the Original Inhabitants Society; Cappers; Kretchen.*

MASOUF. The general who finally defeated Stretcher Jones and personally slew the great rebel leader. He is said to have wept over the body of his adversary. After so many years of battling Stretcher Jones, Masouf was distraught to have finally destroyed the only man who had been his equal in military skill and tactics. In his journal entry that fateful day, Masouf wrote, "As I stared into that pale, bloodied face, as I cupped his head with my hands as he breathed his last, I felt as if I were staring into my own face, into an ill-fated reflection, and as the life flickered out of his eyes, so too the life briefly seemed to have left me as well." Masouf relieved himself of his own command three days later, and after an unsuccessful suicide attempt left his wife and children and spent the next 20 years as a recluse in the self-imposed solitude of Zamilon. He would eventually take up Stretcher Jones' struggle and for a brief time liberated the Kalif's western-most vassals from servitude, before being defeated by a general more brilliant than even he. Masouf died when his horse, spooked by a rabbit, threw him as he fled the battlefield. See also: *Jones, Stretcher; Zamilon.*

MIDNIGHT FOR MUNFROE. The first volume in Maxwell Glaring's series of novels detailing the adversarial relationship between the anti-hero Munfroe and the criminally-insane Krotch. Voss Bender once considered writing an opera based on this book, but abandoned the idea after reading the complete series. Bender's purported reason? "There is too much Krotch in the world already." The book first appeared as a serial in *Dreadful Tales*, which may explain the staccato "voice" of the book—its high number of cliff hangers and near-escapes. Glaring found the story's success inexplicable and, vowing never again to write a Munfroe-Krotch story, proceeded to churn out a large number of them. See also: *Bender, Voss; Dreadful Tales; Glaring, Maxwell; Krotch; Munfroe.*

MIKAL, DRAY. Randomly chosen to be the Petularch by a ceremonial bull, as is still the custom. Let loose by the Priests of the Seven-Edged Star, the ceremonial bull was allowed to roam free until it had chosen a Petularch. The selection process consisted of any "sign" from the bull deemed sufficiently conclusive by the priests. Although the "sign" from the bull in this case has been lost in the garbage heap of unimportant facts, it is known that Mikal was a fruit-on-a-stick vendor before his Ascension. He had immigrated to Ambergris from a small city north of Morrow called Skaal. Luckily, the position of Petularch has been largely irrelevant ever since the overthrow of the Church of the Seven-Edged Star several centuries ago. See also: *Caroline of the Church of the Seven Pointed Star.*

MONSTER, THE. Depending on the context, either a huge sewer ball or a huge ball of fungus. See also: *Cappers; Fungus.*

MOONRAT. A pure white rat, about the size of a terrier, that gathers at midnight to drink from tributaries of the River Moth. It feeds on honeysuckle nectar and fungi (to which latter food is attributed the fact that some moonrats glow an intense green in the dead of night). Sacred to the Nimblytod Tribes, the moonrat is also of some significance to Manziists, who every year make the dangerous pilgrimage to the southern rainforests to observe the moonrat in its natural habitat. The moonrat's mating call is sonorous and deep, akin to the sound that emanates from the long horns used by the monks of Zamilon. The symphony created by the moonrat in concert with the Nimblytod's mouth-music is said to rival even Voss Bender for its odd mixture of vulnerability and strength. See also: *Bender, Voss; Manziists; Nimblytod Tribes, The; Zamilon.*

MORHAIM MUSEUM. A repository over the years of many strange and eccentric treasures, from first editions of Vivian Price Rogers' Torture Squid books to gray cap knives. Thomas Daffed's priceless five-thousand specimen collection may be the Morhaim Museum's crowning glory. The Morhaim family has remained sharply a-political throughout the years and thereby gained the confidence of many influential figures in Ambergris. See also: *Daffed Zoo; Fungus; Rogers, Vivian Price; Spacklenest, Edgar.*

EXHIBIT 5: A GRAY CAP KNIFE SUPPOSEDLY USED IN "RELIGIOUS" RITUALS; HOUSED IN THE MORHAIM MUSEUM'S "UNLIKELY WEAPONS" GALLERY.

MORROW RELIGIOUS INSTITUTE. Although Ambergris is the city of religions, Morrow is the city of religious studies. As Morrow is in all ways removed from the lustful thrust of real life, so too is it removed from its spiritual heart to the extent that it holds its faith at arm's length, the better to examine faith's anatomy. The Morrow Religious Institute is the most famously able at this

dissection process. However, despite producing some famous religious figures and teachers, a disturbing number
of its graduates, once exposed to religion-in-the-raw, have
either "gone native" or succumbed to the pleasures of this
too mortal flesh. Formerly the Institute of Religiousity. See
also: *Menites; Signal, Cadimon.*

MUNFROE. The ever-weary anti-hero of Maxwell
Glaring's Krotch and Munfroe series, Munfroe is a pro-
tean sort whose past changes from book to book. First the
son of humble farmers who travels to the city to become an
accountant, Munfroe later becomes the son of accountants
who travels to the country to become a humble farmer.
Other incarnations include parents who serve stints in the
circus, the army, as doctors, and as carpenters, variously.
Only one thing is for sure: Munfroe had parents. See also:
Glaring, Maxwell; Krotch.

– N –

NADAL, THOMAS. He who died in infamy, his fate too
sad to relate here. Let him rest in peace as he could not in
life. Faithful to his lover and faithful to his city. A curse on
all of those who would defame him for his sole moment of
weakness. See also: *Jones, Stretcher.*

NEW ART, THE. An oxymoron. See also: *Burning
Leaves; Gallery of Hidden Fascinations; Mandible, Richard;
Shadow Art Movement, The; Sporlender, Nicholas; Verden,
Louis.*

NIMBLYTOD TRIBES. This tree-dwelling people, wiry but strong, has inhabited the southern rainforests for centuries, weaving their bird-like huts in the crooks of sturdy branches. Oblivious to the efforts of Truffidian missionaries to convert them, the Nimblytod still worship the sacred moonrat and the plumed thrush hen. Members of the tribe can make flute-like sounds without instruments and the concerts that often break the silence of the tree cover can seem "like the songs of beautiful angels," as one shaken missionary put it. The Nimblytod confirm their independence by blowdarting anyone who enters their territory. (Most casualties in recent years, however, have been Manziists.) The poison used in their blowdarts results in a prolonged period of fever, followed by malaise and then a sudden and intense passion for whatever object the sufferer happens to gaze upon at that moment. Eventually, dementia and death follow, like sullen cousins. See also: *Manziists; Moonrat.*

NUNK, AUTARCH OF. Although a real historical figure, the Autarch is more commonly known to children and adults as the happy fool of Voss Bender's Nunk poems, which contain such rhymes as "The Autarch of Nunk/ Was a collector of junk/Which he kept in a trunk/Beside his pet skunk" and "The Autarch of Nunk/Loved to get drunk/And, in the grip of a sudden funk,/Pass out fitfully on his bunk." Several critics have complained that a less famous personage would not have been able to get such doggerel published, but the illustrations by Kinsky in the omnibus version amply make up for the simplistic verse. Recently, amongst the few possessions left by Michael

Abrasis to the Manzikert Memorial Library, archivists discovered a second set of Nunk poems, decidedly more adult, as this excerpt demonstrates: "The Autarch of Nunk/Liked women with spunk/To wiggle and tickle/His enormous pink pickle." (Although some historians believe this is a gardening reference.) See also: *Abrasis, Michael; Bender, Voss.*

NYSIMIA. A western city known for death, dust, beer, and, more recently, for ridiculous theories involving pony-riding invaders, old dead men, and the gray caps. See also: *Hyggboutten.*

NYSMAN, MICHAEL. A native of Nicea, Nysman was a high-ranking Truffidian priest. Although ostensibly sent to Ambergris to assuage the suffering of those who had survived The Silence, documents unearthed since his death clearly indicate that the Truffidian Church had sent him to Ambergris for other reasons entirely. Nysman's mission was two-fold: to research The Silence to determine its cause and also to develop a psychological profile of people in extreme distress and deliver a written report to the Antechamber of Nicea on ways to exploit this distress for converts. Nysman's report on psychological distress is less interesting than his report on the cause of The Silence, which includes the following sentences: "With all due respect, I do not know what good it will do us to find out the cause of this affliction. Surely the truth will be too horrible for any of us to hold within ourselves, and yet we could not loose such knowledge upon the world. The only words I can use to describe the utter despair that settles over me in this city are 'without God.' I feel entirely without God in this city." Later in the report, Nysman writes that around the time of The Silence several sheep herders saw strange lights during the night, emanating from Alfar. Nysman finds this fact to be of supreme importance, but instead of visiting Alfar, he abruptly changed his itinerary to visit Zamilon, for reasons that are lost to us. See also: *Alfar; Zamilon.*

– O –

OCCUPATION, THE. The term given to the 100 days during which the Kalif's troops occupied Ambergris. With the exception of The Silence, The Occupation was the bleakest period of Ambergrisian history. If not for the ingenuity and pluck of ordinary citizens, The Occupation would have lasted much longer. As this letter from David Ampers, the owner of a local tavern, The Ruby-Throated Cafe, to his cousin in Morrow (the infamous "fighting philosopher" Richard Peterson) demonstrates, the Kalif's troops did not have an easy time of it:

> Why, I had just said to my old friend Steen Potter (you remember Steen from your last visit—the watch salesman?) as we sat drinking at the Cafe and sharpening our knives to an unparalleled sharpness—I had just said that the city, our beloved Ambergris, had been stuck in a sort of malaise, a doldrums, the whole summer, when what should I and every other citizen of the city find nailed to our doors but a barbaric

sheet of paper from the Empire of the Kalif that read thusly:

"Noblest of the Gods, King and Master of the whole World, Son of the previous Kalif, the new Kalif, to Ambergris, his vile and insensate slave: Refusing to submit to our rule, you call yourselves lord and sovereign. You seize and distribute our treasure, you deceive our servants. You never cease to annoy us with your bands of brigands. Have I not destroyed you? I suppose I must destroy you more utterly than you have ever been destroyed before. Beware Ambergris! Beware!"

Oh, I thought to myself, now this was promising. An ultimatum! This promised to shake us out of our rut—a real threat! And backed up too! So of course Ambergris spread her arms to the aggressor, the better to love him to death. The messenger prior to invasion was a broadsheet boy who ran past screaming, "Armies of the Kalif cross the river, crush the free armies of the Cappan!" In a stroke, Ambergris had fallen, after five years of snapping at our flanks by the Kalif—such a tease. All right, we could live with that, but did the boy have to scream it out to the world? There is such a thing as pride, my cousin, and although perhaps Steen over-reacted a little, no one complained when he took aim, let fly, and dropped the lad with a stone thrown to the head. Pride is very important to us here, although you may not understand that, not having been born in the city . . .

So the Kalif's troops invaded and we all came out to line Albumuth Boulevard for the obligatory Parade of Conquerors. It was a bright, breezy day and the swallows flew through the sky like knives. The Kalif's men formed a supposedly impenetrable wall on either side of the street, armed with spears, swords, and small cannons. It appeared they thought the local population might cause some sort of problem. Steen and I exchanged a meaningful glance. All we wanted to do was welcome the invading army to our city.

The Kalif's general, the Great One as he was called, made for an impressive sight, with his emerald turban, white ostrich plumes, silver spurs, and the eight gray oliphaunts that lurched along behind him. At least, he was impressive until someone in the crowd sent a blade flying through his throat. My, what a lot of blood he had in him—and it certainly seemed as red as anyone else's would have been in a similar situation. Alas, the assassin slipped away in the resulting turmoil.

When order had been restored, we crowded up the palace steps and watched as the mayor, the defeated Cappan at his side in chains, relinquished, in a formal ceremony, the keys to the city, and gave the sacramental sword to the new Great One (hastily recruited from among five resplendent if fiercely sweating officers). The Cappan performed these duties with a slight smirk and a conspiratorial wink to the crowd. The Cappan's personal bodyguards, too, were in a particularly mirthful mood, considering the circumstances. Indeed, one would at times during the ceremony have had difficulty determining who was slave and who was victor . . . The Great One, as he looked out on the crowd, seemed discomfited by the applause, the ready smiles, as we showed our teeth. A flicker of fear flashed across the Great One's face before tranquility once again overtook those fine, western features.

It didn't last long, of course, although I shall, in the interests of saving my hands from gripping this pen for hours and you of reading into boredom, summarize the events of the next 100 days. Inevitably, the second Great One was poisoned and the third found garroted in his palace, so the Kalif had no choice but to order the mayor of our fair metropolis hanged by the neck until dead. I'm sure he did not expect what happened at the hanging: We all cheered as our mayor went to a better (or at least cleaner!) place. We'd never much liked him anyway, and would probably have done the deed ourselves in a few more months. But then, following the execution, we rioted and killed many of the Kalif's soldiers because, after all, he was one of us, even if he had been an incompetent, embezzling bastard.

From then on, it was just a matter of time. Each dawn saw another set of foreigners' heads on spikes down by various city fountains. Each sunset was occasion for mingled screams and pleas for mercy. Everywhere they turned: the confluence of fate and malice in the ancient stone face of the city. When they came to my establishment, why, I treated them like kings, using a slow-acting poison to kill several of them over a period of days. Some trickster they trusted told them that the red flags strewn across the city were flags of defiance, so the Kalif's men tore them up, angering the gray caps, who stirred and clicked amongst themselves before "disappearing" the Kalif's men in droves. The zoo keeper let the big cats free right into the barracks of the Great One's personal guard. Store owners crept up to the Kalif's cannon after dark and poured sand and glue in the muzzles. Priests in the Religious Quarter stoned patrols to death for violating obscure, out-of-date rules and then pleaded exemption from punishment on grounds of conflicting faiths.

Finally, one day, they simply left, cousin, and never returned. We boxed the bones they had left behind into the walls of abandoned buildings. We burned their carts. We appropriated their horses. We scrubbed the palace clean. We re-instated the Cappan. And, once again, we cheerfully settled down to govern ourselves, ever so refreshed by this little interlude, this experiment in occupation by a foreign empire . . . So you should come visit again soon, cousin. The cafe is doing well and we would be glad to have you. The city is beautiful this time of year.

Fondly,
David Ampers

See also: *Banfour, Archduke of; Kalif, The; Oliphaunt; Peterson, Richard.*

ODECCA BICHORAL WHITE WHALE. The most intelligent of sea-going mammals, venerated by the Church of the Fisherman, prized by zoologists, and possessed of a brain so large that its skull is lopsided. Odecca Whales must always swim at a diagonal, their heads preferably resting on the surface while their massive stern fins churn relentlessly. If they stop swimming for even a minute, the massive head will cause them to sink to the bottom and drown. By necessity, the whale is a surface feeder. See also: *Church of the Fisherman; Daffed Zoo.*

OLIPHAUNT. One of Tonsure's favorite mammals, these great gray creatures almost ended Stretcher Jones' rebellion at the outset. Their sudden introduction into battle, brought from the jungle plains of the far southwest, caused such panic at the Battle of Richter that Jones was lucky to escape with his life. Xaver Daffed found this usually gentle mammal so compelling that he devoted two volumes of his *A History of Animals* to it. Manzikert III found oliphaunts so succulent that toward the end of his reign he ate their flesh to the exclusion of all else. The Kalif, upon his temporary subjugation of Ambergris, planned to build a palace that would have represented the apogee of the oliphaunt motif in architecture: a vast structure in the shape of an oliphaunt. The plans included hindquarters fashioned to resemble a glen with its own running brook and a theater in the front. See also: *Ambergris Gastronomic Association; Daffed, Xaver; Jones, Stretcher; Occupation, The.*

– P –

PEJORA, MIDAN. The most famous architect in Ambergris' history. He holds primary responsibility for the grandest buildings in the city, including the Cappan's Palace. Pejora could best be classified as an "idiot genius." From an early age, he erected incredible models of buildings out of wood, sand, and rock, but he could not even graduate from grade school. His parents eventually taught him as best they could at home, and many were the times neighbors would complain because Pejora had erected some new architectural monstro-city in the family's front yard.

PETERSON, RICHARD. Founder of an unnamed faith that preaches the story of the little red flower that grows by the side of the road. The faith uses a calendar of 12 months comprising 30 days each. Each year ends with the five-day Festival of the Holy Little Red Flower, which includes the Day of Seed, the Day of Root, the Day of Stem, the Day of Leaf, and the Day of Bloom. (A splinter faction called the "Scientific Reformists" inserts the Day of Budding before the Day of Bloom every fourth year, rather than the universally symmetrical five-year cycle recognized by the true followers of the faith. Violent confrontations have been known to occur during this false celebration of the Day of Budding.) The Five Volumes of the *Dodecahedron* represent the only true written teachings of the Faith. Each volume is divided into twelve books (Petal, Sepal, Stigma, Style, Ovary, Pistil, Stamen, Pollen, Anther, Filament, Nectar, and Calyx). Each book is divided into 240 chapters with 30 verses each. Adherents are generally recognizable by their trademark red sashes and precise pentagonal tonsures. The Brotherhood of the Red Stamen, an order of the Faith, is famous for its scholarship and teaching. Specializing primarily in geometry and horticulture, the gardens which surround each of the five monasteries of the order are justly renowned and lead many thousands each year to join the faith. An unfinished cathedral devoted to expressing the *Dodecahedron* in physical form may one day supplant the gardens as a mechanism of mass conversions. See also: *Holy Little Red Flower, The; Strattonism; Verden, Louis.*

PORFAL. An inventor best known for his Porfal Memory Capsule, a festival necessity. Porfal also developed a coin shaped like a knife, issued by Hoegbotton & Sons as a commemorative item and hastily discontinued after numerous stabbings occurred at the subsequent Festival. His most controversial inventions were erotic in nature, including the honey-powered Orgasm Machine, the Mechanical Toe-Sucker, and the infamous Inverted Maiden, into which hapless men in search of ecstasy descended only to find the demands of pleasure too great for their hearts to withstand. See also: *Burning Leaves; Cappers; Monster, The; Spacklenest, Edgar.*

– R –

RATS. In sewers. In religions. In words like pirate, desperate, and narrative. Rats infest this glossary as surely as words and mushrooms. See also: *Ambergris; Lacond, James; Manziism; Moonrat.*

REAL HISTORY NEWSLETTER, THE. A fringe publication that has allowed many historians in exile to have their say under the safety of pseudonyms. See also: *Ambergrisians for the Real Inhabitants Society; Lacond, James.*

REDS. Originally founded to oppose the interests of the composer nee politician Voss Bender, the remnants of the Reds ended their days running a small tavern on the southern edge of Ambergris and hosting dart competitions. See also: *Bender, Voss; Borges Bookstore; Greens; Manzikert Memorial Library.*

ROGERS, VIVIAN PRICE. Brought up on a farm as the only girl in a family that included eight brothers, Rogers revenged herself on her unruly, brawling brethren by re-imagining them as the Torture Squid. For many years the Torture Squid books outsold even the works of Henry Flack in Ambergris' many bookstalls. In later years, Rogers accepted an honorary position at the Borges Bookstore while her brothers continued their lives of dawn-till-dusk drudgery back on the farm. See also: *Borges Bookstore; Morhaim Museum.*

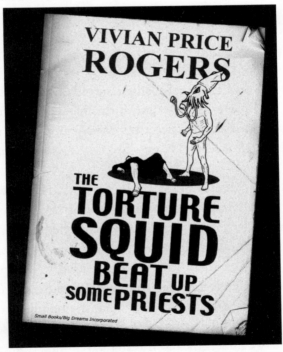

EXHIBIT 6: A RARE FIRST EDITION OF VIVIAN PRICE ROGERS' CLASSIC TORTURE SQUID BOOK; HOUSED IN THE MORHAIM MUSEUM'S "FIRST EDITIONS" LIBRARY.

ROYAL GENEALOGIST. A position in the Kalif's Empire much shrouded in secrecy. Only the Royal Genealogist knows the true identity of the Kalif, but can publish only the vaguest facts about the royal personage. Although the theory cannot be proven, many historians, this one excluded, believe that on more than one occasion the Royal Genealogist has actually been the Kalif. See also: *Kalif, The.*

– S –

SABON, MARY. An aggressive and sometimes brilliant historian who built her reputation on the bones of older, love-struck historians. Five-ten. One-fifteen. Red hair. Green, green eyes. An elegant dresser. Smile like fire. Foe of James Lacond. In conversation can cut with a single word. Author of several books. See also: *Lacond, James.*

SAFE HOUSE. A place, usually controlled by Hoegbotton & Sons, where travelers could seek shelter during the Festival of the Freshwater Squid. Most safe houses provided little packets of useless products and information to assuage the fears of its temporary tenants. This packet usually included some insipid festival "story." See: *Verden, Louis.*

SAINT PHILIP THE PHILANDERER. A Living Saint who was kicked out of the Order of Ejaculation because he bathed too regularly. See: *Living Saints.*

HOEGBOTTON ROYALE SAFE HOUSE
1048 Albumuth Boulevard
Ambergris

Dear Valued Guest:

Welcome to the ancient city of Ambergris, and to the Festival of the Freshwater Squid! An exciting element of unpredictability has entered the Festival in recent decades—we applaud your daring for attending the Festival and your good sense for selecting this establishment, Hoegbotton's premier safe house. For 75 years, Hoegbotton Royale has provided uninterrupted, quality service to its clientele.* We believe you will delight in your choice of a luxury King Squid suite, with its many extra amenities.

We are pleased to provide you, our honored guest, with the following items designed to enhance your Festival experience:

> • *One traditional Festival pamphlet* – Every year, Hoegbotton commissions a delightful, Festival-oriented story for your entertainment. This year, the renowned Sporlender and Verden team up yet again for The Exchange, a rousing tale of dinner intrigues that will whet your appetite for our special Festival buffet.
> • *One votive candle* – This candle's perfect simplicity replicates that of candles fashioned during the reign of Ambergris' founder, Manzikert I. Such candles were originally made from a combination of fungi and chemicals known to repel Ambergris' subterranean inhabitants, the gray caps. Its soft texture has been designed for full-body protection; we recommend you rub it on exposed parts of your anatomy.
> • *One Portal Memory Capsule* – We urge all of our guests, even those who do not plan to roam the city during Festival night, to take a moment now to write their name and the names of next of kin on the paper included inside the capsule, purely as a precautionary measure. Very few guests ever find the time to write down this information later.
> • *Two dried mushrooms* – It is extremely unlikely that you will ever find yourself cornered in a dead-end alley, completely at the mercy of the gray caps. However, guests who do find themselves in an awkward situation may wish to eat the convenient poison fungus. You will feel no pain as you expire; in fact, you will experience unimaginable pleasure as you pass over into the next world. (The second fungus provides an antidote to the first, should you undergo a sudden favorable change in circumstances.)

Rest assured that your peace of mind is our greatest concern. If you have any questions or require immediate unexpected medical attention, please contact us, day or night. (The red emergency bell is conveniently located on the night table beside your bed.)

Sincerely,

The Management

P.S. Please note that the bars on your windows are not solely for purposes of ornamentation; the safety lock should remain in place at all times.

* With the exception of 17 years when fires prompted rebuilding efforts.

EXHIBIT 7: A REPRODUCTION OF THE CLASSIC SAFE HOUSE LETTER INCLUDED WITH SPORLENDER AND VERDEN'S FESTIVAL STORY, *THE EXCHANGE.*

SALTWATER BUZZARD. The main beneficiaries of battles between Stretcher Jones and the Kalif, the Kalif and Michael Brueghel, Michael Brueghel and Manzikert I, Manzikert I and the gray caps, the Brueghelites and the Gray Tribes, the Gray Tribes and the Arch Duke of Malid, the Arch Duke of Malid and the Kalif, the Kalif and Ambergris, Ambergris and the Haragck, the Haragck and Morrow. Scavengers, saltwater buzzards mate for life, have an average wing span of 10 feet, an average life span of 20 years, and are distinguished from other buzzards by the flashes of red and green on the tips of their otherwise black wings. See also: *Brueghel, Michael; Gray Tribes, The; Jones, Stretcher; Kalif, The; Malid, Arch Duke of.*

SAPHANT EMPIRE, THE. As empires go, this one made the Kalif's holdings look pathetic. The Saphant Empire lasted for 1,500 years and encompassed most of two continents at its zenith. Its rulers, elected by an oligarchy, demonstrated an uncanny ability to mix negotiation and ruthless military force to consolidate their successes. Under the centralized stability of Empire, an unprecedented wealth of advances in technology and the arts threatened to make the Empire a permanent institution. However, a series of inbred, weak rulers coupled with crippling attacks on shipping by Aan pirates eventually broke the Empire into five pieces. The last Emperor's chief advisor, Samuel Lewden, did his best to hold the central government together, but the five pieces became 30 autonomous regions and then splintered into even smaller kingdoms. Until finally only ghost-like cultural echoes remained of the once-great empire. For more information, read Mary Sabon's one excellent book, *The Saphant Legacy.* See also: *Bedlam Rovers; Frankwrithe & Lewden; Sabon, Mary.*

SHADOW ART MOVEMENT, THE. Movement was actually anathema to the Shadow Artists, who, with their bodies and the late afternoon sun, created works of great beauty and grandeur in Trillian Square, shaming the Living Saints who also gathered there. See also: *Gallery of Hidden Fascinations; Living Saints; New Art, The.*

SHAPISM. A deviant branch of mushroom science that uses the shape of mushrooms to determine toxicity. Not very popular. See also: *Fungus.*

SHARP, MAXIMILLIAN. Possibly the most talented and yet most obnoxious writer ever produced by the South. Of all the infamous tales told about him by publishers and editors, the only one backed up by actual documentation concerns his association with Frankwrithe & Lewden. Sharp published his work regularly in F&L periodicals and as stand-alone books and pamphlets. On one occasion, he apparently did not appreciate Andrew Lewden (his editor) characterizing him at a dinner party as "somewhat arrogant" and sent Lewden the following missive (Lewden, by all accounts, read it once, smiled, threw it away, and promptly remaindered all of Sharp's books):

> From: Lord Sharp I, Steward of the Sacred Word & Keeper of the Torch of Life.

> To: Andrew Lewden, Lowly Knave, Steward of the Bottom Dollar & Keeper of Writers with No Alternative (currently)

A Missive, To Whit, Responding to Andrew Lewden's last letter and unworthy comment of last week, in the Year 34 of our Lord Sharp. Forthsooth and with haste herewith:

Dear Lewden:

(1) My Lord Sharp thanks you for your appreciated, if rather short and wretched letter of last week and begs me to tell you (as he is himself involved in Extremely Important Matters of Writing and Editing, and has no time to deal with editors hailing from squalid and distant corners of the world) that although he appreciates the copy of your latest magazine with His exalted story "The Glory That Was Me" printed therein, you have failed to place his name in large enough type on the cover—nor have you situated His name first and to the detriment of all other (lesser) names on said cover. Furthermore, His story was not published as the first story in the magazine, nor was it given an elaborate illustration, and, finally, the biography which accompanied the piece was not long enough, did not adequately cover Lord Sharp's career, and did not state (as is common enough custom for Lord Sharp's work, and certainly common knowledge) that Sharp is "The Premier Writer of His, or Any Other Generation."

(2) These are grave misdeeds, Mr. Lewden, and Lord Sharp, while not altogether concerned, owing to the low circulation and low pay associated with your magazine, is perplexed as to why you should seek to draw His Lordship's wrath upon you. Certainly deigning to present to you an Exalted Reprint from several years past, he has laid upon you the gravest of all duties: the proper representation not only of the Sharp Fiction but of the Sharp Image. If no illustration were available, Lord Sharp, through his many underlings, would have been glad to provide you with a glossy representation, in three-quarters profile, of His Famous Visage. This would not only have been adequate, it would have been more perfect, due to the marvelous perfections of the Sharp Visage, than any illustration (unless, of course, such mythical illustration had been of His Lordship).

(3) In any event, due to the Extreme Kindness of Lord Sharp, I am instructed by His Lordship to officially Forgive You Your Trespasses and to let you know that you may, if you ever visit Lord Sharp's estate, be allowed to kiss His hand, and even to keep a crumpled piece of paper from one of His Lordship's abortive rough drafts.

(4) Finally, as you say, Mr. Lewden, mere mortals may include appropriate return postage for a manuscript, but as your sentence implied,

Lord Sharp is, like the unbroken string of Kalifs, most exceptionally Immortal, in that most enduring of ways: through the glory of the written word. Therefore, on a related topic, we ask that you immediately relinquish a tear sheet, to use a vulgar term, of the review of His Lordship's Greatest Book, *A Testament*, for His perusal. (He will not, in fact, read it, but one of His many underlings may read it to Him; or, as is more likely, one of His underlings gifted in the Word shall rewrite the review so that it flows like liquid gold rather than liquid shit and thus shall not distress in any way His noble ears; there is nothing that harms his Lordship more than a badly-turned phrase.)

(5) In closing, I shall simply remind you, Mr. Lewden, that it will soon again be time to pay the annual tribute to His Lordship. This year, as you should know, it consists of three days of reading Lord Sharp's works aloud, two days of studying them silently, and one day of transcribing them by Your Own hand, that you may more fully understand how Genius doth descend upon the World.

Your Obed. Ser.,

Gerold Bottek
(one of Lord Sharp's many underlings)

P.S. His Lordship would like to convey to you His appreciation for your previous (if distant) kind words in various broadsheets which He has, through his underlings, perused; they have, I am told to tell you "a rough eloquence quite unlike the bastard, no doubt inspired by my works." He so appreciates this attention that He has commanded me to tell you that you may skip one of the three days of reading His works aloud.

See also: *Frankwrithe & Lewden.*

SHRIEK, DUNCAN. An old historian, born in Stockton, who in his youth published several famous history books, since remaindered and savaged by critics who should have known better. His father, also an historian, died of joy; or, rather, from a heart-attack brought on by finding out he had won a major honor from the Court of the Kalif. Duncan was 10 at the time. Since then, Duncan has never died from his honors, but was once banned by the Truffidian Antechamber. Also a renowned expert on the gray caps, although most reasonable citizens ignore even his least outlandish theories. Once lucky enough to meet the love of his life, but not lucky enough to keep her, or to keep her from pillaging his ideas and discrediting him. Still, he loves her, separated from her by the insurmountable gulf of empires, buzzards, bad science, and an arrogant writer. See also: *Rats.*

SIGNAL, CADIMON. A most curious man of religion who combined elements of common crime with the utmost respect for the spiritual life. He taught the most successful missionaries ever to graduate from the Morrow Religious Institute and spent 10 years studying with the monks of Zamilon. Famous for his fervent lectures on Living Saints and martyrs. See also: *Morrow Religious Institute* and *Zamilon*.

SIMPKIN, WILLIAM. The head of Ambergris' labyrinthine centralized mental health facilities and the chief psychiatric interrogator for incoming cases. Simpkin wrote fiction on the side, publishing several volumes about an evil imaginary kingdom ruled by a mouse. At base, a heartless bastard. See also: *Bedlam Rovers*.

SIRIN. A writer and editor originally born near far-fabled Zamilon. He is primarily known for his series of fictions supposedly describing various aspects of Ambergris history. Infamously involved in the Citizen Fish Campaign. See also: *Citizen Fish Campaign; Fungus; Shriek, Duncan; Zamilon*.

SKAMOO. A proud, aloof people well-adapted to the snow of the frozen northern regions. Some historians have tried to link the Skamoo to Zamilon, claiming that the forebearers of the Skamoo built the fortress-monastery. See also: *Zamilon*.

SOPHIA ISLAND. An island named after Manzikert I's wife, located in the River Moth, to the north of Ambergris. Long ago ceded to Hoegbotton & Sons by Ambergris' last Cappan, John Golinard, in exchange for much-needed monies, Sophia Island served for many years as a base for Hoegbotton mercantile operations. However, some 50 years ago, H&S leased the eastern half of the island to Frankwrithe & Lewden, in exchange for trading rights to Morrow markets. In recent years, the island has become a battleground between H&S and F&L forces, slowing traffic north and south as both sides exact ever-more ridiculous tariffs on boats wishing to pass through. See also: *Frankwrithe & Lewden*.

SPACKLENEST, EDGAR. Author of the cult novel *Lord Hood & the Unseen Squid*. Spacklenest came from "old money" and lived in a mansion in the marshes to the west of Ambergris with his mother, grandmother, and sister. From his third-story room overlooking the Moth, he would write for hours in a black notebook, every few months sending another tale to *Dreadful Tales*, which rejected his work because the editors did not understand it, or *Burning Leaves*, which rejected it because it was too traditional. Eventually, a friend of the family convinced the Ambergris Department of Broadsheet Licensing Publications to print Spacklenest's first collection of stories, entitled *Scars & Other Weapons*. Published in hardcover, the collection sold only 25 copies and the Ambergris Department of Broadsheet Licensing Publications dropped Spacklenest from their stable of safety pamphlet authors. For several years, Spacklenest did not attempt publication again, instead pouring himself into writing the classic stories that would eventually be issued in the posthumous Frankwrithe & Lewden collections *Nights Beyond Night* and *Dark Sings The Lark Beyond the Veil*. F&L would also publish his *Lord Hood* novel posthumously, a work which sold well and has led to Spacklenest's current cult status. After writing *Lord Hood,* a dejected Spacklenest abandoned both fiction and his ancestral home, relocating to a small apartment off of Albumuth Boulevard and accepting an archival position at the Morhaim Museum. In later years, under the pseudonym "Anne Sneller," Spacklenest published a number of nonfiction books, including *A History of Traveling Medicine Shows & Nefarious Circi. Lord Hood* and his short stories were discovered among his personal

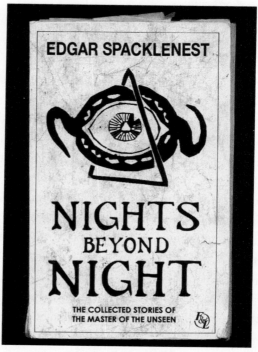

EXHIBIT 8: A FIRST EDITION OF EDGAR SPACKLENEST'S *NIGHTS BEYOND NIGHT,* ON DISPLAY IN THE MORHAIM MUSEUM'S "A HISTORY OF SOUTHERN PUBLISHING" WING.

effects when he died of stab wounds inflicted by a Porfal coin knife during a particularly violent Festival. See also: *Burning Leaves; Dreadful Tales; Frankwrithe & Lewden; Morhaim Museum; Porfal.*

SPORE OF THE GRAY CAP, THE. The tavern in which much of Duncan Shriek's Early History was written. A marvelous hide-away more fully described in *The Hoegbotton Guide to Bars, Pubs, Taverns, Inns, Restaurants, Brothels, and Safe Houses.*

SPORLENDER, NICHOLAS. The author of over 100 books and instructional religious pamphlets, including *Sarah and the Land of Sighs, Truffidian Votives for the Layperson,* and *A List of Daily Sacrifices for Members of the Church of the Seven-Edged Star.* Many of Sporlender's books incorporate the ideas of the "fighting philosopher" Richard Peterson. Sporlender frequently collaborated with the artist Louis Verden before a violent disagreement ended the relationship. In his memoirs, he wrote of the break up: "It's not like we didn't know when it started. It was Verden's obstinence that started it. And his insipid obsession with Strattonism. He simply could not let it be. It was always Stratton this, Stratton that. I'd ask him, 'Please—lay off the Strattonism. I'm trying to write.' Eventually, I took up Peterson's teachings just to block out the Strattonism. But he wouldn't stop." A five-time recipient of the Southern Cities' most prestigious literary award, The Trillian, Sporlender moved to Morrow in later years with his wife and three dogs. See also: *Burning Leaves; Caroline of the Church of the Seven-Pointed Star;*

Dreadful Tales; New Art, The; Peterson, Richard; Stratton-ism; Verden, Louis.

EXHIBIT 9: AVANT GARDE WESTERN PAINTER ORIM LACKPOLE'S MODERN INTERPRETATION OF THE GRAY CAP SYMBOL, ENTITLED "SPORN ZETBRAND 3"; ON DISPLAY IN THE MORHAIM MUSEUM'S "MODERN ARTISTS" WING.

SPORN. The term commonly used throughout the Kalif's Empire to refer to the gray caps. The Kalif's people refer to the gray caps' sacred symbol as the "zetbrand" and their underground land as the "zetland." See: *Fungus; Kalif, The.*

STOCKTON. Even more boring than Morrow. Might as well be populated with monkeys or Oliphaunts than with people. Not even a religious institute to save it from boredom. Incidentally, the city of Duncan Shriek's birth. See also: *Busker, Alan.*

STRATTONISM. Believers in the mythos of the bicameral brain, Strattonists have always been in conflict with the followers of Richard Peterson, primarily because neither religion can understand its own teachings, let alone those of its opponent. A typical entry from the guiding text of Strattonism, *The Consciousness of the Origin of the Bicameral Breakdown*, reads "The compresence and prehension of a monism in keeping with the gravitational relinquiships and syntaptic revolutions of the mind cannot be undersuaged in any discussion of concantimated narratizations or even when considering slorbenkian bilateral mandates." One diagram in the book depicts a brain with arrows pointing to "The Bandaic Hallucinatory Pit," "The Bilateral Convulsive Impulse," and "The Origin of the RP Heresy." The belief that the brain can talk to itself has led to some confusing conversations at Strattonist meetings. See also: *Peterson, Richard.*

– T –

TARBUT, ARCH OF. Richard Tarbut was a wealthy man who liked to have things named after him. The Arch of Tarbut is one of those things. The Tarbuts moved to Ambergris from Morrow, where they sold, among other items, stoves and canaries. Tarbut named only one condition for giving money to construct the arch: that, by means of a ladder, he and his family be allowed to hold a party atop the arch upon its completion. This, indeed, he did, but, bothered by a mud wasp, lost his balance, and fell to his death, attaining a condition very close to that of Brandon Map. See also: *Map, Brandon.*

THRUSH, THE. A doomed ship in the Ambergrisian navy, commissioned during the reign of Trillian the Great Banker. At that time, even oak-built ships succumbed to rotted timbers because the alternate wetting and drying of wood created favorable conditions for the growth of fungi. Reports from the naval command to Trillian stated that "In building and repairing ships with green timber, planks, and trennels, it is apparent by demonstration to the ship's danger and by heat of the hull meeting with the greenness and sap thereof immediately putrefies the same and draws that ship to the dock again to repair within six years what should last 20 years." Directly prior to The Thrush leaving port, an even harsher report stated "The planks were in many places perished to powder and the ship's sides more disguised by patching than usually is seen upon the coming of a fleet after a battle. Their holds not cleared nor aired but (for wont of gratings and opening their hatches and scuttles) suffered to heat and molder until I have with my own hands gathered toadstools growing in the most considerable of them, as big as my fists." Despite this, The Thrush was sent down the River Moth toward Nicea. Within five days, the crew complained of a general itchiness. Within ten days, the ship was so encrusted with fungi that the crewmembers were trapped inside. Forced to eat the fungi for sustenance, they began to mold and the ship collapsed and sank far from shore on the twentieth day. No one survived. See also: *Fungus*.

TRILLIAN THE GREAT BANKER. One of the greatest rulers Ambergris has ever known. Under Trillian, Ambergris became a miniature empire, but more importantly, a center for business and finance. Ambergrisian banks spread across the continent and at one point accounted for 75 percent of all financial transactions in the South. Trillian, more than any ruler before him, was able to snuff out the power of the Brueghelites through a methodical process of depriving them of capital and resources. Strangely enough, his downfall came at the hands of cababari pigs. A slave in love to his mistress, he bristled over a perceived insult handed to her by a cababari breeder and signed an order that cababari would no longer be considered fit for eating and would be banned from the city. Just six months later, a group of Cappan Restorationists funded by a powerful pig cartel ousted Trillian. See also: *Cababari*.

– U –

URINATION, ORDER OF. The most annoying of the Orders. See also: *Living Saints*.

– V –

VERDEN, LOUIS. This talented artist first established his reputation with gargoyle-inspired jewelry (the highlight of many a Festival parade). From jewelry, Verden progressed to book illustration, illuminating such popular texts as *The Physiology and Psychology of the Giant Squid*. He served for many years as the contributing art director for *Burning Leaves*. A fervent acolyte of Strattonism and a prize-winning hedgehog breeder, Verden has for many years headed up the

EXHIBIT 10: THE DELUXE EXCHANGE, A COLLABORATION BETWEEN SPORLENDER AND VERDEN; HOUSED IN THE MORHAIM MUSEUM'S ROTATING "CRUEL FEAST: FESTIVAL MEMORABILIA" COLLECTION.

Ambergris chapter of the Free Thinkers Guild. His most famous quote might be "I'm working on your damn illustrations!" directed at his long-time collaborator Nicholas Sporlender and published in the "Heard in the Mews" section of *Burning Leaves*. Laypersons will be most familiar with his work for the festival booklet, *The Exchange*. See also: *Burning Leaves; New Art, The; Safe House; Sporlender, Nicholas.*

– Z –

ZAMILON. A ruined monastery-fortress still inhabited by monks. This vast complex of buildings and defensive fortifications is ancient beyond memory. No one knows who built

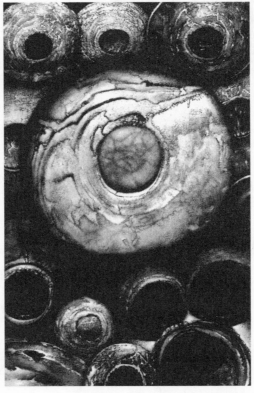

EXHIBIT 11: BADLY DAMAGED PHOTOGRAPH OF GRAY CAP ARTWORK FOUND BY CAPPERS NEAR THE SO-CALLED "GRAY CAP ALTAR" DURING THE REIGN OF TRILLIAN; EXPERTS BELIEVE THIS IMAGE DEPICTS A GRAY CAP FUNGAL "BOOK" EMBEDDED IN A DOOR; HOUSED IN THE MORHAIM MUSEUM'S SPLENDID "SUBTERRANEA: THE HIDDEN WORLD" COLLECTION.

the original structures. The monks who live there possess a page from Samuel Tonsure's Journal and believe that, if the words on that page are read in a particular sequence, the page can serve as a door to another place. See also: *Busker, Alan; Daffed Zoo; Lacond, James; Masouf; Skamoo.*

A NOTE ON FONTS

Caslon Old Face, used for the body text of "The Book of Ambergris" is artfully structured, with classic textures and aromas. Redolent of fine leather, sandalwood, and cinnamon, Caslon is dry yet velvety, its gossamer qualities offset by enough backbone to satisfy even aficionados of such terse fonts as Nicean Monk Face and Cinsorium Ironic. Elena Caslon created Caslon Old Face during the reign of Trillian the Great Banker, while working in Frankwrithe & Lewden's Morrow print shop. Arguably, the most famous book ever set in Caslon is Slothian's grotesque Gorngill Awakened.

"Times New Roman," a font foreign to the Southern Cities, and not currently registered with the font guild, was used by X for his manuscript "The Release of Belacqua." Although some printers feared that this blunt intruder might gain a fonthold in Ambergris, the rejection of "Belacqua" by more than forty of the city's foremost editors is widely seen as a comment on this "pest font" as Sirin has dubbed it, rather than on the quality of X's prose. "Times New Roman" combines the coarse ambiance of a tough steak with the structure of a potato, its flinty bouquet mixed with a moist texture.

Garamond and its constituents, used for "King Squid," contain a hint of orange peel and white pepper, toast and sprinkled chocolate, with an aftertaste of trellised violets and orchids planted in minerals and black earth. Created in the Court of the Kalif by the master Font Vizer Kullart, Garamond has proliferated in the Southern Cities almost as rapidly as the telephones, guns, and cheese graters that are the most visible signs of the Kalif's cultural imperialism.

Officina Sans, which is not a disease although it resembles one, has been used for "The Hoegbotton Family History." Officina Sans has a bouquet of dry leaves and cold earth. The nice black pepper kick to its finish is best expressed by the dots that live inside its 0's. Developed by committee courtesy of the Morrow Department of Naturalization, the font has since been perfected by the Ambergris Department of Broadsheet Licensing, which has added two variants: Officina Deluxe and Officina Tertiary. Officina Sans graces most of the bureaucratic documents produced in Ambergris.

Palatino, the preferred font of Hoegbotton & Sons for such fictions as Sirin's *Details of a Tyrant & Other Stories* (including "The Cage") has a rich, gamey quality that combines the essence of smoked cherry, pepper, and dark chocolate. Brooding and dusky, Palatino reflects the obsessions of its creator, the Truffidian monk Michael Palatino. Palatino spent 20 years in the silence of Zamilon, studying texts buried in basements and subterranean tunnels accessible only by air ducts or crawl spaces. Palatino eventually emerged from the darkness, trailing behind him enlightenment, several rare religious books, and a font he had developed while lost in a cave. Originally called "Palatino Lost," the name was changed to "Palatino" by a font guild already reeling from such previous melodramatic attempts as Venturi's Folly, Bosbane's Glory, and Flounder's God Send.

Bookman Old Style, used for "In the Hours After Death" and all other body text in the arts journal *Burning Leaves*, has a bouquet of dates, figs, herbs, yellow squash, plums, and blackberries. It can be pleasantly earthy, both rich and mellow, with a hint of entangling vines. Created by a printer during the waning days of the Saphant Empire, Bookman Old Style conjures up all the grace notes and subtle decay of that period and remains a reminder, primal yet profound, of that civilization's continued grasp upon the collective imagination. (It is worth noting that this font was not the first choice for the body text of *Burning Leaves*. The first three issues of the magazine were set in Porfal Erogenous, a font developed by the eccentric inventor Porfal. The editors were at first ecstatic to have found a font as decadent as the material they planned to print. In Porfal Erogenous, tiny nude figures form the letters. Some letters, such as "H," "M," and "O" are pornographic, while others, like "t," "r," and "i" are merely erotic—until set in combination with one another, whereupon certain words create depictions of graphic sexual acts. As a result, the editors soon found that readers ignored the stories, instead fixating on individual letters or words, often with a magnifying glass and a handkerchief on hand [presumably to wipe the sweat from their brows]. Circulation swelled. Shaken by the reaction—and driven to action by protests from both their writers and the Truffidian Antechamber—the editorial board settled on Bookman Old Style as a replacement. Today, Porfal Erogenous is used for little other than posters that advertise squid clubs and houses of ill-repute. The font has a bouquet of honey poured over firm, fresh peaches, cucumbers, ripe melons, and asparagus tips, with a hint of creamy oak. What the font lacks in backbone it makes up for in flexibility.)

The font Dr. V uses for his correspondence is known as "Mother's Typewriter" because it is indeed generated on his mother's typewriter, which he has borrowed because the glacially-slow disbursement of funds from the monolithic Ambergris Psychiatric Studies Division (Dr. V has often wondered what ASPD is a division of; the thought of an even more monolithic institution behind ASPD makes him tremble) made it necessary to personally replace his Sophia 300 model when it finally died. Dr. V blames Dr. Simpkin, ten years his junior and three promotions his superior, but, really, what machine that requires the clacking together of metal parts will fare well in a city as fungus-riddled as Ambergris? In any event, "Mother's Typewriter" is a cranky font with a lecturing, brittle ambiance and enough backbone for ten fonts. The briny aftertaste is particularly unpleasant, reminiscent of the frequent (and didactic) postscripts Dr. V's mother added to the letters she sent him when he was a student at the Blythe Academy so many years ago.

ART CREDITS

Frontispiece – Eric Schaller

Book of Ambergris title page – John Coulthart

Dradin, In Love
Title page – Scott Eagle
Illuminated letter – Eric Schaller

The Hoegbotton Guide to the Early History of Ambergris
Title page – Scott Eagle
Illuminated letter – Eric Schaller
Mushrooms illustration – Jeff VanderMeer
Gray cap symbol – Jeff VanderMeer
Broken gray cap symbol – Jeff VanderMeer
Haragck relief – Eric Schaller

The Transformation of Martin Lake
Title page – Scott Eagle
Illuminated letter – Eric Schaller

The Strange Case of X
Title page – Scott Eagle
Illuminated letter – Eric Schaller
"Disneyfied" gray caps – Eric Schaller
Appendix title page – John Coulthart

X's notes
Voss Bender sketch – Mark Roberts
Martin Lake sketch – Mark Roberts

King Squid
Collages (and layout) – John Coulthart
Fig. 1. Communication – Mark Roberts

The Exchange
All illustrations by Eric Schaller

Glossary
Burning Leaves cover (Exhibit 1) – Eric Schaller
View of Festival Fireworks (Exhibit 2) – Eric Schaller
Hellatose & Bauble cartoon (Exhibit 3) – Eric Schaller
Kodfan cartoon (Exhibit 4) – Eric Schaller
Morhaim Museum knife (Exhibit 5) – Dave Larsen
Rogers Torture Squid cover (Exhibit 6) – Mark Roberts
Safe House Letter (Exhibit 7) – Jeff VanderMeer, Eric Schaller
Spacklenest *Nights Beyond Night* cover (Exhibit 8) – Mark Roberts
Lackpole's "Sporn Zetbrand 3" (Exhibit 9) – Mark Roberts
Deluxe *Exchange* photograph (Exhibit 10) – Eric Schaller
Zamilon gray cap artwork (Exhibit 11) – Hawk Alfredson

"Author" photo (author played by Simon Mills) – Mark Roberts

All layout not attributed to John Coulthart by Garry Nurrish, except for "The Early History of Ambergris," by Robert Wexler

Note: Alas, due to generally poor Ambergris photographic technology, some images from the Morhaim Museum have a quality similar to Victorian-era stills.

ACKNOWLEDGMENTS

Thanks

Thanks to two patient, long-suffering individuals: my beautiful monosyllable (and first reader) Ann and designer Garry Nurrish. I have, in so many ways, stolen irreplaceable time from you with this project. My appreciation of the unflappable Juliet Ulman, my editor, and the entire Bantam staff is boundless—thanks for your tireless efforts, and for bringing a new audience to this book. (Thanks to the ever-patient Glen Edelstein in Bantam's design department as well.) Thanks also to Eric Schaller (my long-time Ambergris conspirator, whose work sparked some of these stories), John Coulthart, Scott Eagle, Dave Larsen, Mark Roberts, Wayne Edwards, Stephen Jones, Jeffrey Thomas, Michael Moorcock (for your continued generosity and untiring energy), Brian Stableford, Richard & Mardelle Kunz, Ellen Datlow, Terri Windling, Bill Babouris, Tamar Yellin, Dawn Andrews, China Miéville, Jeffrey Ford, Neil Williamson, Keith Johnston, Henry Hoegbotton, Tom Winstead, S. P. Somtow, Rhys Hughes, R. M. Berry, Scott Thomas, Robert Wexler, Forrest Aguirre, Andrew Breitenbach, and anyone I have inadvertently left out. Thanks for confirmation of encryption to Ann, Rudi Dornemann, Peggy Hailey, and Jason Erik Lundburg. Thanks to Erin Kennedy and Jason Kennedy. Thanks to my dad, Robert VanderMeer, his wife Laurence, my mom, Penelope Miller, my sister, Elizabeth, and my two brawling brothers, Francois and Nicholas.

Thanks to Richard Peterson and Scott Stratton for being good sports (as well as the leaders of major cults). Finally, thanks to the Squidophiles who provided many of the entries in the King Squid bibliography and whose names, albeit in altered form, have thus become permanently embedded in the firmament of Ambergris. – J.V.

Credits
"Dradin, In Love" first appeared as a trade paperback from Buzzcity Press, 1996.

"The Hoegbotton Guide to the Early History of Ambergris" first appeared as a chapbook from Necropolitan Press, 1999 (including portions of the Ambergris Glossary).

"The Transformation of Martin Lake" first appeared in the anthology *Palace Corbie 8*, 1999.

"The Strange Case of X" first appeared in the anthology *White of the Moon*, 1999.

"The Exchange" first appeared as a booklet from Hoegbotton & Sons. The text commenting on the Exchange is original to this edition.

"Learning to Leave the Flesh" first appeared in the U.K. magazine *Dreams from the Strangers' Café*. It also appeared as a performance art piece from Russia's Projekt Trotsky (Moscow) in 1999.

The versions set out in this collection constitute definitive revisions.

Notes

"The Hoegbotton Guide to the Early History of Ambergris": Some text has been adapted from material written by such ancient chroniclers and leaders as the Byzantines Michael Psellus and Theodore of the Studium; Ruskin; the Romans Eusebius and Lactantius; the Papal diplomat Liuprand; and the Venetian Doge Andrea Gritti. My thanks to David Griffin for allowing me to steal an idea from an unpublished short story for Tonsure's final journal entry. I am also indebted to John Julius Norwich, a magnificent historian, for his style, which I have perhaps appropriated, lovingly, for this novella.

"The Transformation of Martin Lake": Quotes attributed to "Leonard Venturi" were adapted from commentary by Lioneli Venturi in his book *Chagall*.

"King Squid": The opening lines of the novella were adapted from the beginning of the Austrian writer Fritz von Herzmanovsky-Orlando's 1920s novel *Masque of the Spirits*.

"The Ambergris Glossary": Much of the "Calabrian Calendar" entry was conceptualized by Richard Peterson. Peterson also wrote the "Richard Peterson" and "Holy Little Red Flower" entries. Scott Stratton provided invaluable support materials for the "Strattonism" entry.

Contacting the Author
vanderworld@hotmail.com
www.vanderworld.redsine.com
www.jeffvandermeer.com
www.ambergris.org

ABOUT THE AUTHOR

Jeff VanderMeer (1968 - ?) spent his childhood in Pennsylvania, the Fiji Islands, France, and Mongolia. His father Robert, an insect taxidermist, and his mother Penelope, a graveyard performance artist, traveled constantly for a variety of reasons, some nefarious. A 1986 graduate of Ulan Bator University's School of Writing, where he studied under the great fiction mystic Jugderdemidiyn Gurragchaa, VanderMeer drifted through several professions—instigator, landrician, maniacist, English instructor, opera singer's assistant, and dog care professional—before settling down to publish his first fiction, *The Book of Frog* (1991). Due to its international success, he was able to take up writing full-time.

After appearances in a number of notable periodicals and a famous "call to arms" aimed at complacent writers of fantastical fiction (rudely received), VanderMeer published his second book, *Lyric of the Highway Mariner* (1992). Although popular, *Lyric* failed to capture the public imagination. Little is known of VanderMeer's movements during the next four years, a few random sightings doing nothing to dispel the mystery. A French tourist claimed he saw VanderMeer in Samarkand in July of 1993. On the 10th of August 1994, the American Embassy in Uzbekhistan received a garbled cell phone call from a man claiming to be VanderMeer, asking for what sounded like an "emergency shipment of paper." A traveling priest saw VanderMeer in Timbuktu in October of 1994 and asked him to autograph his worn copy of *The Book of Frog*, but the man the priest approached angrily denied being VanderMeer. Further VanderSightings in Cairo and Sydney appear to be erroneous.

In 1996, VanderMeer resurfaced in Tallahassee, Florida, recently married, sporting dual degrees in fungi and cephalopod studies from Florida State University. When questioned by an interviewer from *Modern Fantasy Studies*, VanderMeer refused to explain his absence, but indicated that new fictions would be forthcoming. Indeed, *Dradin, In Love* and a story collection, *The Book of Lost Places*, appeared in that very year.

Throughout 1997–98, VanderMeer abandoned writing for a career in the field of cephalopod studies. His controversial findings on the Florida Freshwater Squid were published in the journal *Mollusca* in 1998 and, coupled with a paper entitled "The Empirical Evidence for the Squid-Fungi Connection," firmly entrenched him on the "exciting lunatic fringe" of both disciplines, as reported in an article published by *Scientific American*.

However, bored by science and thwarted in an attempt to join the professional racquetball circuit by an injury suffered while swerving to avoid squashing a bullfrog, VanderMeer returned to writing for good. According to his wife, Ann, VanderMeer wrote for 18 or 19 hours a day from January

1999 until July 2004. The results of this intense flurry of writing activity are, of course, now widely known: six novels, publication to be staggered every three months as part of an extended PR campaign by Bantam's new U.S. imprint Hoegbotton & Sons, the first novel published in July 2005 to acclaim and respectable sales. A trip to New York City to meet with his agent Howard Morhaim culminated in a very public breakfast at Martha's Vineyard with Paul Auster, John Irving, and a vacationing Martin Amis. A series of readings in major cities also attracted favorable media attention, a photograph of VanderMeer and his wife appearing in *Entertainment Weekly*.

However, in late January 2006, on the eve of the publication of this very edition, VanderMeer disappeared from his house. He left no note. He did not confide in his wife. The only clue: the galleys of the four main novellas included in this collection, found on his work desk, cut into sentence-sized sections and profoundly rearranged—pieces of "Transformation" stuck together with "Strange Case," pages from "Dradin" inserted into "The Early History." The purpose of these juxtapositions remains a mystery, although his wife believes that VanderMeer was attempting to communicate in some new and arcane manner. Regardless, VanderMeer remained missing. The only evidence of any kind as to his whereabouts is the photo accompanying this bio note, taken by the owner of a bookstore in Prague. Although the owner claims the photograph is of VanderMeer, experts who have examined it cannot conclusively identify the silhouette as the author in question. Bantam Books would appreciate receiving any information about VanderMeer's whereabouts, although no cash reward is being offered.